"This community could be your home..."

"I'm going to stay," Jeb said, meaning it. "I'm Amish. I've been an Amish man lost in the world."

"You're not lost anymore," Rebecca replied, her eyes telling him the secrets she couldn't voice.

"No, I'm not alone, but I still have many roads to walk before I can be completely at peace."

"You did talk to the bishop. That is a start."

"It is. I have to let him know if I'm committed. Now, after your words to me, I am committed more than ever."

"I'm glad," she said, her hands clutched over her apron. "I like having you around."

He smiled. "I like being around you, but, Becca, we have to accept that before I can be true, I need to find God again. Then I'll work my way toward the other part of why I'm staying."

"And what would that be?" she asked, her breath held on the air.

"You, Becca," he whispered. "You make me feel this peace inside my soul."

With over seventy books published and millions in print, **Lenora Worth** writes award-winning romance and romantic suspense. Three of her books finaled in the ACFW Carol Awards, and her Love Inspired Suspense novel *Body of Evidence* became a *New York Times* bestseller. Her novella in *Mistletoe Kisses* made her a *USA TODAY* bestselling author. Lenora goes on adventures with her retired husband, Don, and enjoys reading, baking and shopping…especially shoe shopping.

Emma Miller lives quietly in her old farmhouse in rural Delaware. Fortunate enough to have been born into a family of strong faith, she grew up on a dairy farm, surrounded by loving parents, siblings, grandparents, aunts, uncles and cousins. Emma was educated in local schools and once taught in an Amish schoolhouse. When she's not caring for her large family, reading and writing are her favorite pastimes.

New York Times Bestselling Author

LENORA WORTH

&

EMMA MILLER

Hidden Hearts

2 Uplifting Stories

Secrets in an Amish Garden and
Their Secret Courtship

LOVE INSPIRED
INSPIRATIONAL ROMANCE

LOVE INSPIRED®
INSPIRATIONAL ROMANCE

Recycling programs
for this product may
not exist in your area.

ISBN-13: 978-1-335-50834-8

Hidden Hearts

Copyright © 2023 by Harlequin Enterprises ULC

Secrets in an Amish Garden
First published in 2022. This edition published in 2023.
Copyright © 2022 by Lenora H. Nazworth

Their Secret Courtship
First published in 2022. This edition published in 2023.
Copyright © 2022 by Emma Miller

For questions and comments about the quality of this book, please contact us at CustomerService@Harlequin.com.

Harlequin Enterprises ULC
22 Adelaide St. West, 41st Floor
Toronto, Ontario M5H 4E3, Canada
www.LoveInspired.com

Printed in U.S.A.

CONTENTS

SECRETS IN AN AMISH GARDEN

Lenora Worth

To my dear editor Patience Bloom for always
helping me through the writing life. You are the best!

Consider the lilies how they grow: they toil not, they spin not; and yet I say unto you, that Solomon in all his glory was not arrayed like one of these. If then God so clothe the grass, which is to day in the field, and to morrow is cast into the oven; how much more will he clothe you, O ye of little faith?
—*Luke* 12:27–28

Chapter One

"April showers bring May flowers."

Rebecca Eicher smiled at her seven-year-old niece's solemn statement. "And who told you that, wise little Katie?"

"Daed," Katie said with a snaggle-toothed grin. "He's always telling me things."

"That's what makes *daeds* so special," Rebecca replied. She sure missed her parents, especially during spring. Glancing at the old clock on the kitchen wall, she said, "And it's time for you to run home. Your *mamm* will be wondering if Aunt Becca hid you under a honeysuckle bush."

"I won't fit under a bush," Katie said with her elbows out and her hands on her blue dress. "I'm getting taller every day."

"You for certain sure are," Rebecca replied as she took Katie's hand and guided her and the bag of snickerdoodle cookies they'd just finished baking toward the front door. "Now, don't run or you'll break all the cookies and then the chickens will peck at them."

"I'll walk really slow," Katie retorted, walking like a creature from the forest, her steps wide and exaggerated.

"Perfect," Rebecca said. "I'll watch you across the road."

"And I'll watch for cars or buggies," Katie said, knowing the rules. "I promise."

Rebecca walked out to the end of the lane with Katie and gave her a kiss. "Okay, run along now, *liebling*."

She loved her freckle-faced golden-haired niece as well as Katie's three older brothers, Michael, Elijah and Adam. Blessed that her own older brother, Noah, and his wife, Franny, lived across from her place, Rebecca turned back to her yard, the sign Noah had made for her a few years ago now showing a fresh coat of paint:

The Lily Lady.

The sign stated that in big black letters, with a variety of painted daylilies underneath and an arrow pointing to her home and the colorful fields beyond.

Ja, she was the lily lady all right. And right now, she needed what the other sign by her driveway asked for:

Help Wanted.

Dear Lord, send someone soon. Rebecca was having a hard time finding a permanent handyman to help her with not only the lilies but also everything else her parents' small farm required. Her helper of the last few years, Moses Yoder, had decided to move to a community in Ohio to be near his ailing sister. He'd left a month ago and she still hadn't found anyone to replace him.

Most men around here had to work their own land or had a regular job. And the young folks didn't want to work in a hot field most of the summer. They found summer work elsewhere or had to help their own families get through the crops.

She looked toward the sky, expecting more dark clouds full of rain, but the sun shone brightly in the midmorning sky. What a wet week it had been. Hoping her bulbs wouldn't rot away instead of blooming, she made it back to the front porch and turned to see Katie waving to her from Noah's porch.

Rebecca waved back. Then she noticed something else.

A man walking along the road.

People walked by here all the time. Rebecca loved to walk and often did that since she didn't like horses.

But this man looked different.

When he turned toward her house, she gasped and went inside. She had a phone she used for business. She'd use it to call the police, too, if need be.

The man kept walking, his dark hair shaggy around his face, his jeans worn and tattered. He carried an aged olive-colored pack on his back. He wasn't Amish.

Rebecca watched from the kitchen window. He came up onto the porch and stood at the unlocked screen door. One knock. Then another.

"Hello, anyone home? I came about the help-wanted ad." He stopped and Rebecca heard a distinctive sigh. "I need a job."

Rebecca had hoped someone Amish would take the job. She needed a handyman who liked working with the earth, someone who understood the art of growing lilies.

This man didn't look like that type.

More like a beggar wanting a *gut* meal.

"Hello? I have references. Mr. Hartford from the general store showed me your ad," he called again.

References. She'd verify that. And Mr. Hartford wouldn't send someone he didn't trust.

Yet, Rebecca hesitated. She wasn't sure what to do. She needed help now, and here he stood, asking for a job. She watched him turn, his shoulders hunched in dejection, his head down as he eased off the porch.

Her spring season was here. She needed someone, had just prayed about it, and so far, this was the only person who'd shown any real interest. Well, the only person who looked strong enough for what the work demanded. She'd turned down two scrawny teens because she knew them to be troublemakers, and a *grossdaddi* who only wanted to get out of his rocking chair. But he could barely get up the porch steps. No one else had even tried to apply.

What should she do?

Rebecca stilled for two heartbeats, then hurried to the door.

"Wait."

The man turned around and looked up at her, his expression raw and edgy, dangerous. But his eyes— they held a world of hurt and pain. He looked broken. Completely broken.

She let out a little breath. He reminded her of someone—her deceased fiancé, John Kemp. Her heartbeat lifting to a new height, she blinked back tears. John had died when he was eighteen. Fifteen years ago. This stranger looked *Englisch*. He also looked lost.

"What's your name?" Rebecca asked, motioning him onto the porch while she gathered her composure. His features only reminded her of John, but then she thought every day of the man she'd loved and planned to marry. She had to be imagining things. No amount of longing could bring John back.

Jebediah," he said, his voice like splintered wood. "Jebediah Martin."

That name didn't ring a bell with her, so she tried to relax. Pointing him to a rocking chair, she sat down on a nearby bench. "And why do you need this job?"

He glanced out at the yard and then back to her. "Because I need work. I need…money. I've been traveling and I wound up here."

"You have references?"

"Yes, a couple from other jobs."

"Do you know anyone here?"

"No."

"How do I know I can trust you?"

"You don't know, but you can trust me. I need a job."

"What can you tell me that would make me trust you?"

"Nothing. You *can* trust me."

Rebecca tried again. "Do you like working outside, with flowers and gardens? Do you know how to plow— with a horse pulling the plows?"

"I know horses, but as for gardening, I've never done it before, but I can learn." He looked down at his old boots. "I know the earth, the seasons, the crops."

Rebecca lifted her hands, palms up, and let out an aggravated breath. "You're not impressing me."

The man finally looked directly into her eyes. "I told you I need a job. It's that simple."

Then he reached into the battered backpack and pulled out an envelope filled with folded papers. "Here."

He handed her two references—one from a restaurant owner in Indiana and one from a hotel where he'd cleaned rooms in Kentucky.

"These folks seem to think you're a *gut* worker."

"I am."

Trying hard to ignore the deep blue of his gaze, she said, "I grow lilies, you understand? I need someone with a strong back who can work long hours. I need someone to look after the horses—two of them. Red is the roan mare, and Silver is the draft horse. I have a small barn and stable. I have greenhouses and a vegetable garden and soon, my backyard and the lily field and the plant nursery will all be full of people buying lilies, other plants, and fresh vegetables. A lot of them *Englisch*."

"I can handle that."

"Horses?"

"I said I can handle horses. I grew up around horses."

She wondered if he could truly handle anything. With each question she asked, his eyes went dull and then lit up as if he'd just thought of that idea.

"What other jobs have you had besides the restaurant and cleaning hotels?"

He rubbed the dark stubble on his chin. "Let's see. Janitor. Bartender. Dog walker. Apartment cleaner.

Trash man. Lumber company. Painter. Construction. Rented beach chairs to tourists in Florida."

Disbelief warred with curiosity. He'd been all around, it seemed. "But never gardening?"

"No. But… I like flowers. My mom used to grow a lot of flowers."

The way he said that coupled with the longing in his blue eyes told her what she needed to know. He was a black sheep, an outsider, a wayfarer. A man in need of something to cling to—in need of the earth and the wind, the sun and the rain. What should she do?

"Are you hungry?"

"Yes. And thirsty."

Rebecca made her decision, based on entertaining angels unaware. This man did not look like an angel, but he sure needed one. "Meet me around back and I'll bring you some lemonade and a sandwich. Do you like cookies?"

His eyes stayed bright on that question. "Yes."

Jeb walked around the neat, compact white farmhouse, noticing all the colorful flowers in the yard. This place was so pretty and prim, it almost hurt his eyes to take it all in.

But then, he'd seen the ugly side of life for so long now, he'd forgotten that the earth was still beautiful.

He'd wound up here by sheer fate. Or God's will. After not finding work in another Pennsylvania community, Jeb had worked a few weeks with a building crew. But the whole operation got shut down due to outstanding permits. One night in his hotel room, he'd remembered some letters he'd kept through the years. Letters from his cousin who used to live here.

Campton Creek, Pennsylvania. He hopped on the next bus out and planned to find kinfolk here. Only, no one related to him still lived here. He'd gone into the local general store to buy some supplies, and while there he'd heard someone mention a local Amish woman was looking for help. Mr. Hartford had immediately told Jeb he should find out more.

The Lily Lady, they'd called her.

This little bit of earth was nice. This woman was nice, too, despite her many questions. Legitimate questions, but pushy, all the same. She had pretty freckles and sun-streaked dark blond hair covered with a white *kapp*—a prayer bonnet. That *kapp* reminded him of his *mamm*.

He was a long way from home, but this town had sounded so peaceful and serene in his cousin's letters.

This place—the Lily Lady's place—certainly brought that feeling to his soul. But he wasn't sure she'd hire him, and he wouldn't blame her if she didn't.

He came around the house and stopped to take it all in. Daylilies, rows and rows, some with hardy blossoms ready to pop open, some just about ready to grow and bloom. He could smell the mixtures of a thousand scents. Lilies of the field.

He did not want to leave.

"Here you go."

He turned to find her with a wooden tray full of food and a tall glass of lemonade, the condensation on the side of the glass shimmering like teardrops.

Jeb hurried to take the tray.

"Denke," she said, pointing to a table on the porch. "Sit and eat and I'll talk."

He smiled at that, his brain rattled at finding something to smile about. "Thank you for the food."

She nodded and tugged at a rebel strand of hair, tucking it behind her ear. "I live here alone, so I have plenty of leftovers."

After she said that, a wary glaze darkened her eyes. "My *bruder* and his family live across the road."

"So you're not too alone," he replied, hoping to reassure her. Then he decided to be honest. "I don't bite, and I'm not going to rob you or hurt you. As I said—"

"—you need a job," she interrupted, a soft smile on her face. "Let me see a few more reference letters."

Handing her the whole pack, he said, "Read whatever you want."

Jeb bit into the roast beef sandwich with fresh tomatoes. Then he took a swig of the freshly squeezed lemonade. "This is good," he said between mouthfuls.

She leafed through the references. "Don't forget the cookie."

He nodded and finished off the sandwich. "We can walk and talk if you'd like. I'll take the cookie with me."

"Bring your lemonade, too, then."

He got up and followed her. "This is all yours."

"Yes. I inherited it after my *mamm* passed on. We lost my *daed* five years ago, and Mamm and I lived here together until she had a heart attack two years ago. She loved helping me with the lilies."

"How did this come about?"

She laughed at that. "I love daylilies. I started planting ditch lilies, and then I planted more and learned how to cultivate them since they like to spread. At first, we gave them away but after Daed died, we needed money—an income—so we planted different varieties and put a sign on the road. People started coming to buy them. I added different varieties and learned which worked best. With my *bruder*'s help, we planted a small field and he put up the sign. And now, this is my life." She stopped and took a breath. "I'm known as the *alte maidal* lily lady."

"You are not old," he said. And regretted it when her eyes went wide.

"You can interpret *Deutsch*?"

He had to think quickly. "Only a few terms. I've worked with Amish on construction sites."

She didn't look convinced, but she nodded and started back walking. "The creek is back there." She pointed to the right. "We use irrigation from the creek on a limited basis."

"Pretty spot, there by the creek."

"Yes, it is." Her green eyes seemed to lose some of their shimmer. "You'd need to plow—that's where the horses come in. I don't like horses, so I usually have someone else handle them."

"I can do that. Me and Silver will get to know each other. And Red sounds like a nice lady."

"You'd also need to weed, fertilize with natural materials."

"You mean manure?"

"Ja." She laughed and it seemed the sun got brighter.

"I don't mind manure. Been in it a few times here and there."

She shook her head. "You do have a sense of humor."

"Yes." He rarely smiled this much in one day.

"We plant seedlings, we dig up bulbs and fans—the stems. We pamper the lilies, and we are open Monday to Thursday from nine to four. Friday is maintenance day. We open until noon on Saturday and never on Sunday."

"I don't mind the work," he said. "I like it here."

"You might change your mind during peak season when cars are parked all over the yard and children are running through the fields." She lifted her hand. "There are also the spring mud sales and festivals. I have a booth at all festivals, and we bring in a lot of income that way."

"I won't mind that either," he replied. "I'll do any work and I'll find solutions."

She stopped their stroll between the field and the barn. "Well, then, Jebediah Martin, I'm going to go on faith and trust you." She named his salary. "Is that fair?"

"More than fair," he replied, relief and gratitude moving through his frazzled system. "I can start Monday. I just need to find a place to live."

"I might be able to help with that, too," she said. "My *bruder* has an empty *grossdaddi haus*. He rents it out."

Surprised yet again, Jeb was beginning to think God had brought him to this place. "That might work."

"We can walk over to see him now if you'd like."

"Sure."

He put down his empty lemonade glass and hurried

with her around the house. "I'm sorry," he said. "I never got your name."

"Oh, that's my fault. You surprised me and I forgot. I'm Rebecca. Rebecca Eicher."

Jeb's heart dropped to his feet.

Rebecca.

Could this be possible? Was this the woman his cousin John Kemp had planned on marrying so long ago?

Chapter Two

There were a lot of women named Rebecca in the world, especially in an Amish community. He'd ask around to be sure, but while she chatted about rain and pests and pollen, he studied her with covert glances. Older, yes, but John had described a girl with dark blond hair and pretty green eyes.

This couldn't be possible, but the more he glanced at her, the more he became sure this was John's Rebecca.

Becca, John had said in his letters.

But John was no longer alive. Add to that, John and Jeb had kept their correspondence a secret, since Jeb's *daed* had been a Mennonite. His mother hadn't been shunned after she'd married Calvin Martin, but she'd faced an uphill battle between her faith and the man she loved. And so had her two sons. While she'd raised Jeb and his brother as Amish, Calvin Martin had made their lives hard on all accounts. The man might have grown up in a Mennonite home, but he'd had no scruples and no faith in God.

Jebediah had to sneak John's letters into the house, and he'd also had to be careful when replying with his own. While his *mamm* knew how close the cousins had become, she never mentioned the letters to her husband. But she sure enjoyed reading them in private after Jeb had read them, and she made sure it was his job to collect the mail. John's letters were the only way she got news from her sister, who sometimes tucked in her own messages.

Now here he stood, about to go to work for John's once-fiancée, Rebecca.

Should he ask her outright? No, not yet. He needed to work, to get his life back on track, to find himself and God again.

He couldn't hurt her by blurting out something that might *not* be true, or that *could* be true. Either way, he'd bring pain to her. She'd never married, obviously. The timing and her age added up, but he kept denying what he saw with his own eyes.

When they reached her brother's house, a little girl ran out onto the porch and giggled. "Aenti Becca, I got home all by myself. Why are you here?"

Becca.

The woman standing by him said, "I have a visitor. Tell your *daed* to please come out here."

A woman with dark hair appeared at the door. "Becca, so *gut* to see you. Did Katie forget to tell me something?"

Rebecca shook her head, while the other woman stared at Jeb, making him want to turn and walk away. "*Neh*, I need to talk to Noah about renting the *gross-*

daddi haus to my new worker. Jebediah Martin, this is my sister-in-law, Franny."

Franny came out onto the porch. "I see." She kept her eyes on Jeb. "Nice to meet you."

He knew she didn't feel that way. The woman was petrified and curious about him being here. "Same here," he said, not knowing what else to do.

"Franny?" Rebecca's amused smile sprouted a dimple on her left cheek. "Where is Noah?"

"Oh, look at me not minding my manners. He's out back near the barn. Pulling weeds."

"I'll go and find him," Rebecca replied. *"Denke."*

Franny nodded. "Do you want something to drink?"

Jeb shook his head. At least he'd never go hungry here.

"Neh, but *denke*," Rebecca said, motioning him around.

"Can I come?" the little girl named Katie asked.

Her mother grabbed her by the sleeve of her dress. "I need you in the kitchen with me."

Katie's bottom lip protruded in a pout, but she followed her mother all the same.

After they were around the corner of this bigger house, Rebecca whispered, "My *bruder* is the protective sort. He'll question my decision, but he will give in."

"If you say so," Jeb replied, thinking he should just walk away. He had no right to be here and if his guesses were true, his presence could bring pain to this kind woman. She might think he'd purposely come here to find her. He didn't know whether to let what he'd discovered stay unsaid, or just blurt out the truth.

Maybe if he got through the first week or so, then he could explain to her.

"There he is," she said, pointing to where a big man moved a hoe through some tall grass. "Noah?"

The man turned, his long beard holding a hint of gray, his straw hat low over his brow. "Sister, what brings you over? And who do you have with you?"

Rebecca walked closer to her brother. "This is Jebediah Martin, my new helper. I just hired him, and he needs a place to live while he's working for me."

Noah's brown-eyed gaze moved over Jeb like a hawk searching for a ground mole. "Is that right, now?"

"*Ja*, right as rain," Rebecca replied, her hands held together over her apron. "He needs a job and I need a helper."

Noah placed the hoe next to the barn. "And where are you from, Jebediah?"

Jeb had not thought about people knowing of him, but John had promised to keep their correspondence a secret to protect Jeb's mom. He'd be vague on the details, just in case. "Ohio."

"You have people here?"

"Not that I know of."

"But you are *Englisch*?"

"Yes." For now, anyway.

"He starts Monday," Rebecca went on. "Can he rent the *grossdaddi haus*?"

Noah's frown made him look like a hawk waiting for a mouse. "What do we know of this man, Becca?"

She shoved several of his references into her brother's hands. "He comes highly recommended."

Noah read over the short references. Jeb had been meticulous about getting references. They helped him find a lot of jobs. He hoped they'd work on this one.

"How do we know he didn't write these himself?"

Becca gave him a light shoulder tap. "Noah, these are handwritten, and some typed out. They have phone numbers to verify."

Jeb nodded. "They're real. I always ask for references before…before I move on."

"*Ja*, moving on. That concerns me," Noah replied. "Becca, you can't trust how long someone like this man will stay."

"I trust him for now," she said. "I need help. I prayed for help. He came walking up."

Noah handed the references back to her and dropped his hands to his side, eyeing Jeb with that intense frown again.

Jeb held his breath. If he lost this offer, he'd be at the end of the road. No hope left. He was tired of roaming.

Her brother glanced from Rebecca back to Jeb. "Could I have a word with my sister, alone?"

Rebecca stepped toward Noah. "I know what you're going to say. He's *Englisch*. He looks like a criminal. We don't know him. You don't want him hanging around me. Did I miss anything?"

Jeb held his lips tightly together to keep from laughing. But the serious look in Noah Eicher's eyes told him that would be a big mistake.

"That covers most of it," Noah said, his eyes on Jeb. "We can find someone within the community."

"I've tried that for a month now."

"Try harder. I don't like the looks of him."

Jeb held up his hand. "Whoa, I'm right here. I can see you don't want me here. But your sister and I talked all that out. I look this way because I don't have a home and I've been traveling around. But I work when I can find work, just to get back to the place where I need to be. Right now, this is the place I'd like to stay in for a while. I can do this work. I won't hurt your sister or do any damage to her property. I only want a good day's work for a good pay. She has offered me that."

Noah's dark expression softened. Then he shook his head. "You two should work well together. All that stubborn is burning a hole in the grass."

"Is that a yes?" Rebecca asked, her hands on her hips.

Her brother didn't seem so sure. "*Ja*, I reckon it is at that."

"*Gut*, because he's ready to move in on Monday."

Noah opened his mouth to speak, then shut it while he pondered this situation. "I'll have the place cleaned up and ready."

He named the rent price, and Jeb agreed.

Jeb extended his hand. "Thank you."

Noah took it, reluctantly, but held it in a firm warning of a grip. "Don't make me regret this."

Rebecca got up bright and early Monday morning and headed up the hallway toward the kitchen. After setting the kettle on for tea, she stood and looked out the kitchen window, marveling at the sunrise lifting out over the foothills and valleys. Her kitchen had windows on each side, front and back. Her *daed* had built it that way for her *mamm*.

"So you can see the day coming and see it ending," he'd told Mamm. Her mother had loved telling that sweet story.

Rebecca was sure glad he'd been so thoughtful. Because while the sun did remain in one spot, the earth revolved around it, and her world revolved around her morning prayers by this window and her evening prayers at the one across the way by the old dining table and buffet. She was allowed the afterglow of dawn and dusk, almost every day, and the full sun on special days. This helped her remember the afterglow of her parents' abiding love. She might not ever have that, but she had her windows.

After she'd stood silent, her prayers a mixed bag of hope tempered with a lonely grief that never ended, she moved to the dining room and checked the fields. The buds just peeking out of the green field would open all the way in a few weeks. They'd bloom mostly from May through October, and some would keep blooming. The variations of her lilies, especially the hybrids, always amazed her. So much color, so much beauty. Some were more fragrant than others, but they were all perfect.

"*Denke*, Father."

She turned to make her tea and toast and brought her meal to the table. But something out the window caught her eye.

Jebediah Martin stood, dressed in Amish clothes, staring out over her lily field, his hands down by his side, his back to her.

Rebecca's breath caught in her throat and a swift piercing shot through her heart. She couldn't stop staring at the man she'd hired, but she wished with all her heart that her John was standing there, ready to start his day.

Before she could turn away, he pivoted and glanced toward the house, his gaze meeting hers. Rebecca stepped back from that intense glance. This man made her remember she was alone and lonely. She reminded herself that she had family to love, and she had a busy, blessed life.

Why should that change now?

She left the window and tried to eat her breakfast.

But she couldn't finish, so she took her tea and walked out to where he waited. "Have you eaten?"

He nodded. "Yes. I found food on the counter when I got to the house. You have a kind family."

"We like to feed people. Let me finish up inside and I'll be out to get you started."

He nodded. "Mind if I go to the barn? I'd like to learn my way around."

"Go," she said, relieved that he'd found something to occupy him. Also relieved that she didn't have to give him a tour.

All weekend long, she'd wondered about hiring this man. She knew nothing about him, and he knew nothing about daylilies. They made a strange pair. The whole community would be gossiping, but Rebecca had learned to let gossip run its course. How was she supposed to do all this by herself? It was hard enough with someone helping her. She hired local youths during the summer months, but right now she needed a capable adult who didn't mind the work involved in preparing before her loyal customers came from all over to buy their lilies.

Did I do wrong?

She watched Jebediah go into the barn, her heart always escalating with fear when anyone got close to the horses. Sad, since she used to love the horses. But not now. Not after she'd witnessed John being thrown from an excited roan.

Thrown and killed.

Even though John's own horse had thrown him when a vehicle backfired on the road near his house, she had not been in the barn near her family's horses since then. Her brother and others kept up the stables for her. Relieved, she was glad this man didn't seem to mind dealing with that part of his job.

Rebecca turned toward the fields. She had two small ones, but between them, they yielded about two thousand rooted stems with fans per year. She'd try more if she had help.

Maybe this season.

Grabbing a hoe and basket, she hurried to the field, intent on getting rid of weeds before the day became warm. She loved late spring into early summer. The smell of lilies would wake her each morning and send her to sleep at the end of her day.

Lilies of the field, morning and night. She'd been content with that for so long.

But today, her contentment wasn't as serene as it had been last week, before he'd shown up. What an irony, that the Lord would send her someone to help, but that someone, that stranger, only reminded her of the life she'd lost the day she'd lost her John.

What kind of summer did she have ahead of her with this mystery man? She'd hired him on an impulse and out of a fear of failure. Those traits could do her in one day, but Rebecca remembered that *Gott*'s will would keep her steady. She also tried to convince herself that she didn't hire him on the spot because he resembled her deceased fiancé. That would make her truly pathetic.

She tore into her pruning and hoeing—sending weeds and trimmings flying into her basket, her mind recoiling from the longing in her heart.

Until a bronzed hand touched her aching shoulder. "Let me."

Jebediah knelt beside her at the end of a row.

She'd been so lost in her musings, she hadn't even noticed him or the time of day. "What?"

"It's noon and you've been at this all morning. Rest. I can finish these rows."

She stood, her hands automatically reaching for her tired back. "I'm sorry. I left you in the barn too long."

"It's okay. I introduced myself to the horses, put them out in the corral, cleaned the stalls and freshened the hay. I'll get back in there later at feeding time. I want to organize everything."

Rebecca glanced at the barn and then back to him. "You've for certain sure been busy, ain't so?"

He gave her a direct gaze, his blue eyes battling with the sky. "I like staying busy."

She blinked, thinking too much sun had gone to her head. "*Denke.* I'll make dinner."

"Rest first. And, Rebecca, you don't have to feed me."

"Part of your pay," she said, glad to have someone *to* feed. Glancing around, she smiled. "Besides, I have a vegetable garden behind the barn. I'll need help with that, too. We get to eat the fruits of our labor."

"I like that idea. Do you have fruit trees, too?"

"Apples, blueberries, blackberries, cantaloupe late in the summer, pumpkins, turnips. I grow lots of vegetables. Beets—"

"I hate beets."

"I'll try to remember that," she said with a grin. "Do you like cranberries?"

"I do."

"I don't grow those."

"Too bad."

Rebecca motioned to him. "Before you finish what I started, *kumm* to the house and let's eat. I have cold chicken to make chicken salad. With sweet pickles and my secret ingredient."

"Not beets?" he asked, following her toward the house.

"No. Just a dash of paprika. Another sandwich on fresh sourdough. With chips."

"Chips?"

"I love potato chips," she said with a shrug.

"You are a woman full of surprises, Rebecca."

"We have that in common, then," she said on a saucy

note. Maybe this would work out, after all. Jebediah seemed to like keeping to himself, same as her. But she hoped he'd open up about his own life and why he'd chosen to wander the earth, rather than plants roots in it.

Chapter Three

Day's end.

Jeb took a long breath. He'd sure enjoyed working again. He'd only been here a week, but this might be the best job he'd ever had—considering he got fed by everyone. He walked out of the barn and shut the big doors.

He'd taken care of the two horses. The roan, Red, was docile and sweet and the big draft, Silver, had a gray coat and white mane. Silver seemed spirited but dependable.

"Why don't you like horses?" he'd asked, curiosity getting the best of him.

Her pretty eyes had gone dark, a shutter falling across her smile. She'd glanced out at the barn. "They frighten me."

He'd left it at that, but he knew something bad happening usually caused people to fear animals. "I'll take care of them," he'd said. "You don't have to worry about that anymore. I've cleaned and rearranged all the bridles and harnesses and mended some of the reins that are worn. Saddles look good, but I polished them. And I washed the summer buggy and checked the wheels."

"You have been busy," she'd replied, a faraway look in her eyes. "I've neglected the barn for a long time."

Now, he turned away from the brilliant sunset that had become a mixture of clouds warring with color just over the tree line. Puffy gray had turned to muted yellows and pinks. The prettiest sunsets usually came with low-hanging clouds, because the clouds and clear, clean air reflected the sun in those brilliant hues.

He could spend the rest of his days here, watching the sun rise and set. This was a peaceful, beautiful place. But he'd only been here a few days. He and Becca were getting along. Each morning, she'd give him coffee and food if he hadn't eaten, then tell him what needed to be done. They worked together at times and alone at other times. She was a gentle boss. Things could change. He knew that.

Rebecca came down the back steps with a basket in her hand.

"What's that?" he asked, liking the easy way they could talk to each other.

"Your supper," she said with a soft smile. "Beef stew and potatoes with string beans. No beets."

He laughed. She made him laugh. "I have to remember that with the Amish, lunch is dinner, and dinner is supper."

"*Ja*, we like to eat, same as most."

"Now, I like to eat," he said. "But you don't have to feed me supper all the time. I can cook."

"Was that one of your jobs?"

"Yes, I've worked in a few restaurants and cafés." He shook his head. "I'm a wanderer."

"A wayfaring stranger?"

"Yes."

"Do you want to tell me a little about how you wound up here?"

"No. Not yet."

She looked away, as if she already knew she'd find him going up the lane to the road one day. "As long as I have you through the summer."

"I think I'll be here a good long while," he said, realizing that he meant it. "Especially for the meals."

She giggled. "Take your supper and go get cleaned up. You had a long first week."

"I liked my first week," he replied. "I'll see you tomorrow, early. More weeding?"

She nodded and lifted her arms. "Always weeding and pruning, sorting bulbs, planting bulbs and watering everything. But only a half day." Then she pointed to the basket she'd just handed him. "I know we've talked, and I've tried to explain everything to you, but I put some papers in there, about lilies and our schedule. That might help or you might leave in the middle of the night."

"I won't do that," he said. "Thank you."

She nodded and walked with him toward the front yard. "My *bruder*'s been busy with crops this week, but he will probably pay you a visit soon. He's protective." She waved her hand in the air. "I'm sure he managed to get in touch with some of those names on your reference papers."

"I'd expect that, having met him."

"He means well, but we have different mindsets regarding outsiders. He will worry that you and I work here alone together. But I think I'm far past needing a chaperone."

"And I was taught how to respect women."

She smiled at that, her eyes full of questions he wasn't ready to answer.

Jeb wanted to tell her he wasn't really an outsider. He'd left the Amish close to twenty years ago after a horrible accident and a disagreement with his rigid father, and he'd never dreamed he'd want to return. But would she understand and accept that, or that he was her John's long-lost cousin? He'd find the right time to tell her all of this, all about his life. But not yet. This would be a long summer, with plenty of daylight left to talk about the past.

They made it to the front and he turned to her. "I'll see you tomorrow, Rebecca."

"I'll be here, Jebediah."

"You can call me Jeb," he said, again not really thinking.

"Oh." Her eyes filled with shock and the darkness fell across her expression again. "Jeb. Only if you call me Becca."

"I can do that."

He turned, realizing his cousin John had called him Jeb. Had John mentioned that to her before?

Jeb Martin.

That nagging wonder she'd felt when this man first walked up the lane made Rebecca stop and stare out toward the orange-tinged afterglow of the sunset. Why did he have to remind her of John? Why did Jeb seem so familiar to her?

You are imagining what you can't have.

She'd had men court her since John died, but she'd never gotten past a first outing or two. Telling herself she'd rather be alone, Rebecca had been so adamant on that, her friends and family had finally given up on trying to find her a husband.

Some frowned on her running a business on her own. But when she pointed out she was capable of taking care of herself, they usually quieted. She refused to live on handouts or the kindness of friends. She and her mother had made a nice enough living selling lilies. What was so wrong with her continuing to do that on her own?

This was what was wrong—this knowing she'd be alone for the rest of the day. With the sunlight, she had her work to keep her busy. But nighttime was lonely. She read by the propane lamp, mostly the Bible, a few novels and bulb catalogs, *The Budget* newspaper, and other weekly papers.

Boring. She had a boring, but peaceful existence. Now that existence had been shifted and rearranged by this man showing up out of the blue to ask for work.

Shaking her head, Rebecca went about getting her supper on a plate. She glanced at the calendar she kept on a small desk in the living room and saw that tomorrow, her sister, Hannah, was coming by to help with canning some early vegetables. They always had fun together with their Saturday frolics. Hannah was younger and newly married to Samuel.

That usually didn't bother Rebecca, but all the longing she'd managed to hide so well for the past fifteen years came back full force. She'd never be married. She'd missed her time for marriage and a family.

Gott's will.

She shouldn't question the Lord's plans for her, but today she'd certainly been near to doing that. She took her plate out onto the back porch to enjoy the last of dusk while she nibbled at the food. At least she had someone who seemed capable to help her through the summer. Would Jebediah—Jeb—decide to stay longer?

Did she want that?

You don't know this man.

No, she didn't know him. But she felt she should know him. He'd done all the work she'd heaped on him and done it without complaint. They worked together, but he left her alone once she issued him a task. She'd had a few early customers this week and he'd stayed in the background, absorbing and learning, then offering to load up the purchased plants.

He learned quickly and seemed to be well educated.

He'd made it clear he might wander off again. She needed to remember that and maybe start looking for a permanent solution while he was still available. Surely someone in the small community of Campton Creek needed a steady job.

She wanted to ask him more about what had made him become a nomad, a wanderer, a loner. But that was none of her business.

She'd ask around in a discreet manner. Well, as small communities went, she'd try.

She wondered if people passed on her job offer because no one wanted to work with the old maid lily lady. Why did marriage have to define a woman's status? She knew her faith demanded certain things and she understood that but being alone wasn't much fun at the end of the day. Was it prideful to want to be strong and self-sufficient so she wouldn't need to rely on the kindness of others?

The food tasted *gut*, but like most things, food was better when shared with company. Rebecca thought about the few meals she'd had with Jeb. He made her laugh and challenged her with his worldly talk and all the occupations he'd tried.

She needed to know why he liked to roam around. She wanted to understand why he made her think of John.

She set her plate down and put her hands in her lap, her unfinished food on the table beside her, her head down in silent prayers.

Then she heard a voice. "Rebecca?"

Looking up, she saw Jeb standing there.

Startled, she stood. "What is it?"

"Nothing," he said, his hair clean and combed back off his face, a new shirt smelling of her sister-in-law's detergent. "I… I need a haircut and… I thought maybe you could help me with that?" Shrugging, he went on. "I meant to ask earlier and well, I forgot."

Rebecca bobbed her head, while her heart came to a skidding halt. The man needed a haircut, so why was she being a ninny. "I have scissors. We can set a chair in the grass, and I'll give you a trim."

"I'd appreciate that," he said. "Will you be able to see?"

"I think we have a few minutes before full dark," she replied. "If not—we'll see how I do when daylight returns tomorrow."

He grinned. "Okay, then."

Rebecca rushed inside to get a towel and her scissors.

She prayed her shaking hands didn't give Jeb the worst haircut ever.

Jeb sat in the high-backed chair and waited. He should have put this off until later, but after he'd cleaned up for the day, he realized his hair was too shaggy. Since he had no way into town to find a barber, he'd thought of Rebecca.

Dumb idea.

Now the pretty woman who was his boss would be running her hands through his hair. At least it was clean and smelled like some sort of flower garden, thanks to the goat's milk soap Franny had left for him by the kitchen sink in his tiny house.

Rebecca came back out of her house with a towel and scissors. "Do you want me to take off a lot or a little?"

He grinned. "I don't want a shaved head. Maybe just an inch or so and trim my bangs."

"I promise I won't put a bowl over your head," she teased, her laughter like wind chimes in his head. "Sit up straight and don't move."

"Yes, ma'am."

She shook her head at that, then started combing his hair. "You have a lot of hair."

"I know. Do you see that little bit of gray?"

"I think we all have that."

He thought about her hair and wondered how pretty it would look if she could wear it down. Which was forbidden, of course. Only her husband could see that. And obviously, she didn't have a husband.

As a teenager, he'd chafed under the Amish tenets, but after some of the things he'd witnessed through the years out there in the world, he didn't find it so bad now. Maybe, like his strict *daed* had suggested he should do long ago, he'd finally become a mature adult.

"Okay, here I go."

He felt her hands on his neck, a little jolt of awareness going down his spine. Jeb blinked and refocused, his eyes on the rows and rows of green lily leaves across from them. He'd read over her reports while he'd enjoyed the home-cooked meal she'd given him. Growing lilies required nature's blessings and a human's hard work. But he thought it might be the best work for him, since he could gather his thoughts and process what he wanted to do next, while he gathered lilies and pulled up weeds. His mother used to say God was in all gardens.

He prayed God would touch his heart in this garden and show him the way when he reached the end of the row.

Rebecca's nearness brought him back to the gloaming. The sun shimmered over the trees, hovering in regret, not wanting to slip away. The air was soft and silent, as if a lightweight blanket had come down to comfort the world. Peace. He felt an intense peace sitting here.

Rebecca snipped and brushed his damp hair while he

tried to ignore the feeling of her fingers against his skin, her touch as soft and quiet as the very air they were breathing. Maybe this had been a bad idea, after all.

She came around front. "Now your bangs. They like to curl, *ja*?"

"Uh-huh." He pretended to be looking out beyond her, but she was so close he could smell lavender and a hint of jasmine.

More of that homemade soap, he figured.

She'd just finished trimming his bangs, her comb flying through his new cut, when someone came stomping across the yard.

"Becca, what do you think you're doing?" Her brother Noah came charging toward them, a mad rage in his dark eyes. "This is not acceptable behavior. You need to stop right this minute."

Becca stood back, her eyes going wide. "Noah, calm down. He needed a haircut."

"He could have let me do that," Noah said, his hands on his hips. "You know this is not right."

"I'm all done," Rebecca replied, her blush showing even in the waning light. "And I dare say, I think I've done better than you would have."

"I don't like this at all," Noah said. "I'm going to ask around to find you more suitable help."

"Neh," she replied, her scissors clutched in one hand. "I have hired someone, and Jeb has proved he's capable of taking care of things for me."

"He might be capable of a lot more," Noah said, his words thrown out like rocks. "And that will not go over well with me, and probably not with the bishop."

Jeb stood and moved away from Rebecca. "It's my fault. I asked her to trim my hair. I didn't think it would cause any trouble."

"You are trouble," Noah said. "I don't like this."

Rebecca moved to stand between Jeb and her brother. "Noah, do you think I'd do anything to dishonor myself or you, or anyone who knows us? I certainly won't stray from our ways. Jeb knows that. I was only cutting his hair and no harm came to anyone. I didn't even nick his skin."

"I'm not worried about his skin," Noah replied, his tone firm. "You mark my word, no good will come of this."

Jeb held up a hand. He had to stop this, or he'd be out of a job. But he wouldn't let Rebecca's brother make her feel bad on his account.

"Understood," he replied to Noah's heated words. Then he turned to her. "Rebecca, thank you. Noah, I get that you don't trust me but there's something you both need to know about me. Something that might help in relieving your concerns."

"What's that?" Noah asked, his eyes still blazing with distrust.

Rebecca shot Jeb a confused glance. "What is it, Jeb?"

Jeb took a deep breath and prayed he was doing the right thing. "I…know your ways, I know all the rules, I have read the *Ordnung*. I used to be Amish."

Chapter Four

Rebecca couldn't speak. All the signs were there, but she'd somehow ignored or missed them. He could understand some *Deutsch*, he knew his way around a barn and a farm, and he was humble and worked hard. Could those traits and mannerisms be the reason he reminded her of John?

She cleared her throat and looked at Jeb. "Why didn't you tell me that sooner?"

Noah held his hands on his hips. "*Ja*, that would have been a *gut* starting point."

Jeb sank down on the porch steps. "I've been away from the Amish for twenty years. I left my community in Ohio during my *Rumspringa*." He shrugged. "My *daed* and I didn't see eye to eye on anything. I left after we had an argument, and I never went back." He wouldn't tell them the rest now. They'd probably ask him to leave if he became completely honest.

Noah's anger moved from boiling to a simmer. "Why did you come here? Why not go back to Ohio?"

"I have no one in Ohio," Jeb said, his eyes dark, a forlorn expression on his face. "My *mamm* passed when I was a teenager, and I lost my only brother. He was thirteen when he died."

"Oh, Jeb, I'm so sorry." Rebecca knew his pain, had seen it in his eyes. It reflected her own torment. "That must have been so hard on your parents and you."

"It was, for me and my dad. My mom had passed already." He stopped and shook his head. "After Pauly died, things got worse between my dad and me. So… I left. I regret that now. Leaving my *daed* alone like that—it was wrong."

"You could still go to him," Noah suggested, his tone full of understanding. "My *daed* and I had fights, but we forgave each other. That is the Amish way."

"I tried that," Jeb said. "He became ill about five years ago, but he died before I could get home. The farm went into foreclosure and was sold at auction. I have no home now."

This explained some of his sadness and why he roamed around so much. He must blame himself terribly for losing his father and the farm, and after he'd lost his mother and brother, too. What a heavy burden for a person to carry.

"*Ja*, you do have a home," Rebecca said. "You have a home here in Campton Creek. We will make sure of that, won't we, *bruder*?"

Noah looked doubtful. "Do you want to return to the Amish for *gut*?"

Jeb nodded. "That is why I came here."

"Why here?" Noah asked, still being stubborn.

Jeb sat silent for a moment, then pushed at his new haircut. "I've been all over this country and a…friend told me about Campton Creek and the small community here. I don't know why I came, but I'm glad I found my way to this place."

He glanced at Rebecca, his gaze moving over her with renewed hope. "I like the work, and I can be good at it once I learn what I need to know."

Noah grunted. "We still have to consider you working here with Becca, day in and day out. Staying at my place means when the day's work is done, you do not return to visit my sister."

Rebecca tried not to roll her eyes. "Noah, I don't turn away visitors. And I don't mind feeding someone who works hard all day. Or cutting their hair."

Noah huffed and nodded. "Then it's settled. I'll be sending Adam over to work for you—as long as needed. That is the only way I'll agree to Jeb's staying. Adam and he will return to my side of the road at sunset every day, or I'll *kumm* checking."

Rebecca wanted to stomp her foot in frustration. "You need the boys to help you."

"I can spare one. Adam is the youngest at twelve. But he has *gut* eyes and *gut* ears. He will report back to me."

"I will not have you forcing your son to spy on me," Rebecca said, her hands now on her hips.

Jeb stood and held up both hands as if to separate them. "Enough. Noah, I've tried to tell you I will not dishonor your sister or my job. She would fire me on the spot if I tried anything *dumm*. Since I like this job and want to work, I will not be stupid. Either you accept that now, or *I* will have to walk away."

Rebecca gave him an imploring glance. "I haven't fired you, Jeb. You can't leave in the middle of my busiest season. Noah has no say on that regard."

Noah glanced from Jeb to Rebecca. "I should make you do just that. But Rebecca is of her own mind on these matters. Probably why no man will come near her."

Rebecca let out a shocked gasp, then whirled and headed for the house. "So, what are you fussing about? No man wants me, ain't so. I should be completely safe with Jeb."

She grabbed up her unfinished meal and held her scissors up with her free hand. "I'm surprised Jeb hasn't already left."

Then she went inside, the door slamming on her discontent.

Noah gave Jeb a long stare. "Well, that went as expected. She is easy to anger sometimes. Most times."

"You hurt her feelings," Jeb replied, angry on Becca's behalf. "You should know not to speak like that to a woman."

"I should, but I guess I'll never learn," Noah said. "Women have unpredictable ways, and I don't need unsolicited advice from a stranger. You're the reason she's angry."

Jeb bristled. "I'm not the one who made a rude remark about her. We've been getting along fine." He shook his head. "Go ahead and tell me I'm fired. See how she reacts to that."

Shrugging, Noah glanced toward the house. "You don't need to quit. She does need someone, and you seem willing to return to the brethren." Then he reached out his hand to Jeb. "I'm still sending Adam over to help out."

Jeb shook Noah's hand, silent. He worried about Rebecca more than he worried that Noah would send him packing. "I don't mind having a youngie to help out here and there, and Rebecca will be glad for it, too, I'm thinking."

Noah let go of his hand and smiled, surprising Jeb. "I'm beginning to think this situation will take care of itself. If you mean to stay here, you'll need to see the bishop and brush up on our ways. You'll have to go before the church and ask forgiveness." Then he leaned in. "And you will surely have to follow our tenets. If you show me how badly you want that," he said, glancing toward the house, "I might begin to believe you could be one of us. And that it will do my sister some *gut* to have a strong, purposeful man around."

Jeb got the message, but he would not be bossing Rebecca around. She seemed to have her confidence under control. "I'll show you more than that. I'll work hard on all fronts. This is the most beautiful spot I've seen in a long time."

He didn't tell Noah, but he also thought Rebecca was the most beautiful woman he'd seen in a long time.

But Jeb would keep that particular observance to himself.

Rebecca hadn't slept well. Finding out Jeb was Amish had been both a blessing and a shock. While she celebrated his return to the fold, she had to wonder why he'd withheld that from her when she'd hired him.

After she slammed into the house, he and Noah had walked home. She'd watched them out the window, her mind reeling with all that Jeb had told her. He'd never opened up before, so she knew his admission had been hard on him. He'd been forced, since her brother wouldn't stop pestering them.

Jeb had confessed as a last resort so he wouldn't be fired, but if he'd been honest up front, she would not have held that against him. Maybe the shame of being away so long had kept him from explaining. Or was there more to his story?

Her brother had taken the news much better than Rebecca, but as was the case with Noah, he had stipulations. She knew Adam needed work to keep the boy calm but sending him to her seemed like a punishment and a shout of mistrust from her well-meaning brother.

After finishing the cup of tea she'd made to eat with the slice of apple pie she'd decided to have for breakfast, Rebecca gathered her garden tools and headed to the herb bed she'd started in a raised box near the back door. She loved cooking with fresh herbs, so she'd planted basil, oregano, mint and parsley, along with rosemary, dill and thyme, and a few sweet peppers. Sometimes, she'd take a bit of bread dough and make her own pizza, covered with her own fresh sauce, goat cheese, vegetables, and herbs. Her treat to herself.

She wondered if Jeb liked pizza.

Why did that matter? Her brother would make sure he was fed at the house, just to keep Jeb from hanging around to have supper with her after the workday had ended. Noah's words to her last night still hurt. Why did people judge her for not having a husband? And why would they judge her for finding a strong, hardworking man to help her?

It didn't matter. She'd have to stay professional with Jeb, so her brother would stop having tantrums about her being alone with a man. Now that Jeb had admitted he was once Amish, maybe Noah would back off a bit. Or that could make matters worse.

Her mind whirling with that predicament, Rebecca didn't hear Jeb approaching until he was right up on her.

"Oh," she said, putting a hand to her chest. "You scared the daylight out of me."

He backed away, a frown darkening his face. "I didn't mean to startle you. Just reporting for work."

"Grumpy this morning?" she asked as she put down her trowel and took off her gardening gloves. "My brother does that to people."

Jeb's smile held a bit of understanding. "He's only trying to protect you. And you did warn me about that."

Rebecca crossed her hands over her stomach. "Jeb, why didn't you tell me right away?"

He looked down at his brogans. "I wanted to say a lot of things to you, but I wasn't sure how to go about it. I decided if you gave me this work, I'd keep quiet and do my job. And I hoped I could ease my way into my past."

"I don't think that worked for you," she replied, turning back to the tiny buds of green covering the foot-square sections of the long garden box. "Honesty is important in any relationship. We work together, so if there is anything else that I need to know about you, tell me now. I want the truth. That's all I ask of you."

Jeb couldn't look at her. He wanted to explain everything, but he'd jumped one hurdle by telling Becca and her overbearing brother that he was Amish. Or had been Amish at one time.

Did he really want to do this? Return to this world and make a life for himself here among strangers?

So far, the answer was yes, but the confrontation last night only reminded him of all he was hiding. Not just that he was related to Rebecca's beloved John, but all the secrets Jeb held closely to his heart. Would she want him to stay if she knew everything about him?

He couldn't risk that, not yet.

He lifted his gaze to Becca. "I have nothing much left to reveal. I have no money, no family, and no future unless I start right here and now. I want to make enough money to get me started, then I hope to find a place of my own."

He wanted to add that he could be happy working here the rest of his days, but that would only make things worse at this point. He'd work the summer and then leave. She'd never need to know he was related to the man she'd loved and lost. "I don't want to jeopardize my job, Becca."

"Your job is safe," she said after a moment of eyeing him. "I'll handle my *bruder* and his concerns."

"I think he'll be better now," Jeb said. "We had a good talk when we walked home together. I think he now regrets what he said to you."

"That's fine," she said. "He was so kind to point out that I'm blessed to have you, since I'm such a bitter old maid."

"You are not old," he reminded her. "We're practically the same age."

She gave him a confused, questioning glance, as if she wanted to ask him more questions. Then she looked out over the lily field. "Some days, I feel old," she admitted. "My brother has a point. I've missed my prime. He knows I'm bitter. I was about to be married, long ago. But one horrible accident ended that."

Jeb wanted to take her in his arms and tell her to stop listening to her brother. Instead, he grabbed a hand tiller and started helping her weed the herb box. "You are only as old as you feel inside," he told her. "Let's pretend we're young again. It's a pretty spring day and we have the afternoon off. I'd like to go fishing."

She looked up at him, then glanced out toward the creek. "I have poles and you'll have to dig for bait but do whatever you wish."

"I was hoping you'd come with me."

Rebecca pushed at her *kapp.* "Oh, I have things to do. All day."

Disappointed, Jeb thought it was for the best. Noah wouldn't like seeing them fishing together. "Okay. I'm sure I'll catch the biggest fish you could imagine and then you'll be sorry you missed it."

"You can brag about it all you want," she retorted, her tone firm. "But I can cook whatever you catch. Hope you like frog legs."

"Oh, you think I'll only catch frogs?"

"I don't know yet, but maybe."

They both worked their way around the long rectangular garden box, clearing weeds and pruning heavy plants so the herbs could grow better. The scents of the tiny buds and unfurling greenery made Jeb think of home cooking and Sunday dinners. He'd had a lot of meals in greasy-spoon diners and fast-food places, so all the fresh, organic food here tasted even better than he remembered from his *mamm*'s cooking.

"I can't wait to use some of these," Becca said. "I'll sneak you meals when my brother isn't looking."

"That's a great idea."

Jeb went to grab a trowel at the same time she leaned over to get the watering jar.

They bumped heads.

"Ouch," she said, lifting up to rub her forehead.

He held her arm with one hand and his head with the other. "We both have hard heads. That hit me on my temple."

"Ja." She started laughing, her eyes prettier than the green grass and trees. "I've been called hardheaded at times."

"Me, too."

Jeb laughed with her, his hand still on her arm. Giving her a careful once-over, he asked, "Are you okay?"

Becca nodded. "I think we'll both have a knot."

He leaned close, studying her forehead. "Red right now."

She did the same with him. "Yours, too."

Then their eyes met, and Jeb's heart stilled for a moment.

Becca's eyes widened, a soft gasp escaping her mouth.

A current sizzled like a sweet longing in the air between them. He'd never felt anything like it, and he didn't want this moment to end.

Then a female voice called out, "Sister, what are you doing?"

Becca whirled so quickly, she almost hit Jeb again.

"Hannah, I thought you weren't coming until later."

"It is later," the woman said with a wide grin. "And not a minute too soon, from the look of things."

Chapter Five

"So this is the hired help," Hannah said with a grin while she watched Rebecca run around the kitchen to fix their noonday meal. "I had heard a lot about him already. Noah is fussing and stomping like an old bull."

Rebecca shoved a glass of iced tea toward where Hannah sat in a high-backed chair at the dining table. She'd planned to feed Jeb, too, but he'd taken off to his place to "eat a sandwich."

"Noah stomps around fussing about everything I do," she retorted. "Does he pester you about your choices and your household?"

Hannah nibbled on a sliced carrot. "*Neh*, but I'm married. I have a husband to do that."

Rebecca let out a sigh as she sliced cold chicken to go with the potato salad she'd made last night. "So that's the reason Noah watches me like a hawk?"

"I think so," Hannah said, her hazel eyes wide with understanding. "He means well, but he worries."

"I'm fine," Rebecca said, "but he upset me last night.

Jeb asked me to cut his hair and I did so, out in the back-yard. You'd think I was walking out with him without a chaperone or something." She told Hannah what Noah had said. "He's never talked like that to me before."

Hannah waited for Rebecca to join her for their light meal. "Sister, we both worry about you. I know you're independent and capable, but don't you want someone in your life?"

Rebecca looked at her plate. "Of course, I'd like that. But I haven't found that someone. I fear I might not ever find anyone, and I have to be okay with that. I have family. You and Noah, Franny and the *kinder*, and our community. I love my work here. I'm content."

"Content is one thing," Hannah replied. "Being happy is another."

"I was happy once," Rebecca said. "I'm as happy as I can be these days."

"Jeb makes you smile," Hannah said before she scooped up a spoonful of chicken salad and chewed, her eyes bright with mischief.

"We get along," Rebecca replied, shocked at her sister's antics. "He works hard and he's easy to be around."

"And not bad on the eye."

"You are a married woman," Rebecca admonished. "Don't let Andrew hear you talking like that."

"You know I love Andy. But I wish the same for you."

Rebecca ate some of the potato salad. "Are you suggesting Jeb would be a *gut* match?"

"From what Noah told me this morning, he was once Amish," her sister replied. "He could be again with a little coaching."

"So, you're suggesting that I coach Jeb into becoming Amish and then becoming my husband?"

"I might be…"

Rebecca put down her fork. "Did Noah put you up to this? Did he hurry to your house early this morning to ask your help in planning out my life for me?"

"You're angry," Hannah said.

"You haven't answered my question."

"He might have mentioned that Jeb seems to be a *gut*, strong man. And that there's really only one tiny problem."

"Jeb is not Amish anymore."

"Yes, that is the concern, but he has indicated he'd like to come home to his roots, to become one of us again. You could help in that area."

Rebecca shook her head and laid her hands on the table to keep her temper from erupting. "Let me get this straight. The *bruder* who fussed at me and told me no man would want me anyway has decided that the very man he's so worried about being around me is now the perfect man to be my husband?"

Hannah bobbed her head. "*Ja*, that sums things up. What do you think?"

"I think you are both *lecherich*."

"I'm not being ridiculous, Becca," Hannah replied. "This could be a *gut* solution for both you and Jeb."

Matchmaking seemed to be the pastime around here, especially when a new man came to town. Was she that pathetic?

"Not if Jeb and I don't want it." Rebecca gave up on finishing her meal. "I can't believe you let Noah talk you into such a foolish task. Jeb has been here a little over a week and has just now admitted what he hopes for his future, and you two already have our lives planned."

"Noah feels better knowing Jeb wants to make amends and come back to the Amish way of life."

"*Ja*, I'm sure he does. He's found a man to pass off his lonely, bitter sister to." She wanted to scream, but she refused to upset her sister. Hannah had been a pawn in Noah's persuasive hands. "I will discuss this with my *bruder* as soon as I see him again. If I ever speak to him again."

"You don't mean that." Hannah shook her head. "He lives right across the way. That would be hard to do since you see him almost every day."

"I can avoid him, but you are right. That would be hard to do since I love Franny and the *kinder*."

"You love Noah, too," Hannah said, giving Rebecca a wry smile. "He loves us even when he oversteps. Remember how he followed Andrew around, telling him exactly what he could and could not do around me?"

Rebecca had to laugh at those memories. "He didn't want Andrew to even look at you or hold your hand. Makes courting a bit difficult, ain't so?"

Hannah giggled. "Imagine if you and Jeb were truly serious about courting. Noah would sit between you in every buggy ride."

They started laughing, both of them wiping at their eyes.

When they heard a knock at the back screen door,

Hannah actually snorted. "Probably Noah wanting to know when the wedding is."

Jeb stood there, staring at them with an inquisitive glance. Rebecca looked up and saw him, her laughter ending as she poked her sister.

"Jeb, *kumm* in," she managed to sputter.

He looked so distraught, she feared something had happened.

"Are you planning on getting married?" he asked, glancing from her to her sister.

Hannah burst out laughing again.

While Rebecca blushed, her face going hot.

"Not anytime soon," she replied. Then she gave her sister a warning glance. "My sister was telling me a bad joke, that's all."

Jeb looked confused and maybe a little curious. Or she could be imagining things since her sister had planted that seed in her head. Jeb wasn't ready for marriage. First, he needed to find himself again and return to his faith. That could take a while. And second, she was in no hurry to marry just to please her siblings and this community.

But Hannah still had a big smile on her face.

Jeb had never understood women. Laughing one minute, in tears the next. They scared him with all the drama and emotions. His own *mamm* had been kind and quiet, following his *daed*'s every word or order. For a long time Jeb thought all women acted that way, but when he realized his mother was not happy, but just pretended to be, his heart hurt for her. His *daed* had not been a kind man. Not even before his brother, Paul, had died. Even more so after.

After his *mamm* passed away, Jeb tried to so hard to take care of Paul. Pauly, as they nicknamed him, had some issues. Slow, his *daed* called the boy. Mamm always said Pauly was a true blessing from *Gott*. After she passed from a rare disease, Pauly got even worse with tantrums and outbursts. Daed didn't like that. Then as Pauly grew older, things escalated. Jeb had to work to keep his family together. Pauly would run away and show up at Jeb's workplace, a buggy repair shop down the road.

Then one day he came to the shop and Jeb had been busy. He was harsh to his brother and Pauly ran toward home…didn't show up. Pauly didn't come back home. He'd been hit by a vehicle—ran right out in front of it. The driver kept telling everyone that the kid just came running across the road.

Jeb stopped remembering. He couldn't go back and change things. His family was gone. With God now.

But he could work on the weeds in the yard, and he could get a head start on pruning the lilies. Rebecca had told him they'd start potting the healthier plants to sell on the road and at festivals.

He'd gulped down a thrown-together sandwich with some tea for his noon meal. Now he hoped the sisters were over whatever they'd been discussing earlier. He couldn't figure why the thought of Rebecca possibly being engaged had taken him so by surprise. She would have mentioned that to him. But then, they'd been wary of each other from the beginning, and he still held his secrets close. Why would he expect her to share the details of her life?

Maybe they *had* been telling a bad joke and he'd come in on the punch line. He'd see how Rebecca acted when her sister left.

He only had to work till noon, but he'd stayed to get some things done and he had to check on the animals anyway.

And maybe, just maybe, he wanted to see how Rebecca was doing since they'd bumped heads. Then he smiled.

Probably wouldn't be the last time that happened.

Rebecca waved to her sister, then turned to head to the back of the house. With an afternoon off from work, she felt at odds. She had some mending to do, and she'd promised Katie a new summer dress for church. She and Hannah had cut out the pattern and she'd sew the dress together. That task could wait. She'd walk the perimeters of the lily field and see if anything needed her attention. The next few weeks would become busy. Locals and tourists alike would show up for lilies. Some wanted several to plant beds in their gardens. Others just wanted one to put in a pot or a special corner. She loved seeing people smile when they found the perfect hybrid. She had a special garden for shows, as many of her returning customers liked to display their plants in the local garden shows.

When she reached the back porch, she stretched and glanced around the property. Then she saw Jeb down at the creek with a fishing pole. He had invited her to go with him earlier, but she'd declined.

Should she at least walk down there now? Would that only add fuel to her brother's wishes for her?

Deciding to defy Noah and just be a friend to Jeb, Rebecca grabbed two glasses of lemonade and two oatmeal cookies from the batch she and Hannah had baked, and slowly made her way to where he stood by the bench she'd had the local furniture maker, Tobias Mast, build for her. She loved to watch the sunset from there. The wooden bench had a lily carved on the high back.

Maybe Noah wouldn't come running around the house, demanding a wedding, if she sat on the bench while Jeb fished.

"Hello," she called as she neared where he stood near a short pier. "I thought you might be thirsty."

He held his pole but turned to smile at her. "I am at that. I did some weeding and walked the field. I like walking through the lilies." He glanced back at the grid of rows, all with a different variety of lily. "I'm learning to identify the names, based on the charts you gave me. Some are really fragrant, and others hold a faint scent. *Hemerocallis*, day beauty. That's the technical name from the Greek." Then he added, "But daylilies are different from lilies, right? They got that name because they only bloom for a day or so."

"You have been studying," she said, impressed. "And yes, you are correct. Most lilies started in Asia, but the *Englisch* especially loved them—the Eng*lish* in England that is. America got a late start, but now they are highly popular. Obviously, or I wouldn't be in business."

She glanced back at the field. "That's why I have two fields. One is purely daylilies, and the other is more exotic lilies that need pampering and watching closely. I've come up with some unusual hybrids."

"I hope I can learn all the varieties," he said. "We could do hybrids this summer—come up with our own lily."

"What would we call it?" she asked, her heart thumping against her apron. Their own lily?

"The JeBecca," he teased.

"Or the Beccediah," she shot back.

"Or just the Becca," he replied, his tone soft and low.

"I never thought of naming one after myself."

"I'll name it—that way I get all the credit."

She pushed at his shoulder, noting how firm his muscles were. Quickly pulling back her hand, she grinned at him. "We'll see about that."

"But we can call them *Tetraploids*, too." He laughed. "It's confusing when they are really just beautiful flowers."

Rebecca nodded in agreement, gathering her scattered emotions. "You didn't have to work overtime."

"I didn't mind. You needed the time with your sister."

"I did," she admitted, trying to put what he'd suggested out of her head. Hybrids with their names joined. A wild suggestion. Naming a lily after her, even more so. Getting back to earth, she said, "Normally, Hannah comes by on Saturdays since I sometimes get last-minute guests who can't wait to buy lilies. She helps me with the money and such."

"She seems like a nice girl."

"*Ja*, wait until you get to know her. *Mischief* is her middle name." Rebecca laughed again. "She's married to Samuel Yoder. He's related to Moses Yoder, the man who used to work here."

Jeb nodded at that. "She surely had you laughing this morning."

How much had he heard? Rebecca didn't dare tell him what they'd discussed. Noah sending Hannah to push Rebecca onto Jeb. It was *baremlich*—terrible.

"We like to tease each other, and we compare notes on our overbearing brother. She's married now, so I'm the one he finds fault with most. I'm surprised he hasn't *kumm* running to fuss at us for fishing."

"Noah?" Jeb grinned. "I saw him leaving with his family a little while ago. I reckon they have plans for the day."

She wanted to say that was *gut* to hear.

Instead, she replied, "They go to the Hartford General Store to buy supplies. It's a perfect day for a buggy ride."

"A perfect day for fishing, too," he said. "I've caught two nice bream and I have a frying pan waiting for them."

She sat on the bench and offered him a glass of lemonade. "Sounds like a *gut* supper to me. You can take some tomatoes to add. Do you have potatoes?"

He put down his pole and took the lemonade and a cookie. "I don't have any potatoes. I could stir-fry them and slice the tomatoes."

"I'll gather them when you're finished fishing."

"*Denke.*" He glimpsed back toward the house and

then looked at her. "May I sit here with you for a moment or two?"

She nodded. "Longer than that, Jeb, if you'd like."

He slid onto the bench, leaving a measure of space between them. "So if you were engaged, you'd have mentioned that, right?"

She decided to tease him a bit. "*Ja*, in the same way you mentioned you were once Amish." Then she smiled. "Gotcha."

Jeb shook his head and bit into his cookie. "I can see your sister is not the only one who has mischief on her mind."

Rebecca laughed and ate her cookie. "You'd better keep an eye on your pole. I've heard there is a big bass roaming this creek."

"He might already be in my fishing net, floating just beneath the surface."

"Ah, so you can make jokes, too."

"Every now and then," he admitted.

She laughed and wished this kind of day could last forever. The buzz of bees, the wind singing through the trees, the scents of spring. For the first time in a long time, Rebecca felt hope in her heart.

Then she looked into Jeb's eyes and saw John there.

John should be here on her bench, not a stranger who was lost like a prodigal. Jeb was a kind person, and a handsome man. But could anyone ever measure up to her John?

Her laughter died down and she looked out over the water, no words forming on her lips. Tears formed in her eyes while she remembered how happy she'd once been. Why did this man have to remind her of all she'd lost?

"What's wrong?" Jeb asked, a frown on his face, questions in his eyes.

"I was engaged once," she admitted, the streaming water blurring as her eyes misted over. "But that was a long time ago."

Chapter Six

Jeb wanted to tell her he knew all about that engagement. But he couldn't find the words. He'd bring hurt to her either way. If he brought up John, and told her he was his kin, it would hurt. If he sat here and stayed silent and she found out later, it would still hurt.

"Do you want to talk about it?" he asked, deciding that staying neutral might be the best plan for now. He might not be here long anyway, and once he was gone, she'd never need to know.

Rebecca gave him a quick glance, then looked at the gurgling water that flowed through this small community. "What is there to say? We were engaged and about to be married. He was riding a horse, one his *daed* had just purchased and brought home. The horse was fidgety and skittish and a vehicle on the road backfired near where they were riding."

"It scared the animal," Jeb said, closing his eyes to the worst, and quickly opening them to see the horror in her expression She'd gone pale, her lips trembling.

She nodded, her hands held tightly together in her lap, her knuckles white against her blue dress. "I was there. I'd been watching him, my arms dangling over the fence rail." She shook her head, as if to get the memories out of her mind. "The horse lifted up and took off so fast, John lost the reins and... He was thrown. He landed too hard and hit his head against a fallen limb." She stood and stared at the water. "He...didn't wake up. I ran to him, and he wouldn't wake up. He was already gone."

Jeb tried to find air. He knew his cousin had died young, but he'd never heard the details. Her description was so close to what had happened to Pauly. "I'm so sorry you had to witness that, Rebecca. This is why you're afraid of horses?"

She bobbed her head. He stood up and moved close. "And this is why you never married?"

She whirled then. "*Ja*, how could I ever marry anyone when the man I loved so much died before we ever had a chance to be happy together?"

Jeb realized two things standing there, the scent of her milk-and-honey soap wafting out around him. She would never get over losing John, and Jeb could never reveal that he was John's cousin. He couldn't bring her any more pain when he wasn't even sure if he belonged here.

Father, what should I do? How do I pray for this woman? Help me see the way.

It had been a while since Jeb had turned to God. He'd cried out to God a lot, blaming the world for his problems, and railing at God for creating them. But he'd learned his problems were because of his own doings and the consequences of his choices.

But Rebecca, what had she done to deserve such a cruel turn of events? She'd say this had been God's will.

Why would God do that to her?

You're here now.

Jeb took in a breath. He *was* here now. When he'd seen the sign on the road and walked up that lane, weary and drained, he'd immediately felt a sense of home.

I am here now.

"Rebecca," he said, wanting to say so many things, "I'm sorry for that horrible loss. Sorry that you had to witness the death of the man you loved. You've done something remarkable, though. You've created a thriving business and made a life for yourself. A good life. You managed, even with tremendous grief, and you should be proud of that."

She wiped at her eyes. "*Ja,* I am content most days. But… Remembering is never easy. Remembering what might have been, that gnaws at me and stays with me every day of my life. I know John is with *Gott* now, and that there has to be a reason why this happened. I will find out that reason one day."

Jeb almost reached for her but drew his hand back. He had no right to let her think they could be anything but friends. He was drifter, a wanderer, a lonesome soul. Lost.

And she was a beautiful soul. Lost.

Would it be so wrong to think they could be together?

Maybe not wrong, but first he'd have to find a way

to help her forget the man she truly wanted to be with. John, the man who'd left her all alone.

And Jeb would have to make some life-changing decisions. Did he want to stay here? In his heart, he did. But his head didn't think he could ever be worthy of a woman like Rebecca. He should pour out his heart to her, tell her everything. But then she'd never trust him again. It might be too late for the truth between them.

Jeb decided he'd leave all of it in the Lord's hands.

He'd do the work, be a friend to Rebecca and try to show the world he could be more if she ever hinted as such.

But would she ever see beyond her grief? And could he be more to her, as damaged and doubtful as he was?

He glanced back at her. "Do you want me to catch that big bass?"

She laughed at that. "*Neh*, let him be. He's been around a long time." Then she looked into Jeb's eyes, her heart showing in that beautiful gaze. "But I will be happy to fry the fish you did catch."

"You mean, for supper?"

She nodded. "With me. I'm inviting you to supper with me. Would that be okay?"

Jeb thought that would be wonderful. "Yes, that would be great. I hate eating alone."

"So do I," she said. "Fish a bit more and we'll go get things started. We'll have a feast out on the old picnic table under the oak."

"I'll try to catch another big one, but not Old Man Bass."

Smiling, she said, "I'm hungry. You might need to

catch two." Then she headed back toward the house. "We can talk about our lilies. Next week, we start transferring them to pots."

Jeb could think of nothing better than a good meal with a pretty woman who loved to talk about lilies.

"This is so good," Jeb said after he'd eaten his fish. "Crispy and perfect."

"I'm glad you caught several," Rebecca replied. She poured more tea into his ice-filled glass. They'd fried potatoes with sweet onions and sliced the tomatoes. She had apple pie that Hannah had brought.

"It's a nice night," Jeb said when she passed him his slice of pie. "You have good spot to watch the sunset."

"I do." She told him the story of the two windows in the kitchen. "My *daed* was always so proud he could do that for my *mamm*. She was able to see most of the sunrises and sunsets, depending on the season."

"That was thoughtful," Jeb said. "So your parents were happy here."

"They were. We all were. They loved each other so much, and they loved us." Curiosity made her bold. "How about your family?"

Jeb put down his fork and looked out at the glow of pink and purple over the water. "My folks pretended to be happy, but they had a hard time of it."

Rebecca could see the deep pain and regret in his eyes. "I'm sorry, Jeb. Is that why you left?"

"I left for all the wrong reasons," he said. "I felt guilty after my brother died."

"Why?" she asked, figuring it had been hard for him to admit that.

He had to trust her. He knew he could, but he wasn't ready to let go of his shame. "It was my fault."

"How can that be?"

He sighed and gave her a look of resolve, as if he knew she'd keep asking. "He looked up to me. Paul— we called him Pauly—had issues. I didn't understand at the time, and neither did my parents. But now, having been out in the world, I found some answers. He had a birth defect that left him with the mind of a four-year-old. He was sweet one moment and angry the next."

He stopped, his eyes on the flowing water off in the distant. "My *daed* would beat him."

Rebecca put her hand over her mouth. *"Neh."*

Jeb shook his head. "It's hard to understand. Mamm loved Pauly so much. She always said he was a special gift. He'd be young forever. Only after she died, he changed even more. We all did. Daed got worse. He stopped with the verbal abuse, but he shunned Pauly. It was up to me to take care of him."

"And you tried?"

"I did, but I was a teen. I had a job—we needed the money. Daed wasn't the best farmer." He took a sip of tea. "I worked at a buggy-repair shop not far from our house. I usually walked to work. Pauly didn't like being with Daed, so he'd sneak out and run away. Usually, he'd come straight to the buggy shop."

Rebecca put a hand on his arm. "You don't need to tell me the rest." She could imagine what had happened and she didn't want the details. Not yet. Not until he was ready to tell her everything.

Jeb let out a sigh. "Good, because I usually don't go further, even when I relive that horrible day in my nightmares."

She glanced at the creek and then back to him. "We share similar grief, ain't so?"

He nodded. "Becca, as Amish we learn that everything is *Gott*'s will, right?"

She nodded. "Correct."

"Do you ever question that?"

"I have, especially after I lost John."

"I did the same after Pauly's death. My *daed* and I never got along and being just the two of us—well—he used that to pick on me and blame me and tell me how worthless I was. So, I left. I've been running ever since."

Rebecca's heart caved in. What this man had suffered—no surprise why he had been roaming the earth in search of peace. "You find it hard to believe that could possibly be *Gott*'s will?"

He nodded, his eyes full of torment. "I've been wandering for twenty years. My entire family is gone now. Did God put me through all of that, knowing I'd wind up here one day?"

Rebecca wasn't sure how to answer that. Had the Lord let John die, so she'd be sitting here with this man one day?

Anger pieced through her heart. She wanted to get up and go into her house and shut all the curtains. Why did Jeb bring this out in her, this need to let go of her bitterness and sorrow and find joy again? She wasn't ready for joy again. Not the kind between a man and a woman.

She'd had enough joy living here alone.

Hadn't she?

"Why do you think he brought you here, Jeb?" she asked on a sharp shrill.

"I've upset you," he said, standing. "And it's getting late. I should go."

"Neh," she said, her hand in the air. "Sit back down. You can't ask me something like that and then just get up and leave."

Jeb put his hands on his hips. "I shouldn't have shared all that and I know I asked a stupid question. I wound up here out of desperation."

"Maybe," she said, calming a little. "Why did you come here?"

He stared out toward the waning sun. "I've been to so many different places, some Amish and some *Englisch.* I guess because I'm getting older and I no longer have a home in Ohio, I thought I'd cross to the other side of Lake Erie and see what Lancaster County had to offer."

"It is one of the biggest Amish settlements," she said. "At least that's what the tourists like to repeat."

"Yes, and Campton Creek sounded perfect. Not too big and not too small. Beautiful."

"You did your homework on that, too."

He hesitated, then looked down at the ground. "I asked around, yes."

"So why would you ask me if *Gott* brought you here?"

"Look, it was a dumb question," he said as he started gathering dishes. "I got too deep. Never mind."

Rebecca stood back. She shouldn't push him when he'd been asking an honest question. "Jeb, we can't out-guess the Lord. If He brought you here, He had a *gut* reason. But we'll have to see if that reason is ever revealed. Maybe He just wanted you to come home to your faith."

"Maybe," Jeb said. He went quiet as they gathered dishes and walked toward the house. "I enjoyed supper. I'll find my answer one day. I have to believe that."

After they'd placed their dishes on the old farm sink counter, Rebecca turned to him. "If you mean to stay in Campton Creek, I think it's time you go and talk to the bishop. He's a kind man who offers advice and wisdom. Were you baptized?"

"No. I left before I took that step."

"Then you'll need some preparation so you can go before the church and ask forgiveness."

"And then it will be over. I'll be a true Amish again."

"Ja," she said. "If that's what you really want."

"It is," he said. His eyes stayed on her for too long. "That and so much more."

Before she could ask any more questions, Jeb turned and headed out the front door. Rebecca walked around the kitchen, the last glow of the sunset glistening through the trees and beaming a good-night to the creek stream.

"Why did You send this man to me, Lord?" she asked before she turned out the lamps and went up to bed. That was the burning question now. A question she might not ever understand. Jeb had shown up out of the blue, but he'd also picked this spot, out of all the Amish communities in this area.

Did he know more about Campton Creek than he'd told her? Would he stay and become strong in his faith again? He sure was the best worker she'd had, but then she'd only had an older man before. He had not been inclined to talk, and he'd stayed out of her way most days.

Jeb had stepped into her heart from the moment she'd seen him strolling up the lane. She told herself she was only caught up in offering a stranger help and getting help in return, and she had to admit, because he reminded her of John, she'd been intrigued by him.

She needed answers in the same way she tried to figure out growing lilies. She had to have proof of what worked.

"I will keep praying for those answers," she told the Lord before she drifted off to sleep. Just like her beautiful lilies, Jeb needed to be cultivated and pruned a bit so he could shine brightly and find his faith, and so he could put down roots.

Chapter Seven

Jeb woke up the next morning still wondering why he'd blurted out his past to Rebecca. She was just so easy to talk to. He'd never felt comfortable around women, maybe because his father had not been a good example of how to treat women. His mother had tried to teach him to be kind and respectful of women.

"You are not your *daed*," she'd whispered one late night after his father had been on a rant. "You are a kind boy and I know you'll grow up to be a *gut* man. Kindness and respect will take you a long way in this world."

Jeb wished that to be true, but it wasn't in all circumstances. He'd tried so hard to forgive his father and turn the other cheek, but after Pauly died that had been almost impossible. If only he'd done the right thing that day.

After they buried his little brother, Jeb gave up on forgiving his *daed*.

He'd left his home believing that kindness and respect didn't always win out. He'd met some wonderful people out there in the big world, but he'd also met some cruel ones who would do anything to make others suffer. He didn't want to be that kind of person. When he gave someone his word, he kept it.

At least now he was home, and he had a job he really enjoyed, even with the hard work it required.

Even with the woman he couldn't help but be attracted to—his boss. Rebecca was kindness personified. An amazing woman. And so pretty at that.

Stop it, he told himself. He hadn't finished his story and he never would. Rebecca wouldn't want him here if she knew the whole story. The saddest part of that day Pauly had died.

Besides, Jeb was John's cousin, and he couldn't even bring himself to tell her that. Maybe that made him selfish, because he wanted her to like him on his own merit, not because he was related to the man she'd loved and lost.

I loved him, too. I just don't know how he'd feel about this. And Jeb sure didn't know how Rebecca would feel about him withholding something so important.

Jeb finished dressing and went to make breakfast. A knock on the door of the *grossdaddi haus* brought him out of his thoughts. He went to see who had come to visit this early in the day.

Noah stood there, dressed for church. "Are you ready?"

"Ready for what?" Noah asked, squinting into the morning sun.

"Church," Noah said, bringing himself on into the room. "I'll wait while you change."

"I hadn't planned on going," Jeb admitted. Amish

church started early, around eight thirty in the morning, and lasted till noon. Jeb didn't mind that, but he wasn't sure if he was ready for being exposed to the whole community. Most Amish didn't judge and forgave easily, but just like the world out there and his *daed*, some did not.

"Oh, you're going, and you'll meet the bishop," Noah replied. "I mean—if you're serious about returning to your faith, of course."

Jeb wanted to be angry, but he was so confused he decided talking to the bishop might be for the best. "Is everyone in your family this bossy?"

Noah laughed. "*Ja*, better get used to it." Then he tugged at his Sunday hat. "I'll be waiting by the family buggy."

"The whole family?" Jeb asked, wondering if that included Rebecca.

"Sure," Noah said with a glint in his dark eyes. "My wife and I and Katie. And Becca always rides with us to church. The boys follow on their bikes or horses. Don't worry, we've got room for you."

Jeb stood there after Noah shut the door. What was up? Noah forcing him to go to church and yet, knowing he'd have to sit in the buggy near Rebecca. Noah sure was in a hurry for Jeb to meet the bishop. Rebecca had mentioned that last night, too. While Jeb knew it had to be done, he'd rather meet and talk with Bishop King in private.

But Noah had not asked, he'd told. Jeb didn't want to start off on the wrong foot on a Sunday morning, so he changed into the black pants and white shirt Franny had given him, telling him he might want to go to church now and then.

"I guess it's now," he mumbled as he grabbed a dark hat, hoping it was the proper one for church.

He had not been to any church in a long time. He'd entered a few when they were empty, just to hear the silence. He loved the way a still, silent church felt, so safe and protective. He loved the scent of sweet flowers and burned candles, the perfume of a hundred blossoms left over by women who wore hats and used fans and walked around in their dresses and suits. Then he'd found other churches where everyone wore flip-flops and T-shirts and smelled like coconuts and pineapples. Where the women wore shorts and not much more than bathing suit tops. Some of the worst bars in Florida held church on Sunday morning. What was that all about? Maybe a bit of forgiveness for Saturday night transgressions?

The Amish didn't consider church as a building but rather a state of mind. That was why they held the service from place to place, home to home, moving around the community in a time-honored rotation. Jeb had missed that steady routine, too. It would be good to sit and listen to the old hymns and get acclimated to the old language, too.

He finished dressing and walked out into the warm morning, the buzz of bees humming in his ears.

He didn't have to look up to know what Rebecca would be wearing to church. But he couldn't keep his head down, so he took time to smile at her when she approached the buggy. Her green dress smelled fresh like her fields, the scents of sun and wind mingling with a slightly fragrant something. Peach, maybe?

"Jeb?" she asked, her eyes bright as he walked toward her. "Are you going with us?"

"Yep," he replied. *"Ja."*

She gave him a once-over. "Did Noah make you *kumm*?"

Jeb grinned. "Kind of, but he also told me I had to sit by you in the buggy, so I agreed on that stipulation."

She hid a giggle with her hand. "My *bruder* is so… difficult."

"He wants me to talk to the bishop, same as you suggested last night."

He saw fear in her eyes and a hesitancy. "What's wrong?"

"My *bruder*, going all around *me* to find someone for *me*."

Jeb shook his head. "I don't understand."

Her smile turned into a feminine pout. "Noah has decided to make a match for me—with you."

Jeb couldn't believe what he was hearing. Jolted down to his feet, he shook his head. "But Noah doesn't like me."

"I know," she said, whispering as the family came out to the waiting horse and the big buggy. "But when you told him you used to be Amish and you wanted to return, he got it in his head you'd make a fine match for me—his poor unmarried sister. Now he's determined to make that happen."

She must have seen his shock on his face. "Jeb, think nothing of it. I…we…can't listen to my misguided *bruder.*" Shrugging, she said, "I won't let him force us into something we'd regret, and you shouldn't either."

Noah and Franny came out the door with Katie on their heels. Rebecca shot Jeb a warning glance. "Don't mention this."

"Are you two through passing secrets?" Noah asked, grinning. "It's time to go."

Jeb took the covered basket Rebecca held and placed it in the storage area of the open buggy. Then he helped her up onto the wide back seat. Katie jumped in between them. "Daed said I could sit with you, Aenti. He said between. Between."

Rebecca shot Jeb a wry smile. "Your *daed* always thinks of me, ain't so?"

Jeb wasn't sure if he should get in the buggy.

Katie nodded and grinned at Jeb. "I always get to sit with Aenti Becca, but never between before."

The three boys came charging out. "Getting our bikes," Michael called.

Noah nodded. "Do not be late. Stay right behind us."

His sons elbowed each other, scrambling for their bicycles, and took off ahead of the buggy. "We'll get a head start," Elijah shouted.

Katie giggled. "Can Jeb sit with us? Does he get on the side of me?"

"I can," Jeb said, thinking he still had a brain in his head after all.

Rebecca shrugged and mouthed, "Sorry."

He gave her a returning, "It's okay."

At least he was sitting close to her, even if Noah had

forced his young daughter to be a temporary chaperone by stuffing the sweet child between them.

Katie, blissful and full of life, pointed out flowers and trees as they went along. Her chatter kept him from being able to talk to Rebecca.

But he was confused. Did Noah want him to marry Rebecca, since he was available and about to return to the fold? Or did Noah want him to bolt and run like the coward he was, knowing he couldn't marry her. That would break her heart, even if she didn't want to marry Jeb. She'd think she wasn't worthy of any man. Jeb told himself he couldn't fall in love with Rebecca. That would never work. He'd brought too much of his past with him, and he was withholding an important part of that past—the letters from John and his relationship to John.

Noah had backed him into a tight corner. Either get on with being Amish or get going.

And now, Jeb wasn't exactly sure which of those two choices he should pick.

Rebecca placed the container of roast beef sandwiches she'd made for the church meal on one of the broad tables the men had set up under the old oaks of the Weaver place. Jeremiah and Ava Jane made such a sweet couple. They now had four children, Ava Jane's older boy and girl, and now a younger boy and a baby girl. Their house was a four-square nestled on the property by the creek that Jeremiah's family had owned for generations. Jeremiah kept the place spic-and-span, and Ava Jane had made a lovely home inside the house and out. They often bought lilies to plant along the well-tended beds Ava Jane worked on all year long.

While Rebecca held joy in her heart for her friend, her own heart ached like a festering wound. Her brother schemed to pass her off on her employee. Jeb had looked so shocked earlier, she wanted to go home and curl up in bed. But Rebecca had learned a lot, being on her own. She had to be tough and gentle, determined and flexible, and she had to take care of the things no one else could tackle. She'd explain to Noah that he needed to stay out of her love life, or lack thereof. Neither she nor Jeb would be pushed into something so ridiculous. She'd make that clear to Jeb, too, so he need not feel obligated.

"Hi, Rebecca," Ava Jane said in passing. As the hostess, she had to be frazzled but Ava Jane handled it easily. "How are you these days?"

"I'm…all right," Rebecca replied. "My busy season is about to start, so I'm a bit preoccupied."

"I heard you found a helper," Ava Jane said, her blue eyes matching the perfect, cloudless sky. "And just in time, at that."

"I think everyone has heard about Jeb, both *gut* and bad." Rebecca placed napkins and utensils on the table. The men would eat first.

Ava Jane stopped bustling about and touched Rebecca's arm. "Jeb seems like a nice person. Jeremiah can sniff out anyone who's faking in the same way he can sniff out fresh cookies. He likes Jeb. And if you hired him, you must trust him, right?"

Rebecca nodded, thinking of how kind Ava Jane was. "You've heard the rumors?"

Ava Jane nodded, her golden hair peeking out from her *kapp*. Placing a plate full of peanut-butter-and-marshmallow sandwiches closer to the other trays, she said, "About him being Amish, even though he came here as *Englisch, ja*." She scanned the table, then, satisfied everything was in place, turned back to Rebecca. "There were many rumors when Jeremiah returned after being away for twelve years. You can imagine how he was scorned and judged. I was the one who judged him the worst."

"And now you are happily married."

"*Ja*, over five years and still going." Ava Jane ran her hand over the tablecloth. "Just remember, *Gott* knows how things begin and he knows how they will end. I've always admired your courage and your wisdom, Becca. Stay the course and forget the *blabberwauls*." Then she leaned close, "And don't let those who think you should be married worry you. *Gott* has that figured out, too. Trust me on this—Jeremiah and I are living proof."

"Denke," Rebecca said, touched that Ava Jane had been so honest with her.

Ava Jane nodded and whirled when one of her youngies screamed too loud.

Rebecca finished helping get the food out, her thoughts streaming along like the gurgling creek. She'd felt Jeb's eyes on her during the short buggy ride to church and then later, across the aisle through the hymn singings and the ministers preaching. She'd tried to focus on the sermon, but it had been extremely hard, knowing her brother wanted her to make a match with the first man who'd shown up to work for her. She was surprised he hadn't tried to finagle old Mr. Yoder.

She wished she hadn't blurted out Noah's grand plan for them, but she had to be honest. Now she'd probably frightened Jeb right out of being her friend.

Because she couldn't imagine him wanting to be anything more.

Chapter Eight

Jeb walked up to Bishop King and nodded. "I'm guessing you'd like to talk to me, sir."

The bishop smiled and shook his hand. "I'm guessing you are the one who needs to talk. And don't call me sir."

Jeb nodded. "When could we speak? In private?"

Bishop King chuckled. "Anxious?"

"I guess I am at that," Jeb admitted. "I had not planned to get going on this right away."

He didn't know how much the bishop knew about Noah's interference in this decision, but he did know that if he didn't do something to prove he was an honorable man, he'd have to quit his job and leave Campton Creek behind.

Leave Rebecca behind. Which he should probably do on his own. Just go back to wandering around like a nomad. Only he wasn't ready to go back out into the world, so he had to do this.

Bishop King motioned for him to move over to where a giant oak shaded them and gave them some space as people began to leave for home. The familiar sounds of horses being hitched up and buggy wheels squeaking mingled with children laughing and mamas calling. The spring air held a hint of warmth, a promise of summer, hope for a new beginning.

Jeb wondered if Becca was looking for him so they could leave. He wondered when he'd become so indecisive.

The bishop waited until Jeb gave him his full attention. "Why are you holding back on returning to your faith, Jeb?"

Jeb hadn't realized he'd been holding back, even though he obviously had taken a long time to reach this decision. "I'm afraid," he admitted, glancing around to see if anyone was listening. He figured everyone still here after church knew to steer clear when a newcomer and the bishop were standing alone and in conversation.

He was right on that account.

The bishop's shrewd dark eyes pinned him to the spot. "What are you afraid of?"

Jeb tried not to squirm under that solemn stare. "I've been away for twenty years." He explained the situation. "I don't have anyone left. I knew this place from a relative who is no longer with us, so I came here."

"And you like our community?"

"I do. I found work that I enjoy, and so far, everyone has been kind to me."

"That is our way," the bishop replied. "Are you willing to work on returning to *Gott*?"

"I never left God," Jeb said. "I thought at times He'd left me, but I can see now He was there, but He was waiting for me to do what I needed to do." He shrugged. "He led me here, I think."

Bishop King's dark eyebrows lifted like curling fence wire. "You need to be sure."

Jeb took in a breath. It was now or never. "What is required of me? I was never baptized."

The bishop's smile held wisdom and kindness. "You'll have to do a refresher course on our ways— read the *Ordnung*, study your Bible and mind your manners. Once you've completed your learning, you'll go before the church and confess and ask for forgiveness and a return to the way of life you left. Your past will not be mentioned again."

Jeb didn't want to ask how long all of that would take. What if he decided to leave at the end of summer?

The bishop sensed his trepidation. "This is a firm commitment, Jeb. If you can't follow our ways, you won't be able to return. You will have to live in the *Englisch* world."

Jeb nodded. "I'm going to ponder what you told me. I knew as much but hearing it from you makes it real."

"Take time to think on this," Bishop King suggested. "*Kumm* and see me next week." He gave Jeb his address. "I have faith in you, Jeb Martin. I've already heard *gut* things about you."

"But if I go through with this, you might hear bad things."

The bishop touched a hand on his arm. "All the more reason to be reborn in your faith, ain't so?"

"Yes," Jeb said. "The very reason I've been roaming around. I didn't feel worthy of ever returning."

"*Gott* will be the decider of how worthy you are," the bishop replied. "I feel confident that he has deemed you so."

"I want that," Jeb said. He did want that. He turned and looked up for the first time. And saw Rebecca across the way.

She waved and he waved back.

Bishop King chuckled again. "I think you want a lot of things, young Jeb. God did bring you here. Now I have no doubt of that."

Rebecca didn't ask any questions on the way home, since Katie was back between them and chattering like a little magpie.

"Aenti, did you like the sandwiches? Peanut butter and marshmallow is my favorite. I could eat them all day long."

"I had a bite or two," Rebecca replied, giving Jeb a smile. "I enjoyed all of the food."

"I had peach cobbler," Jeb said to Katie. "It was sweet."

"My *daed* says I'm sweet," Katie replied.

"You are at that." Jeb looked over at Rebecca, making her wish she had children of her own.

Noah glanced back. "Katie, aren't you tired yet?"

"*Neh,*" his daughter said. Then she yawned.

They all laughed at that, but Rebecca could see the tension in Jeb's face, even when he smiled. She'd have to talk to him about his meeting later.

Once they were home, Jeb and Noah went to take care of the buggy and horses, leaving her with Franny and Katie. "I'm going on home," she said, watching as the boys biked up to the house. After they hurried to do chores, she turned back to Franny. "I'm tired."

"I'm sure you're more than tired," Franny replied, glancing toward the barn. "Noah should mind his own business."

"He told you of his wild scheme, then?"

"He told me of his *wunderbar gut* idea," Franny said on a snort. "In his mind, anyway."

Rebecca shook her head. "He's forcing Jeb into something he might not be ready for. Being Amish again is a big step and he's been away a long time. That's enough in itself, but now my bossy *bruder* throws me into the bargain, too."

"I tried to reason with him, but you know how he can be," Franny said. She stooped to deadhead a geranium. "I'll try again. Don't let him force you or Jeb into something you don't want, Becca."

"I don't plan on that." Becca thanked her for the ride and then started toward home. She'd have to talk to Jeb some more tomorrow. Today, she was too weary to think about her interfering brother. She'd make sure she talked to Noah, too, but in private. She needed him to understand she was happy with things the way they were.

She went inside the coolness of her empty house, then cleaned and put away the casserole dish, made herself a cup of mint tea and decided to walk out to check the fields. It was her daily habit, to go back out and just…be still.

Gott would want her to be still and think things through. Then she'd have to trust Him. Not anyone else.

Just as the gloaming came in a wave of burnished sunset, the air became cooler, and the wind died down to a sweet melody that played through the trees. She stood by the lily field, thanking the Lord for His provisions, for her love of flowers and for sending her a helper who could keep up with her.

Rebecca breathed deep and accepted that she had no control over any of this. She'd have to wait on the Lord to show her the way from here on out. Jeb had come into her life when she needed someone to help her with her work.

But she had to wonder if he was meant to be here. When she looked back on the last few months, and the day she'd heard that her longtime employee would have to move on, she'd felt a sense of panic. But she also trusted that she'd know when the right person came along to replace him.

She'd known that day she'd seen Jeb walking up the road. She couldn't send him away when he desperately needed to be needed.

And she had so desperately needed someone.

Not just for these beautiful budding lilies, but for her own peace of mind, too.

She sighed, turned around to go into the house and saw Jeb standing there in her yard.

She'd take that as a *gut* sign she'd made the right decision.

Jeb had waited until near dark to go for a walk. That walk had brought him to Rebecca's backyard. Afraid Noah would see him if he came up the front lane, he'd snuck out through the woods like a thief running from the law.

But this place calmed him and gave him time to stop and think of everything that had brought him here. He wished John could be here, married to Rebecca, with children running around. Then Jeb could feel right, more at home again.

But John wasn't here. He was with God now. Guilt filled Jeb's soul. He shouldn't have erratic feelings for his cousin's girl. But he also knew marrying again after becoming a widow was not frowned on in an Amish community. More like, it was expected so no woman had to go it alone. Would John approve of him now, however? Technically, John and Becca had never married. And yet, it felt as if they had. It felt wrong, even when it felt right.

He saw Rebecca on the edge of the lily field. She looked as if she belonged there, like one of the slender, elegant lily buds that would soon be bursting with color. She was a burst of color, a taste of spring, a ray of hope.

Stop that mushy-head talk, he told himself. He cleared out his brain and walked toward her.

"What are you doing?" she asked, her voice breathless.

"I don't know," he admitted. "I needed some air, and this is the best place to find that and some space."

"So, you decided to claim my favorite spots as your own. First the bench by the creek, and now my lily field?"

"I can leave." When she didn't speak, he turned, feeling at a loss.

"Jeb."

Her voice carried over the wind like a prayer.

He whirled back around. "I can leave. I mean really leave. Pack up and move on. That might be for the best."

"Is that what you want?" she asked, her tone low and full of that small question.

"I don't know," he said again. "I've never been this confused in my life."

"Are you warring with *Gott*, then?"

"I could be. I want so much to just be at home again, but is this where I stop? Is this where I need to stay?"

She moved closer, the last of the sun's glow set behind her like a painting. "I think home isn't a physical place. It's where you feel the most *at* home. It's a place inside your head, and your heart. But to be here, to be Amish, you will be making the most important decision of your life. I don't believe you left the Amish, Jeb. I believe you left a life that was not best for you. You couldn't save your *mamm* or your brother, Pauly, but you could save yourself in the only way you knew."

"To run."

"*Neh*, to walk away from everything and try to find some peace. And that action spanned twenty years and brought you here. This community could be your home, your place to live, your place that comes to mind when you think of home."

She was close now, so close he could reach out and touch her. He didn't. He stood a foot or so away, enjoying the lilt of her words, accepting the truth in those words, and accepting that he did feel at home standing here with her.

"I'm going to stay," he said, meaning it now, knowing it now. "I'm Amish. I've been an Amish man lost in the world."

"You're not lost anymore," she replied, her eyes telling him the secrets she couldn't voice. He believed she wanted him to stay, but maybe she also wanted to deny that.

"No, I'm not alone but I still have many roads to walk before I can be completely at peace."

"You did talk to the bishop. That is a start."

"It is. I have to let him know if I'm committed. Now, after your words to me, I am committed more than ever."

"I'm glad," she said, her hands clutched over her apron. "I like having you around."

He smiled. "I like being around you, but Becca, we have to accept that before I can be true, I need to find God again. Then I'll work my way toward the other part of why I'm staying."

"And what would that be?" she asked, her breath held on the air.

"You, Becca," he whispered. "You make me feel this peace inside my soul."

She gasped and put a hand to her mouth, tears forming in her eyes. "I have prayed for us, Jeb. Prayed for you to stay and find your faith again, prayed for myself to accept what comes, if it is *Gott*'s will. I don't want you to be forced into something you'd regret."

Jeb's heart opened at the agony in her words. She seemed sure about her feelings. They could only be friends. "And I don't want that for you either."

"We need to let things take a natural course. Nothing can be pushed or rushed."

"I have the rest of my life," he said with a smile, thinking being a friend of this woman would be an honor and a blessing.

"So do I."

He turned then and walked back toward his little house. But he pivoted at the corner of her porch. "I'll see you tomorrow."

"I'll be here," she replied with a wave.

The sun settled for the night and the sky turned to a deep blue shot through with creamy oranges and vivid pinks that made the whole horizon sparkle like a bright quilt over the trees.

Jeb walked home, a peace coming over him. He smiled and took another look at the beauty around him. He could almost hear a sigh going out over the land.

Chapter Nine

"I'm here, Aenti Becca."

Becca looked up from her *kaffe* and toast to find Adam standing at the screen door, grinning at her. "Daed told me I get to help you all summer."

Even though her brother wanted her to make a match with Jeb, provided Jeb followed through on becoming Amish, he'd still sent Adam as a chaperone of sorts to work with her and Jeb each day. Now that school was done for the year, Adam needed to stay busy. Amish children had plenty of free time during summer, but they were taught chores and work all year long.

"*Kumm*," she said, tugging at his hat. "Did you have breakfast?"

He nodded. "Jeb is on his way. I saw him before I ran over." Her nephew tucked his straw hat low. "I like Jeb and if I work with you in your big garden, I don't have to muck stalls."

"A *gut* trade-off, ain't so?" She ruffled his long bangs. "I'll feed you and Jeb lunch, too."

He bobbed his head, joy on his youthful face. "What are we doing today?"

"Ah, today we'll start moving the harvest into the pots and containers I ordered a month ago. They're in the barn. We'll set up a worktable and get going. I'll be selling them on the road and also here on-site." She pointed out the window. I usually set up the potted plants just on the outskirts of the field, so customers might ask me to dig up more."

"And you do *gut* at the mud sale," Adam reminded her. "Two weeks from now."

"*Ja*, and I need to prepare for that, too. You are a *gut* helper already, reminding me of that important event."

A knock at the back door brought her head up. "Jeb, *kumm* in."

Jeb nodded to her. "We have acquired a hard worker," he said, poking at Adam's arm. "Let's see how much we get done."

The twelve-year-old beamed. "I can outdo you."

"You think so, huh?"

Rebecca shook her head. "Don't make me regret hiring you two."

Jeb gave her a quiet smile, his eyes telling her nothing. Maybe it was a *gut* idea to have Adam here to break the tension and force her to focus on work.

"First, I need the big long table in the barn to be brought close to the house. Then I need the wheelbarrow and a shovel. Adam, you can bring the compost to and from the compost bed behind the barn."

"That stuff smells," Adam said, twisting his nose.

"That's because it's a natural mixture of food scraps and—"

"—manure," Adam finished, giggling. "I'll have to wash *meine* boots for sure."

"And your clothes," she added. "This is what we do. I know you'll be fine."

Adam grabbed a biscuit and headed for the door. "I'm going to find the wheelbarrow."

Jeb smiled after him. "He's a good boy."

"The best of the three," she said. "He's kind and sweet, while his older *bruders* are at that age where they think they know better than anyone."

"I remember that age," Jeb said after taking the coffee she offered him. "I was trouble from the get-go."

She wanted to ask him more about those days, but decided he'd talk about it if he wanted to do so. "I think we all have times in our youth we'd rather forget. Being a teenager is hard—that transition from child to adult comes with a lot of drama and doubt."

"Were you trouble, Becca?"

She gazed at him, wishing she could tell him how she'd felt when she was young. "I had my moments."

They finished their coffee, neither ready to give up any past indiscretions.

"Are you ready?" she asked.

"I am." He smiled and put on his straw hat. "Lily field, here we come."

They worked together in the morning sun, transplanting lilies from the ground to the pots. Jeb learned the names and varieties of each one. Becca showed him how a bigger bulb could produce a stronger plant and bring more blooms. She smiled each time she held a hardy bulb in her hands.

He smiled because she smiled. Adam worked back and forth bringing what they needed to get several different varieties potted.

"I pot a lot of what is called Asiatic lilies—Stargazers are one of our most popular ones. People can use them for cuttings, or they can take them from the pot and plant them in a cutting garden. A lot of hostesses like to have that as a separate garden, so they can have fresh-cut lilies inside and not bother their blooming lilies, which can return next year."

"The best of both worlds," he replied. "How deep should I plant these, then?"

She held up a clay pot and gave him the measurements and depth that would be best for the bulbs. "This one will work well for the section we're potting today."

"And we leave them along the back of the house, in the pots, until we're ready to sell them?"

She nodded. "*Ja*, but we water them often and let them do what they do best. Grow and bloom." Then she grinned. "Sometimes, I talk to them."

Jeb shook his head. "You are a constant surprise."

"Then you don't find me *lecherich*?"

He had to stop and remember the translation of that word. "No, you are not ridiculous. You're smart and you're passionate about your work."

She blushed and went back to work. "That I am. Let's get back to it."

"They love the sunshine," she said later, right after they'd had lunch underneath the great oak by her back porch. She kept glancing at the three-row-deep cluster of potted lilies lining the area by the porch.

"I think you love sunshine, too," he told her while they watched Adam playing with a stray dog that came to visit daily, but never stayed. Adam named the dog Lily since the little thing seemed to like catching varmints around the fields and in the barn.

"I do love being out in nature," she said, laughing at the tan-colored dog and Adam tugging at a thick string of old rope. "I especially love midsummer when the different varieties begin to fully bloom. It's like… a rainbow sent by the Lord. Heaven surely smells like this field in summer."

Jeb couldn't take his eyes away from her. She glowed with the kind of contentment and hope that he'd longed for all of his life. She glanced back at him, her eyes going wide, and then she started laughing.

"What's so funny?" he asked, the lump in his throat making his words husky.

"These days, Jeb. They are so beautiful and so rare. I haven't smiled so much in a long time. But watching Adam and that little dog and having a picnic under my favorite tree with you—it's a blessed day."

"The best day," he replied. "I will remember this for a while to come."

Lily ran right into their picnic, then skidded to a stop when she smelled ham. Then she became pristine and sat to stare at them with begging brown eyes.

Rebecca threw a small piece of the meat out from where they sat. Lily took off and gulped it down in one bite.

"That's all you get until supper," Rebecca said.

Jeb was almost glad the dog had interrupted them before he said something he'd regret. Becca was a lot like her lilies. She needed to be cared for and she needed air and sunshine to keep her happy. Strong but delicate, she might crumble if he told all he already knew about her. He had envied his cousin back in the day. John's letters had held happiness, while Jeb's life had only held hopelessness. Now, the guilt of his feelings for Becca made Jeb draw back. It would be best if he never shared that time with her. John's letters would only bring her pain.

And Jeb's confession to her would surely do the same.

Adam finished watering the potted lilies and turned to Becca. "I only gave 'em a little water, just like you said."

"You've done a fine job today, Adam. Think you'll like doing this all summer?"

Adam bobbed his head. "*Ja*, for certain sure. I don't have to put up with my *bruders* nagging me, and Katie wanting me to play dolls with her. I like being here on my own."

Rebecca laughed at that. "Sometimes, it's *gut* to have a little time to ourselves."

Adam grinned and ran a dirty hand over his face, leaving a black streak. "Jeb is smart. He's showing me how to care for the horses—I mean—Daed has taught me a lot, but Jeb lets me do things right off. And he doesn't stand there watching every move I make so he can correct me."

Becca hid her smile. Her brother had a way of micromanaging everyone. She only knew that word from hearing her *Englisch* customers complaining at each other. Husbands and wives didn't always agree on how many lilies they actually needed to plant, but one customer had told her his wife worked in finance, so she liked to micromanage both her employees and her family.

When Rebecca had obviously looked confused, he'd whispered, "She thinks she has to oversee the whole family, and check every little detail, or we'll mess things up. Her staff fears her, but they get frustrated with all her suggestions and abrupt decisions. Me, I just love her anyway. She means well, most of the time. You know anyone like that?"

Noah had come to mind that day, same as right now. She'd only nodded to her customer and now she only smiled at Adam. "Your *daed* has a big heart and he loves you. Jeb has a big heart, too, and he likes having you around."

"I guess I am nice," Adam said so seriously, she did laugh then. "Jeb told me I'm *gut* with the horses."

Jeb might be training his replacement. That made her both happy and curious. Would he leave once he had Adam trained in all his duties? Had that also been part of her brother's plan if they refused to go along with his arranged marriage for them?

Maybe they were all micromanaging things around here.

"You are indeed nice and also kind," she replied. "Now, go wash up and we'll have cookies before you go home."

Adam took off toward the pump, little Lily trotting after him before she pounced at his feet, wanting him to play. He'd worked without complaining, so her brother had taught him some things about hard labor at least. Noah had never sent any of the boys over unless she really needed them. He had to depend on them to help with the milking and care of the livestock. Noah raised dairy cows and sold their milk. Franny and the older boys took care of the goats. Franny made goat milk soaps to sell. Rebecca always received supplies of the good-smelling soaps and lotions on her birthday or Christmas.

Franny had a regular shelf in Raesha Fisher's Bawell Hat Shop. While a crew made hats in the small factory behind the storefront, Raesha's staff sold local products of all kinds—the kind of genuine Amish products tourists loved. The shop carried Franny's soaps and lotions and took a small commission right off the top, but Franny got most of the profits. Several of the retailers around the community took in Amish products on consignment. Hartford Hardware always carried local foods and produce and handmade items, and also provided a garden section where Rebecca's lilies took center stage.

When Jeb walked over to help her finish tidying up, she told him about Adam's compliments. "He really looks up to you."

"I think that's good," he replied, his eyes going dark. "My little brother looked up to me, but I let him down when he really needed me."

She saw pain in that darkness. Jeb's guilt weighed him down. "You couldn't help the accident, Jeb."

He heaved a breath and gave her a longing stare. "I wish I could go back and change that day."

"What really happened?" she asked, hoping he'd trust her enough to explain.

Jeb glanced at the lily field and then back to her, his expression full of regret and torment. "Rebecca—"

"Hey, me and Lily found a lizard." Adam came running up to show them the squirming prize before Jeb could speak, and the moment was lost.

What secrets did he hide behind those compelling eyes?

Chapter Ten

They soon had a routine going. Potting, pruning, weeding, fertilizing, watering. Jeb loved the ebb and flow of the days, even as spring turned to summer, and the days grew longer and hotter. Customers trickled in and out and some days got really busy, but Becca handled her clients like a pro, and let him stay in the background doing the physical work, while she chatted with her returning buyers.

He liked to eavesdrop on her conversations regarding the lilies. He learned a lot this way, and he got to hear her sweet voice lifting out over the countryside.

"*Ja*, that one's okay. That blue mold on the bulb won't hurt a thing. And this is a *gut*-size bulb to replant in your garden. It will produce a fine showoff as the years go by."

"If you want fragrance, try the Fragrant Returns. It lives up to that name. Lemony and it reblooms."

"Now, Miss Amelia is a more creamy-yellow but with a nice mild fragrance, but one of my favorites is

Lullaby Baby. It's a white-pink blushing lily with a sweet fragrance. It really adds to your garden."

She knew all the names, the history, the scientific names, the award winners, and the everyday ditch lilies that had started her on becoming a prominent master gardener.

Jeb thought of the blushing lily with the sweet fragrance. Did she think of holding babies when she sold that particular flower? It sure made him think of that— a surprise since he'd resigned himself to the fact that he might not ever be a father.

Pushing such thoughts away, he took a glance at the dark sky. Today, rain had kept the buyers away and forced her two bored employees inside.

On rainy days, he stayed in the barn, and Adam took to hanging alongside him. He showed the boy everything he knew about livestock, because Jeb wanted to earn his pay even if he didn't work much on bad days. Adam had a general knowledge since Amish youngies were trained from birth on how to care for their livestock. While Becca only had the two horses, they still required daily attention.

"We have goats," Adam said this morning. "But we have to watch them. Aenti Becca does not like them in her lilies. Besides, if they eat too many, they can get real sick, real quick."

"Huh, I thought goats were notorious for eating everything and anything they wanted."

Adam did a little head shake. "Most people think goats will eat anything. They might try everything, but they get picky when they want a real meal. Mostly they forage until they find something tasty. But they can destroy whole gardens before they decide. The deer love lilies, too. But Aenti only shoos them away. She loves the fawns and does, so she makes sure she leaves them some feed to keep 'em out of her plants. But the goats—she's not too fond of them."

"So no lilies for goats, and be kind to the deer," Jeb said, thinking he learned something new every day. "My folks never raised goats. Just a couple of cows and some pigs."

"Pigs are messy, and they slide right through your hands," Adam said, his tone one that showed he'd had firsthand experience with fleeing pigs.

Jeb liked to quiz Adam. The boy was smart. Plus, that took Jeb's mind off Becca and helped Jeb get to know people around here without actually speaking to them. "So how do you protect your goats and keep them from straying toward those tempting lilies out there?"

"We have high wire fences—the kind they can't chew through—and we feed them hay and some feed first thing each morning, while they're still in the paddock. That way they're full enough to roam around the big pen. My *daed* had to cut down all kinds of trees and shrubs—pines, rhododendrons, rhubarb, sumac, honeysuckle, any blooming or ornamental plants—just so they'd have a clear paddock and pen. We let them out there and they can't reach anything beyond what's healthy for them."

"You sure know a lot about taking care of goats."

"We learned the hard way, as Daed says. Lost a few goats to ferns and such. That's why Aenti Becca doesn't want them in her garden. It's bad for her plants and bad for the goats." He shrugged. "She might not like the goats, but she'd cry if anything happened to them."

"I'll keep that in mind," Jeb replied. He never wanted to make Becca cry.

"Look, the rain's stopped," Adam replied, grabbing his hat. "I'm gonna see what else I need to get done today."

Adam nodded, smiling at Adam's work ethic. "*Denke* for helping me clean the buggies." Then he said, "Hey, Adam, I have a project, but I want it to be a surprise for Becca. I want to build her a potting shed close to the fields. If I let you help, can you keep it a secret?"

Adam's brown eyes lit up. "*Ja*, I can keep a secret, even when my *bruders* do something I don't like. Course, they kind of make me promise to keep their secrets—or else. Just let me know when you're ready to get going." Then the boy pivoted around like a top. "Uh, how do you plan to keep something so big a secret?"

Smart. Jeb grinned. "I'm going to cut the boards and make the frames, piece by piece, here in the barn and maybe at your *daed*'s place if he'll let me. Then I'll ask your *mamm* and Hannah to take her somewhere— a frolic or a shopping trip to town for an afternoon."

Adam's eyes brightened. "And we'll haul it all to the spot, and have it together before they get back? Like a barn building, but smaller!"

Jeb nodded and put a finger to his lips. "Not a word."

Adam did a silent zip with his fingers. "This'll be so *gut*."

Jeb hoped so. He was anxious to start his secret project.

After all the hauling they'd done to pot several varieties of lilies, he wanted to save Becca some steps by creating a work building closer to the field. He'd make it enclosed with a window on each side, and with lots of shelves for displays and storage. But he'd create two big doors that could be opened wide, so customers could walk right up to buy their lilies. Later, he hoped to build her a small shed out by the road where she could be available there to sell lilies, produce and other products. He'd already altered a hauling buggy to hold more plants. It'd be easy to load one up and hitch a horse to take everything to the road. Her old wheelbarrow was about out of steam.

Those projects should keep him busy all summer. The more he worked, the more tired he'd be each night. So instead of lying there thinking about Becca, hopefully, he could fall asleep.

Becca had mended everything she could find, but the rain kept up. Now she'd turned to baking. Four loaves of bread sat cooling on the table. Two schnitz pies rested on the old sideboard, the scent of orange juice, cinnamon and the dried apples she'd boiled earlier filling the damp air.

She took her tea and stood looking out toward the fields. This had been a gentle rain, the kind that begged for a book to read and a hot cup of tea to sip. The drip-drip of the rain falling off the old roof soothed her soul, while the homey smells in her kitchen made her wish for a family of her own, so she could share the food.

She'd send some home with Adam if she could catch

him. The boy shadowed Jeb like a young buck following a stag. As much as she'd objected to Noah sending Adam over so she and Jeb wouldn't be alone, she did appreciate Adam's willingness to work hard. Jeb could be a *gut* influence on the boy, considering Adam learned way too much of what not to do from his older brothers.

Jeb had been a great influence on her, too. He'd reminded her of John when she'd first seen him, but now, he was just Jeb. He still had the same build and the thick, dark hair that stayed unruly, but his features were harder, more jagged and craggy. Still handsome, but he wasn't John. Jeb Martin filled his own skin and his own personality very well. She could appreciate him for who he was, not because of the man he reminded her of.

She'd heard from Franny he'd had several visits with the bishop, but Rebecca hadn't pressed him for details. That was between him and the bishop. That meant, however, that he was serious about joining this community. She hoped and prayed for that, not because of her confused feelings for Jeb, but because he needed a home, and this community could be the perfect place for him. This job could be his as long as he needed it, too.

She turned from the window, thinking she'd have a quiet supper and go to bed early. But a knock at the back door brought her around. Jeb and Adam stood there looking sheepish.

"Ask her," Adam said, poking Jeb's ribs.

"You ask her," Jeb replied, grinning. "She's your aunt."

"We smell pie," Adam blurted. "And we're hungry."

Becca couldn't hide her smile. She let them stew

there on the covered porch for a while. Then she lifted one of the pies from the sideboard and deliberately let them see it. "You mean this pie?"

Adam bobbed his head. "Told you, Jeb. Schnitz." He touched a finger to his nose. "I have the gift of scent and I smelled cinnamon and orange, and a whole stew pot of apples."

Jeb rolled his eyes and glanced at Becca. "Well, I have the gift of a grumpy stomach. That looks and smells delicious, whatever you put in it."

She laughed and motioned them in. "Wash your hands and make sure your boots are passable."

"We checked our boots," Adam replied as he almost knocked Jeb out of the way to get into the kitchen. "And Jeb makes me double-wash all over every day."

Becca sniffed. "You both smell clean enough. Have a seat and I'll pass the pie. Jeb, would you like *kaffe* or milk?"

Adam lifted a hand. "Milk is real *gut* with schnitz pie."

"Then milk it is," Jeb said, his gaze moving over Rebecca's face.

She blushed, thinking she'd missed him. This visit was a surprise and a joy. She didn't even mind that Adam was with him. She'd send pie home with her nephew. Really, she was almost glad Adam had come inside. She could be with Jeb, but not be alone with Jeb. Because her heart might do something stupid like make her flirt with the man if they were alone.

His eyes told her he might be thinking along the same lines. That, or he really just wanted some pie.

* * *

Jeb enjoyed every bite of the pie. He enjoyed watching Rebecca even more. She moved around her kitchen like a dancer doing a choreographed waltz. When she turned and saw him staring, he lowered his head. "This is really good. I haven't had schnitz pie in many years." He glanced out the window. "I think this crust is even better than my mother's."

Adam's head shot up. "Jeb, why did you jump the fence?"

The question, asked with such earnest curiosity, threw Jeb, and surprised Rebecca.

"Adam, do not be so nosy."

"It's okay," Jeb said. He'd give the boy the honest truth. "I was mad at the world, and I think I was mad at God, too. I had a bad home life. Then I lost two people that I loved."

Rebecca shot her nephew a warning glance. Adam looked from her to Jeb. "I'm sorry, Jeb. I reckon that could make anybody mad."

Jeb fought against the lump in his throat and the hot mist forming in his eyes. "I shouldn't have blamed anyone," he said. "And I shouldn't have stayed gone for so long."

He pushed the pie plate away, leaving a big chunk of crust.

He didn't tell the boy that he blamed himself more than anyone for not taking care of the two most fragile people in his family—his mother and Pauly. He failed them…and his father, too, in every way.

"I'd better get home," Adam said, giving Rebecca a

worried glance. "Did I ask too many questions? Mamm says I'm too chatty for my own good."

Jeb stopped the boy with a hand on his arm. "You did nothing wrong, Adam. I enjoy our conversations. It's just difficult to talk about those who've gone on before us. But take this as a lesson from me. Never abandon the people you love. Family is more important than anything. Remember that."

"I will." Adam swallowed, his eyes going wide. "I hope you can stay here and be part of our family, Jeb. I sure do like you. And… You make Aenti Becca smile."

Then he grabbed the extra pie Rebecca had cut and wrapped and turned to head out the door, leaving Jeb to stare over at Rebecca. "Is that true? Do I make you smile?"

She wiped at her eyes and sank down across from him. "Most of the time, *ja*, but right now I just want to cry. You've been carrying a heavy burden, Jeb. Don't you think it's time to let it go?"

Jeb stared over at her. He wanted to let it go, so much. He wanted to let it all go, tell her the truth, and then take her in his arms and hold her tight. He wanted to feel the goodness and pureness that flowed through her, needed it to cleanse his sins and his soul.

Instead, he stood. He had to get out of here before he made a big mistake. He couldn't blurt out the truth. Not yet. "Thank you for the pie. I'll see you tomorrow."

Then he went out the door and walked home in the gentle rain, his sins still burning at his soul.

Chapter Eleven

Noah was home when Jeb got there. Normally, he'd dread seeing Rebecca's overbearing brother, but today he needed to talk to him.

"Noah," he called, thinking if he started his secret project as soon as possible, he'd feel better about everything. "I need to ask a favor."

Noah waved him into the barn since it was still sprinkling rain. Once Jeb was inside, Noah stood staring. "What do you need?"

Jeb explained what he wanted to do for Rebecca. "I thought I'd work on it here, mostly so Rebecca won't see it. Then we'll ask Hannah and Franny to get her out of the house for a few hours, so we can bring in people to help put it together while she's away."

Noah gave him a confused stare. "That's a mighty ambitious project, but she does have a birthday coming up. Do you have enough lumber for such a project?"

"I found some in the barn and it's in good shape. I might have to add a few pieces, but it's not going to be a big shed. Just a place where she can work—like a greenhouse."

Noah's fierce stare didn't evaporate. "Why are you doing this?"

Jeb felt the fire of that stare. "Because she needs a shed close to the field. She wasted a lot of steps yesterday and today, going back and forth with plants and pots. I tried to fix the old wheelbarrow and it's not going to do. She shouldn't have to stoop and bend all day long when she can have a nice place with shelves and stools and a whole wall full of any kind of tools she might need."

Noah burst out laughing.

"Is this funny to you?" Jeb asked, anger and frustration mounting. Was he wrong to want to make Rebecca's whole operation more efficient?

Noah put a hand on his shoulder. "You really do care about her, ain't so?"

Jeb shifted on his work boots. He might have known Noah would get the wrong impression. He'd never understand the man. "Of course. She's my boss and she works hard. Adam has been a big help, but honestly I don't know how she did this with the old man she told me about being her only helper most of the time."

"I've encouraged her to hire more help, even offered to help her pay for it, but my sister likes her solitude and the quiet," Noah replied, serious now. "I'm glad you want to do something nice for her. How are the lessons with the bishop going?"

And there it was—the reason Noah was so pleased with this idea.

"We aren't talking about me," Jeb replied, wishing everyone would stop trying to pair him with Rebecca. "I need your permission to use the barn and I'd like to borrow some of your tools to plan out the shed pieces and have them tagged and ready so we can get this built. Adam wants to help, and he's promised to keep it a secret."

Noah laughed again. "Did he, now?"

"He promised."

"I'll speak to him." Noah glanced around, then turned back to Jeb. "My sister lost the man she loved before they were married. Right before they were to be married. She's never quite recovered. I don't want her to get hurt again. Understand?"

"I do understand," Jeb replied. "More than you'll ever know." Then he got bold. "But explain to me, if you're so worried about her getting hurt why are you insisting that I consider marrying her?"

Noah looked surprised and then he looked sheepish. "Well, she has a lot of love to give, and she needs someone who can match her, step by step. I keep my eye on her, as you well know, and it irritates her to no end, as you've probably noticed. I'd rest better knowing she has a *gut* man in her life. You fit the bill, except for you needing to reaffirm your faith, of course." Noah paused and let out a sigh. "I know I've been hard on you, but this is what I mean—if you and Becca become close and then you just up and leave, she'll be devastated all over again."

Jeb could see the love and concern in Noah's eyes.

He looked over at Rebecca's house. "I like the work,

Noah. It's helping me in more than just financial ways. A good day's work makes a man feel worthy and hopeful. I won't mess that up by hurting the woman who was willing to give me a chance. The only person in the world, really, who was willing to give me a chance."

Noah stayed silent, his hands holding to his suspenders, his dark eyes solemn. "I will help you build the potting shed, as a gift to my sister. We will make sure it's a surprise." He shrugged. "And I have some lumber here in the barn that needs to be put to *gut* use. If you need more, let me know. I'll buy some at the lumberyard in town."

Jeb breathed a sigh of relief. "I'll pay."

Noah gave him an appreciative stare. "No, you're doing enough. Sometimes, Jeb, the thought is worth much more than the cost."

This would cost Jeb a little bit more of his heart, which he was willing to give. But Noah's warnings still rang loudly inside his head. Could he follow through and stay the course?

He prayed he could, and he would talk to the bishop about his fears and concerns.

"Denke." Jeb nodded and shook Noah's hand. "I'm glad we've come to an understanding. I want this to be a work shed Rebecca can use every day. I believe she will find the shed efficient and accommodating."

Noah chuckled and hurried toward his house. Then he called back, "I have no doubt she will appreciate it."

The next week was a busy one as the whole community prepared for the upcoming mud sale. Jeb helped neighbors put finishing touches on the things they wanted to sell at auction and also helped set up the grid for the sale to run smoothly.

On Saturday, Jeb and Adam loaded up the hauling buggy with potted lilies and a few other perennials and took off to the third sale of the season. Rebecca, Hannah and Franny had all kinds of foods and crafts to showcase, and Noah had some farm tools to be auctioned, so Noah packed the family buggy with their wares, including two quilts to be auctioned off, too.

Noah had told Jeb this particular sale went toward the volunteer fire department, and since several Amish men volunteered, the whole countryside came to show their appreciation. "It's like a big festival, with food and celebrations."

"I heard Becca and her sister talking about the quilts they'd made."

"Some of the quilts go for hundreds of dollars," he'd said. "The *Englisch* get intense about handmade Amish quilts."

Jeb had liked Campton Creek from the moment he set foot in the quaint little township. Everyone here from the *Englisch* to the Amish had been kind to him. He didn't mind helping to pay it back somehow. He might even volunteer himself.

Soon, the two buggies were heading into town, where the sale would be held in the big park by the creek, Jeb and Rebecca in front with Noah's family following.

While the horse trotted leisurely, Rebecca explained how the town came to be and pointed out the Campton Center, which used to be a private home. Majestic and big, the brick house with the grand white columns took center stage on the main thoroughfare. The *Englisch* Camptons were the original founders of the town and still had relatives here. Judy Campton, the matriarch who had lived in the house, was now in an assisted living facility that she'd funded to be built not far from here. It served both *Englisch* and Amish. But her friend and assistant Bettye still lived in the carriage house apartment and often helped out in the offices.

The house and grounds were pretty, but he rather enjoyed looking at Rebecca. She wore a light green dress that matched her eyes, and her hair was perfectly parted down the middle, not a strand out of place underneath her shining white *kapp*.

"A lot of people have been helped there—with legal issues, heath issues and financial issues. They serve the Amish mostly, but anyone in need is welcome. You might see Jewel running around. She's the manager and… Well, she's a bit eccentric but she has a heart of gold."

"I take it this Jewel person is not Amish."

"Neh." Rebecca giggled. "She used to be a bouncer at a bar, and she went through a lot—drugs, assaults, depression. But she got herself well of all that and now she likes to say she's high on Jesus." When he frowned, Rebecca added, "Jewel is one of those rare people who loves everyone, no matter their flaws. So, we in turn love her back."

Jeb listened in awe, wishing he had someone in his life to love him unconditionally. He had the Lord. He knew that and Bishop King had encouraged him to remember his faith, to breathe it and accept it, rather than trying to force himself onto it. "Let the faith grow from your heart, Jeb. Don't pretend. That won't work. You have the foundation, but you lost your way. You'll know it's in your heart the minute you accept *Gott*'s love fully back into your life. Your heart will burn with such joy." Then the bishop had smiled. "And you will be worthy of that joy."

Jeb could feel a burn right now. It happened each time he glanced at Rebecca. The day was beautiful and bright, with low humidity and the kind of spring breeze that made a man feel alive. And hopeful. A new life, a new beginning.

He felt it, all right. And he thanked the Lord for providing such moments. But how could he ever be worthy of such hopes, of a new beginning? He wanted so much, but he couldn't risk hurting Rebecca. She loved John, still loved John, or she would have married by now.

He'd not told her the truth—about John—and about what had truly happened the day Pauly died. Jeb's hope sank. If he were to be honest with her, Rebecca would send him packing.

He'd have no new beginning. Just another tragic ending.

Rebecca wondered about Jeb. They'd been laughing and talking, then he'd gone quiet on her. She'd noticed that about him. Sometimes, he'd go to a place in his mind, a faraway place. The place where he kept his secrets and his pain.

She wished she could help him, but she had her own dark times, her lonely times full of regret.

She wished they could help each other.

Lord, I pray You will show us the way.

Her silent petition on their part would stay between *Gott* and Rebecca. As they pulled up the wagon full of plants, she turned and checked to see if Noah and Franny were behind them. Katie waved to her and smiled. Rebecca waved back, then she looked over at Jeb. "Are you ready for this?"

"As ready as can be. I'll do whatever is needed."

"Is something wrong?"

"No." He gave her a crooked smile. "I guess I'm feeling homesick and missing those I love."

Ah, that would explain his sudden quietness. "They are safe with *Gott* now. And you are here on earth, on this fine day. I hope you have *gut* memories of today."

He gave her a soulful smile. "I think I will."

"Everyone is here and accounted for," she told Jeb. "The boys came early in the summer buggy to help set up. We hope. Those three manage to get right into trouble just standing still."

"Adam says his brothers keep him in trouble."

Rebecca couldn't argue with that. "I think that's part of why Noah sent him to help us. That and the poor youngie is a distraction for us."

"Oh," Jeb said, back to smiling. "Do I distract you from your work?"

She gave him a quick glance and caught the smile he tried to hide. "At times, yes."

After they found the big open booth where they'd

set up their plant nursery, he laughed and hopped down to get the horse situated. Then he started helping her unload the plants. "So, I'm a distraction," he reminded her. "So are you at times."

Rebecca shook her head. "We are so concerned with distracting each other that it's becoming another distraction. Why don't we just accept that we are friends?"

Hiding his disappointment, he said, "I thought that was a given."

She pursed her lips in a teasing way. "I need something official."

He grinned. "I took this job because I needed money and a purpose. You've given me that and more. I'd like to be your friend."

"Then you are my new friend, Jeb."

"Ah, then call me Jeb, the way you've been doing."

"And you call me Becca, the way a friend should."

They stood with a white lily between them. An Easter lily.

"To new beginnings," Jeb said, watching how she held tight to the plant.

"To new sunrises and sunsets," she replied. Then she sniffed at the lily, her eyes closed in bliss, her smile shining a light on his heart.

Jeb had never wanted to kiss a woman so badly, but he stood and took in the lemony scent of the lily, along with the sweet perfume that seemed to surround Becca.

That joy burned another warm thread through his heart, a thread that warred with the secrets of his soul and bound him to this woman forever.

Chapter Twelve

Rebecca's nursery booth stayed busy all day long. She could hear the auctioneers calling out, their gavels hitting against the podium each time an item was sold. Hannah came to help and told her their quilts had sold quickly.

"Both went to sisters who live next to each other in Florida. They were so happy to get them and know that sisters had quilted them together. One loved the wedding ring quilt and the other had to have the tiger lily." She poked Rebecca's arm. "When I told her how you'd made it and also grow lilies, she said they'd come by here soon."

"The threads of life," Rebecca said with a smile. "They flow through all of us. It's nice to know what we created together might be shared with their daughters one day. Or that lilies I grew will grace their gardens."

Hannah glimpsed at her, then waved to an Amish couple as they strolled by. "You're sounding wise, sister, but I think I hear a bit of resolve in your observation."

"I'm not wise, just beginning to see more and more how we're all connected. But I am resolved. I have to remember I am content, and *Gott* knows my future."

Hannah moved some colorful pots of Gerber daisies closer to the front row so customers could see them better. "Does this resolve have to do with the man over there loading lilies into that tiny car?"

Rebecca glanced to where Jeb moved back and forth to help Jewel place several White Lemonades into the trunk of Jewel's vehicle. Jewel planted a new garden of lilies just about every year at the Campton Center. The ruffled, creamy lemonade flower would open early with lush, hardy blossoms, and it tolerated the winters.

"It might," she admitted, after considering her sister's question. Keeping her voice low, she watched Jewel and Jeb having a lively discussion. "Jeb and I had a *gut* talk on the way here. But I don't expect him to stick around, even if he does become Amish again."

"Where would he go?" Hannah asked. "He says he likes it here."

"Onward," Rebecca said while she fussed and plucked at her plants. "He's a wanderer."

"Might he settle one day, if he found the right place and the right person?"

"That's what I have to be practical about," Rebecca said. "I have to accept whatever *Gott* has planned for Jeb. But I'd like it if he stayed. He and I have reached an agreement. We will be friends."

Hannah almost snorted but held her hand over her mouth instead. "Friends? Well, that's so practical I can hardly stand it."

"Don't tease," Rebecca cautioned. "There can never be more between us, and I must accept that."

"Because you have feelings for him?" Hannah asked, surprised.

"Because he needs a community and *Gott* back in his life," Rebecca said. "That is his priority right now. But… I do like him. A lot."

"Does he know that you like him a lot?"

"Shh, he's coming back. Of course not. I can't tell him anything when I'm not even sure myself. Now, hush up and help me line up the Stargazers."

Hannah nodded. "*Ja*, while I try to ignore those stars in your eyes."

"Who has stars in their eyes?" Jeb asked from the corner.

Rebecca shot her sister a warning glance. "I do. We should make a fair amount of money and be able to contribute more this year to the Volunteer Firemen's Fund."

"A good cause," Jeb said. "I talked to Jeremiah Weaver about joining up."

Her sister smiled at Jeb. "You're settling in nicely, ain't so?" Hannah's voice held that mischievous tone Rebecca knew so well.

"For now, I'd say so," Jeb replied, his eyes on Rebecca. "I'll go find us a quick lunch. Anything in particular you'd like, ladies?"

"The roast beef hoagies are great," Hannah said. "I'll have one of those."

"I'll take a chicken salad sandwich," Rebecca told him.

"Okay, I'll be back soon with that and some drinks."

"I can give you some money," Rebecca offered, digging through her tote bag.

"No, my treat," Jeb replied. "My boss pays me well."

They all laughed at that, but after he strolled away, Rebecca gave her sister a playful slap on the arm. "You are so bad."

"I can ask a person a simple question," Hannah replied with a smirk.

"It is interesting that he's thinking about becoming a volunteer fireman," Rebecca said, her gaze following Jeb as he greeted people.

"So interesting," her sister teased. "I think Jeb's wandering days will soon come to end. Think about how many people come here, some to come home, some to hide away from the world, but most always stay."

Rebecca shook her head. "I have given this over to the Lord, sister. If Jeb stays here, it will be *Gott*'s will, and it will have to be Jeb's decision. We are friends, and that will have to suffice."

She wouldn't hold him back from moving on, because she wasn't sure she could give her heart to anyone again. No matter how much Jeb made her feel as if she'd already lost part of that heart.

"Aenti Becca, I bought a doll," Katie said as she rushed up to Becca's booth.

The little faceless doll wore a light blue dress and tiny apron. It had no face because the Amish believed everyone was alike in the eyes of God. They didn't believe in graven images of any kind.

"That is a pretty little doll, for certain sure."

Katie swayed and hummed. "I named her Becky after you. Mamm said that name is a lot like Becca."

"Well, that's mighty sweet of you," Becca said, giving Katie a hug. "Where have you been all day?"

The crowd had dwindled to just a few strollers, and she only had a few potted lilies and plants left. It had been a nice day.

"I had to stay with Mamm," Katie said, shrugging. "She fretted about me getting lost. My *bruders* don't like me tagging along."

Her cute pout only reminded Rebecca of the days to come. Katie would be a heartbreaker one day. Rebecca wished she could prepare her sweet niece for the hard parts of growing up.

"Does your *mamm* know you're with me now?" she asked Katie.

Katie danced back and forth with her faceless doll. "Uh-huh. She watched me and said to *kumm* straight here and stay put, while she cleans up and gets ready to go home."

Becca glanced down the way and waved to Franny. Her sister-in-law nodded and waved back. Franny's thoughtfulness in allowing her children to spend time with Rebecca made her thankful, but also hit her with a bittersweet pain.

Thinking about John, she remembered how kind and sweet he'd been, always with a smile or a joke. He made her laugh. He made her want to be a better person. She'd dreamed of the day they'd have a child together. When she lost him, her world had gone dark and even now, she preferred being in the shadows. She craved a quiet life. But lately, she'd become restless, her heart yearning for something she might not ever have.

Jeb had changed her way of thinking and lightened her loneliness. He'd brought their lunch and sat to eat with them, in between customers. Hannah helped there while they finished their meal. The food fulfilled Rebecca's hunger, but each time she glanced at Jeb, she thought again of how much she'd lost. She could never forget John. But Jeb was different—world weary and aged, but still handsome. He'd brightened in both spirit and looks since the day he'd come walking up to her house.

Thank You, Father.

Now, she began to pack up her plants, handing them off to him one by one, so he could carry them to the waiting buggy. When he returned for another round, Katie showed him her doll.

"That's nice," he said, glancing from the *kinder* to Rebecca. "My *mamm* used to make those dolls. She only had boys, so she'd give them to her friends for their daughters."

"You didn't have a sister?" Katie asked, surprise shining in her eyes.

"No, just a brother."

"Where is your *bruder*?"

Jeb looked at Rebecca, helpless on how to answer.

"Katie, do not pester Jeb. He has to finish his work."

"Can I help?" Katie asked, on to another scattered thought.

"Why don't you put Becky here by my tote," Rebecca

said, giving Jeb a quick glance. "Then you can carry the small herb pots back to the wagon."

"Okay." Katie carefully lifted one clay pot of mint. "I'll be so careful." Then she tiptoed her way to the buggy.

Jeb smiled, then let out a breath. *"Denke."*

Rebecca nodded. "She is inquisitive."

"As she should be at that age."

He grabbed more pots and hurried to the buggy. Soon, he and Katie were in a deep conversation about butterflies.

But Rebecca could see the darkness falling back over his features. He somehow blamed himself for his brother's death. She prayed he'd be able to talk to the bishop about that and hand it over to the Lord. Sometimes, forgiveness didn't *kumm* easy, especially if a person couldn't forgive himself.

She had a feeling Jeb would not quit wandering until he could do that very thing.

Katie managed to get permission to ride home with Rebecca and Jeb, but she didn't squeeze between them. She sat in the back with what was left of their supply of plants.

"I like lilies," she said in a singsong voice. "Consider the lilies of the field…" Katie went on humming and talking to her doll. "My *aenti* grows pretty flowers. She has a gift."

Rebecca shot a quick glimpse toward Jeb and smiled. "Her *mamm* teaches her Bible verses in both Deutsch and *Englisch*," Rebecca whispered. "She is a good learner."

"She is wise," Jeb replied, his gaze on Rebecca for a moment. "God takes care of the lilies of the field and all creatures."

"He does, indeed." She settled back, tired but content, the lingering scent of Easter lilies—*Lilium Longiflorum*—wafting out around them. "He gave us such a beautiful earth. I'm honored to be able to work with His world."

"We had a profitable day, didn't we?"

She nodded. "*Ja*, better than I'd expected." Then she added, "*Denke* for your help today."

"Just doing the work you pay me to do."

"You will receive extra for the overtime."

He took a glimpse at her as they turned the big buggy onto her lane. "Then I can buy you a meal again."

"Or I could cook us a meal, to celebrate."

"That would work."

They dropped Katie off and watched for traffic as she crossed the road and ran home, Noah waiting for her with a smile.

"Your brother didn't even fuss at me today," Jeb said after they'd unloaded the few remaining plants from the buggy. "He kept me busy, though, probably so I wouldn't spend too much time with you."

Rebecca had seen Jeb helping out wherever he was needed. Noah would call him to do a favor in his stall, then send him to take over for someone else so they could go on a break. Noah's way of getting Jeb involved in the community, and it seemed to have worked. People had commented to Jeb each time he helped load pots and flowers onto their cars or vehicles.

As they pulled the buggy up to the stables, Rebecca turned to face Jeb. "Well, my *bruder* isn't here now, is he?"

Jeb gave her a look that told her about many things without him saying a word. Then he leaned toward her. "Are you saying you want me to stay and visit for a while?"

She glanced at the dusk. "The sun is about to set. It would be a shame to watch it all by myself."

Jeb looked from her to the creek. "I wouldn't mind seeing the sunset. Let me get the animals settled and I'll meet you back there."

Rebecca watched as he hurried to the barn.

Now, why did I do that?

She should have said good-night and sent Jeb on his way.

But as much as she loved watching the sunsets to the west, she hated sitting on that bench alone.

Would it hurt to enjoy just a few more minutes with a man who had become her friend?

Chapter Thirteen

Jeb hurried with taking care of the horses and made sure the chickens were fed. Since Rebecca had no other animals, he made quick work of his chores, then washed up at the pump near the barn. He was tired, but in a good way. He'd met a lot of nice people today. Some frowned at him, but the bishop had made a special visit to their booth to talk to Rebecca and him, probably to see how they acted around each other.

"You are a great help to our Rebecca, Jeb," Bishop King had told him after buying two bright yellow lilies.

Jeb thought about how this place settled him and kept him calm. It would be hard to leave if he did decide to do that. Rebecca made each day so easy, and he had meant what he told her. He wanted to stay in Campton Creek. But wanting and doing were two different things. And even the best plans could change in a heartbeat.

When he came out of the barn, he saw her sitting on the bench, the old oak nearby shading her from the last of the sun's rays. She held a small tray with lemonade and two small plates of what looked like cake.

"What do you have there?" he asked as he approached. She smiled and scooted over.

"I had one loaf of apple bread left. Thought we could have a bite."

"That's nice. I like apple bread. But then, I've never turned down any food you've offered, in case you haven't noticed."

"I have noticed. *Gut* thing I like to bake."

He took the glass of lemonade and a chunk of the moist cake. "You are a kind person, Becca."

"*Denke.* I could say the same about you."

He chewed another chunk of cake, wondering what she'd think if he blurted out all his secrets and fears. "I have not always been kind. Bishop King has helped me to find a way to let go of all of the things holding me from my faith."

"Such as?"

"Anger, bitterness, regret and my need to fight starting over in a new place."

"That's a lot to let go of and straighten out." Rebecca gave him an earnest appraisal. "Would you like to tell me why you're so angry?"

Here was his opportunity to come clean, but Jeb held back. They'd had such a nice day and he didn't want to ruin it now. "I guess I'm angry about my home life not being so good, and that I tried my best and still failed. I seem stuck in the past, but I can't go back to fix it."

"You can't blame yourself for everything, Jeb." She sat silent, her hands in her lap. "When you're ready, will you tell me more about Pauly and what happened to him?"

She wanted the truth. He needed to give her the truth. "I want to tell you everything, but could we just be friends while we sit here? Could we enjoy each other's company and this evening?"

"I did say whenever you are ready," she replied on a soft whisper. "I want you to know you can tell me anything and I won't judge you."

He nodded, his appetite gone, his fears like talons clawing at his skin. "I'll remember that."

They finished their apple bread, and she set the tray down on the grass. Then Rebecca did something that made him wish he could be honest with her.

She took his hand and held it in hers while the bright yellow orb of sunlight slipped over the trees and the whole sky glistened and shimmered in a cascade of pink and purple.

As the last of the sun's rays descended, Jeb knew one thing for sure. They had gone past the friendship mark.

Something more was going on with them now.

The next week, Jeb started on cutting the boards to build the potting shed he'd planned out for Rebecca. She rarely came into the barn, so he managed to saw several boards and number them before he stacked them in a corner.

Adam ran back and forth to alert Jeb if Rebecca was nearby.

"She's hanging wash."

"She's hoeing the vegetable garden. I'll go help and distract her."

"She's playing with Lily. That dog likes the treats she bought for her at the general store."

"Aenti Becca walked over to see Mamm. We're in the clear."

Today Jeb stepped out of the barn with Adam, since he'd just reported Rebecca had gone with his *mamm* to see a sick neighbor.

"Okay, so we'll measure the square footage underneath that old live oak that borders the corner of the field closest to the house. I've already cleared the ground since she doesn't want weeds growing on the edge of her garden."

"She's mighty thankful for that," Adam told him.

"But you didn't let anything slip, right?"

"*Neh*, I'm not going to spill the beans. Mamm and Daed know, 'cause I heard them talking about it the other night. Daed told me if I ruin the surprise, I'll have to clean the chicken coop for a month."

Having cleaned a few chicken coops, Jeb could commiserate with the boy. "Try not to mention it when she's around," he said. "You've been a great help. On Saturday, after half day, we'll work in your *daed*'s barn to build the frame for the roof."

Adam bobbed his head. "Then we just tote it over here and frame it up. Only after Mamm and Hannah take her to town."

"That's the plan," Jeb said. "Now let's measure this ground to be precise."

They hurried and figured out the dimensions and Jeb wrote them on an old slab of wood he kept out of sight.

They finished and went to prune the herb box so Rebecca would have fresh herbs to dry and some to use in her cooking.

By the time she came home, they were done with work and fishing at the creek.

She marched out and did a quick inspection, glancing over the growing lilies, then back to the vegetable garden, then the herb box.

"We did it all," Adam called. "Everything on your list is finished, Aenti."

"That's *wunderbar gut*, Adam. You can go home early."

Adam shook his head. "I wanna catch some fish first."

Jeb sent Rebecca a big smile. "He's already caught two nice breams."

"Okay, then," Rebecca said. "I have things to do in the kitchen. I will talk to you later."

Jeb waved and watched her walking toward the house, Lily Dog at her feet. It was a beautiful picture to see her there beside the blooming lilies, a dog dancing at her feet. A homey, welcoming picture.

One he thought of every day.

Since she'd held his hand the other night, something had changed between them. They were shy at times and laughing at other times. He had to wonder if this was what it felt like to fall in love. He smiled more, had more patience, tried hard to please Rebecca, enjoyed his talks with the bishop and slept better every night.

It could be the work and the sunshine. Or it could be the food and fellowship. But Jeb knew in his heart, he was changing because of Rebecca's sweet disposition and her tolerance of a stranger showing up on her doorstep. Rebecca showed people grace and kindness, things he'd not always had at home or out in the world.

But this week, he'd felt a shift in her that concerned him. Did she feel the tug and pull of feelings, just as he did? Was she fighting those feelings, too?

After Adam went home, Jeb lingered to water some plants and hopefully see Rebecca again.

She finally came out on the porch. "All done for the day?"

"I think so," he said, noting she looked tired. "How about you?"

"I'm done here. We had a good crowd this morning. Thank you for taking the buggy of plants up to the road. I sold all of them." She studied her blue sneakers. "I like the bench you fixed and placed up there. I can sit and read while I wait for any customers."

"Well, you are welcome, but you don't have to sit there in the sun all day."

"*Neh.* I only sell there during heavy traffic times— morning rush is a *gut* time to catch people."

"Is there such a thing as morning rush in Campton Creek?" he teased.

"*Ja,* it gets a little busy now and then," she retorted with a smile. "A lot of buggies heading out for the day."

They laughed together, then Jeb asked, "Rebecca, are we okay, you and me?"

"What do you mean?"

"Are we friends?"

"*Ja*, but why do you ask?"

He couldn't blurt out his feelings, so he said, "I would never do anything to upset you."

"You haven't."

He wasn't handling this right. He tried again. "You held my hand the other night. It was nice."

Realization colored her eyes. "Oh, I did, didn't I?"

Jeb waited.

"I enjoyed holding your hand, but Jeb, you know how it is. We have to be careful. Noah is always watching."

"Noah had nearly given us his blessings."

"But he has to be sure… And I have to be sure."

"I see. You're all waiting for me to fail?"

He turned to leave, but she ran down the steps. "That is not what I said. Noah might be waiting for that, but I'm not."

"But you still aren't sure about me?"

"I'm sure of you, Jeb. I'm just not so sure of myself."

"Well, the same goes for me," he retorted, holding his disappointment tight. "I reckon we can keep working on it."

Rebecca gave him one of her soft smiles. "We are like those lilies out there. Growing, changing, blossoming. A work in progress."

Jeb wasn't sure he liked being compared to a flower, but he did see one correlation between himself and the lilies. "I aim to put down roots, Rebecca."

"*Ja*, and that's *wunderbar gut*," she replied. "But the question is—will you put down roots here or will you keep wandering and try again somewhere else?"

"I'm talking with the bishop weekly. Doesn't that prove something to you?"

She smiled again, which only made him more agitated. "It proves you are working hard to find your way home—to your faith. You can take that with you anywhere as long as you're truly back among us."

"Or I keep my faith right here in Campton Creek and be a content man."

Her next smile held a bit more mirth. "And that would make me a content woman, Jeb."

"Right now, you are a confusing woman," he retorted. But he said it with his own smile widening. "I'm going across the road now, Becca. See you tomorrow."

"Good night, Jeb."

He chuckled and waved as he walked away, the glow of their banter giving him new hope, even while the old fears pushed at his heart. He'd find a way, some way, to stay here and he'd also find a way to tell her what he'd held on his heart since the day she'd let him into her kitchen.

He wanted to spend the rest of his life as near to Rebecca as he could be. If that meant just being her employee, he'd have to accept that and consider it a gift from God.

Chapter Fourteen

❧

As summer progressed, Rebecca's field of lilies grew and developed, the scent of the blooms filling the air from dawn to dusk. She opened her bedroom window as night settled over the yard and gently sloping hills. The scent of the lilies, along with the magnolias her *mamm* had planted years ago, and a few gardenias she'd managed to keep in pots and bring in during the winter, surrounded her. Inhaling, she thanked God for his beautiful world.

But summer also brought tourists, and today had been a busy day. Some just stopped to take pictures of the symmetric rows of lilies covering the countryside in shades ranging from white to lemon and orange, followed by reds and burgundies and deep purples. She tried to plant her lilies so the lighter shades would show off and lead to the deeper shade. It made for a beautiful field, almost like a colorful quilt.

She also mixed up a few in a special area, so they could hybridize and produce new variances. Most people came to buy but weren't sure where to begin or how. The mixed garden gave them an idea of which colors worked together. It had become a popular new addition to her garden.

Jeb had suggested she have pamphlets made up, explaining the basic steps of planting, growing and hybridizing the exquisite flowers. He'd helped her draft a sample, and he'd taken his design to the Campton Center where Jewel studied it and created a mockup on the fancy laptop that she used to keep the center running.

Jewel had delivered the big box of pamphlets this morning.

"See what you think, Rebecca," the sturdy woman with short, cropped hair and dangling red earrings had said, her smile shining bright with joy. "I had so much fun designing this for you. I found stock photos online and bought us a few. I even came to your field the other day when you'd gone visiting and snapped some photos. Jeb had a great idea with the handout information. That one, he's a keeper. Hardworking and easy on the eye."

Jewel had winked when she'd said that, causing Rebecca to blush. "He sure brags on you," the eccentric woman had whispered. "I think he's got a big old crush on you."

"We are friends," Rebecca tried to explain. "But I do appreciate his knowledge on such things. I never thought to create a pamphlet on growing lilies. I can hand them out, rather than repeating myself over and over. Progress."

Jewel, wearing a bright floral long tunic over blue

jeans, had agreed. "Jeb is smart. You let me know when these run out. I'll order more."

"How much do I owe you?" Rebecca asked.

"It's paid," Jewel replied. "The man who has a crush on you covered the tab, but don't fret. I gave him a supergood deal." Another wink, which Rebecca interpreted to mean Jewel had saved Jeb from giving up too much of his pay.

Now as she stood looking out at the moonlit field, which showcased her moon garden lilies nicely, she felt a bittersweet ache in her soul. Her loving parents were gone to heaven, up there with her beloved John.

But she was still here on earth, and a new man had come into her life. A confusing, complex, tormented man who seemed to be running from himself more than from the world. Yet, he'd stopped here, had come to her door begging for work. And he'd done a lot of things to improve her little farm. He worked with the horses and cleaned and polished everything from the bearing reins to the saddles and back straps and fixed up broken buggies and even the old wheelbarrow. He'd cleaned and organized the barn and he planned to repaint it when things settled down after the spring rush.

So many little tasks she'd neglected, Jeb had found and taken care of. He never complained and he loved having Adam around. Did Adam make him think of his own brother, Pauly?

Rebecca closed her eyes and prayed to the Lord to help her make her way through this maze of feelings that shifted and shined in the same way her lilies did. Why did she feel this pull toward Jeb? Her feelings had gone from a soft pastel to a deep burning fire red. What was she to do?

She had no answers. She'd have to wait on the Lord with this predicament. But it was hard to wait sometimes.

She was about to go to bed when she saw a white flash moving along the outer row of lilies.

A goat.

Rebecca grabbed a shawl and ran down the steps and out into the yard, her hands flapping, her shouts sounding over the night. The big billy goat ignored her as he sampled some of her prettiest Farmer's Daughter circular-shaped blooms. Rebecca screamed and stomped her foot, but the old goat ignored her.

She went closer, hoping to scare him. "Get away. You'll be sick."

Then she heard footsteps running behind her. "Rebecca!"

Jeb. She whirled and motioned to him. "Old Billy's out and he's messing with my Farmer's Daughters."

Jeb went to work. He ran to the barn and came back with a broom and hurried to hit at the goat. The animal lifted his head and hurled his body toward Jeb, but Jeb was ready. He sidestepped and slapped the broom lightly on the goat's backside, causing the animal to careen away and back toward the pen from where he'd obviously escaped.

Jeb ran up to Rebecca. "Are you all right?"

"Ja," she said, out of breath, her braid of hair slipping over her shoulder. "I don't want him to be sick. He rules the roost over there."

Jeb glanced at the road, and then turned back to her, a smile cresting his face. "But he ruined the Farmer's Daughters."

Rebecca realized the implications of what she'd shouted out, then she smiled, too. Soon, they were both laughing so hard, he held her arms to steady her.

"I suppose that did sound strange," she managed between giggles. "But he'll be the one to pay. He's going to be sick."

"I'll find him, and I'll let Noah know what happened," Jeb said, still snickering. "Do we need to check on the...uh... *Farmer's Daughters*?"

They started laughing again. Rebecca shifted to turn and hit a stump. She went right into Jeb's arms.

Jeb stopped laughing, his eyes on her, his breath coming in huffs. "Rebecca..."

Rebecca's heart burned for something she couldn't describe. A need, a longing, a wish.

He leaned in and pulled her head to his, his hand on the thickness of her braid. Then he put his lips on hers and kissed her in a slow, sweet, lingering way that had her sighing into the moonlight.

She didn't want to let go, but logic took over. She pulled away. "I... I should get inside. It's late."

And her hair was down, her head bare of her *kapp*. She still had on her old work dress, but her apron was in her room.

Jeb nodded, his eyes dark in the grayish-white light. "I'll go find Old Billy."

They both stood still.

"Rebecca?"

"*Ja?*"

"Do you regret me kissing you?"

"*Neh.* Because I kissed you back."

"I noticed that," he said, his smile showing.

She tugged her shawl around her. "I might just thank Old Billy on that account, but I won't forgive him for ruining, I mean, tearing up my lilies."

Jeb grinned again. "And I will always remember the name of that particular lily."

He walked her back to the porch. "I might want to kiss you again, just so you know."

Her heartbeat raced, her pulse hummed, her hope soared. "And I might let you, just so you know."

She went back inside and checked her field again. No more goats. If Old Billy had broken out, more might come.

But Jeb and Noah would take care of that.

She wondered if Jeb would mention he'd helped her scare the ornery goat off her property.

He surely wouldn't mention what else had happened.

Jeb had kissed her in the moonlight mist. And she'd liked kissing him back.

The next morning Noah showed up on her doorstep.

"I'm sorry about Old Billy getting out. The fence near the edge of the goat pen has been damaged, probably from him trying to break out. It's fixed and he's gonna be okay, but he had a bad upset stomach. Doc King came to check on him this morning."

Samantha Leah King was the only female veterinarian in this part of the county, and she was also the only

Amish vet available for miles around. She'd returned to the fold a year or so ago, after surviving a tornado and criminals trying to silence her, and married Micah King. They lived on the other side of Campton Creek on Micah's farm, where she had an office and kennels out back.

"I'm glad he's okay," Rebecca said as she guided Noah inside and gave him a cup of coffee. "I hurried the moment I saw him out there."

"Jeb told me."

"*Ach*, is that why you're here?" she asked, giving her brother a questioning glance.

"He told me he heard you screaming—that he was sitting on the stoop at the *grossdaddi haus*."

"Do you believe him?"

"I do," Noah admitted. "I'd seen him there when I was making my final rounds, but I didn't bother him. A little while later, I heard shouts and then I saw him sprinting across the yard. Before I could get to him, I saw one of the nannies trying to break through. I had to go and fetch one back and get the others and the kids settled. I'm surprised they didn't all escape."

"Did he bring Billy back?"

"*Ja,*" Noah said. "And told me what had happened."

"You didn't come to fuss at me, or warn me against him?"

Noah let out a sigh. "*Neh*, and I was wrong on that account. I can see he's a good, trustworthy worker, but he is still an outsider, sister."

"He's trying, Noah. At your request. Don't pressure him."

"Are you afraid he'll leave?"

"I'm not afraid. I know he'll leave if you keep pushing him. Let it be. *Gott* will show him the way. You move between forcing us together or wanting him to just go. None of this can be your doing, or mine. It's Jeb's decision." Then she touched Noah's arm. "*Gott*'s will."

Noah's dark eyes softened. "I will stop, then. You need to understand, I only want the best for you."

Rebecca put her hand over his. "Then let me be, *bruder*. I'm content and I'm fine. Jeb is an honorable man who still knows our ways, even if he's been out there on his own for a long time."

"You'll wait to see if he follows through?"

"I know he's following through. He meets with the bishop once or twice a week. He's learning and he's willing to return to us."

"To us?"

Leave it to her brother to misinterpret her words.

"To his Amish ways, and to *Gott*."

Noah finished his coffee. "He helped me last night and I will remember that. He's a big help to you—so I will consider that. I have no quarrel with Jeb if he does what he's saying he wants to do. Either staying or going, he'd best do right by you, too."

Rebecca stood and took their empty cups to the sink and pumped some water over them. "Then we both need to let him do his work and finish what he's started. I have faith that Jeb will make the right decision."

"We cannot make it for him, as you say," Noah replied, nodding, his hand tugging at his beard. "I'm sorry

I've tried to arrange things to suit *mein* self. I had *gut* intentions."

"I know you had the best intentions," she told her brother as he stood and tugged at his straw hat. "Now let's find out Jeb's intentions and *Gott*'s intent."

After Noah left, Rebecca got ready for another busy day. When she heard Jeb and Adam laughing and talking, she watched them from the kitchen window. Jeb carried a huge blue umbrella and a white chair, heading for the lane.

She moved from the back window to the front and watched, amazed, as he dug a small hole at the end of the lane, near her sign, and placed the umbrella's pole into the earth and secured it with some boards and big stones. Adam, grinning, then opened the bright blue umbrella wide.

Jeb had made her a better place to sit when she sold lilies and herbs on the side of the road. Adam put a small ice chest down beside the umbrella. She guessed it held water and other drinks.

Rebecca sat down and accepted the tears rolling down her face. A simple gesture, a thoughtful surprise, from a man who wanted so much to be seen, to be loved, to be a part of something.

"Please stay, Jeb," she whispered. "But not for me, *neh*. Stay for yourself, and for your faith."

She said a silent prayer to the Lord and asked Him to guide Jeb, and to help her. She wanted to be a friend to Jeb, but now she knew her feelings had changed to something more.

She wasn't ready to admit what that something was,

but her heart burned like a field of dirt in the stark sunshine.

Rebecca remembered how she'd felt with John. This felt much the same, but different. Stronger, intense and overwhelming.

Did she ever really know this kind of love before, even with John? They'd been so young. Now, she was a mature woman who'd witnessed births, weddings, life and death.

Her feelings too overwhelming to think about, she wiped her eyes and went out to thank Jeb and Adam for this thoughtful gift. She could never tell Jeb whom he reminded her of. That would put a wedge between them and make him think she was only being kind because he seemed so familiar.

"What have you two been up to so early in the morning?"

Adam beamed. "For you, Aenti. Jeb says you don't need to sit in the hot sun. I'll sit here and help you sell your lilies while he takes care of anyone wanting to see the field. It's our new Saturday morning tradition, ain't so, Jeb?"

"That's right," Jeb said, nudging Adam with his elbow. "We'd better get started, huh?"

"*Ja,* I can't have any slackers around here," she teased to hide the tremendous emotions rushing over her like the creek's gurgling waters.

But when her gaze met Jeb's and he smiled his soft smile, her thoughts settled into one realization. She was beginning to care about him as more than just a friend. It might even be love.

Chapter Fifteen

Jeb stood with the men at church the next Sunday, watching across the way for Rebecca to enter Noah's big barn. After the ministers had entered, the married men came next, then the married women. The single men filed in, so Jeb fell into place, being one of the older single men. He kept his eyes on the open doors. When Rebecca walked in with the other single women, she shot him a quick smile, then lowered her gaze. The younger girls and boys then entered. The men removed their hats and soon the service began.

As they sang the old hymns in High German and without music, Jeb thought about how he would eventually have to stand up in church and ask for forgiveness so he could return to the Amish way of life. Here in Campton Creek. He'd been happier here than he'd been in his whole life. Rebecca was a big part of that happiness, but there was more. He felt at home here. This place seemed to bring people home, to reunite families and sweethearts, no matter their flaws, or the past, or their secrets. Maybe some of that goodness would rub off on him if he stayed. Being around Rebecca made him want to be more faithful, more truthful, more focused on community and Christ.

But before he could do any of that, he would have to tell Rebecca the truth about his relationship to John. Her John. Would she understand why he hadn't told her from the beginning?

He couldn't even understand it himself, so how could he make her see his reasons for keeping that from her? It had come time to reveal his secret to the bishop. He couldn't honestly confess without telling the bishop and Rebecca about the letters John had sent him, especially about the last letter he'd received from John telling Jeb he was to be married. It would look like he came here purposely to find Rebecca, but he'd come here because his cousin loved this place.

Then God had dropped him right into Rebecca's world.

Coincidence or God's—*Gott*'s—will?

After the service, the men ate sitting on benches set up underneath the old oak trees by Noah's barn, not far from where Jeb stayed in the smaller house. Jeb went to sit with Jeremiah and Micah, two men he'd already become friends with because Rebecca knew their wives, Ava Jane, and Samantha the vet, who some called Leah, the name her grandmother called her.

A couple of other men showed up, their gaze hitting on Jeb with curiosity.

"Where'd you come from?" an older man named Shem asked. "You remind me of someone."

Jeb lowered his head. He didn't want to lie. "I grew up in Ohio, but I moved around a lot, doing odds and ends."

"But you've been in the *Englisch* world, correct?" another man asked. "We don't get a lot of Martins around here."

"*Ja*, I've been moving around for a long time but I'm more Amish still than *Englisch*." Then he added, "My *daed* was a Mennonite. My *mamm* stayed Amish, and he... He tried to be Amish."

"There is no trying," Noah said as he settled next to Jeb. "Jeb here is going through the steps of returning to his faith—completely." He sent Jeb a determined smile.

Jeremiah laughed and looked at Noah. "I had to study with some youngies while working on the process of getting back to my faith. If I can sit and take the teasing I had to endure, I'm sure Jeb will make it all the way through."

Micah nodded. "Leah, as most of you know, had to do the same. She had been out in the world for a long time. But she fell right back into her Amish ways, although she did have to get approval to continue her veterinarian practice."

"We are all thankful for that," Noah added with a chuckle. "She is really *gut* with the animals."

Jeb smiled as the stories were told. Then he leaned toward Jeremiah. "I'm thinking of volunteering as a firefighter."

"We can always use another hand," Jeremiah said. "Let me know and I'll give you a tour of the station *haus*."

The conversation moved on, but after they'd eaten and now stood mingling, the older man who'd questioned Jeb before came up beside him.

Shem Yoder grinned at him. "Minna Schlock married a Mennonite close to thirty-five years ago. I know 'cause I had a crush on her. That might be who you remind me of, except I can't remember the man's name."

Jeb's heartbeat danced out of control. This man remembered his mother. He was about to come up with an answer when Noah called him to help with packing up the buggies.

"I must go," he said, nodding to Shem.

Shem stared after him for a moment and then turned and walked away. But Jeb had a feeling this was not over yet. He'd need to tell Rebecca the truth, and soon.

Two days later, Noah found Jeb inside the barn back at Noah's house. "Can I speak to you about something?"

Jeb lifted a long board and turned to Noah. "*Ja*, what is it?"

Noah let out a sigh. "Have you been completely honest with us about your reason for coming here?"

Jeb's heart accelerated into a high beat. "I believe I've told you all the important stuff."

"Shem Yoder thinks he knows you."

Jeb looked down at the board he'd been staining for Rebecca's potting shed. He worked here most afternoons when he got done with his paying work. Today, he'd loaded enough lily plants for the many buyers streaming in to make him never want to see a lily again.

But he did want to see those lilies, Rebecca's field of

beautiful flowers, again. He wanted to finish this project and see how she'd react to it. He wanted so many things.

"He mentioned something about that to me Sunday," Jeb replied. "I'm not sure what's he's talking about. I could look like someone he knows."

Noah's shrewd gaze stayed on him. "Shem has a *gut* memory for his age. He says you remind him of a girl he walked out with, until a man named Calvin Martin, a Mennonite who was just passing through, took her away."

Apparently, Shem's memory had returned, or he'd done some asking around. Jeb couldn't lie. Noah had begun to trust him. "Calvin Martin was my *daed*, Noah."

Noah looked surprised, then he became angry. "So, you did *kumm* here for a reason. But you couldn't have lived here before."

Jeb stopped his work and laid the staining rag down, then wiped his hands. Turning back to face Noah, he heaved a great sigh. "I never lived here. My *mamm* did, but she left when she was nineteen. She and my *daed* got married and moved to Ohio. Her family was not pleased that she'd married a Mennonite."

Noah let that soak in. "You grew up in Ohio, so that much is true, at least."

"I did, but I did not have the best childhood. I had a brother named Pauly. I've told Rebecca most of this."

"Except the part about your *mamm* being from here," Noah retorted.

Jeb decided to come clean. "There's more, Noah."

"I was afraid of that. You'd better get to the truth, Jeb."

They leaned back against the work counter, the soft hot wind of summer washing over them, the sounds of animals snorting and birds chirping making this seem like an ordinary day.

Jeb felt anything but ordinary.

"My *mamm* had a sister," he began. "Aenti Moselle was a bit younger than my mother, but they were so close. Aenti Moselle visited Mamm a lot, but she married a man who lived here in a nearby community. Emmett Kemp. They settled here in Campton Creek and had two children, a boy named John and a girl named Sadie."

Noah frowned. "The Kemps. Moselle was your *aenti*?" Gasping, he stepped back. "John Kemp was your cousin?"

Jeb nodded, his eyes burning with a hot moisture. *"Ja."*

Noah got in his face. "What are you doing here, trying to take his place? If Becca finds this out—"

Jeb held up a hand. "I didn't know, Noah. I did not know who she was until she'd already hired me. Then she told me her full name."

"But you did recognize the name? How?" Noah's face reddened with anger. "You didn't live here, and your grandparents have passed on. John's parents took Sadie and left. So how did you know to find her?"

"I didn't come here to find her," Jeb replied, trying to make sense of it. "I came here because John and I were close, and we visited each other when we were boys. Mostly he and his *mamm* would come to Ohio to visit. My *daed* didn't like to travel." He took off his hat and ran a hand through his hair. "John and I wrote to each other secretly for several years—because my *daed* didn't like my *mamm* getting letters from home. The last letter I got from him came just a few weeks before he died. He told me about being engaged to the most beautiful girl in the world."

Noah gasped again. "Rebecca. She was so in love with him, and I don't think she's ever recovered from seeing him being thrown from that horse."

"She told me about it and her fear of horses," Jeb said. "She knows most of what I've told you. Seems we both are still grieving things."

"But you have not told her the truth of you being John's cousin. Now I know who you remind me of— John. Almost like twins. Your mothers weren't twins, but they resembled each other, ain't so?"

Jeb nodded. "They were like twins and *ja*, they looked almost the same, but after a few years, my *mamm*'s health went down. They looked nothing alike by the time she died."

"I'm sorry for that," Noah said. "What happened in your home, Jeb?"

Jeb let out another sigh. "Alcohol. My *daed* drank too much and took his sorriness out on my mother, Pauly and me."

He explained his life to Noah. But still, he couldn't bring himself to talk much about the day Pauly died, or how he'd died.

When he finished, Noah stood staring at him, the sympathy in his eyes as clear as the anger he'd held earlier.

"And you say you've told Becca most of this?"

"I've told her everything but...me being John's cousin. I wanted to tell her a hundred different times, but Noah, I like my job and I mean Becca no harm. I was afraid I'd add to her pain and make things worse for her."

Noah studied him, shaking his head. "I don't see how she missed you looking so much like John. I'm surprised she's never mentioned that to you."

"It might be the same as me never bringing him up. Too painful."

"And she might have held back because she wouldn't want you to compare yourself to him," Noah replied.

"I'm nothing like him," Jeb admitted. "I left after Pauly died and I never looked back. I didn't make it home in time to make peace with my *daed*. I was too bitter and angry. I regret that, but I can't go back there. This was the place that stayed in my head. I still have some of John's letters. But I don't have much else."

Noah patted him on the shoulder. "First, you talk to the bishop, and then, Jeb, you talk to Rebecca. She believes in honesty above all else. You must tell her the rest of your story." Then he stood back. "Or I will."

Chapter Sixteen

Something was bothering Jeb.

Rebecca watched him now while he moved through the field alongside her, checking for spider mites and slugs. She had natural products to help combat pests, but it was a constant battle. Her lilies were hardy and resistant to most anything, but they had to be checked for every little thing. She liked pampering her crop. She'd explained this process to Jeb, and since he'd worked in fields before, he knew what needed to be done.

But he wasn't joking with her as he usually did or talking to Lily Dog in a low sweet voice, or mentioning Noah fussing at him about something, their usual workday banter.

Did he regret kissing her?

That thought popped into her head, coming from a place where she'd buried her own feelings about their kiss. She'd loved kissing him, but she'd also accepted that it was wrong. He'd lived out in the world, and now he was forbidden until he'd finished his sessions with the bishop.

Jeb must have buried his own feelings deep, too.

He was pulling back, shutting down. The kiss had made him realize he couldn't stay here. He didn't want to give her the wrong impression. He didn't want to hurt her or bring shame on her. That was Jeb, always trying to do the right thing.

So noble. But neither of them could deny the intensity of being in each other's arms.

Those thoughts played through her head as swiftly as the wind played through the hundreds of blossoming lilies.

She was so lost in thought, her heart hurting while her head decided this was for the best, she didn't hear Jeb calling out to her.

"Becca?"

Rebecca stood and found him on the far side of the field by the woods. He motioned for her, so she started out at a trot to reach him.

He was in what she called the breeder plants section, seedlings that could be used to breed new plants even though the seedlings hadn't been given a name themselves. These were used to hybridize, and she usually suggested them to customers who wanted to experiment with cross-pollination.

When she ran down the slope of the hill, she saw why Jeb had called her. Half of that row of plants and some nearby had been destroyed.

Jeb motioned to the woods. "I found animal tracks—most likely deer."

"Ach," she said, frustration coloring the one word. "I've been so distracted, I haven't had time to check down here. Deer do love daylilies."

"You mentioned this could happen," he said, staring down at the trampled, half-eaten plants. "But I didn't know to check here."

"It's not your fault, Jeb. I need to put up a fence or use some kind of deterrent, but I need money and time to do that."

She placed her hands on her hips, wondering what could happen next.

"I'll handle it," he said. "I can build a sturdy fence."

"But we can't fence the whole field."

He looked from the front of the field to the back, where the Green Mountain hills sat against the horizon. "No. We will take it one row at a time, if need be."

"That will take a long time, Jeb."

He stopped and stared over at her, realization making him frown. "Rebecca…"

"Don't," she said. "I know you might not be here forever, but for now, *ja*, I need some sort of fence. We'll clear this up and then I'll sit down and go over the budget."

She turned and hurried toward the house before he could tell her the truth. He had obviously decided to leave soon. Maybe sooner than he'd planned. She wished she'd never let him kiss her. And she wished she'd never kissed him back.

Jeb went into town and bought as much fence wire as he could find, then he loaded some fence posts onto the hauling buggy. He wouldn't have much time to work on the shed project. This new fence would take up most of the week and next week.

Mr. Hartford came out the back door of the general store. "Jeb, you got another project going on?"

"*Ja*. I'm going to try and fence up the back part of Becca's lily field—the section closest to the woods. The deer have found it."

"I see," Mr. Hartford said. "You'll need some help with that. It'll have to be a mighty tall fence to keep deer out."

"I can do it," Jeb replied, hoping that he wouldn't be proved wrong. "I'm buying tall posts and I'm going to wire it tight and high."

"All you have to do is put out the word," Mr. Hartford said. "You know your neighbors will show up."

Jeb finished loading the fence posts. "You are correct," he said with a grin. "I tend to forget that."

"Well, I hear you're back for good," the storeowner said. "Make the most of it and don't break your back. Then you won't be able to help anyone." After looking around, he added, "The Amish like to be helpful and since you're new around here, you'll become more endeared to them if you don't shun that help."

Jeb laughed and turned to his friend. "I'll do that. Thanks for the reminder. If I get a few able bodies, I can get this done much faster."

"Then you can return to your secret project," Mr. Hartford said with a wink. "And besides, anyone around here would want to help Rebecca. She's one of the kindest people I know."

"I cannot argue with that," Jeb said, wishing he could

shout it to the rooftops. But other than anything work related, Rebecca had been avoiding him. She must have decided that kiss was a bad idea. Or… Noah had said something to her about Jeb being related to John.

Jeb left and headed home. He'd get the word out that Becca needed help. Her good name would bring people, but his hard work could get the back fence in place. The deer would have to take a long detour if they wanted to nibble more lilies.

By the time he'd made it home, he had enough men to help. He'd first stopped at Micah's house. Micah had readily agreed.

Then Micah told him he'd help get the word out.

Noah showed up just as Jeb was unloading the fence posts.

"I heard Becca had deer trouble, and I'm not referring to you."

"Funny," Jeb said. Then he explained what he planned.

Noah listened, nodding. "I told her last time this happened I'd get her a fence up, but I got busy and neglected that. So, I'm here to help today."

Soon, buggies pulled up with more posts and fence wire.

Jeb saw Rebecca hurrying out of the house, her expression full of surprise. "What is all this?"

Noah chuckled. "Your worker here is going to fence up the back side of the property, to hopefully keep the deer away. Word got out that he might need some help."

Rebecca glanced from her bemused brother back to Jeb. "Is this true?" She looked out over the field and then back. "That would mean from the road to the creek."

"Ja," he said, wondering if she'd get mad. "Now I can fence up almost half of the open field, and after we save up a bit more, I can finish fencing the whole field, almost up to the creek. I'll put a fence there with a gate but leave room to walk along the creek. Mr. Hartford suggested I find some help to get this first phase going, and, well, word got around pretty quickly."

"I can see how the word spread," she replied. "I'm amazed that you thought of everything—even leaving the creek walking trail open. You sure make a good assistant, Jeb. I'm not sure what I'll do when you're gone."

Then she turned to head to the house.

Jeb glanced at Noah. "Does that mean she approves or that she's mad?"

Noah shook his head. "I can't figure women, but I think she's grateful, and if I know my sister, she's getting a pitcher of water or lemonade for us and probably finding some snacks, too."

"You could be right," Jeb replied, still worried. "I haven't had a chance to talk to her, Noah."

Noah gave him a disappointed stare. "I can tell you've been busy. But soon, Jeb. Better make it soon because Shem is a *gut* man and a *gut* friend, but he likes to stick his nose in everyone's business. Wouldn't you rather she hears this from you than from someone else?"

Jeb nodded, but the others were gathering, ready to work. "I promise, I'll tell her the truth, Noah. You have my word on that."

Noah gave him a slight nod. "Let's see what we can get done on this fence today. But I'll hold you to that promise."

* * *

Hannah showed up to help.

"How did you know?" Rebecca asked her sister when she met Hannah at the door to help her carry in some food.

"How does anyone know anything around here?" Hannah asked, laughing. "That grapevine keeps growing."

"*Denke* for coming over."

Hannah hugged her. "Of course. I brought some sandwiches and chips. Samuel will *kumm* later when he gets home from work."

Rebecca glanced out the back window. "I can't believe this is happening. I have to fight off deer every season."

"That's because you never asked for help," her sister said with a shrug. "Apparently, Jeb didn't either. But Mr. Hartford gave him a nudge since you never listen to his advice."

"I always thought Mr. Hartford was being kind, and felt sorry for me because I'm all alone," she admitted.

Hannah made a face. "No one feels sorry for you. You're an established businesswoman and your business brings in tourists and locals alike. That benefits all of the companies around here, Becca. You need to see your own value to this community."

Rebecca sat down, shocked. "I've never thought of it that way. Mr. Hartford knows if I succeed and have an easier way of doing things, I'll benefit him and the entire town."

"You can't see the good you do," Hannah replied, her

tone gentle. "But we can, and Jeb surely can. He's already improved things around here."

"He has done so much," she admitted. "But I still don't know if I can count on him to stay."

"He's doing everything he can to settle down, from what I hear," Hannah replied. "Everyone's talking about him getting ready to commit to his faith again. Why can't you believe that?"

Rebecca stood and went back to work. "I want to believe he means to stay, but I don't want to get my hopes up. Things can change in the blink of an eye."

She couldn't bring herself to tell Hannah that she and Jeb circled around each other—sometimes talking and laughing, other times avoiding each other. They'd done that since that one kiss.

She didn't plan on sharing that information either. If Noah got word of that—he'd set the wedding date for certain sure.

Hannah came to stand by her. "I know you'll never get over losing John, but you can't base every decision on what might go wrong. Try trusting *Gott* and yourself, for a change. Try focusing on what could go right. And try focusing on Jeb doing the right thing instead of wondering when he might walk away."

"Are you through?" she asked her sister with a teasing smile.

"*Neh*, I'm just getting started," Hannah shot back. "You're too stubborn for your own good at times."

Rebecca nodded. "I suppose I am at that. I won't forget what Jeb—and all of you—are doing for me. I'll ask for help from now on. If I need it."

"We all need it," Hannah said. "Now, let's get this food in place out on the porch. You know those men will be hungry once they finish this task."

Rebecca gathered trays and drink cups. "What a *wunderbar* thing—no more deer, or maybe even no Old Billy breaking out to sample my lilies."

"And a new understanding about yourself," her sister added.

"I'm not sure how you became so wise," she told Hannah, "but I love you for it."

"I love you, too," Hannah said. "And I like that light that sparkles in your eyes when you're looking at Jeb."

"I do not have a light or a sparkle," she retorted. "Jeb and I are friends. He's a *gut* worker."

Hannah snickered. "Just keep telling yourself that."

"I will."

They both giggled like teenagers, making Rebecca remember the days when they were young.

"I miss Mamm and Daed," she said. "I could use their wisdom these days."

"They are always with us," Hannah reminded her. "They taught us well."

"*Ja*, they did at that."

Rebecca watched as Jeb and the other men dug holes and stretched fence wire. While she appreciated the help, she also realized she needed someone around here to help her all the time.

She needed Jeb, in more ways than just for work.

But she'd keep that secret to herself for now.

Chapter Seventeen

Two days later, the weather turned nasty. Thunderstorms shook the earth with lightning, and rain fell in heavy silver sheets of mist. Jeb had to shut down the fencing, but with the help of most of the men in the community, they'd managed to complete the high fence directly next to the woods. The deer gathered there most nights, so the fence had become a way to hinder them from eating the lilies. But he needed to get the rest of the fence up, and soon.

"Your fence helps with so many issues," Rebecca told him as they sat on the porch that afternoon, waiting for the rain to lift. "Now if we could find a way to keep the *kinder* from crashing through the rows, too. They are like little lambs after the pretty blooms."

He laughed at that image. Children running through the fields. Somehow, that made his heart ache more than it made him mad. "You're right, there. Children are less inhibited than adults."

She glanced over at him. "Are you thinking about your brother?"

He nodded. "I guess I was. Pauly stayed childlike... up until he died at thirteen. Everything was a joy to him. Everything but our *daed*."

Shock darkened her eyes. "I can't imagine how that must have been. My parents were so gentle, so kind. I'd like to think I'd be the same if I ever had a child."

"You'd make a great mother, Becca."

She lifted her head, her gaze on him. "You did the best you could with Pauly, I'm sure."

Jeb stared out as the wind picked up and the trees swayed. "I tried, but I wasn't always patient with him."

He closed his eyes and asked God to help him. Then he looked over at Rebecca. "I'm the reason he's dead."

"What?" Yet another jolt of shock—because of him telling her the truth. But Jeb felt he had to tell her something about his past. Maybe he'd get up the nerve to tell her about John's letters, too.

"He'd run away when Daed got really mean, usually to where I worked in a buggy repair shop."

"What happened?" Rebecca said. "I won't judge you, Jeb. You've been punishing yourself enough for the both of us."

She saw so many things not spoken, he thought. "*Ja*, I have at that."

"Then let go of some of your pain. Tell me and it will stay here between us."

Jeb stared at his glass of tea. "I was busy when he came running in, crying. When Pauly got in that kind of frantic mood, he was hard to contain." He stopped, gathered his emotions. But the lump in his throat wouldn't go away. "He was crying and stomping. My boss had been kind about these episodes, but on that day, we had some important visitors from a furniture place in Pittsburgh. They were interested in having us do a huge order for wardrobes and rocking chairs."

"You needed to focus on work, and your upset *bruder* showed up?"

He nodded. "My boss wasn't happy. It was the worst possible time for Pauly to have a meltdown."

"What happened?"

"I excused myself and took him out back. I tried to get him to settle down and wait there at the picnic table. I promised I'd get him a hamburger—his favorite food."

Rebecca smiled at that. "I like hamburgers myself." Then she nudged Jeb. "Go on."

"I left him there, fuming and crying. He kept repeating, 'I don't like Daed. I don't like Daed.'" Jeb swallowed again, his heart burning with sorrow and guilt. "I hurried back inside to finish up with our customers and when I finally went back out, Pauly was gone."

Rebecca put a hand to her lips. "Oh, no."

Jeb studied her, looking for condemnation. When he saw none, he decided he needed to tell her the rest of the story. "I went searching for him along the roadside. After a few minutes, I spotted him up the way and ran toward him, calling to him."

Rebecca put a hand on his arm, her eyes meeting his.

"When he saw me, he ran toward me." Jeb gulped in air, his heart hammering. "But he didn't look both ways, Becca. He didn't look. He only wanted his brother. The pickup truck never saw him coming. It all happened in a few seconds and then… He was gone."

Rebecca stood and then kneeled in front of Jeb, her hands grasping his. "This is not your fault, Jeb. Pauly was a special child and *Gott* knew that."

He lifted away and stood. "Then why did *Gott* let that happen to him? He was upset and he was innocent. Pauly didn't care if I had work to do. He needed me and I failed him."

Rebecca was there by him, the rain and wind slashing at their clothes, water falling off the eaves to wet them. She turned Jeb to face her, then she put a hand on his jaw. "Jeb, you did not cause this. It was a tragic accident, a horrible accident. You have to see that."

Jeb looked into her misty eyes and shook his head. "What I see every day and every night is my Pauly flying through the air and then landing on the asphalt road. Then he didn't move. He never moved. He never woke up."

"Jeb," she whispered. "Jeb." Then she tugged him into her arms and held him. "I'm here. *Gott* is here. You've found a home now, and you can seek forgiveness and comfort."

Jeb's emotions exploded with as much fire as the pounding rain. The wind washed at his tears while Rebecca held him and hugged him. He sobbed until he had no tears left.

But Rebecca didn't move. She didn't walk away. She didn't ask him to leave her property. Instead, she stayed with him.

Finally, he lifted his head and wiped at his eyes. "Rebecca?"

"*Ja?*"

"You are an amazing woman."

Her bashful expression showed she didn't believe that.

"I mean it," he said. "I've never told anyone about this—about my part in this. Daed, of course, blamed me and acted as if he really cared. After the way he'd treated Pauly, his reaction made me angry, and we had words—horrible words said to each other. Once I'd buried my brother next to my *mamm*, I left Ohio. I've been searching for something since then."

"You were searching for redemption, Jeb. And now you've found it."

Jeb saw by her earnest expression that she meant those words. He held her, their eyes meeting, and with a sigh Rebecca lifted up and pressed her lips on his. The kiss was soft and welcoming and full of that redemption he'd needed for so long.

When she pulled away, she studied his face and gave him a soft smile. "How do you feel now?"

Jeb touched her wet hair, one finger tracing a loose curl. "I feel as if I've been washed clean. I feel…hopeful." He was about to tell her the rest—about John.

But a clap of lightning filled the sky, and the world went dark.

Becca automatically tugged him close, more from fright than anything else. Then they both stepped back and checked the clouds.

"This weather is about to get worse," he said. "Let's get inside."

Grabbing her hand, Jeb rushed Rebecca into the house and shut the door. The trees leaned sideways as walls of water and wind pushed over the land and lashed at the earth. Small limbs twisted from the trees and catapulted across the yard.

"My lilies," she said, her voice hollow with fear. "This could ruin my whole crop."

Jeb tugged her away from the window. "Let's pray that won't happen."

They sat on the stairs, holding tight to each other while the world outside screamed and thundered with a mighty rage.

Jeb could understand that kind of rage, but while the storm hissed and sneered, he managed to let go of some of his own rage. And he had Rebecca—and God—to thank for that.

After the storm ended, leaving a soft drizzle behind, they put on muck boots and rain capes and went to check on the crops. Sure enough, Rebecca found some damaged stems.

"If the blooms are broken past about two-thirds of the stem, that plant might not produce again. I need to check on the cutting plants. Remember when I explained I have customers who want to have fresh-cut lilies in their homes. They come back each year to buy more just for cutting and displays, so those plants are considered annuals. Those might be damaged the worst since they're near a low spot that rushes with water in storms like this one. They won't like being too soggy either. That causes the bulbs to rot."

"Remind me the spot and I'll go check those," Jeb said, a new reassurance between them now.

She pointed to a corner near the barn. "I'll be there in a moment or two. I want to check my more-expensive plants, the ones people like to grow for shows. I have some beautiful Casablanca lilies that should bloom later in the year if they didn't get too damaged."

They parted, her going toward the best of her hybrids, and Jeb rushing toward the plot of lilies growing near the barn and the rushing creek.

Lily Dog came running from the barn, her yelps showing she didn't like storms either. The shaggy little mutt shivered in the cool air as she trotted along with Rebecca.

"It's okay," Rebecca said, bending to pat the wet dog on the head. "Just a big blow over, is all."

Rebecca hurried through the showstoppers, as she liked to call them. She got top dollar for these cultivars. She'd lose a chunk of her profits if they'd been damaged. Such was the way of any farmer. The crops depended on the weather, but the weather could turn on the crops. Nature was always something awesome, and it required a lot of respect.

After walking the rows, she found a few spots where the early blooms had been snapped off, and several plants that had been bruised or crushed by the heavy wind and rain. Some of the taller stems had broken, so she would have that to deal with.

Finally, she emerged and looked toward where Jeb stood near the other plants. Lily Dog woofed and took off toward Jeb. Rebecca followed, too tired to hurry.

"These look bad," he said, nodding toward the short rows of lush plants. "Most are damaged or broken."

"We'll replant and hope for the best," she said. "It could have been a lot worse. We'll clean up, prune and get things going again."

"How can you be so calm?" Jeb asked, his eyes on her now.

"I'm used to this," she replied. "One year I had aphids so bad, I lost half my crop. Another, a tornado flattened everything in Campton Creek, and that's how Micah met Samantha, or Leah, as we all call her. The tornado lifted her car and it landed in his wheat field. She has a little dog named Patch—reminds me of our Lily Dog."

"I've got a lot of catching up to do," Jeb said with a grin. The dog barked in agreement.

"*Kumm* inside," she said, her voice hollow and tired. "I'll fix us some *kaffe* and we'll make a quick dinner."

"Are you sure?" he asked, his gaze still on her.

Rebecca took his hand. "I'm sure, Jeb. You've done so much for me. I owe you more than I can say."

"What if I want more than gratitude?" he asked.

Rebecca's finger tightened over his. "We have all summer," she said. "Let's see how we feel when fall arrives."

Jeb squeezed her hand back. "I hope fall takes its dear sweet time getting here."

Chapter Eighteen

Jeb had the damaged part of the garden replanted and reworked in a few days. He suggested they build up the soil there to keep that patch of lilies from being flooded with water after each rain. This project had kept him busy, and it had given him time to think hard on what he should do next. He'd shared the worst part of his past, and Rebecca had kissed him during the storm. His heart filled with joy in that moment, but he had tried since to avoid her as much as possible. He wouldn't let this go any further with his one last secret standing between them. It wouldn't be fair to her.

But he sure did like being with her, helping her, making her livelihood stronger and more secure. And he could tell she was beginning to feel the same. Would she forgive him after he told her the truth?

He prayed so and hoped to find the right time to come clean. It had been a few days since the storm, so he'd had limbs to clear away and lilies to pamper. They'd both been hard at work. Rebecca's garden was overflowing, so she'd been over at Franny's house most of the week, canning and freezing vegetables and making fruit preserves.

The day was coming to an end. He'd have to stop and go take care of the animals.

Now, he stood back and checked the new grid. He'd moved wheelbarrows of soil from the outskirts of the fields to this area, building it up until he'd managed to level it off. Then he'd made a dirt drain full of rocks beside the grid, so any rainwater should flow away from the lilies planted there. It looked different, but clean and ready to go. He'd taken the bulbs with stems Rebecca said they could transplant from the big garden and planted them deep into the soil. Rebecca said they should start producing in a few weeks.

"I see this project is done," Noah said as he strolled toward Jeb. "That's a much better layout than the original. This part of the garden was an afterthought that turned into a new responsibility for Becca."

"Well, now it's my responsibility," Jeb said, wondering what Noah was doing here so late in the day.

"You are taking on a lot more of the everyday tasks," Noah replied, holding his suspenders.

"What's wrong?" Jeb finally asked, his instincts telling him he probably did know why Noah was here.

Noah looked him over. "You haven't told her yet, have you?"

"No," Jeb said, since he had no excuse except hard work and a deep dread holding him back. "I took some time earlier in the week to tell Bishop King and he agrees she should know. He thinks she'll appreciate my being kin to John once the dust settles."

"If the dust settles," Noah replied. "The longer you wait, the harder it will become."

Jeb nodded. "I know. But I'm finishing up her garden shed. I have all the boards marked so all we have to do is haul them to the spot I've measured and get going on putting the whole thing together. Are you still willing to help?"

"Are you still willing to be honest with her?" Noah shot back.

"I will tell her everything," Jeb replied, "after her birthday and after she sees the shed."

"And then what?"

"And then I'll either be a forgiven man, and I can stay. Or I'll be in a bad spot again, and I'll leave." He stopped, took in a breath. "As a heartbroken man. Still."

Noah shook his head. "I can't be the one to tell her. And I cautioned Shem on passing what he'd figured out to anyone because he wasn't for certain sure, but we don't want Shem messing around and letting it slip if he runs into Rebecca."

"I know." Jeb took off his straw hat and swept a hand through his hair. "I know. I've made a mess of things, but, Noah, Becca and I are growing close. There will come the Sunday I'll go before the church and confess all."

"Even this last secret."

"Even that, but I want her to know before that happens."

"So do I," Noah replied. "She'd be mighty upset to

hear this with all the brethren around her. She'd be humiliated."

Jeb didn't want that to happen. "I could go and talk to Shem. Would you go with me?"

"And aid you in keeping this a secret?" Noah asked. "I'm already doing that. I won't keep adding to the lie."

"It's not a lie. I'm only trying to protect your sister."

"Neh," Noah said. "You're only protecting yourself and that's the worst thing you can do at this point."

After Noah left, Jeb stood staring at the creek. Noah was right. He needed to get this one last hurdle out of the way and then he could truly feel free and clear—cleansed and complete. He had run out of excuses.

He prayed Rebecca's gracious heart and her promise of not judging him would still hold when he told her the truth.

"Noah, have you said something to Jeb again—about me?"

Rebecca knew something was wrong. She'd sensed a change in Jeb now that they were back to their routines and clearing away the storm damage. He and Adam stayed busy, of course. But Adam followed him into the barn in the late afternoon and then they walked home together. No more suppers alone with Jeb.

He'd kissed her there on the porch the other night, with the rain falling all around them. Rather, she'd kissed him. Why had she gone and done that? Now he'd shut down again and managed to avoid her at every turn. He stayed in the barn until late in the day, after they'd done their chores. Was he ashamed that he'd told her what had happened to Pauly? Or had her brother some-how seen them and told him to stop kissing Rebecca?

"Noah?"

Noah frowned, then he looked away. Then he frowned again. "What do you mean?"

"I mean, he is barely talking to me and after work, he heads to either my barn or yours. How many harnesses can a man mend?"

Noah almost smiled, then he shook his head. "I think, sister, Jeb is at a crossroads. He likes it here and he aims to stay, but whatever he's been through is causing him to doubt. He's afraid he'll be hurt again. Heartbroken even."

"Then you have been talking to him!" Had Jeb told her brother all that he'd shared with her about his past, his *daed* and Pauly?

Flustered, Noah tugged at his beard, a sure sign he had something on his mind. "We talk, *ja*. He's around a lot, so I talk to him. Surely you aren't upset about that. I thought you wanted me to be nice to him."

Rebecca started walking with Noah toward her house. She'd come over to visit with Katie and Franny and to help process some of the first crops of wild blue-berries and blackberries, and the fresh vegetables from both of their thriving gardens.

Today, they'd blanched beans and peas, and shucked and cleaned fresh corn to store in the propane-operated refrigerator. Noah was helping her carry her baskets full of jars of jam and vegetables back home to put in the storage room in the basement.

"I do want you to be nice to him," she said. "I don't want you pestering him or pushing him off on me."

Noah's thick eyebrows lifted like a set of wings. "Well, I thought you were beginning to like him, same as me."

She had to be careful what she told her brother. He'd get the wrong impression and meddle even more. "I do care about Jeb. He's one of us and he's been fighting a hard battle. He and I get along, but he's been acting strange lately. Not as friendly and talkative. Now I think I understand. He's still struggling, ain't so?"

"Struggling how?" Noah asked, surprised.

"You just said it yourself. He's reached a time of no return. He either comes back to the Amish life, or he has to move on. Is that what you've talked about?"

Her brother looked both ways when they reached the narrow ribbon of road. "*Ja*, sure. We've talked about that and a lot of things."

"So… This is why he's been so distant? He's still having doubts even though he says he's going to be okay?"

"*Ja*, that could be it."

Frustrated, Rebecca shifted her basket of blueberry preserves. Noah answered her in riddles. He was either protecting her, or he was protecting Jeb. Maybe both of them.

"Well, thank you for making all this as clear as mud."

Noah carried the jars of beans and crushed tomatoes into the kitchen. "So now you're cross with me?"

"I'm not cross with anyone," she said. After placing her basket on the table, she turned to Noah. "I'm having doubts, too. I don't know how I feel about Jeb or anything else these days."

Noah's eyes widened, and he twitched like a newborn foal. "Has he done or said something to hurt you?"

"*Neh,* I'm fine. He's respectful in every way, he works hard, and your little chaperone hangs on his every word."

She hoped she wasn't blushing, but each time she thought of their kisses, she got all warm and dreamy. Her brother didn't need to know that. "I'm just used to having Moses Yoder following me around. He rarely talked, mostly grunted and nodded and mumbled."

Her brother grinned. "Jeb is quite different from Old Moses."

"*Ja,* and there's the problem. He is my friend, and he works for me. It's a lot different."

Concern rimmed Noah's face, causing her even more worry. "In a good way, or a bad way?"

Her brother's genuine sincerity touched Rebecca. "That's the confusing part. In a good way, and in a bad way. Jeb is a *gut* man and he's doing all he can to come back to his faith. But just like Jeb, I don't want to ever be heartbroken again either." Then she put her hands on her hips. "Which is why you need to stop playing matchmaker to us."

Noah nodded, his fingers moving down his beard. "And that means I must not worry about the both of you being here alone with each other so much. I miss Old Moses, for certain sure."

Rebecca patted her brother on the arm. "Noah, you do not need to worry on my account. I'm grown now, remember?"

"Every day, I remember this," he said. "I dread when Katie grows up and starts walking out with boys. I will not like it, not one bit."

"But you won't be able to hold her back either," Rebecca said. "I can figure out my life, and you go and take care of your *wunderbar* family. If I have doubts, I promise I will *kumm* to you. You are so much like our *daed*."

Noah's eyes misted. "I will take that as a compliment."

"You have been *gut* to me and you've watched over me for a long time. I know I can depend on you."

"Even when I overstep?"

"Even so," she said with a smile.

Noah looked uncertain, making her suspicious all over again. But she knew him well enough to think she wouldn't get any information out of him unless he wanted her to know it.

"Now, go," she told him. "I'm tired and it's almost suppertime."

Noah nodded. Then he turned at the door. "I won't force you and Jeb together. I think this is something you two have to decide on your own, with prayer and consideration. If *Gott* wants you together, it will work itself out."

"Denke," Rebecca said. "I'm glad you've come to that conclusion."

Noah nodded, started to speak and then shook his head. With a sigh, he turned. "I'll see you later, then."

Rebecca watched her brother go, still not sure. Something was up. Noah knew more than he was letting on. She'd never seen her brother so befuddled or *verhud-*

delt—confused. Noah always spoke his mind, and especially about Jeb. But he'd hesitated today.

She had to wonder what her brother and Jeb were hiding from her.

Jeb finished the fence, doing most of the last bits of work after he'd completed his other chores. Adam helped, talking away about fishing, riding his bike, milking cows and goats, and just about any subject. Jeb let the boy talk, and he answered when asked a question. That gave him time to his own thoughts, mostly about Rebecca and how much he appreciated this job.

"Hey, Jeb?"

He looked up to find Adam holding a hammer. *"Ja?"*

Adam scrunched his nose. "Are you mad at me?"

Jeb stopped tugging at the leftover fencing wire and turned to the boy. "What makes you think I'm mad at you?"

Adam put his hammer on the fence post next to him. "You ain't been talking much lately, is all."

Jeb had so much on his mind, he'd shut down a bit. His young helper must have picked up on that. "Well, I'm letting you do most of the talking. You entertain me and that keeps me from wanting to take a nap."

Adam grinned at that. "My *mamm* says my talking puts her to sleep."

"Well, it keeps me awake," Jeb replied, thinking the boy might splutter along, but he was observant. "I do have a lot going on—things I have to fret about."

"So you're not mad, you're just stewing in your head?"

"Exactly. Stewing a lot."

"You're gonna stay here, right?"

Jeb took a sip of the big water jug Rebecca always provided. "I haven't decided, but I'm ninety percent sure that I will be staying past summer."

"I'm glad," Adam said. "You're like one of my best friends. I want you to be one hundred percent for certain sure."

Jeb was so touched, he had to blink and look away. He prayed for 100 percent. "I'm glad we're friends," he said, his voice husky because of the big lump stuck in his throat. "You know, I had a brother who followed me around all the time."

Adam's eyes got big with surprise. "You did? I didn't know that." Then his expression changed, and he hung his head. "You said once you'd lost two people you loved. Was your *bruder* one of them?"

"Ja," Jeb said, his heart burning. "My *mamm* died when I was a teenager. My *daed* wasn't an easy man to live with, so I tried to take care of Pauly—my brother. I didn't do such a good job."

"Well, most kids need a *mamm,* ain't so?"

"You are right there, my friend. Pauly and I sure needed our *mamm.*"

Adam stared over at him. "I'd be sad if my *mamm* passed. Is that why you don't tell about it much? Cause it might make you cry?"

Jeb loved this kid. "I don't talk about it much because it still hurts and because I've made a lot of mistakes in my time of grief. Pauly died when he was a bit older than you."

Adam leaned over the nearest fence post. "That's a shame. Terrible. My *bruders* get on my last nerve sometimes, but I'd be sad if something happened to either of 'em."

"It does make me sad," Jeb admitted. "I've been angry about it, so sometimes I get quiet and…moody. But you need to know I'd never be mad at you. You're right—we're best friends."

Adam's grin made all the bad thoughts go away. Jeb had to wonder what it would be like to have a son like Adam, so inquisitive, so full of life and promise.

Then he thought about Rebecca, could see her holding a baby. If they were to marry, could they have a child? Or had they already missed that time in their lives?

He didn't dare dream any further. There was still a lot he needed to work through before he could even contemplate marriage and a family. But he already knew in his heart, he wanted to be with Rebecca, children or no children.

Chapter Nineteen

"You have a birthday soon."

Rebecca glanced at her sister. Hannah always showed up on Saturday to lend her a hand or help her with customers. Now that she had Jeb and Adam, Rebecca had more time to keep things organized. This morning, she and Hannah were watching over the gardens while Jeb and Adam sold plants and produce up on the road.

They'd pulled two lawn chairs out into the shade of the old oak near the field, with a small wooden table between them serving as Rebecca's desk. Rebecca let her customers roam on their own until they needed her help. Hannah had made a huge container of honey lemonade to offer their visitors, and she'd brought paper cups to serve the sweet, refreshing drink. Rebecca handed out the pamphlets Jeb and Jewel had created, so customers could read her tips and pass that information on to others. That one gesture had brought her a lot more business.

"I'm trying to forget my birthday," she told her sister

while she kept her eyes on the half-dozen people milling around her gardens. The fields were at their prime, so she expected a lot of business today. "I'm getting older by the minute."

"You still look young. Mamm always looked so young. You take after her." Then Hannah shrugged. "The *Englisch* don't think being in your thirties is old, you know."

"The *Englisch* are different from us, you know," Rebecca shot back with a smile.

"*Ja*, they just have fancy doctors to lift everything," Hannah said with a giggle.

"Hannah!" Rebecca never knew what would come out of her sister's mouth. But Hannah did make a valid point. "I'm past worrying about wrinkles and such. I'm thankful I've made it this far."

"You and Jeb are about the same age."

"Really, I hadn't noticed," she quipped. Did everyone around here want her to marry Jeb?

"Have you thought about him anymore?"

Rebecca wanted to say she thought about nothing else, but she wouldn't give anyone fodder or hope. "I work with him, so *ja*, I think about him a lot when I'm planning out the daily tasks around here."

"That's not what I meant."

Rebecca gave her sister a frown. "I know what you meant, and I have no answers. I care about Jeb. We've grown close, but that information is between you and me. Noah has backed off, at least. He knows I like Jeb and that's all he needs to know."

"So if you and Jeb were to become really close, it won't be because our brother demanded it, ain't so?"

"That is correct. It will happen naturally and because it is the Lord's plan for our lives." Rebecca watched her customers and then she turned back to Hannah. "Have you heard Noah talking about Jeb? Our brother seemed skittish the other day when he came by to talk."

Hannah shook her head. "Noah doesn't confide in me. He thinks I can't keep a secret."

Rebecca raised her eyebrows and they both started laughing.

"Okay, so maybe I do find it hard to not repeat things," Hannah said, "but Noah won't tell me any gossip, so I can't repeat what I don't know."

"Noah likes Jeb now, same as me. I'm beginning to think those two are in cahoots about something."

"You know how men are—they hold everything in, trying to be all manly. Maybe Jeb shared something with Noah that he didn't want to talk about with anyone else."

Rebecca stood, her mind reeling with possibilities. "That is the best answer anyone could give me. Men do talk, but they speak differently than women."

"*Ja*, and we are all thankful for that," Hannah replied.

"So, if Noah and Jeb have been talking and passing secrets, that means our brother trusts Jeb, at least."

"And that also means Jeb must hold trust in our stubborn, well-meaning brother," Hannah said, proud of herself.

"This could be *gut*," Rebecca replied, relief washing

over her. "Whatever those two have going on, I will stay out of it. Just to keep the peace around here."

A customer approached with a question, so she hurried off to help. Hannah poured more lemonade and then went to help another customer. Soon Rebecca got so busy, she didn't worry overmuch about how strange her brother had been acting. But if Noah and Jeb were growing closer, why did Jeb seem to be avoiding her at every turn? Noah might have befriended Jeb, but he might also still be trying to push Jeb toward her.

Would she ever understand how Jeb really felt about her?

He'd tried.

Jeb let out a sigh as the last of the marked timber was put away. He could finally build the potting shed he'd imagined for Rebecca. Meantime, he'd tried every which way to find the courage to tell her about John. Her John, his cousin. He had letters written by the man she'd loved.

Why can't I just be honest with her?

He finished up in the barn, hiding the last of the wood he'd managed to saw and shape into a passable puzzle that had to be put together in a few hours while she was away.

Noah was in charge of making that happen. He'd explained to Franny that she should invite Hannah and Rebecca for a town day. They'd buy fabric for dresses and quilting, thread, anything they needed to make Franny's soap and candles and anything that could keep them away for a few hours. Next Saturday afternoon, after they'd done their half day of work.

Franny would use Rebecca's birthday as an excuse to get her away from the house. It just happened to fall on a Saturday this year.

Noah had given him a grace period.

"You don't want to upset her before or on her birthday. So get this done and then, Jeb, you have to be honest with her. Or I'll have to be the one to tell her, and that will make it twice as humiliating for her."

Jeb's head hurt from lack of sleep, trying to keep a secret surprise, and having a bombshell secret he'd kept from Rebecca.

"You look sad."

Surprised, he found Franny standing in the barn door with a glass heavy with sliced lemons and tea.

"I have a lot on my mind," he admitted. Noah's wife was quiet and steady, like the creek behind Rebecca's house. She didn't gossip and she kept her four children under control. But she rarely talked to Jeb. "Did you need something?"

She offered him the drink. "I need to speak to you."

Jeb got that feeling of dread in his stomach. "All right." He took a sip of lemony-sweet tea with mint. "This is *gut*."

"I'm trying new versions," Franny admitted. "I read about mixing tea and lemonade in a magazine at the doctor's office. Sounded refreshing, *ja*?"

"It is that."

Franny's shy smile changed to seriousness. "I know

what you have planned for Rebecca. I think this is truly kind of you, Jeb. She will be so touched."

"I hope so. I want to make her life easier."

Franny nodded. "I wanted to apologize for judging you when you first showed up here. I've heard nothing but the best about you from day one. Most of that coming from Adam, of course. He really looks up to you."

"Adam is a *gut* kid, and we're best friends."

"He has learned a lot from you," Franny said, smiling. "Noah is so busy, and he tries to take time with all the boys, so letting Adam work with you has also helped him become closer to his *daed*, too."

"How's that?" Jeb asked, wishing he could have discovered some way to help his *daed* and Pauly become closer.

"Adam is a talker, inquisitive and smart. Noah doesn't often have the patience to deal with that. But now that Adam has been around you, he has also learned to speak to Noah in a different way, with understanding and respect. I owe you for that, Jeb."

Jeb's heart swelled with pride for Adam. Not for himself. "It's easy being around Adam. We've had some great conversations."

"Maybe I should send the other two over to take lessons from you, *ja*?"

He laughed, afraid Franny might be serious. When she grinned, he breathed a sigh of relief. "You had me there for a minute."

She laughed again. Then she said, "Don't worry. I'll get Hannah and Rebecca away so you can build the shed. Hannah only knows I want to take them into town to celebrate a bit. As you know, we don't go all out for birthdays. But I can't wait to see Becca's reaction when she comes home to find it there."

"Let's hope she'll be pleased."

Franny gave him a knowing smile. "She will be pleased because you are a thoughtful person, someone she admires."

"*Denke*, Franny," he said, handing her back the almost empty glass. "I hope she'll like the new shed."

Franny left, and Jeb stood there taking in a breath. He'd won over so many doubters. But how could he win over the one person he wanted to believe in him and trust him? How could he win over Rebecca after being dishonest with her for weeks now?

One more week until her birthday and the shed being built. Could he wait another week? He had no choice. He wouldn't mess up her surprise. If she told him to leave later, at least she'd have that gift to use and maybe to remember he did have a good, caring side to him. He wanted her to remember the good in him, not his one sin of omission.

The days seemed to flow for Rebecca. She kept thinking about her birthday. She'd long ago given up on a husband and children, letting her niece and nephews give her the joy of what must feel like mothering her own child. But each time she glanced at Jeb, she wished she could be ten years younger.

Silly, but he'd make a great father.

That could be the thing between them that no one talked about—that she might be too old to have children. Did he think about that? Just one more reason for them to remain friends.

He'd been a bit more talkative lately, but she felt as if they were walking a fine line. So she decided to take matters into her own hands. She'd learned long ago if you want something done, do it yourself.

"Jeb," she said late on a Thursday after they'd had a busy day in the heat of summer, "I'd like you to stay for supper tonight."

Jeb had been gathering vegetables, as he liked to do at the end of the day. The asparagus and cabbage were both exploding, so they had to constantly gather buckets full of both. She and Franny would make sauerkraut with the cabbage, and they could eat the asparagus fresh and sell most of it. He glanced up in surprise, his cutting scissors in one hand. "Are you sure?"

"I wouldn't ask if I weren't sure," she retorted, the sting of his words hitting their mark. "Unless you have other plans."

"My only plan is to wash up, find food and collapse," he admitted. "I've cut a whole row of cabbage and cleared off the outside leaves. And this asparagus is ready to clip so I want to finish this row."

"*Denke* for doing that, but if you're tired, you might not want to linger or eat a real meal."

"I didn't say that."

She took one of the buckets and started clearing heavy green cabbage leaves from the sturdy stems. "Why are you avoiding me, Jeb? Is it because I was bold enough to kiss you? Did that make you think less of me?"

Jeb put his bucket down and stared at her. "Kissing you would never make me think less of you, Becca. It only made me want to kiss you more."

She blushed but blamed the heat rising up her face on the warm day. "I see."

"*Neh*, that is the problem," he said, his brow wet with sweat. "You do not see. You fight against what we are feeling because you are just as afraid as I am, aren't you?"

She set her bucket down with a thud. "What do I have to fear, Jeb?"

"Everything," he said, frustration echoing out behind that one word. "I'm a stranger. I need to confess everything to become Amish again. I'm a hard man to deal with, a man who has a past. That's a lot to have to accept."

"I have accepted you in every way," she replied, anger and frustration boiling over. "Is there anything else I need to know? Is it me? Because I'm old and I can't bear children? Is it because everyone wants you to marry me, so they can all stop feeling sorry for me?"

"Becca…" He started for her, but Lily Dog chose that moment to come running toward them from the creek.

Rebecca turned to keep the dog from shaking creek water all over her, but Lily Dog kept coming. Then next thing she knew, the dog ran around her leg and accidentally tripped her up, causing her to start a fast fall.

Right into Jeb's arms.

Cabbage and asparagus flew through the air.

Together, they stumbled and fell to the ground, Lily Dog dancing and barking all around them, enjoying this new game.

Becca hit his chest with a thump, her breath leaving her body. Then she glanced down at him, saw the need in his eyes, and felt that same need inside her heart.

"Becca," he said again. "I need—"

Rebecca pushed away, not daring to kiss him, although she wanted that badly. She pushed against the ground and managed to stand. Grabbing enough fresh asparagus to feed two, she said, "I'm going to make supper. You can stay or not. It's up to you."

"I'm staying," he said. "And Becca, I'm not just talking about staying for supper. I'm going to find a way to stay here in Campton Creek for the rest of my life."

Rebecca's heart lifted at that passionate declaration, but it sank fast when she thought of all the things still between them. "Biscuits or corn bread?" she asked, thinking she sounded *dumm*.

He blinked, got up and wiped his hands down his pants. "Biscuits sound *gut*. And I do like asparagus."

Rebecca marched to the house, thinking between his mixed signals and her constant state of confusion, it would take something big to ever bring them together.

Or something big to destroy both of them all over again.

Chapter Twenty

Jeb thought this would be the time to come clean, except he and Noah had agreed to wait until after Becca's birthday.

So now here he sat, his hair still damp from sticking his head under the cool pump water, his skin smelling like lemongrass and heather soap, watching Becca move around her kitchen. She'd barely spoken to him, but he heard her humming as she worked. Somehow, this felt right. Better than any of the places he'd worked and lived before.

He wished with all his heart he could have supper with her for the rest of his life. Surely, God hadn't brought him here and let him fall for this woman, just to have him leave again. He'd tell the bishop he was ready to go before the church. He knew in his heart he needed to be right here.

"That sure smells good," he said. "Do you need any help?"

She whirled, her expression showing he'd insulted her in some way. "I don't mind cooking for you, Jeb."

"I didn't mean you're not capable," he said, his tongue becoming tied. "I love your cooking. I guess I'm used to batching it, is all."

She finished checking on the steamed asparagus and then checked the baked chicken and rice in the oven. Wiping her hands down her apron, she fixed tea for them and came to sit at the table. "It will be ready in a few minutes."

Jeb took a sip of tea. "Franny brought me some tea the other day—tea with lemons, mint and honey. It was good."

"Would you rather I added those items?"

"Neh," he said, getting more flustered by the minute. "Why are you so mad at me?"

Rebecca looked sheepish. "I don't know. I don't want to be mad, but… I can't name why I'm feeling this way. I wanted us to have a nice dinner. I made a cake—strawberries and white cake with whipped cream."

"I like that kind of cake."

"Gut."

"I don't think you're mad at me, really," he said. "I think we're trying hard to not like each other, but Becca I do like you. A lot."

She stared over at him, her hands in her lap, her eyes as pretty as any forest he'd ever seen. "What are we to do, then?"

"We can continue as we've planned, and let God show us the way," he said, meaning it. Wanting it.

"I like that plan, and I'm sorry I've been…mad."

"Does that mean you care about me?"

She nodded, looked down at her hands. "I don't want you to feel obligated, Jeb."

"Obligated?" He couldn't believe she didn't see how much he'd fallen for her. Yet, he couldn't tell her that. Not yet.

"I know Noah has been pushing you toward me. It's pathetic that my brother is constantly trying to match me with anyone who comes along." She twisted her apron in her hands. "I told myself I'd just ignore him, and I even warned him to stop. He did seem to stop, but now you're acting strange and he's acting strange, and I know something is going on with you two. Is my brother hounding you about me? You don't have to sacrifice yourself for me. I can take care of myself. I've learned that. I will be okay."

He saw the tears she'd tried so hard to hold back. Jeb got up and lifted her out of her chair. "Becca," he said, taking her hands in his, his eyes on her, "no one is hounding me, and you are not pathetic. You are one of the strongest women I've ever met. I've had every opportunity to marry—either Amish, Mennonite or *Englisch*. But none of them have compared to you, do you understand me?"

She bobbed her head and wiped at her eyes. "But I kissed you and messed things up—I was too bold and reckless."

Jeb shook his head. "I told you I liked kissing you."

"But—"

He stopped her, his nose lifting in the air. "But... I think something is burning."

She whirled and ran to the stove. "Your biscuits."

"*My* biscuits?"

She grabbed a potholder and opened the oven to grab the pan of slightly singed biscuits. "And the chicken and rice will be dry now."

"My biscuits," he repeated, a smile cresting his face. "You have burned my biscuits."

"This is not funny," she said, fussing with getting the chicken and rice out. "I've ruined our meal."

He held a hand to his lip to keep from laughing.

"What is wrong with you?" she asked, glancing around.

"It's just between Old Billy ruining the Farmer's Daughters and you burning *my* biscuits, we seem to always be in trouble a lot, don't you think?"

Rebecca put her hands on her hips and tried to be mad. But instead of pouting, she started giggling. Then they both started laughing. Jeb came to her and grabbed her hands again, dancing her around the kitchen.

They stopped, both out of breath, and he looked into her eyes. "I like burned biscuits, Becca. I like the way you make me laugh. I haven't laughed this much in such a long time."

He held her there, savoring having her in his arms. Then he leaned over and whispered, "This is the part where you kiss me again."

She did kiss him again. When she finally pulled away, Jeb stepped back and smiled. "Don't ever think anyone feels sorry for you, Rebecca. I think everyone around here admires you. I know I do." Then he looked at the food. "And I can't wait to eat burned biscuits and dry chicken."

She slapped at his arm, but her smile countered that action. "Then help me get our food on the table and we will enjoy our messed-up meal."

Jeb smiled and helped her finish up. "Nothing with you is messed up," he said. "And just so you know, Noah has not been after me about marrying you. Other things, yes. But not that."

She gave him a puzzled glance. "Then what's wrong with both of you lately? You've avoided me and he's acting like a cat in a roomful of rocking chairs. What is he after you about now, Jeb?"

Jeb seemed to like the cake. She sent some home with him, watching him out the front door. She half expected Noah to *kumm* running with either a knowing grin or a stern frown. But her brother seemed subdued these days.

Rebecca was more confused than ever.

Jeb hadn't really told her anything to ease the nagging dread she felt in her heart. After her question, he only said that Noah liked to pick at him about almost everything, but that lately they'd been getting along a lot better.

So why had Jeb avoided her so much before their supper together?

True, they had been busy, and they couldn't stand around flirting while customers kept coming on a daily basis. Today, a whole bus full of tourists had arrived and they'd asked a lot of questions. She and Jeb, and sometimes Adam, had done their best to answer all the questions.

Now as she looked out over the yard and fields, she could see all the improvements Jeb had helped her with. The barn looked fresh from a new coat of red paint. She knew it was in tip-top condition inside, too, since Adam went on and on about helping Jeb fix it up. She'd peeked in once or twice, but she still couldn't bring herself to go near the horses. It wasn't that she was so terrified of them, but the trauma of seeing John go flying through the air and then never waking up was just too much to remember all over again.

John.

She felt the guilt of not remembering him as much now. It had been so long, and yet, she didn't want to forget him. Jeb reminded her so much of him at times, she had to turn away. But Jeb was different, more confident, and older, strong, and dependable. John would have been all those things if he'd lived.

She had to stop comparing the two of them. It wasn't fair to Jeb. Since their dinner the other night, he'd been kind and considerate and he found ways to make her smile. He and Adam were *gut* at doing silly things to get her attention. Lily Dog always went along with the fun, causing all of them to giggle.

But Rebecca still had that feeling that something wasn't right. Maybe it was because she'd forgotten how it felt to be in love. She had fallen for Jeb. It was an easy fall, a soft, delicate drifting, as a leaf would let go of a tree and fall softly to earth. She couldn't come out and tell him, but he had to know. He had to feel her heart beating against his chest when he held her, he had to feel the warm intensity that flowed over her when he kissed her. He had to see it in her eyes each time he looked at her.

Especially after the burnt biscuits episode. She still giggled and got all dreamy—over biscuits! He'd eaten them with butter and declared they were the best biscuits ever.

That had to mean he loved her in some small way. He just had a lot to work through to come to his own conclusions. But the bishop had stopped her at church the other day.

"Jeb is a *gut* man, Rebecca. I hope whatever his future holds, that he will stay here among us. I'm praying for you, and your part in that decision."

Bishop King never pushed, and he never made demands. He usually laid out how things should be and the consequences of anyone's actions if they strayed. Then he guided that person into making the best decision. He wanted Jeb to stay.

And so did she.

But Jeb and *Gott* would have to have that discussion.

She stood on the porch now, taking in the late afternoon sun that shifted in a golden glow across the trees and fields. Jeb had gone home, Adam trailing by his side, talking away about the snake they'd found and sent to the woods, and the big fish he'd seen jumping in the creek.

She loved hearing their conversations.

When she saw a shadow coming around the side of the house, her heart expected Jeb. But Franny waved to her and smiled.

"What brings you over?" Rebecca asked, thinking they'd done enough putting up and canning to last for years.

"I want to go into town Saturday afternoon," Franny said. "I thought you and Hannah might want to ride with me. It can be your birthday outing. Then when we get home, we can have a picnic supper out under the trees."

Surprised, Rebecca stared at her sister-in-law. "That's a lot for one day. We usually just have cake and punch."

"Oh, we'll have cake," Franny said. "I ordered one from Ava Jane Weaver."

"Oh, she makes the best cakes," Rebecca said, touched that Franny was being so kind. "You don't have to do this, you know."

Franny glanced around. "But I do. I mean I want to give you a special day. You've worked hard and helped me with getting all the jellies and jams made, and the produce put away. We won't starve this winter. Let's have some fun, okay?"

"I really didn't want to dwell on my birthday."

"You won't dwell. You'll be having fun with your sisters."

Rebecca did consider Franny a sister, same as her real sister. "What does Hannah say?"

"She's excited to be included. We'll leave after you shut down for the day. I have meat for burgers and Noah said he'd help with preparations—something he rarely offers."

"A real picnic, for my birthday. I can bring a side dish."

"*Neh*, you are the birthday girl. You don't have to worry about anything."

Franny seemed so set on doing this, Rebecca couldn't refuse. "I will be ready after dinner hour," she said, smiling. "*Denke*, Franny. This is so thoughtful, and it sounds like fun."

"*Gut*," Franny said. "No church on Sunday so we can rest up then."

Rebecca hugged her sister-in-law, then Franny took a glance at the lily field. "Oh, my, Rebecca. This looks so pretty with the late sun shining on it. You and Jeb have done wonders."

"Adam helped," she said, smiling. "This summer has been my best so far. I've had more customers than ever."

"You're so smart and I'm so happy for you," Franny replied. "You've helped me with the youngies so much. *Denke*."

Rebecca smiled. "I'm thankful to have you and Noah so close."

"And now you have help, *ja*?"

Rebecca chuckled. "Jeb is certainly strong and hard-working. Moses Yoder reminded me of a tortoise, but he did try."

Franny chatted a little more and picked out a pretty apricot-colored lily with curly, plush blooms. "Take it," Rebecca said. "On the house."

She waved her sister-in-law home, smiling as she thought of the fun day they'd have on Saturday.

Her life was settling into a nice, pleasant routine.

And Jeb had become a part of that routine. She only hoped her peace could last past summer.

Chapter Twenty-One

Saturday turned out to be a beautiful day, warm with a gentle breeze and blue skies for miles. The kind of day with many possibilities.

Jeb went through the morning eagerly awaiting the time when he and his friends would meet in Noah's barn to move wood slats, and then do the same in Rebecca's barn. They'd piece together the numbered boards to quickly build Rebecca's shed.

Jeb had made a sign for it—Rebecca's Lily Garden— that he hoped she'd like. Franny had painted a bright burgundy lily with a yellow throat on the small piece of wood. He'd hang it over the double doors that he'd already had Tobias Mast smooth and polish at the furniture shop where he worked. Noah had kept them in his barn and Tobias had come there to finish up his work. Just about everyone except Rebecca was in on this surprise.

He only hoped his grand plan wouldn't backfire on him.

The day passed with vehicles coming and going up

and down the lane leading to the gardens and fields. Not only did they sell all the potted lilies, but Adam and Jeb had dug up a few and potted them on the spot. Rebecca patiently answered the many questions people asked, handing them one of the pamphlets Jeb and Jewel had created. They seemed to do the trick, especially since Jewel had added several good websites on growing lilies.

They needed to set up their own website, he thought as he hurried around to clean up everything and make sure the lilies hadn't been trampled by all the folks who'd been here.

A lot of their visitors only wanted pictures, so last week he and Adam had set out benches and made designated trails for the lookers to follow. He'd noticed several parents taking pictures of their children sitting on one of the benches, lilies blooming like a rainbow in every color behind them.

He thought of the bench by the creek, smiling when he remembered being there with Rebecca. Maybe after today, after they'd celebrated her birthday, she'd see that he cared for her deeply. And she'd understand why he hadn't been honest with her.

He was headed toward the barn with the wheelbarrow when he heard her calling.

"Jeb?"

Jeb set down the wheelbarrow and turned to greet her. She'd changed her work dress for a mint green fresh frock and a crisp white apron. She looked so pretty as she walked toward him.

"Ja?"

"I'm about to leave with Franny and Hannah for our town trip." She gave him a shy smile. "Are you coming to the gathering later?"

"Oh, you mean, will I be at your birthday celebration?"

"It's not a celebration, just people getting together. Family."

He wondered if he would be part of her family one day.

"I plan to. I wouldn't miss it."

"You want cake, right?"

"Right. That's why I want to be there."

Her eyes lit up while her smile shot hope straight to his heart. "I'll be back in a few hours. Try to stay out of trouble."

"I will," he said, his heart beating so fast, he had to take a deep breath. "You do the same."

She laughed and waved, looking so young and happy, his guilt kicked at him like an old mule. He would hate to destroy that happiness.

A few minutes later, Noah and the crew showed up. Adam came running toward the barn. "Are you ready, Jeb?"

"I'm so ready," Jeb said, waving to Jeremiah Weaver, Tobias Mast, Josiah Fisher and Micah King.

"We have others on the way," Jeremiah said, ready to get to work. "But we can get the framework set up."

Jeb nodded and showed them where the slats and boards had been hidden in the back of the barn. Noah and his sons went back to his place to load everything they had hidden there.

Soon the fields echoed with hammering and men

shouting and talking. Jeb stopped and glanced around, making sure no women were approaching.

He wanted this to be the best surprise Rebecca had ever had. And the best birthday.

Franny held tightly to the buggy reins, occasionally turning to check on Rebecca in the back, while Hannah rode up front with her. "How ya doing back there?"

"I'm okay, Franny," Rebecca said. "I know you're a *wunderbar gut* driver."

"And I'm right here," Hannah said, smiling over her shoulder. "This was such a sweet idea, Franny. I haven't been on a girls' outing in so long."

"Noah suggested it," Franny said. "He's getting mellow in his old age."

"Wait," Rebecca said, leaning up. "Did you say my brother suggested this?"

Franny checked the reins, but she looked *ferhoodled*. "I mean, he asked if I'd like to take you both into town. Just a thought."

Rebecca smiled at her sister-in-law's confusion, but she got that feeling inside that something was off. Why would she think that just because her brother and his wife were thinking of her on a special day?

"That was thoughtful of our *bruder*," Hannah said.

At least she hadn't been acting strange. But then, no one told Hannah their secrets. Rebecca was surprised her sweet but talkative sister hadn't blabbed about Rebecca's feelings regarding Jeb.

"I thought we'd start with a quick bite at the Campton Creek Café," Franny said. "It's that new place that

Jewel and some of our friends have opened. A lot of Amish are employed there. Jewel helps when she can, but she has her hands full with the Campton Center."

"That would be nice," Rebecca said. "But I must save room for supper tonight, too."

Hannah grinned. "I'm hungry already." She looked so shy, Rebecca now had to worry about her, too. What was she hiding?

Franny parked the buggy across from the new café, secured the horses and marched them across the street. The café was in what used to be a small Victorian-style house. It was past lunch hour, so they found a nice table on the big porch where they could sit in the shade of an aged oak tree.

Once they were seated, Rebecca glanced at her sister. "Hannah, are you feeling poorly? You're pale today."

Hannah shook her head. "*Neh*, I mean… I'm feeling a little faint is all." She took a sip of the water a young Amish girl had brought them. "I'm feeling…different."

Franny stared at Hannah and then put a hand to her mouth. "Are you with child?"

Rebecca glanced at Hannah, and then she saw her sister's apologetic eyes. "You're expecting?"

Hannah nodded. "I didn't want to spoil your day, but I'm a little shaky. I need food."

Rebecca got up and came around the table to hug her sister. "Why would you worry about me? You know I'm thrilled for you."

"Are you?" Hannah asked. "I was afraid…it would make you sad."

Rebecca touched a hand to Hannah's face. "Silly, I'm happy. I will be the first to spoil this child."

Hannah hugged her tight. "I'm so glad you're okay with this. I…miss Mamm so much right now."

Franny got up to hug her, too. "You have us, sister. We will pamper both you and the *bobbeli*."

The waitress came back, concern on her face. "Can I help?"

"We're fine," Franny said, a smile on her face as she wiped her eyes. "We are celebrating a newcomer to our family."

The girl clapped her hands together. "We have cupcakes. I'll bring a big one for dessert."

Rebecca laughed and nodded. "We'll let the expecting mother eat most of it."

They ordered salads and laughed and talked.

Rebecca kept smiling at her little sister. A new baby for her to spoil. She couldn't wait to tell Jeb.

That thought made her heart burn with a need she had tried to hide. She wished she could experience having a child of her own. But she prayed for God's guidance and wisdom.

Being married to Jeb would be more than enough.

Three hours later, Jeb stood back and smiled.

"We did it, Jeb," Adam said, slapping Jeb on the back. "It looks real pretty, too."

"It does look nice," Jeb replied, ruffling Adam's hair.

"I need some water and a snack," Adam said. "I'm tired."

The other men had left for home. Now Jeb had to

get cleaned up for supper at Noah's house. But first, he wanted to finish cleaning up things around here. Becca should be home before sundown, so he wanted to be here when she spotted the fresh new shed near the old oak. He'd found an old wooden picnic table at a garage sale a couple of weeks ago and taken it to the Furniture Mart in town where Tobias worked. Together, they'd spruced it up and Tobias had brought it today.

Now, it was centered off to the side of the shed with a potted lily—a Farmer's Daughter—sitting on the table.

He finished up, pleased that everything was coming together. The minute he saw the buggy returning from town, he'd walk over and ask Rebecca to come back here with him for just a few minutes.

He'd get through today, and his gift to her. Then tomorrow, he'd tell her the last of his secrets.

"We are running out of room."

Franny and Hannah laughed as Rebecca tried to find a spot for all the bags and boxes they'd loaded into the buggy.

"But we have so much—our fabrics for dresses and quilts, more jam jars for canning, some new books to read. Did I miss anything?" Franny asked, laughing.

"I need to run into the general store," Rebecca said. "I remembered I need some more pots. We've used so many more this season. I can buy up what is in stock and order a new shipment through Mr. Hartford and get a discount."

"Okay, I'll go in with you," Franny said. "I'm sure I can find something I need."

Hannah got out of the buggy and sat on a bench out front. She had grown tired. "I'll be here, napping like an old man."

Franny and Rebecca hurried in and headed back to the garden section. Franny went one way and Rebecca went the other.

Rebecca was trying to decide how many pots to order and which colors when she ran into Shem Yoder. He and Moses were related in some way, but she rarely saw the reclusive widower.

Smiling, she said, "Hello, Shem. I haven't seen you in a while."

The older man stared at her. "Rebecca?"

"That's me," she said, thinking he'd aged a lot.

"I was just thinking about you the other day," he replied, his face squinting into a grimace. "You and John— so sad that."

She blinked, surprised to hear that coming out of his mouth. Nodding, she turned back to her pots. But Shem kept standing there. "Did you need something, Shem?"

He scratched his beard. "Minna had a sister, Moselle."

Confused, Rebecca nodded. "Yes, John's *mamm* had a sister named Minna, but she moved away before I ever met her."

"Minna married a Martin," Shem went on. "John's cousin sure looks just like him, ain't so?"

Rebecca thought she'd heard wrong. "What did you say?"

Shem's eyes widened and he turned so quickly, he almost knocked over a shelf full of gadgets.

"Shem, are you all right?"

Shem looked confused. "You know, the man who works for you." Then he put a hand to his mouth. "I'm sorry. I've said too much."

He lifted his hat and slowly walked away, leaving Rebecca so shocked, she dropped the plastic flowerpot she was holding.

John's cousin looks just like him, ain't so?

You know, the man who works for you.

Rebecca couldn't move. John's cousin? Martin. Minna Martin. Jeb Martin.

Franny came rushing toward her. "Becca, what happened?"

Rebecca grabbed her sister-in-law's hand. "I need to get home."

"Are you ill?" Franny asked as she reached down to pick up the cracked pot.

Rebecca held a hand to her head. "*Neh*, but I need to talk to Jeb. Right now."

Franny set the pot back on the table and took her toward the front door. "We'll pay for the busted flowerpot later, Mr. Hartford," she told the surprised owner. "Becca isn't feeling well right now."

Rebecca could barely get into the buggy. Her hands were shaking, and a cold sweat inched down her spine. Hannah kept asking what had happened, but Franny just shook her head.

Rebecca sank back on her seat, her stomach roiling and lurching with each bump of the buggy.

Could it be true? Could Jeb be John's cousin?

And if so, why hadn't he told her that from the beginning?

:ied Katie toward the house, her husband, Samuel, hurrying after her.

Franny glanced toward Rebecca's house. "I don't know. She was talking to Shem Yoder in the general store, and she looked so…shocked. She wanted to come home immediately."

Noah sent Jeb a knowing glare. "We knew this would happen. Now what are you going to do?"

Jeb knew what he had to do, and he also knew it was all over now. He'd have to leave. If Shem had told her the truth, Rebecca would never forgive him.

Franny's gaze moved from him to Jeb. "What are you talking about?"

Noah motioned to Jeb. "Go after her."

Then he took Franny by the arm. "I'll explain everything."

"*Ja*, you will," his wife said. "I've never seen Rebecca so shattered. At least not since John died."

Jeb took a deep breath, went inside the *grossdaddi haus* and found the letters from John. Then he walked up the lane to Rebecca's house. It was the hardest walk he'd ever made.

Rebecca made it as far as the kitchen, where she sank down on a chair and held a hand to her mouth. It all made sense now, of course. Jeb looked so much like John. She'd seen that, felt that in her heart. But she'd :ecided she just missed John and she'd imagined the :st. How silly, how naive she'd been.

When she heard a knock at the front door, that day :'d seen Jeb walking up the lane the first time came back to her. She wouldn't allow him into her house again, and she'd get him out of her heart. Somehow.

"Becca." He called her name like a plea. "I'm so sorry. I wanted to tell you a thousand times, but I had an excuse for not telling you—any excuse I could find. I didn't know, Becca. I didn't know until you told me your name. And by then, I didn't want to go. I wanted this job and later after we'd worked together and I got to know you and your family, and this community, I wanted to stay here with you forever."

Rebecca gulped a sob, her head falling into her hands. She'd never been betrayed in such a cruel way. Never. This hurt almost as much as losing John.

"Becca, please. I... I have letters from John. I'll let you see them. I wanted to tell you so many times."

Letters? He had letters from the man she was meant to be with, the man she'd longed for all these years. All this time, he'd had letters. Every time she'd mentioned John, Jeb had known. He'd known what he was doing.

She sat, her hands shaking, her lungs burning, her eyes streaming silent tears—tears of grief, anger, disbelief and heartache.

She was living it all over again because she'd trusted a man who reminded her so much of John.

John was in heaven.

Jeb was here on earth.

In her whole life, she'd only loved two men.

One she'd never forget, and one she'd never forgive.

She got up and went upstairs and fell across her bed. Then she remembered it was her birthday, and the tears came all over again. Her heart hurt so badly, she felt the burn of it all the way to her soul.

There was no getting over this. Ever.

Jeb didn't know what to do. She wouldn't open the door, so he went around back. He didn't try to go up on the porch or into the house. Instead, he took the bundle of letters to the new shed, the smell of fresh wood and lilies merging around him with what seemed like a taunting scent.

What have I done?

He stood in the shed, praying to the Lord. Asking for true forgiveness, from the Master. Asking for redemption from the One who could give it. He'd do anything to make this up to Rebecca. Anything.

Even leaving her if that's what it would take.

But he didn't want to leave. He wanted to comfort her and hold her and tell her how much he loved her. He'd fallen for her the moment he'd seen her. Before he even knew her name.

He should have left then, after he'd figured things out. But coward that he was, he'd stayed and withheld the most important thing he could tell her. Now, she'd heard it from an old man who got confused, but who also had a memory that seemed as sharp as ever. He couldn't blame this on Shem, though. The man knew what he knew. And so did Jeb. But Shem told the truth in his misguided way.

Jeb had held the truth away because he didn't want to wander anymore. Now he'd have to do that very thing anyway.

He stood in the little building he'd created to show Rebecca how much he cared. Turning, he stared up at the house for a long time, hoping she'd come outside.

But the sun began to set, and she still hadn't opened any doors. Jeb left the letters there on the small counter he'd made for her. Then he turned and headed for the barn. He'd make sure the animals were taken care of for tonight at least. Because he'd be gone by morning's light.

Rebecca heard someone knocking at the back door.

Groggy and confused, she sat up and realized she'd fallen asleep with her clothes on. Outside, the sunset shot ribbons of purple and gold across the lily field. She went to the window and looked down, thinking Jeb was back. The whole place looked like a painting—a painting done by the Master, the One who watched over even the lilies of the field.

Then she noticed the shed.

How was this possible? There had been no shed there when she'd left all those hours ago. Her heart hammered the answer while she tried to ignore it.

Jeb. It had to have been Jeb.

When she saw her brother walking away from the house, she hurried down and came out the front door, so she could speak to him about the new building on her property. And about Jeb.

"Noah."

Her brother whirled as she called from the front porch. "There you are. We were fearsome worried about you."

Rebecca straightened her *kapp* and wiped at her tear-swollen eyes. "Were you worried when Jeb told you the truth?"

Noah looked so guilty, she almost felt sorry for him. "Why didn't you say something? You were the one who warned me against him."

"I only found out a few weeks ago, not all of it, mind you. But Shem had put things together and asked around. I came to Jeb and confronted him. He told me the rest—about John."

Her anger returned, burning like lightning down her stomach. "You should have told me."

"It wasn't my place, Becca," he said, his hands out. "Jeb promised me he'd tell you everything—after your birthday."

She sank down on a rocking chair. "Why would it matter which day he told me?"

"He wanted… He made you a gift…" Noah stopped. "The man is in love with you, Becca."

As much as those words jolted her heart, she couldn't accept that now. "Well, he has a funny way of showing it—keeping this secret from me the whole time, Noah. The times we worked together, laughed together, chased your goat, ran off deer, every little thing we did together, and he knew, he knew how much this would hurt me."

Noah came to her and patted her shoulder, tears in his eyes. "He did know this would hurt you, sister. He fought with it day and night. He told the bishop and Bishop King urged him to be truthful with you. Jeb was afraid it would destroy you."

"Well, Jeb was right," she said. "I don't know if I can ever get over this."

"But he built you a garden shed."

"That won't help my broken heart," she replied. "Nothing can help that."

Noah nodded and stood. Then he said, "Katie is asking after you. She wants you to have your birthday party."

"I ruined the day for her, didn't I?"

"We explained that you felt ill," he said. "Hannah and Samuel entertained her. Hannah wanted to come and check on you, but I told her I'd do it. We can celebrate another day."

"Tell Hannah to go home. She needs her rest. Or did you know that secret, too?"

Noah shook his head. "She told me a little while ago. Oh, and Adam came over to help Jeb in the barn. I think the boy wanted to find out what was going on. He sure was looking forward to you seeing that shed. We all helped build it. Jeb mapped out the pieces and had it all planned out. We had us a regular shed-raising while you were in town."

"I suppose everyone was in on that, too," she said, her heart too bruised to thank him.

"*Ja*, because we all love you and because we thought—"

"Don't say it." She stood. "I'm going to check on the lilies and then I'm going to bed."

"But it's almost dark."

"I'll just stand on the porch and make sure the fields are quiet."

She watched her brother walking away, then turned and went inside. There was just enough light left for her to go out to that shed and have one look at it. Before she told her brother to tear it down.

Jeb pivoted when the barn door creaked open, hoping Rebecca had come to talk to him. But when Adam stuck his head in, Jeb swallowed his disappointment. Only because the boy looked so dejected. Lily Dog pushed past Adam and ran up to Jeb, barking hello. Jeb rubbed the dog's head.

"Hey, Jeb," Adam said as he moved up the short stable alley, petting Red and Silver as he walked by. "Is Rebecca feeling better? Did she see her shed yet? Is she gonna be okay?"

Jeb swallowed again. "She's still not feeling well, so I think she went to bed. She'll have to see her shed another day."

Adam's dejection held him like a heavy cloak. "We didn't even get to cut the cake and it's a mighty big cake, round and with a lot of high layers. And white icing with sprinkles and Ava Jane even put little flowers on there, like lilies and petunias or something. Things women like, I reckon. Katie's pouting about not getting her piece."

Jeb couldn't look at Adam. He was too ashamed. Darkness shrouded the barn, but he didn't want to leave this shelter. He reached for a kerosene lamp and lit it with the long matches he kept nearby, then set it on the table. The glow from the lamp showed Adam's confusion.

Adam came closer. "Jeb, are you disappointed that Aenti Becca didn't see her pretty garden shed?"

Jeb nodded, cleared his throat. "I am. But I'm more disappointed in myself."

"Why?" Adam asked, moving to help him put away the scrap lumber they'd saved from the shed building. Lily Dog ran back and forth, wondering what to do next.

Jeb was close to telling the boy the truth about why Rebecca was feeling so bad, but when he turned to face Adam, he accidentally tripped over an extended four-by-four board he'd leaned against the worktable. The table wobbled and the kerosene lamp fell to the floor, landing against some old rags and a pile of straw. Jeb lost his footing and his balance. He went down hard, hitting his head against the thick wooden board. He landed, blinked and saw stars. Then he saw fire running up the wall, before everything went black.

Chapter Twenty-Three

Rebecca stood in the shed, amazed at how beautiful it was. It smelled fresh and clean. New. Two small windows on each side allowed for airflow when opened and…also allowed for seeing both the sunrise to the east and the sunset to the west on most days. The little work counter and the stool behind it were both perfect, and so was the potting table spreading the length of one wall, complete with tools hanging over it and baskets and pots sitting on a rack below. The picnic table off to the side held a lily she recognized immediately. The Farmer's Daughter. Its bright pink petals and soft yellow throat shined against the sunrays covering the yard. How could she forget that day? How could she forget this summer?

But when she spotted the stack of letters tied with a string of twine lying there on the counter, her heartbeat went into a rapid retreat. Jeb had left her the letters from John.

She stood and took it all in, thinking of what might have been if he'd been honest with her.

And how would she have reacted? Would she have accepted him and let it all fall into place? Or would she have turned him away, her heart still broken over losing her childhood sweetheart? She'd never know because Jeb had not given her that choice. How she wished he would have trusted her enough to be honest with her. Knowing he was John's cousin should bring her comfort, but now it only brought her another kind of horrible pain. The pain of feeling betrayed by a man she'd learned to trust.

What am I to do now, Lord?

Then she heard the dog barking—an urgent, swift bark that sounded different. Rebecca turned, the smell of smoke rising through the air. When she heard a scream coming from the barn, she rushed out the door, Lily Dog barking and twirling in front of her. The dog wanted her to go to the barn.

Her breath gasping, her feet taking her forward, Rebecca cringed and put a hand to her mouth. The barn was on fire.

She glanced around, thinking no one was here to help her. But she'd heard a scream. She heard it again.

"Aenti!"

Adam. Adam was in the barn.

Had Jeb already left?

When she heard one of the horses whinnying in a panic, she knew she had to save Adam—and Red and Silver, too. Asking God to give her strength, she pushed at the half-open door and stood staring as fire licked the back wall with a hungry anger. Then she saw Adam tugging on something.

"Adam?"

"Aenti, it's Jeb." Her nephew's hoarse, breathless shouts sent a cold sweat across her skin. "He tripped over a board and the lamp fell. He got knocked out. Help!"

Jeb. She had to save Jeb.

She rushed forward. She and Adam tried to get him up, but the big board that had fallen kept him wedged between the table and the dirt floor.

"The horses," Adam called. "We have to drag him away." Her nephew started coughing again.

She couldn't let Adam stay here. The fire was spreading too fast, its golden flames sparking and flashing heat over their heads.

"Adam, go and get your *daed*. Hurry. I'll get the horses out and I'll find a way to get Jeb."

"*Neh*, I can't leave you."

"Just go. Now. Run fast. We need help."

Adam gave her one last panicked glance, then hurried out the door. Lily Dog ran with him.

Rebecca lifted her apron over her nose, then searched for a rope. Finding what she needed, she kept an eye on the fire behind the worktable. She had to get to the horses and use one to drag Jeb out. Or he would die.

"I can't let that happen," she shouted. "I can't go through this again."

She loved him. She knew in her heart, she loved him. No matter what, she couldn't let him go.

Right now, she didn't dwell on his misguided deceit.

She only wanted Jeb to live. So she dropped her apron and pulled her *kapp* down like a mask, then went to Red and let her out. The roan rushed past her, scaring her almost as much as the fire. Then she found Silver, the gentle draft. Silver, the stronger of the two, would cooperate, she hoped. Grabbing the bit and reins next to the stall, she prayed for God to give her the courage she needed to help Jeb. While the fire clawed its way to the ceiling, she opened the stall and threw an old blanket over the draft's head, then guided him back to where Jeb lay. So still. So quiet.

"Jeb, please wake up."

He didn't move. She'd have to use the rope to tie his feet, but she didn't have time to get the reins and bit onto the horse. She'd have to guide Silver out by coaxing the horse and walking with him.

Rushing around, she steadied the horse with calm words, and threw a rope around Silver's middle, looped it back through to cinch it, then tugged the length of the rope toward Jeb. Silver whinnied and tossed his head back but didn't run away. After tying Jeb's feet, her hands shaking and her fingers working swiftly, Rebecca managed to secure the rope across his work boots. She touched his neck, searching for a pulse.

He was breathing. Somehow, she had to make this horse help her get Jeb to safety.

With a tug and all the strength she had, Rebecca got the heavy beam of wood moved enough to drag Jeb away without hurting him more. When she saw blood near his temple, she went into full panic mode.

"Silver, I know you can do this. You're a *gut* boy." She kept talking in soothing terms to the frightened horse while she tugged at the lasso around the animal's big girth. Clicking her tongue the way her *daed* used to do, she held the blanket over Silver's head and urged the horse forward, her prayers centered on saving Jeb, instead of fearing she'd get knocked out by the horse.

Silver's fear increased as the smell of smoke and the heat from the fire leaping behind them caused him to balk and lift up his massive front legs.

Rebecca stepped away, her heart dropping. "C'mon, Silver. We can do this. We have to do this. I need to tell him I love him, I forgive him. I don't want him to die."

Silver neighed a high-pitched whine, but when the horse heard voices coming from the yard, he bolted forward, almost knocking Rebecca down. Rebecca stepped back, watching as the rope she'd tied to Jeb's feet held enough for him to come flying up the alleyway.

"No," she shouted, her hands gripping the heavy rope. If the horse went too fast, Jeb would be dragged and hurt even worse. "Silver," she shouted, "wait."

Tugging at the rope with all her might, Rebecca managed to control the nervous animal, her hands burning from the heat and from the rope searing into her palms. But she couldn't let go. Silver practically dragged both Rebecca and Jeb out of the open door.

Then before she knew what was happening, her brother and his three sons surrounded her and took the rope from her.

"Becca, let me," Noah shouted, taking her hand away. "Go, get out of here."

Becca looked into her brother's eyes and then she looked at Jeb. "Don't let him die, Noah."

Adam guided her out into the night air. Gasping, she didn't realize she'd been holding her breath—but not against the smoke. *Neh*, she'd been holding steady for Jeb's sake.

Franny came running and tugged her to the picnic table. The table Jeb had set up for her with the pretty lily centered on it.

Rebecca held to her sister-in-law. "Franny, he can't die. I can't let him die. I have to tell him I love him."

Franny held her tight. "He won't die. He won't. You saved him, Becca."

Katie ran to her mother. "Aenti, don't cry. It's okay. We saved the cake, too."

Becca laughed and took her niece onto her lap. Then she cried all over again, and she and Franny sat and prayed silent prayers while the volunteer fire department came and tried to save the barn.

When the paramedic walked by, Franny ran to one of them. "What about the man in the barn? My sister-in-law Rebecca needs to know if he's going to be okay."

The paramedic nodded and motioned to Rebecca. "Why don't you go see for yourself. He's been asking for you."

Rebecca hurried to the stretcher they were about to lift into the ambulance. "Jeb?"

He groaned and turned his head. "You're here."

"I'm here," she said, taking his hand. "Jeb, I forgive you. I love you. I'm sorry."

She saw the tears in his eyes, saw the bump over his left temple. "Don't die on me."

"I'm not going to die," he said, his words weak. "I have so much to live for now. I hope you like your shed."

She started crying, her hand touching his smut-covered face. "I love my shed. I love you. I'm sorry."

"*Neh*, I'm the one who's sorry, but, Becca, I love you so much."

Rebecca watched as they lifted him into the ambulance.

"He's going to be fine," Noah told her. "He has a slight concussion and a twisted ankle. You saved his life, Becca."

"And he saved mine," she replied.

A week later

Rebecca stood near the lily field, taking in a thousand scents while up at the house her belated birthday celebration was going strong.

Noah had finally cooked their hamburgers over a firepit grill that Mr. Hartford had sold him. They had potato salad, fresh cucumbers and several other side dishes. Franny had stored the cake at the Campton Center in a big freezer. Jewel had picked it up and kept it there until they were ready.

Today, they were all ready to celebrate. Jewel, with her usual energy, had helped with the whole gathering.

The neighbors had pitched in to rebuild the part of the barn that had burned. It looked new and fresh and strong. Rebecca could step inside now, her old fears burned away with the fire. Silver and she had a new beginning, a bond that brought them together.

A few days ago, Jeb had returned from the hospital, thanks to Jewel picking him up and bringing him home. He'd been resting so his foot and his head could heal. But today, he was well and at home for good.

Home. This would be his official home come this fall.

He'd told Becca in the hospital that he loved her and wanted to marry her.

"But we won't make it official until we're back home," he'd said, after he'd apologized over and over.

"Jeb, I was so angry at you, but I can understand why you did what you did. I loved John and I wasn't ready to let go of him. There was no easy way for you to tell me the truth."

She'd read the letters that night after the fire, and she'd cried with each word. But they had become a gift to her, a gift from the man she'd lost, brought to her by fate, from a man she'd found. She loved both of them.

One man in heaven.

One here on earth.

"What are you thinking?"

She turned as Jeb walked up to her and took her hand.

"I'm thinking about everything. About us, about the future, about the past. I'm so thankful for all of it."

He pulled her close. "I was an idiot."

"I was a bitter *alte maidal.*"

"We make a *gut* pair, right?"

"I believe so."

He glanced at the new shed and then back to her. "Becca, will you marry me?"

"Ja," she said, smiling, happy, glad.

"Okay, then. This fall. Meantime, I'm free and clear and I'm Amish again."

"That you are," she replied.

He'd stood up in church just yesterday and confessed all of his sins, including his connection to John.

He was forgiven. They would never speak of this again.

Rebecca wondered about all those who had to constantly pray for forgiveness. She sure had to do her own praying.

But now, she was content and at peace, and she thanked God for his perfect timing.

Only one thing held back her joy.

"I can't give you children, Jeb. I wonder how you feel about that."

Jeb turned her in his arms and kissed her. Then he drew back and smiled. "I'll tell you how I feel about that. *Gott*'s will, Becca. It took me twenty years to find you. We'll just have to see if he has one more blessing planned for us."

"You think?"

"I hope and pray, but if not, then I will still be the happiest man here on earth."

She nodded, unable to speak.

Then Katie and Lily Dog ran up.

"We really need to cut that cake, Aenti Becca. Please?"

"Please?" Jeb echoed.

Lily Dog barked.

Then they all walked together to join the rest of their

family as the sun settled over the lily field and the air smelled like a wedding garden.

The Lily Lady had never been happier.

They were married in September, and a week before Christmas of the next year, they had a beautiful, healthy baby boy and named him John.

* * * * *

THEIR SECRET COURTSHIP

Emma Miller

Two are better than one; because they have
a good reward for their labour.
—*Ecclesiastes* 4:9

Chapter One

"Whoa, easy, Sassafras!" Bay murmured when the mare shied as a minivan laid on its horn and sped past them. The iron-wheeled wagon swayed ominously, but she held tightly to the reins and guided the dapple-gray back to the middle of the blacktop lane. She didn't understand how *Englishers* didn't know that beeping their horn could startle a horse, but she always tried to be charitable. Not everyone, she reminded herself, grew up with farm animals.

Bay let out a sigh of relief as Sassafras found a steady stride again, and she relaxed on the rough-hewn board that served as a bench seat. She'd been driving a horse and wagon since she was ten years old, but Sassafras was nearly thirty and more skittish than she once was. If Bay hadn't left in such a hurry, maybe she would have considered taking one of the surer-footed horses from her stepfather's barn. She gazed overhead at the dark clouds gathering and wished she hadn't acted so impulsively. Especially with a potential storm blowing in. But she'd been so eager to get away from her mother that she hadn't been thinking clearly when she decided to go into town for gardening supplies.

Gripping the leathers firmly in her hands, Bay gave Sassafras more rein, urging the mare into a faster trot as a rumble of thunder reverberated in the sky. The first raindrops began to fall. "Good girl," she soothed.

A disagreement with her mother was what had pushed Bay to get off the farm even knowing a storm might be coming in. She didn't need the supplies today; she'd just used that as an excuse to cut a conversation short with her mother. It was the same argument at least once a week, and she was tired of it. Ever since her twin, Ginger, had married last spring, their mother had been fussing about it being time for Bay to wed, too. At twenty-six years old, it was time a girl started thinking seriously about a husband, her mother had told her. They had just finished the midday meal, and Bay was expected to remain in the kitchen to help her sisters Nettie and Tara wash dishes. But Bay knew that if she stayed, her mother would start talking about an Amish woman's responsibility to have a husband and a house full of children, and the conversation would go downhill from there.

Bay had been short with her mother, insisting she didn't have time to help with the dishes because she needed to get into town to buy more vegetable seeds and potting material for the family's gardening business. The greenhouse and shop had originally been her stepbrother Joshua's idea, but Bay had quickly discovered that she not only liked commercial gardening, but she had the head and the hands for it. Working with Joshua as an equal partner, she'd seen the business expand quickly in two years' time, and she'd done less and less housework. These days, Bay was more comfortable in the greenhouse or at the cash register than in the kitchen.

But then she had always been different than most Amish girls. When she was younger, she was the one that neighbors called a tomboy, and she'd always preferred outside chores. After her father passed away, she was the one who'd cared for their horses and cows, and tilled the garden. She'd carried her love of gardening with her when her family moved from upstate New York to Kent County, Delaware, four years ago.

Bay enjoyed getting her hands into the rich soil she made to pot seedlings and later to grow healthy vegetable and flower plants. It might have been sinful pride, but she secretly considered herself a match for any man in the county when it came to having a green thumb. It just seemed natural that she would work in the family's gardening business rather than in the house. She wasn't a very good cook, anyway, something her sisters teased her about. She could follow a written recipe well enough, but she didn't have the instincts her mother and sisters had. She barely knew the difference between white sugar and brown, and she never knew what spices to add to soups or stews.

The occasional raindrop began to turn into a pitter-patter on the wagon bed and on her head, covered only by a navy blue scarf. Bay looked skyward to see dark clouds coming in faster from the west. She should have taken one of the family buggies, but along with the seeds, she wanted to pick up several bales of peat moss and vermiculite, and she needed the wagon for that.

Glancing ahead, calculating how long it would take to get to the lawn and garden store in Seven Poplars, Bay wondered if she ought to turn around and head home. She was getting wet and she hadn't grabbed a raincoat. Instead, she was wearing one of her brothers' old denim jackets.

Ahead, she spotted a road that went off to the right, and she wondered where it came out. It seemed to lead north. Would it be a shortcut to Seven Poplars? she wondered. When she first started working in the gardening business, she and Joshua had spent lots of time wandering the local roads. Both of them enjoyed discovering new ways with less traffic to get around the county. But then he'd gotten married, and he no longer had as much time to spend with Bay as he used to.

On impulse, Bay urged Sassafras right, onto Persimmon Lane. As she turned, she noted a large drainage ditch to her right; the water was higher than usual due to heavy rain earlier in the week.

They weren't a quarter of a mile down the road when she heard a motor vehicle come up behind them and begin to pass. She caught a glimpse of the white pickup truck as it kicked up water off the road and sprayed the wagon.

Sassafras laid back her ears and snorted.

"Easy, girl," Bay murmured, gripping the leather reins tighter in her hands. Just as she spoke, the spray from the truck struck the mare and Sassafras let out a shrill whinny and reared in the traces.

"Whoa!" Bay cried as the wagon swayed and she fought to gain control of the startled horse.

The mare reared again and threw herself sideways, sending the wagon sliding off the road and down the ditch bank. Bay heard a loud snap and leaped off the wagon, managing to get free before she was caught in the tangle of thrashing hooves and the leather harness.

She landed hard on the bank on the far side and lay sprawled in the wet grass for a moment, the wind knocked out of her.

In his side-view mirror, David Jansen saw the horse rear, and he slammed on his brakes. Pulling over, and putting on his flashers, he threw his pickup into Park. He jumped out as the wagon slid off the road in what seemed like slow motion and tipped onto its side in the ditch. But where had the Amish woman in the green dress gone? She'd obviously been thrown from the wagon, but she wasn't lying on the road.

He was fast, but not fast enough to reach the overturned wagon before the young woman popped up and began making her way down the other side of the bank toward the thrashing animal. She must have been thrown clear, and appeared unhurt.

"Don't get near her!" David shouted above the sound of the flailing, whinnying horse.

But the woman didn't listen. As she scrambled to get to the animal, she spoke patiently to it, calling it Sassafras.

Heart in his throat, David ran toward her. "Wait!"

"I have to help her!" the woman cried. Now that David was closer, he could see that she was a woman close to his own age, with bright red hair. When he passed her on the road, he remembered she'd been wearing a wool scarf tied beneath her chin to cover her hair. It was gone now, and her hair tumbled wet down her back.

"Listen to me," he pleaded. He understood her need to help the animal, but he also knew how dangerous a frightened horse could be. He might be driving a pickup now, but he'd grown up Amish and had driven his share of horse-and-wagon teams.

Through the falling rain, David could see the mare trying to get to its feet, its eyes rolled back in its head in fear so that only the whites showed. It thrashed and neighed pitifully in the muck of the drainage ditch as it tried to find sure footing. "You can't do it that way!" he hollered.

"Help me, then," the woman cried, lifting her wet skirts as she reached the horse. "If I don't get her up—"

At that instant, his boot slipped on the wet grass and David fell hard, sliding down the bank into knee-deep water. "Just wait. I can help you," he shouted as he clumsily got to his feet, water filling his boots.

But she was paying him no mind as she waded through the cold water, brushing her hand along the horse's back and talking quietly to it. "Whoa, Sassafras. Easy, girl. Just give me a minute and I'll get you out of this."

The mare stilled, its head held at an awkward angle

as the woman spoke soothingly and stroked the horse's haunch. David hoped that the old horse didn't have a broken leg. If a bone was shattered, it would be the end of the road for it. He knew from his farming days back in Wisconsin that sending an old horse off to some fancy veterinary hospital was beyond what an Amish family could afford. When a horse broke a leg, the animal was put down.

The woman reached the horse's head and stroked between its ears, using the same unruffled tone. "That a girl." Without looking at David, she said, "You have to help me get her out of the traces. I'll tell you what to do."

"You think that's wise?" Reaching the mare, he put out his hand to stroke her. "What if she's broken a leg?"

"I think she's all right." The woman began working a buckle on the harness. "I just have to—"

"I'll get the traces off. I've harnessed a few horses in my lifetime. You keep her calm." He moved slowly through the water, taking care to maintain his balance and not splash the horse. He didn't want to startle it. A frightened horse in this situation could kill a man trying to get free. Or a woman.

"My name's David. David Jansen. I live just up the road." He nodded in the direction of his farm, hoping his words would put the woman at ease. It had been his experience that some Amish women were uncomfortable around *English* men. Of course, he wasn't exactly an *Englisher*, but she didn't know that. "What's your name?"

She looked up at him and he was taken aback by how beautiful she was. She had a heart-shaped face with the most startling green eyes. And hair that was a striking, bright red. Being a redhead himself, he'd always had a thing for gingers.

The woman hesitated as if she wasn't sure she wanted to tell him her name. She returned her attention to her horse. "Bay," she responded. "Bay Stutzman. I live over in Hickory Grove. My stepfather, Benjamin, owns Miller's Harness Shop."

"Sorry, I don't know it." He bowed his head to get a better look at the harness. It was interesting, as he moved straps and tugged on buckles, how quickly the process came back to him.

In five minutes' time, the rain had eased and David had the harness off Sassafras. "You think you can lead her up and out or would you rather I did it?" he asked as he grabbed the horse's halter. "She might bolt when she comes to her feet."

"Just get back," Bay said, her tone short. "She won't hurt me, but she doesn't know you." She gave him a quick glance. "We wouldn't be in this ditch if you hadn't sped by and splashed water on her. That's what scared her." She shook her head. "You *Englishers*, you're always in such a hurry."

David wanted to defend himself; he hadn't been speeding. In fact, he'd taken his foot off the gas when he spotted them. It had just been an accident. And he wanted to tell her he wasn't an *Englisher*. That he'd grown up Amish and become Mennonite as a young man, but it didn't seem to be the right time. Instead, he moved up the bank, far enough to be out of the way, but close enough if Bay needed his help with the horse.

He watched the young Amish woman as she murmured into the mare's ear, then snapped a lead line
onto the halter. The horse came easily to its feet in the
ditch and stood patiently while Bay ran her hand down
each of its legs.

"I think she's fine," Bay said without looking at
David. "Back up. Here we come."

He moved over to where the wagon lay on its side
in the ditch and watched as Bay led the horse up the
slippery bank to the road. Once they were safely on
the blacktop, he threw the harness on the wagon's seat
and began looking over the vehicle. He was certain he
could pull it out of the ditch with his truck, once it was
righted...but it looked like there was damage to the
rear wheel.

He looked up at Bay on the road now. It occurred
to him that maybe he ought to get the reflective emergency triangles out of his pickup and set them up. But
Persimmon Lane was never busy; sometimes only a
dozen cars passed his place in a day. "Wheel's busted,"
he called up. "Not sure what else. We won't know until
we get it out of the ditch."

He came up the bank, approaching Bay. "Do you
have any way to call your husband? We could go up
to my place so you can use the phone. Does he have a
cell phone?" he asked, knowing that these days, some
Amish men, particularly the younger ones, *did* have
cell phones for work and emergencies.

"Don't you have a cellphone?" she asked, her tone
indicating she was still annoyed with him.

"Accidentally left it home," he told her sheepishly. He

kept stealing glances at her, telling himself he shouldn't, but he couldn't help it. Despite the annoyance in her voice, he had liked her at once. She was different than other Amish women he'd known. She was very sure of herself and he liked that.

She watched him as if trying to decide if he was trustworthy or not. Which was smart. David believed that most folks in the world were good people, but that didn't mean there weren't bad people out there, too.

The rain was beginning to fall again, and he adjusted his Clark Seed ball cap to keep his face dry. He cleared his throat. "Bay, I'm really sorry about this. I wasn't speeding. I guess I caught the water from the trough made in the road by buggy wheels—"

"You're saying this is our fault?" Bay's green eyes widened with further irritation. "Everyone thinks that the Amish don't pay taxes, but we do. Our taxes pay for roads, you know. We have a right to the roads the same as you."

David looked away, pressing his lips together so he wouldn't smile. He liked the fire in her spirit. When he had control of his facial expression, he returned his gaze. "Anyhow, I'm sorry." He looked up at the sky that was darkening by the moment. "Do you have someone you can call from my house?"

She pursed her rosy lips in thought. "There's a phone in my stepfather's harness shop. I can call there and someone will come for Sassafras and me." She glanced at the wagon. "You think it will be safe here until morning? It looks like the weather is only going to get worse."

He nodded and glanced up as a streak of lightning

zigzagged across the sky. "Let's put Sassafras in a stall and get her rubbed down. I imagine she'd appreciate a scoop of oats after what she's been through." He tilted his head in the direction of his farm. "I'm a quarter of a mile up the road, just around that corner." He put out his hand. "You want me to lead her?"

Bay frowned. "I can lead my own horse." She made a clicking sound between her teeth and started walking. The mare fell into step.

David hesitated, then began walking on the other side of the horse.

Bay looked at him over the mare's back. "Aren't you going to take your truck?" she asked as they went by his Ford parked on the side of the road.

"If you're walking in the rain, I'm walking in the rain." He stopped to open the driver's side door and grab the keys. Then he locked it and closed the door. "I'll come back for it."

Her mouth twitched almost to a smile. But not quite. "I can get her to your place on my own. I won't melt, you know."

He smiled at her. "Neither will I."

They fell into silence then, leaving the wagon and his truck behind. His wet boots were making a squeaking sound with every step he took. Anne had told him to take his rain jacket. Why hadn't he listened? But the walk wasn't far. He would dry just fine and so would his boots.

The horse's hooves made a rhythmic clip-clop as its metal-shod hooves hit the pavement, and David felt a wave of nostalgia wash over him. When he had left the

Old Order Amish, it had been the right thing to do, but there were still times when he missed the slower pace of life. And the soothing sound of hoofbeats.

The rain began to come down harder and David and Bay both lowered their heads as they walked. At last they rounded the corner in the road, and he spotted his driveway ahead. "There's my place." He pointed.

"I appreciate your help." Bay's tone wasn't quite as cool now. "And I'm sorry about saying this was your fault. Sassafras can be skittish. If it's anyone's fault, it's mine. I chose to bring her out with a storm coming in." She lowered her head and kept walking. "I don't usually snap at strangers. I had a disagreement with my mother and—" She exhaled. "You don't want to hear about this."

Bay halted suddenly at the entrance to his driveway, and David heard the sounds of loose gravel, kicked up by Sassafras's hooves, skitter across the pavement. "Wait, this is your place?" She stared at the sign hanging from a post: Silver Maple Nurseries.

"It is."

She looked at him over the back of the horse. "You have a commercial nursery?"

"I do. I sell shrubs and trees. Mostly wholesale, but I've been playing with the idea of selling to the public."

"I have a greenhouse and garden shop," she said, her face lighting up.

And then she smiled, and David felt his insides flutter.

Chapter Two

Bay glanced again at the white-and-green sign that swung in the wind. How had she not known David had a commercial nursery only four miles from her? She'd thought she knew all of the local growers. She and Joshua had checked out the greenhouses and nurseries in their immediate area before starting their own business two years ago.

Thunder rumbled, followed by a crack of lightning that zigzagged across the sky, and she began walking again. David walked on the other side of Sassafras but didn't attempt to take the horse's halter. Most men, even her stepbrothers, would have insisted it was a man's job. The idea that David thought she was capable of leading her own horse in a thunderstorm intrigued her. Was it just because he was an *Englisher*, and it was their way? She didn't know many *English* men.

"Have you been in Kent County long?" she asked, the sound of Sassafras's horseshoes clanging on his paved driveway.

"Nope." David flipped up the collar of his corduroy coat that was wet with rain. "I moved here from Wisconsin just after Christmas. Had a nursery business there, too."

She nodded, trying to ignore how cold she was all of a sudden. She supposed the shock of the accident and her concern for the safety of the mare had kept her from feeling the temperature dropping, but now that she no longer had adrenaline rushing through her body, she was shivering. "We've got good soil in the area." Her gaze flicked to his as she wondered how old he was. Older than her, for sure. Maybe thirty? *And handsome.*

But also an *Englisher*, she reminded herself.

And more likely than not, he was married.

She was surprised at her thoughts. She never considered men that way. More fuel for her mother's concern she would end up an old maid.

She glanced at David. He had a strong jaw and was clean-shaven. He was a redhead with blue eyes. "I imagine you had good soil back in Wisconsin, too, but we have a milder climate here. And a longer growing season." She chuckled. "My family moved here from upstate New York a few years ago. We used to shovel a lot of snow."

David grinned, nodding. "Definitely a milder climate here. And I have to say, I didn't miss having to shovel my way to the barn in January and February."

The rain began to fall harder, and Bay walked faster. Stealing another glance at David over the mare's back, she reached out and stroked the horse's flank. "Good girl. Almost there. You'll be inside, warm and safe, soon enough. Not a great day to be out," she directed toward David. "I was headed to the new feedstore over in Seven Poplars—Faulkner's. You know it?"

He met her gaze, and she felt the strangest sensation, something like a tickle at the nape of her neck. It wasn't unpleasant, but it was definitely unfamiliar.

"I do know Faulkner's. I like them as well as Clark's." He slid his hands into his coat pockets; he looked as cold as she felt. "Been there a couple of times for vermiculite. They have good bulk prices."

"I was going for vermiculite," she responded, appreciating their shared interest. "And bales of peat. That's why I took the wagon instead of the buggy." She shook her head. "Guess I should have checked the weather forecast."

"Day like this," David said, "I'd think you'd have sent your husband."

Bay laughed aloud. Why, she wasn't sure. Maybe because the argument that had led to her leaving the house so imprudently had been about the very fact that she *didn't* have a husband. Or maybe because there was a strange, nervous excitement rippling through her, making her feel off-kilter.

He frowned, his dark red brows moving closer together. "I say something funny?"

She shook her head, surprising herself with a giggle more suitable to one of her younger sisters than herself. "*Ne*, I'm not laughing at you. I'm laughing at myself." Her gaze strayed to the trees that lined the driveway.

The row nearest to the driveway looked like dogwoods. White dogwood, probably. Her favorite. They grew well in the area and had the most gorgeous white flowers. And there was a second line of trees that were easy to identify because they were about to burst into bloom. Cherry trees, also a favorite of hers.

David waited, watching her over Sassafras's back, a hint of a smile on his face.

She glanced his way, then shifted her gaze to look forward again, wondering what her mother would think if she knew she was alone with a male stranger. It wasn't the Amish way. And to make matters worse, she'd somehow lost her headscarf when the wagon went into the ditch. An Amish woman was never supposed to be without a head covering except in the presence of her husband. Her mother wouldn't be pleased about that, for sure. She wished she'd looked for it back at the scene of the accident, but she'd been more worried about Sassafras's safety than proper attire.

"My mother and I argued today," Bay heard herself say. "About me still being single with no prospects. I left the house with the excuse of going for supplies, but I really just wanted to get away from her."

"I'm sorry to hear that. I know from experience that can be hard, being an adult, living with your parents."

"*Ya*, yes," Bay corrected, adjusting her speech for the *Englisher* the way she did when she waited on them in her garden shop. "That's for sure. My twin sister got married and ever since, my mother has been pushing me to 'find a good Amish man to make me his wife,'" she said, using her mother's words. "It seems like that's all she wants to talk about."

He was quiet for a moment and then asked, "You

don't want to marry?" She could detect no judgment in his tone, just curiosity.

"No, not…well, I don't know. Definitely not yet." She exhaled. "It's not that I'm too old. That's my mother's fear, I think, that no one will marry me, so she wants me to start looking. She thinks I'm too independent to suit most Amish men. *Mam* is afraid I'll be an old maid like her aunt Dorcas, who lived with her family when she was growing up."

"She thinks no one would want to marry you?" David chuckled. "I hardly think that's a concern."

She felt herself blush. *Was he complimenting her?* "I think she's worried that my greenhouse business will be off-putting to Amish men, and I don't want to give it up. But it's not really our way. Women working."

He frowned, wiping the rain from his forehead. "But plenty of Amish women work. I see them in Byler's and at Fifer's Orchard, too."

"*Ya*, but they're mostly unmarried women or women whose children are grown. And that's working at a counter. Those women aren't running their own businesses. They're still home in the mornings to make breakfast and then back by late afternoon to make supper. And clean. And do wash. And make bread, and… and all the things we do in a day."

"I would think your mother would be proud of you, owning your own business."

"Oh, it's not just mine. I own it with my brother."

"Still, even owning *half* a business, I'd think your mother would be pleased that you're so capable."

She laughed. "I think she'd like me to be a little more capable in the house. In the kitchen, in particular."

"Not much of a cook?" he asked, the amusement in his tone again.

"I can follow a recipe well enough, but I get distracted and put in too much baking powder or not enough." She shrugged. "Just not all that interested in cooking, I guess."

He nodded thoughtfully. "And your father? What does he think of you being a businesswoman?"

"My father passed years ago. Benjamin is my mother's second husband. I'm not sure what he thinks about me working. Probably whatever my mother thinks— just to keep her happy." She flashed him a smile. "I didn't intend to get into the gardening business. It just sort of happened. The greenhouse and shop were my stepbrother Joshua's dream, but then we realized I had a knack for it, and somehow, I ended up part owner."

"Right, I guess that is unusual. An Amish woman owning a business, running it."

"It is, especially since we're Old Order. I mean, I know women who sell poultry or eggs, or make quilts to sell so they have their own pin money, but— You know what pin money is?" she asked.

"I do. It's a woman's personal money. My mother embroidered Bible verses for her pin money. She framed them herself and sold them in a little country store where I grew up, near Madison."

She was impressed that he knew the term. And was curious about his upbringing. She wanted to ask him to tell her more about growing up in Wisconsin, but it didn't seem appropriate. It was likely she'd never see this man again. She didn't even know why she wanted to know those things.

Ahead, the lane opened up in front of them and a barnyard appeared. It looked remarkably like every Amish barnyard in Kent County: a big, gambrel-roofed barn and several outbuildings, all well cared for. And there was a white, two-story farmhouse with a big front porch. There were goats in a small pasture on one side of the drive and three horses in a larger one on the other side. In the distance, she heard the bleat of goats and the cluck-clucking of chickens. There was even a shiny, new windmill. The only real difference between her place and David's was the wires over their heads that stretched from the road to the house and some of the buildings, carrying electricity. And the three huge greenhouses she saw in the distance in a field on the back of the property.

David met her gaze. "I'm sorry about the disagreement with your mother."

"Thank you." Bay gave him a quick smile. "It'll be fine. She only wants what's best for me. And what's best for our community. It's important that we keep up our Amish traditions."

"And going against that can be very hard," he agreed. "I know. I've been there."

She glanced at him, curious as to how he knew about going up against traditions, when thunder clapped loudly overhead. The boom was followed immediately by another streak of lightning in the sky. And then the rain fell harder.

"Come on, let's get her in the barn and rubbed down," David said, heading in the direction of the main barn.

Twenty minutes later, Sassafras was tucked in a stall of David's immaculately kept barn, a scoop of oats in a trough in front of her. The rain had let up a bit, and Bay and David dashed across the barnyard toward his back porch. As they hurried up the steps, the door swung open and a pretty woman about Bay's age, wearing a calf-length dress similar to hers and a lace head covering, stepped out onto the porch.

She had to be his wife.

And she was Mennonite. She knew a few Mennonite women and they all wore a small bit of lace on the back of their head rather than a full prayer *kapp* like Bay and her family wore.

They were Mennonite, she realized. David was Mennonite. She should have guessed. A man driving a white pickup truck, living on a farm that looked like an Amish farm, and just how he carried himself. He was polite and friendly in a wholesome way.

"David?" the young woman said, wiping her hands on a pale blue full apron tied over her protruding belly. "I didn't hear the truck come up the lane. Is everything all right?"

"Fine. Anne, this is Bay. She lives down the road. She had a little run-in with a ditch in her wagon. We put her horse up in the barn until someone can come for them. She needs to use the phone."

A little boy of maybe three years old peered out from behind David's wife. David's son, obviously. When Bay made eye contact with the boy, he hid behind his mother again.

"Oh my, are you all right?" Anne moved aside, almost stepping on the little boy. "Matty, get inside," she told him, though not unkindly. "You've got bare feet. You'll catch a chill."

The little boy darted back into the house.

"Come in, please," David's wife said. "You're soaked through." She stepped aside, waving Bay past her. "Why did you walk home, David? You should have brought her in the truck. She's soaked. The both of you are."

"It's not his fault," Bay said, stepping into a large mudroom that looked similar to her mother's. A clothes dryer was running, and the room smelled of wet shoes, fabric softener and gingerbread. She saw a basket on the floor with a mother cat inside, nursing several black-and-white kittens. "I had to walk my mare here," she told Anne. "He didn't want me walking alone."

Anne followed Bay into the laundry room. "You're brave to walk a horse in this storm. Please, come into the kitchen and I'll get you something hot to drink. Would you like tea or coffee?"

Bay stepped out of her soaking wet black sneakers, wondering why she hadn't had the sense to put on her rubber boots when she left the house. Next, she peeled off her coat, which Anne took from her and hung on the wall hook. "I don't want to trouble you."

"No trouble at all. The kettle's already on."

"Tea would be nice, then," Bay said.

"Tea it is." Anne turned to David. "Don't you even

think about wearing those boots in the house. I just mopped the kitchen."

He lowered his head sheepishly, then winked at Bay and sat down on a bench to unlace his work boots.

Bay was so surprised by his wink that she froze for a moment. What kind of man would wink at another woman right in front of his wife?

"Please come in," Anne said again, walking into the kitchen. If she had seen David wink at Bay, she gave no indication. "I'll have that tea ready in just a minute. Tea, David?"

"Coffee," he called from the bench where he was still wrestling with his wet boots.

"You've had enough coffee for today." Anne flashed Bay a smile as she walked toward a kitchen counter where an electric teakettle was beginning to whistle. "He'll be up half the night if he drinks anymore coffee." Then to David she called, "Tea or hot chocolate?"

The country kitchen was almost as big as the one at home, with a big, six-burner gas stove with two ovens. The floors were polished hardwood, the walls white, the countertops some sort of shiny stone, and the cabinets were all painted a cheery yellow. Gingham white-and-yellow curtains were pulled back from the windows, which looked to have been recently cleaned.

"Hot chocolate sounds good," David hollered from the laundry room. "With *mashmallows*, right, Matty?" He mispronounced the word, obviously for the benefit of the boy who was now under the table. "We like *mashmallows*."

The boy said nothing.

"Matty, come out from under there," Anne ordered. When he made no attempt to move, she said, "Come out and you can have hot chocolate with Uncle David. With *mashmallows*."

David was Matty's uncle?

Which meant Anne was his sister, not his wife. Bay glanced at David, now standing in the doorway. *If Anne wasn't his wife, where was his wife?*

Or maybe he was single.

The moment the thought went through her head, she tamped it down. It was so unlike her to be concerned whether a man was married or not. What did she care? She wasn't looking for a husband. And certainly not one outside her faith. Bay only knew one person who had left the Amish community to become Mennonite and that was Hannah Hartman's daughter Leah. Leah had married a Mennonite and gone to South America with him to do mission work.

"I'm going to run upstairs and change," David said, his wet socks leaving spots on the wood floor as he crossed the kitchen. "I'll be right back, Bay. The phone's there on the wall." He pointed to a dial wall phone. "Anne, can you find Bay a blanket or something?"

Anne poured the hot water into a white teapot painted with blue and yellow flowers. When the sound of David's footsteps echoed on the stairs, she turned to Bay. "Go ahead and call home. I imagine your family must be worried about you."

Bay dialed the phone number to the harness shop and one of the girls who worked at the front counter answered. She told Emily what had happened, assuring her that she and the horse were fine when the girl got flustered. Then she gave her the directions to David's place and hoped for the best. Emily wasn't always the best at relaying phone messages, because she never seemed to get them right. She either missed a digit of a number or forgot to write down the reason for the call in the first place.

"Someone's coming for me," Bay told Anne when she hung up.

"Good. In the meantime, can I get you some dry clothes?" Anne asked.

Bay touched her wet hair and felt her cheeks grow warm with embarrassment. She didn't know who would come for her and the mare, but she doubted any of the men in her family would appreciate her being bareheaded. "I lost my headscarf when I had the accident. My dress will dry, but if you have a scarf I can borrow, I'd appreciate it." Out of the corner of her eye, she saw Matty peeking out from under the round table, which was covered with a tablecloth with buttercups embroidered on it. "We don't let our hair go uncovered. But you probably know that."

Anne smiled at her as she carried the teapot to the table. "Ah. So, David told you that we grew up Amish?"

That surprised Bay, but then she realized it shouldn't have. Many Mennonite families had once been Amish. "*Ne*…no. He didn't."

Anne shook her head as she went into the laundry room and came back carrying a dark blue wool headscarf that looked similar to the one Bay had lost. In her other hand, Anne had a pair of blue socks. "At least put on some dry socks," she told Bay, offering both items. "You'll feel warmer."

Bay considered saying *no, thank you*, but the practicality of Anne's offer overrode any sense of awkwardness she felt. She was always so sensible, always making good choices. Taking the wagon out when bad weather was coming in was so out of character for her. She didn't know what had gotten into her. "Thank you," she murmured, accepting the items.

"Matty, come out from under there," Anne ordered, pointing her finger. "This is our new friend, Bay. Can you say hello?"

The little boy peeked out from under the tablecloth and then slowly pushed out one of the chairs.

"Is this for me?" Bay asked him.

Matty nodded slowly, watching her with big brown eyes.

"Thank you," Bay told him as she sat down to change her socks.

"It's not you," Anne said, carrying two mugs to the table. "Matty's shy. Has been for some months now." Her eyes started to tear up and she turned away. "Milk and sugar for your tea, Bay?"

"Just sugar." Wondering what had made Anne sad, Bay remade her bun and covered her wet hair with the scarf, tying it at the nape of her neck.

Anne wrinkled her nose. "You sound just like me. I don't care for milk. I know. A girl who grew up Amish on a dairy farm who doesn't drink milk." She tilted her head, looking under the table. "Matthew, if you want cookies with that hot chocolate, you'd best run and wash your hands. I saw you playing with those kittens when I turned my back. We have new kittens," she explained, returning her attention to Bay. "A stray female some-one dropped off at the end of the lane. David is such a softy. He brought her inside and made a nice bed for her in the laundry room and two days later, we had six cats instead of one."

The ladder-back chair opposite the one Bay was seated at scraped the floor, and Matty darted out from under the table and ran out of the kitchen.

As Bay was putting the dry navy knee socks on, Anne brought over a plate of homemade gingerbread cookies. "I hope you'll excuse my son's behavior. He's very wary around strangers and doesn't really talk any-more. Not since his father passed."

"I'm so sorry," Bay breathed, glancing at Anne's round abdomen. "And you—" She cut herself off be-fore she said *expecting*. Among the Amish, one didn't bring up pregnancy with strangers. She didn't know if it was the same with Mennonite women.

"Thank you." Anne sighed and stroked her belly. "It's been bittersweet. I lost my husband, Matthew, to a car accident last fall, but God saw fit to bless us with another child all the same."

Bay balled up her wet socks and carried them to her shoes in the mudroom. When she returned to the kitchen, Anne was spooning cocoa mix from a big blue tub into two mugs. "I can't imagine how hard it's been for you," she said quietly. "You moved here from Wis-consin, too?"

"When Matthew and I married. He has a brother who

lives in Greenwood. We were renting an apartment in Dover, looking for the right property. Matthew had always wanted a greenhouse business and when this place came up for sale, we bought it. He had big plans for this spring." She pressed her lips together, going quiet for a moment. "But it wasn't meant to be." She flashed a smile at Bay. "I was trying to decide if I was going to have to sell and move back to Wisconsin." She leaned against the counter. "I knew I'd need help when the little one arrived, but I didn't want to leave our church. Kent County had just begun to feel like home, and I didn't want to leave my friends or my midwife. Then David offered to sell his place and come here to live with us and take over the business and..." Tears filled her eyes. "I'm sorry." She lifted the hem of her apron and patted her eyes. "You don't want to hear all of this. I don't know how I started down this path." She sniffed. "Hormones, I guess."

Bay stood in the middle of the kitchen for a moment, not sure what to do. Her impulse was to give Anne a hug. Anne just looked like she needed it. It occurred to Bay as she moved toward her that Anne might not want a hug from a wet stranger, but when she opened her arms, Anne looked relieved.

"I'm sorry I'm wet," Bay murmured.

Anne put her arms around Bay. "Thank you," she whispered.

The two stood, hugging for a moment, and then Anne took a step back, pulling a hankie from her apron pocket to wipe her nose. "Matty," she called. "Your hot chocolate is ready. I'm just trying to figure out if you want marshmallows or not." She flashed Bay a mischievous smile. "He hears just fine, just not interested in talking again yet. His pediatrician said to give him time. Losing a father at Matty's age is traumatic. We were hoping that when David moved in, Matty might find his voice, but so far..." She sighed, then looked up at Bay. "All in God's time, right?" She picked up the two mugs of hot chocolate she'd made and carried them to the table. "Enough of this talk. Tell me about yourself, Bay. Do you have children? Please have your tea before it gets too cool." Anne motioned to the table.

Bay slipped back into her chair, thinking how much she liked Anne. She was so positive for a woman who had been through so much. And she seemed like she'd be fun. There was a sparkle in her eyes that made Bay smile. "No children. No husband."

Anne had just turned away from the table but turned back, her calf-length skirt swishing. "Oooh, single? And no beau?" she asked, narrowing her gaze coyly.

Bay laughed and took a sip of tea. "Funny you should say that. The fact that I have no husband or beau is how I ended up in the ditch." She tipped her head to one side. "In a roundabout way."

Just then, Bay heard the sound of David's footsteps as he came down the stairs. A moment later, he walked back into the kitchen with Matty trailing.

"Did you know Bay is single?" Anne asked her brother as he took the chair opposite Bay at the head of the table. Matty climbed into the chair to his uncle's left.

David smiled from across the table at Bay and, against her will, she felt a little flutter in her chest.

"David's single, too," Anne announced, sliding into the chair on the other side of her brother as she looked from him to Bay and back at him again.

Any other man would have been embarrassed, but David just threw his head back and laughed, and Bay was almost glad she'd driven into the thunderstorm.

Chapter Three

"'The end,'" David read softly. Closing the book, he looked down at his nephew in bed, his little hands tucked beneath his head as if praying as he slept. The sight of the boy sleeping so soundly brought a lump of emotion to his throat. He wondered what it would be like to have his own son or daughter. Because if this feeling of joy was what children brought into his life, maybe it was time he thought about looking for a wife. He always knew he would marry someday, but he'd never been in a hurry to take that next step. Why was he thinking about it tonight?

He gazed at Matty with a smile. The boy had the same red hair that David and his sister had. Would his own child be a redhead? The three-year-old looked so much like Anne that Matty's father, Matthew, had joked that their child was a Jansen through and through. But David saw Matthew in the boy's brown eyes, in his facial expressions and in his kindness to all creatures from the tiniest insect to their massive Clydesdale horse.

David set the Laura Ingalls Wilder picture book on the nightstand, adding it to a whole stack of them that he and Anne had found at a local flea market. One of Anne's friends from her Mennonite church had brought the first one to Matty after his father died, and the boy had clung to it for days. He had David and Anne read them over and over again. When David found another one of the books, he'd brought it home and he and Anne had laughed that he had bought it for his own sanity. He didn't know how many times more he could read *Little House in the Big Woods* to Matty. Now there was a whole stack of them to read to the boy. In fact, they owned two copies of a couple of books because Matty carried them around the house, out into the barnyard, the fields and the greenhouses, and the original copies had gotten too tattered to read.

David swept the hair off Matty's forehead and slid back in his chair, his thoughts drifting from the boy to his day. More specifically, to Bay Stutzman.

A smile lifted the corners of his mouth. "A good thing I saw the accident in the rearview mirror, wasn't it?" he said softly to his nephew. The boy hadn't spoken since he learned of his father's death six months ago, but David made a point of talking to him, anyway. Even when he was asleep. "I feel terrible enough as it is for unintentionally causing Bay's accident, but I'm afraid to think what might have happened if I hadn't been there."

He smirked. "Who am I kidding, Matty? She'd have been just fine. She'd have gotten her mare out of the traces. Probably walked all the way home in that thunderstorm."

He couldn't stop smiling. "She was nice, don't you think? Spirited." He leaned forward and tucked the handmade log cabin quilt around the boy. "And pretty."

David continued, keeping his voice low. "You thought she was pretty, didn't you? I saw you looking at her from under the table. You liked her, too." He nodded thoughtfully. "You're a good judge of character, little man. At least for a three-year-old," he added.

He shifted his gaze to the curtained window on the far wall. "There was just something about Bay that made me feel…good. You know, happy. In here." He tapped his chest over his heart. Then he exhaled. "I know. I know what you're thinking. She's Old Order Amish. She would never be interested in a man like me. When she marries, it will be to a man in the Old Order church. The two of us? It can't happen." He closed his eyes. "But Matty," he whispered. "I wish it could. A woman so smart and beautiful and independent. And she loves plants like me. She—"

The bedroom door that David had left half-open creaked, and he turned around in the chair.

"Matty, what are you doing still—" Anne stepped into the room and glanced at her son, a look of surprise on her face. "Oh, he's sound asleep."

Slightly embarrassed to have been caught talking to a sleeping child, David rose from the chair and moved it to its place on the far side of the nightstand. "He is. He was out by the time we got to Pa and the bee tree."

She frowned, looking tired. "Then who were you talking to?" she asked.

He shrugged. "Myself, I guess," he answered sheepishly. Something he had been doing frequently since his arrival in Delaware. He hadn't made any friends yet and he missed having friends or family to talk with. Sure, he and Anne talked. A lot. But there were some matters, like his worries concerning her health, that he couldn't talk to her about. Also topics like pretty, single women, too.

He followed Anne out of the bedroom, sliding the dimmer light down until the lamp on the nightstand beside Matty's bed barely glowed. Since his father's death, Matty had not only stopped talking, but he had become afraid of the dark. In the first days after his father's passing, he hadn't been able to sleep unless it was in his mother's bed. Only after David had moved in had Matty been convinced to return to his own room.

"I thought you'd gone to sleep," David said, redirecting the conversation. "You said you were going to bed. You know what the midwife said. You can't be on your feet all day without resting. Not with the hours you keep. At the very least, you need to be getting to bed earlier."

Standing in the hall, she pulled off her apron that was dusty with flour, likely from the buttermilk biscuits she had made to go with the ham and scalloped potatoes and roasted Brussel sprouts they'd had for supper. "I'm going. I just have to get the dried beans soaking to make a soup with that ham bone tomorrow."

"I'll do it."

"David, you already do so much. I hate to—"

"What? You think I can't dump a bag of beans into some water?"

"And add salt, or they won't taste right," she added.

"I've got it, Anne. So…" He opened his arms wide. "Go on, get to bed."

"I'm going. Stop fussing over me," she said, as she headed down the hall.

David was turning to go in the opposite direction when Anne turned back to him.

"I liked her. Bay," she said. "And I think you did, too," she added, a hint of playfulness in her voice.

He didn't look back as he strode toward the staircase landing. "She was nice enough," he answered, trying to keep his tone neutral.

"She's very pretty," Anne called after him. "You should ask her out."

He stopped, his hand on the staircase rail. "Anne, she's Amish. And we no longer are. Bay and I…that would be impossible."

She gave a little laugh. "That's where you're mistaken, Davy," she responded, using his childhood nickname, one she knew he disliked. "Anything is possible with God."

David didn't answer, but he lay in bed awake for a very long time that night, thinking about Bay, and imagining what it would like to love and be loved by a woman like her.

That night, Bay lay awake in bed into the wee hours of the morning, listening to the sounds of her sisters Nettie and Tara sleeping. She couldn't sleep because her thoughts were all a jumble in her mind. She kept rehashing the conversations she'd had with her mother and with David.

That evening, after returning from David's with her brothers, Bay had waited until after supper to have a private conversation with her mother. Something that wasn't easy in their household. She'd found her *mam* in the pantry after the kitchen was clean and her family had scattered to finish their tasks of the day before gathering in the parlor for evening prayers. Her mother, Rosemary, was adding flour to the sourdough starter she'd been keeping since she was a new bride nearly thirty years ago. She had brought her starter from her first marriage to Bay's father, to her second marriage to Benjamin Miller. While Bay wasn't much of a baker, it was a comforting continuation in a world that seemed to be changing quickly, a world where she no longer knew exactly where she belonged.

Bay's father and Benjamin had been the best of friends. It only seemed right that Benjamin, also widowed, would eventually come calling on Bay's mother. Both had a houseful of children and a farm to care for on their own. It had been logical to the Amish way of thinking that the two should join their two households. What had been surprising was that they had fallen in love. It had been a daring move, trying to meld two families with adult or nearly adult children together, but they had made it work.

Bay rolled onto her back in her bed.

As she had stood in the doorway of the pantry that evening, she'd wondered if the reason she was so opposed to marriage was that she was afraid. Her mother had found love not once but twice in her lifetime. Bay's sisters Lovey and Ginger and her stepbrothers Joshua, Ethan and Levi had all married for love. Benjamin's only daughter, Mary, had, as well. But what if no one ever fell in love with Bay? What if her liberated ways made her unlovable? She knew that some women in their community married for reasons other than romantic love, but Bay wanted to love and be loved and if that weren't possible, she would rather remain single for the rest of her days.

Her mother had taken a proofing jar from a shelf and removed the flat, glass lid. She was a pretty woman still, even on the downside of her forties, as she liked to say. She had a comely face with a clear complexion and no visible wrinkles. Her eyes were nearly the same color as Bay's. She wore her brown hair in a bun at the nape of her neck, a pristine white prayer *kapp* on her head, and she was nearly as slim as Bay. For years she had been a little plump, but after the birth of Bay's two little brothers after they moved to Delaware, she had slimmed down to the body of a much younger woman. It was chasing after the boys that had brought down her weight, she insisted. Whether that was true or not, Bay thought she looked far younger than a woman nearing fifty.

"There you are," Bay had said softly. "I was looking for you."

"And here I am," her mother had replied. She hadn't looked at her, but there had been no crossness in her tone.

Bay had watched her pour off part of the starter

so she could add fresh flour to keep the *mother*—the pre-fermented dough—alive. "I wanted to—" She had sighed. Apologizing had never been easy for her. It wasn't that she never regretted things she said and did, only that she found it trying to find the words to say so. "I'm sorry about our argument earlier today."

With the sourdough *mother* divided, Bay's *mam* had measured out flour from a five-gallon plastic tub. "I wasn't aware we argued, *Dochter.*" She'd glanced at Bay in the doorway.

Bay had hung her head. "It felt like we did." She'd looked up: "And it felt like you were criticizing me for who I am."

Her *mam* had sighed and wiped her hands on her apron, turning to her. "I'm sorry if it sounded that way." Green eyes had met green eyes. "I didn't mean to criticize you. I love your free spirit, Bay. We all do. It's only that Benjamin and I worry about you. About your future. This time in your life is so crucial, and I don't want to see you make mistakes that could affect the rest of your life. This is when you should be going to singings and frolics and taking buggy rides with eligible young men." She had rested a hand, dusty with flour, on her hip. "Do you want to spend the rest of your life in your mother's home, never having one of your own? Your own family?"

"You and Benjamin *are* my family. My sisters and brothers are my family."

Her *mam* had put the lid back on the flour container. She had been wearing a peach-colored dress and even in the dusky light of the pantry, it made her skin look rosy and fresh. "You know what I mean." She'd given Bay an all-knowing eye.

"*Ya*, that you're afraid I'll never marry. That I'll be an old maid." Bay had studied her slippers, trying not to grow impatient with her mother the way she had earlier in the day. "Would that really be such a terrible thing, I mean, if I didn't marry," Bay had asked. "I'd be around to take care of you and Benjamin. We care for our own when they get old. You say that all the time."

Her mother had laughed. "Old, are we? Tell those little brothers of yours that." In the direction of the toddlers' bedroom, she had pointed upward to where they were, hopefully sound asleep. "Maybe they'll stop running me ragged."

Bay had looked away, a lump rising in her throat. She admired her mother. She loved her deeply, but she didn't feel like her mother really listened to her. "You always take what I'm saying in the wrong way. I didn't say you were old. But one day you will get old, *Mam*." She had let out a frustrated sigh. "Not all women marry, you know. Some stay home and care for their parents."

"Hmm," her mother had intoned. "And here Benjamin and I were looking forward to, someday, many years in the future, having some time to ourselves. The way we had at the beginning of our first marriages— before we had children."

Bay hadn't been sure how to respond, so she'd said nothing.

Her mother had stared at her for what seemed like a long time before she had spoken again. "I just want you to be happy, Bay. I want you to live a long, happy life of faith and good deeds."

"And I can't have faith in God and do good without a husband wrapped around my neck?" The moment the words had come out of Bay's mouth, she had regretted them. She had gone to apologize, not start another quarrel.

Her mother hadn't taken her words poorly, though, in fact, she had chuckled. "When you say it that way, it doesn't have a lot of appeal, does it?"

Bay hadn't been able to resist a little smile as she had lifted her gaze to her mother again. "I'm not saying I will never marry. I'm only saying that…" She had exhaled, her thoughts darting back to her accident earlier in the day. To David. She had pushed them aside. "I haven't met anyone I like well enough even to consider marriage. You wouldn't want me to marry someone I didn't want to live the rest of my life with, would you? You want me to find someone I'm suited to."

Her mother had narrowed her gaze. "It seems to me that a certain young woman told me today in my kitchen that she was never, *ever* going to marry and that I couldn't make her do it." She had gestured. "As if I was going to drag you to your wedding by your apron strings."

Bay had felt her cheeks grow warm. "I was upset, *Mam*. You know how I can be. I say things sometimes that I don't mean."

"Oh, *Dochter*." Her had mother crossed the short distance between them and put her arms around Bay. "I'm so glad that you weren't hurt today. I feel as if it were my fault, you taking off the way you did with a thunderstorm coming in."

Bay had returned the hug, breathing in the scent of her mother, a mixture of flour, vanilla and love that she knew would always be present. "It wasn't your fault. I'm a hothead. Or becoming one," she had admitted, stepping back. "And I'm fine. The mare's fine."

"And the wagon?"

"Not quite as fine. Jacob said he and Jesse would go in the morning and try to pull it out of the ditch. It was raining too hard by the time they arrived to get Sassafras and me, and he wanted to get us home."

"That was kind of those folks to help you."

"*Ya*, Anne was so nice." Bay had pressed her lips together, not sure why she'd mentioned Anne's name and not David's. "She gave me socks to wear because my feet had gotten wet." She left out the bit about the scarf, thinking there was no need for her mother to know that David had seen her bareheaded.

Her mother had returned to the counter to finish the sourdough starter. "I plan to make cinnamon rolls in the morning." She had begun to stir the flour into the pre-fermented dough. "You said Anne's Mennonite? I bet the family would appreciate homemade cinnamon rolls. You should take them some."

"I'm sure they would. I was thinking I would go with the boys to get the wagon and…return Anne's socks." As she spoke, Bay realized she really wanted to go back to David's place. To thank him and Anne. In fact, her need to go almost felt desperate. "I could take the rolls, too."

"I think that would be lovely."

Their conversation had ended with Bay's mother giving her a peck on the cheek as she left the pantry. It was decided. Bay would go back to Anne and David's home with the cinnamon rolls to say thank-you.

Bay rolled over in her bed, pulling the patchwork quilt, which her mother had made her, to her chin. That was what was keeping her awake now. Thinking about David. She kept going over every word he'd said, every gesture he had made. His wink. What had that been all about? No one had ever winked at her before. Which had her intrigued.

She closed her eyes, wondering if it would be wrong to pray to God that David would be there again in the morning.

The following day, one that had turned out to be sunny and reasonably warm, Bay found herself standing beside her stepbrother Jacob and brother Jesse, staring at the drainage ditch on Persimmon Lane. David's road. Where there was no wagon.

"I don't understand," she worried aloud. "I'm sure this is the place." She pointed. "Look, you can see the ruts the wheels made as I slid into the ditch." She'd been going over and over in her mind what she was going to say to David when she took the cinnamon rolls to him. Them, she corrected. She had planned out everything she was going to say and how she was going to say it. She even had a contingency plan for what to do if he winked at her again. She was going to call him on it—ask if he'd winked at her or if he'd only had dust in his eye. He'd likely laugh. She liked the idea of making him laugh because she had loved the sound of it. She had the whole morning planned out. What she hadn't planned on was the wagon not being there where they had left it the night before.

Jacob glanced around, taking in the field beyond the drainage ditch and the woods behind them, across the road. "I know this is the place. It was here last night when we went by."

Jesse tugged at the brim of his straw hat, imitating Jacob as he looked one way down the road then the other. While he had grown taller over the winter, her little brother was still small for his age. Wiry. As his face matured, he reminded her more and more of their father. "This is the place, all right. You think someone stole it?" he asked, seeming excited by the idea.

Jacob shrugged. "I guess it's possible, but who? This road isn't well-traveled. And what would an *Englisher* do with an old horse-drawn wagon with a broken wheel? How would they get it down the road?"

Bay stared at the ditch, hands on her hips. "I bet I know where it is."

Five minutes later, Bay stood at David's back door, the disposable pan of cinnamon rolls in her hands. As she waited for someone to answer the door, she glanced over her shoulder. Jacob and Jesse were waiting in the wagon they had borrowed that morning. With the tools they had piled in the back, they were hoping to repair their wagon and tow it home.

Was no one home? Bay knocked again and looked into the barnyard, where there was no sign of their wagon. She had thought David had brought it back to his place to keep it safe until they came. Now it was looking more as if Jesse had been right. Maybe someone had stolen it.

A sound on the other side of the door caught Bay's attention. She saw the doorknob turn and looked up, hoping it would be David. So she could thank him properly. And tell him about the stolen wagon, she guessed.

But when the door opened, no one was there.

Actually, someone was.

When she looked downward, she saw Anne's little boy. "Matty. Hi, there, remember me from yesterday? I'm Bay." She crouched down to look at him eye to eye.

"I brought something delicious for you and your *mam* and D—your uncle." He was an adorable little boy with red hair the same shade as David and Anne's, but darker than her own. She'd always adored red-haired children, maybe because she knew what it was like to grow up a redhead. People made all kinds of assumptions about redheads: they had terrible tempers, were badly behaved and had minds of their own. Well…maybe the last one was true. Anyway, she knew what it was like to be teased in the schoolyard and have your hair pulled while kids called you carrottop.

"Do you like cinnamon rolls?" She showed him the container. "With orange frosting," she enticed.

Matty nodded, his eyes widening with approval.

"Then I think you should have one, but only if your mother says it's okay. Is your mama here?"

"I'm here!" called Anne from inside. "Come on in, Bay."

Bay walked into the laundry room and pulled the back door closed behind her. From the doorway between the laundry room and the kitchen, she spotted Anne standing on the fourth rung of a stepladder.

"We saw you pull up in the driveway," Anne said. "It's just that I—"

"Can I get that for you?" Bay rushed to the kitchen table to set down the rolls.

Anne was trying to lower a stack of colorful ceramic baking dishes, one nested inside the other. The problem was that it appeared they were heavy, and she was having a problem keeping herself balanced on the top of the stepstool.

"No…actually, yes," Anne said with a laugh, half born of frustration, half of relief. "David said I shouldn't put these up here, that it's too high for me." Leaving the dishes on the top of the kitchen cabinet, she slowly came down the stepstool, using the countertop to keep her balance. "But who likes to tell a man when they're right about something in the kitchen?" she joked.

Bay chuckled as she hurried up the stepstool, grabbed the stack of baking dishes and backed her way down to the floor, thankful she didn't keep her dress hems as low as most of the Amish women she knew. "Did you want all of these?"

"Actually, just the middle one." Anne leaned against the counter, seeming a little out of breath.

As Bay fished out the rectangular baking dish, she glanced at Anne. "Are you okay? Maybe you should sit down."

"I'm fine." Anne gave a wave and then pressed her

hand to her chest. "I'd forgotten what it was like, being this far along. Carrying a baby around twenty-four hours a day takes a lot of energy." Her smile was bittersweet, as if she was remembering her previous pregnancy, and maybe her husband.

Bay set the bright orange baking dish down in Anne's workspace on the counter. "Want me to put the others back?"

Anne shook her head. "No. Thanks. I'll find a better place for them. Just leave them on the counter there."

Bay did as she asked, and then folded up the stepstool. "Where does this go?"

"Oh, in the laundry room to the right of the dryer, but you don't need to do that. I'll do it in a second." Anne looked down at Matty, who was standing right in front of her now, looking up at her with obvious concern. "Mama's fine," she reassured him. "Oh my, look what Bay's brought. Are those homemade cinnamon rolls?" Her tone was obviously meant to distract her son and it worked. Matty ran to the table to have a closer look at the treat.

Bay returned the stool to its place and walked back into the kitchen. "I hope you don't mind me just stopping by. I didn't have your phone number. I brought the cinnamon rolls to say thank-you." She reached into her denim jacket pocket. "And I brought back the socks and your scarf." She set them down beside the rolls.

"You don't need to call to stop by. Come anytime." Anne was still leaning against the kitchen counter, but her breath was more even. "I'm so glad you did, Bay. I don't have any friends nearby. All my church friends are farther away and can't just stop by. I'm hoping we can be friends." Her brow furrowed. "That's allowed, isn't it? Even though I'm Mennonite."

Bay laughed. "Of course. Why would that matter?"

Anne gave an exasperated smile. "Well, the church David and I grew up in…" She opened a drawer and pulled out a butter knife. "Our bishop thought Mennonites were fallen souls and we weren't to mingle with them." She gave a laugh as she crossed the kitchen to the table and took the plastic wrap off the rolls. "And you don't even want to know what he said about *Englishers.*" She used the knife to cut out half a roll, pluck a napkin from a holder on the table and set the half piece in the middle of it. "Is this what you were waiting for?" she asked Matty.

He nodded, his eyes filled with excitement.

"Hop up in your chair, then." She set the treat at his place at the table and turned back to Bay. "I'm serious. Stop by anytime. The days are so long sometimes. I'd love the distraction."

Bay nibbled on her lower lip. "I think I'd like that."

"And I'll give you my phone number. You can call from your harness shop, right?"

"Sure can." Bay watched her open a kitchen drawer and pull out a pad and pen. "So my brothers and I came for our wagon, but it's not there anymore. I thought maybe David brought it up here, but… David's not home?" She hadn't seen his pickup but had hoped maybe it was parked somewhere out of sight.

"No, he went—oh my." Anne whipped around, covering her mouth with her hand. "I forgot. I'm sorry. I seem to get scatterbrained when I'm expecting." She sounded flustered now. "I was supposed to tell you if you showed up looking for the wagon that David got it out of the ditch at first light. He took it somewhere to be repaired. Something about the axle? He's got a big flatbed trailer, so he loaded it up and took off. He left a message at your family's harness shop this morning. Did you not get it? He called and talked to someone... Emily, I think?"

Bay rolled her eyes. She liked the young woman Benjamin had recently hired, but she wasn't entirely sure it would work out. Emily was an Amish girl who had just moved to Hickory Grove with her family. She was a nice girl, but what her mother called *whiffy*. Emily was friendly and comfortable with customers, *English* and Amish, but she wasn't much one for details. She never rang items correctly at the cash register, and she struggled to use the credit card machine. And she wasn't good about answering the phone. She either chatted with the caller about the weather and wasted time or totally got the message wrong if someone had a question she couldn't answer. Benjamin refused to let her go, though, no matter how many mistakes she made. His explanation was that the family needed the income, and he needed to share his financial blessings with others in the community.

"He took our wagon to be repaired?" Bay asked, not sure if she should be pleased or annoyed. "He didn't have to do that."

Anne wrinkled her freckled nose. "I think he felt bad about what happened. That the spray from his truck startled your horse, and that's why you went in the ditch."

Because I accused him of causing the accident, Bay thought. Which was impulsive and just plain inaccurate. He hadn't done anything wrong. Horses shied sometimes.

"It wasn't his fault," Bay told Anne. "It just…happened."

"I think he was happy to do it." Anne moved the baking dish Bay had taken down for her, poured a little oil into it, and then used her fingers to spread it across the bottom and up the sides.

"Well…please thank him for me. And I guess he'll be in touch?" She glanced out the kitchen window to see her brothers in the wagon. They were laughing, which made her smile. "My brothers are waiting for me, so I'll say goodbye."

"Oh, I'm sorry you can't stay." Anne wiped her hand on a dish towel and turned to her. "Will you come again? I don't drive. Never learned." She gave a little laugh. "Matthew kept telling me I needed to learn and then…" Her tone was wistful, and when she met Bay's gaze, her eyes were teary. But she was still smiling.

Bay was surprised by the emotion she felt for this stranger. Anne was so strong, so brave. Bay couldn't imagine what it would be like to lose the man you loved, the father of your children. And she realized that she really did want to be friends with Anne. "I'll come back another day. I'll call you and—"

"Oh, you don't need to call. Come anytime. I never

go anywhere but church. Poor David is even doing the grocery shopping these days."

Bay glanced at Matty, who had finished the half of the cinnamon roll on his plate. He was now eyeing the pan. "Goodbye, Matty. Maybe I'll see you in a few days."

The boy looked up and offered a shy smile.

"Wouldn't that be nice, Matty?" Anne asked. "If Bay came back to visit us?"

The boy remained silent, as his mother turned back to Bay. "I'll tell David you were here. I'm sure he'll give you a call or stop by your place, or something, once he knows what's going on with your wagon." Then she surprised Bay by throwing her arms around her.

The hug startled Bay, but then she wrapped her arms around Anne, feeling her rounded abdomen against her own flat one, and it felt…as if she had known her new friend her whole life.

Chapter Four

David had to fight his urge to beep his horn at the minivan in front of him. He understood the need to travel slower on the back roads and the importance of following the posted speed limits, but he didn't understand why people had to drive ten or fifteen miles an hour *under* the speed limit.

He was tempted to pass, but there was a double yellow line because of the road curves, and he wasn't about to get a ticket. He'd had his driver's license almost ten years now, and he didn't have a single ticket; he wasn't about to change that.

He would just have to be patient. He reminded himself of Paul's words in his letter to the Romans. *Patience in tribulation.*

And ordinarily, he *was* a patient man. One had to be, in the greenhouse business. With almost everything he did, whether it was growing perennial flowers, trees or bushes, there were times when action was required by him, and other times when he just had to sit back and wait. Patience was required while the plants germinated from seed, while they grew sturdy enough to be replanted in larger pots. And even once there were healthy plants, one had to be patient while they grew fruits or vegetables, while those fruits and vegetables ripened, or while flowers reached full bloom.

The problem was he wasn't feeling patient today. He wanted to get home in case Bay stopped by. He'd meant to be home more than an hour ago, but it had taken him longer than he'd anticipated at Jared Kline's house, where he'd taken Bay's wagon to be mended. In his early sixties, Jared was a kind man from their church who had been happy to fix the broken axle for free to return a favor David had done for him. But Jared reminded him of his uncle Adam—a nice man who could. Not. Stop. Talking.

Jared chatted about the weather, his neighbor's sheep, and his wife's cousin's friend who, at seventy-eight years old, had fallen from a tree she was climbing. He talked about the leak in his hose that ran to his washing machine, and the flavor of toothpaste he preferred. Honestly, after forty-five minutes of not saying more than ten words, David had been ready to just load Bay's wagon back on his trailer and take it elsewhere. Then, just as he finally escaped from Jared, he received a text from Anne asking that he stop at the drugstore for her. How could he tell her no, that he wanted to get home just in case this smart, attractive, single woman happened to stop by? A woman he had no chance with?

He couldn't. So, even though he had been halfway home when Anne texted him, he'd backtracked, gone to the drugstore and then taken every shortcut he knew home. He could almost see his driveway now. He saw the roof of one of his greenhouses in the distance. He was almost to the house, and maybe, just maybe, Bay would be there.

But the white van seemed to have slowed down even further. David could have walked faster than the mini-van, even pulling his flatbed trailer with a few lengths of corn string and muscle.

Once he'd taken the curve at a snail's pace and could see his driveway, David checked his rearview mirror, saw all was clear, and hit the accelerator. He passed the minivan on two solid yellow lines and wheeled into his driveway. He was half expecting—or at least half wishing—that Bay would be there, but why would she? He'd left a message at her stepfather's harness shop first thing that morning, letting her know he had gotten the wagon out of the ditch and that it was being repaired. In the message, he'd asked the young girl who answered the phone to tell Bay that he'd contact her as soon as he knew when the wagon would be fixed.

With no sign of an Amish vehicle, David parked in front of what had once been a dairy barn. Because he didn't have cows, it was now home to three horses, four goats and a passel of barn cats. With a glance around to see that all was well in the barnyard, he hurried across the driveway toward the house, the bag from the drug-store in his hand.

"Hello?" he called as he closed the back door behind him. From the doorway between the laundry room and the kitchen, he saw Anne sweeping. Matty sat at the kitchen table coloring with crayons. It smelled like she'd been baking. There was a hint of cinnamon in the air.

"Boots off!" Anne warned. "I just swept. Your slippers are in your cubby."

David impatiently stepped out of his boots, shrugged off his barn coat and walked into the kitchen in his socks. "You hear from Bay?" He set the bag on the kitchen table and pressed a kiss to the top of Matty's head. The boy was drawing circles, filling the whole page with them.

"She was here. You just missed her."

Disappointment washed over him. "She was here?"

"She came looking for the wagon."

"She was looking for the wagon?"

Anne stopped sweeping and leaned on her broom. "Is there an echo in this kitchen?" she teased, knitting her brow.

"She didn't get my message?" he asked.

"She didn't get your message."

He chuckled, shaking his head as he realized his sister was doing the same thing he had done. "Yup. Definitely an echo in here."

Anne laughed and tried to lean over, broom in one hand, the dustpan in the other, so she could gather the dry cereal from Matty's breakfast off the floor.

David only had to watch her struggle with her belly in the way for a couple of seconds before he took the dustpan from her. He had no problem sweeping the kitchen, but he knew better than to try to get her to pass the broom to him. His little sister by eighteen months didn't get angry often, but when she did... David preferred not to be the recipient of that anger.

"I guess the message didn't reach Bay before she left her house. She and her two brothers came for the wagon, didn't find it in the ditch, and came here looking for it."

He carried the dustpan to the trash and dumped it. "I knew I should have left a note or something," he fretted.

Anne laughed as she took the dustpan from him and carried them to the mudroom, where she kept them behind the door. "You were going to leave a note in a *ditch*?" she asked.

He ignored her. "What did she say?"

"What do you mean, what did she say?" Anne returned to the kitchen. "She said she'd come for the wagon, and I told her you'd taken it to be repaired."

"That's it?"

Anne shrugged and went to the sink and began to wash the breakfast dishes. "She apologized for stopping by without calling. I told her she was welcome anytime. She needn't call ahead. I really like her. I think we could be good friends."

"She say anything about me?" The moment the words were out of his mouth, he wished he could take them back. He sounded like a teenage boy.

Anne giggled and glanced over her shoulder at him. "Like how handsome and smart and strong you are?"

He opened his eyes wider, not sure how to respond. *Did she really say those things? Was she attracted to him in the same way he was attracted to her?*

Before he could figure out how to answer, Anne turned back to the sink, laughing again. "No, she didn't say anything like that."

Not realizing he'd been holding his breath, he exhaled, trying to see the humor in his little sister's joke. "Very funny."

She was still chuckling to herself as she set a clean bowl in the dish drain. "Oh, but she did bring those cinnamon rolls for us. For you, really, I guess. As a thank-you. Did you tell her how much you like homemade cinnamon rolls? They even have lots of icing, just the way you like them."

Only then did David notice the aluminum foil tray with a plastic lid on top sitting on the table. "I don't think we talked about cinnamon rolls." He lifted the plastic lid and inhaled. There was the cinnamon he'd been smelling. "Wow." He glanced at Matty. "Hey, little man, did you see a burglar here?" He looked one way and then the other as if searching for a masked man. "Because someone stole half of one of my cinnamon rolls."

Matty smirked but kept his head down, licking at the evidence of the white icing on the corners of his mouth. Now he was coloring in the circles he'd drawn all over the piece of paper.

David pried the other half of the roll out and took a big bite. "Mmm," he muttered, closing his eyes. "These might be the best cinnamon rolls I've ever eaten."

"You know what it means when a woman bakes for a man, don't you? It means she likes you, as in *likes you*."

David felt his cheeks grow warm with embarrassment. "I suspect she was just being nice."

Anne crossed her arms across her chest and leaned against the kitchen cabinet. "Men can be so daft. You have to see the subtle hints," she told him conspiratorially. "There was no need for her to come here this morning. Her brothers could have gotten the wagon. And the fact that she made you cinnamon rolls, which is yeast bread and time-consuming?" She lifted her brows. "She likes you."

He grabbed a paper napkin from the table and wiped his mouth. "You think?"

She nodded, smiling.

"So what do I do?" he asked, feeling like that school-boy again.

"You can start by letting her know what's going on with her wagon."

He stroked his clean-shaven face. "You think I should call the harness shop and ask to speak to her."

Anne laughed. "No, silly goose. You should go to her place and tell her personally." She looked at Matty. "Your uncle David, he's a silly goose, isn't he?"

The boy nodded soberly.

"I should go?" David asked. "Now?"

"What else do you have to do?" she asked, hanging a dish towel with a rooster on it on the oven door.

"I don't know, my to-do list is about this long." He stretched out his arms. "And at the top of the list is fixing the drippy faucet in the downstairs bath. You've been asking me to do it for a week."

She gave a wave. "The faucet can wait."

"Are you sure?" he asked, but he was already heading for the door.

"Go!" Anne called after him. "Tell Bay I said hi and not to be a stranger."

David grabbed his boots in the laundry room doorway, stepped over their resident mama cat, and went to the bench near the door to pull on the boots. "Will do."

"And ask Bay to marry you while you're at it," Anne called.

David didn't dignify that with an answer.

Using the register counter as a desk in the greenhouse shop, Bay signed a check she'd written to one of the distributors where she bought plastic growing trays. She licked the envelope, sealed it and added her address and a stamp. There had been a mix-up with the bill, and she wanted to get the payment in the mail as quickly as possible. She checked the clock on the wall. It was nearly noon. If she hurried, she might make it to the mailbox at the end of their driveway before the mail carrier reached it.

"Joshua?" she called to her stepbrother, who was working in the attached greenhouse. He was planting tiny annual flower plants they'd grown themselves from seed. "I'm going to run down to the mailbox. When I get back, I'll mix up the fertilizer."

"Sounds good," he hollered. "The sun's peeking out, finally. Take your time."

Bay slipped into a quilted denim jacket that had once belonged to one of Benjamin's sons. With so many patches on it and a torn cuff, it had been relegated to the rag box her mother kept in her sewing room. Bay had snitched it from the box, making it her own. While she would never be seen off the farm in a ratty men's coat, it was perfect for working in the greenhouse. It was warm and durable and big enough to wear a sweater under it. After fastening the hook and eyes, she picked up the envelope and walked out the shop's door, a little bell jingling overhead.

In the parking lot the greenhouse shared with the harness shop, she spotted two pickup trucks and a horse and buggy. Customers. One of the trucks was white, and for an instant, she *hoped* it might be David's. Which was silly, of course. He was a busy man with his business, and the farm and his sister and nephew to care for. If he had a message to pass on about their wagon, he'd call the harness shop the way he had that morning. And he'd probably ask to speak to Benjamin. After all, it was *his* wagon she'd borrowed. And wrecked. But true to form, her stepfather hadn't been the least bit upset when he heard about the accident. In fact, when she'd arrived home after the incident, he'd given her a big hug, telling how thankful he was that she hadn't been hurt. He told her that wagons and sadly even horses could be replaced, but his Bay never could be. He'd also dismissed her attempt to offer to pay for damages, telling her it hurt his feelings that she would say such a thing.

Reaching the lane that had recently been covered with several inches of fresh oyster shells, Bay turned right, the farmhouse where they lived behind her. Just as Joshua had said, the sun was out at last, and she closed her eyes for a moment, lifting her chin so she could feel its radiant warmth.

It had been a cold winter for Delaware, and then spring had been late in coming. But the temperatures were supposed to continue to rise the rest of the week, with Saturday predicted to be in the sixties. With Easter behind them, she and Joshua hoped the warm weather was just around the corner, but having grown up in upstate New York, she was hesitant to make any predictions. She knew from experience that just when you declared winter to be over, there would be snow again, piled up to the windowsills.

But winter *seemed* to be over. The thunderstorm the previous day was evidence of that, wasn't it? You didn't see thunderstorms in the winter. The idea that spring had finally arrived excited her. Spring was when plants that lay dormant all winter began to spring forth from the soil, when the leaves would pop out in the trees and bushes, and daffodils, tulips and hyacinths would poke from the soil. She had already spotted her *mam's* crocuses in the flower beds around the house.

It was a good quarter of a mile down the lane to the road, but Bay didn't mind the walk. It gave her time to think without worrying about making any mistakes in her woolgathering. The other day while stewing over a conversation with her twin, Ginger, about why she was not attending a frolic at the matchmaker's in Seven Poplars, she'd accidentally mixed marigold seeds with cosmos and now the seeds were in an envelope waiting to be planted in her mother's garden. And two weeks ago, after her mother expressed her disappointment when Bay didn't accept an offer for a ride home with an *eligible* young man, Bay had been so unfocused that she'd combined the wrong ratio of ground limestone to sphagnum peat moss while making potting soil. Such a mistake might seem trivial to a non-gardener, but potting soil that was too alkaline would prevent plants from absorbing nutrients properly. And they would die or grow so spindly that they would have to be thrown in the compost heap.

Halfway to the road, Bay leaned down to pick up a discarded soda pop can. She crumpled it in her hand and stuffed it in her jacket pocket. She didn't understand littering. Who did people who tossed cans into driveways think was going to pick it up?

The sound of a vehicle approaching caught Bay's attention, and she looked up to see the mail carrier speeding past the driveway. She took off at a run, waving the envelope. "Wait!" she cried.

As the postal carrier stuck out her hand to take the envelope, Bay caught sight, out of the corner of her eye, of a white pickup truck signaling to turn into their lane. At first, she thought it was David. But it was undoubtedly just her imagination. In a day, dozens of white pickups came down their driveway headed for the harness shop. And once the greenhouse opened for business in three weeks, the number would double. "Thank you!" she told the mail carrier, out of breath.

The mail carrier plucked the envelope from Bay's hand. "Want the mail?" she asked, all business. They had two mail carriers, one during the week and a different one on weekends. Joe, the weekend carrier, who had to be seventy, was friendly and chatty. But Jazzy, a pretty woman in her forties with little braids all over her head, never said anything more than was necessary.

"Sure. Yes, thank you." As Bay accepted the bundle wrapped in a rubber band, she realized that the man driving the white pickup had red hair. A second later, she recognized him.

It was David!

And he was headed up the drive. A moment of panic overtook Bay, and she froze. The mail truck took off, throwing bits of gravel onto her sneakers. David must not have seen her, his view blocked by the mail truck. She couldn't let him see her looking like this, in a man's old, patched coat and her hair covered with a stained headscarf. Maybe she could just wait until he reached the parking lot, and then she could cut across the lawn and run around the back of the shop, and he'd never see her.

But she didn't want David going up to the harness shop. She didn't want him talking to Benjamin or her siblings, or even the whiffy Emily at the shop's register. She didn't know why; she only knew that she didn't.

"David!" she hollered, taking off after his truck. "David!"

He must have either heard her or seen her in his mirror because he hit his brakes. Bay had to hit her own to keep from running right into the back door of his truck. "David," she repeated.

His window was down. "Bay." He smiled as he shifted into Park.

"What—" She was trying to catch her breath without appearing to be out of it. "What…are you doing here?"

He had a big smile for her, so big that she couldn't resist smiling back. He was looking at her the way she had seen men look at her friends. The way a man looked at a woman when he liked her in a romantic way. The idea was scary and exciting at the same time.

"I came to see you."

"Oh," she exhaled.

He rested his forearm on the open window and leaned out a bit. "I guess you didn't get my message I left this morning. I talked to Emily."

"New hire," she answered. "Sorry about that. She's still working on her phone skills."

He chuckled. "Well, sorry you ended up coming for the wagon and not finding it. I guess I didn't think the whole thing through. A friend from church is a retired welder, and he has all the equipment in his garage. There's an issue with the wagon's axle, but he says it's an easy fix, though you might need a new wheel, too. Depends on whether or not he can straighten it out. He says he doesn't see many wheels with rolled steel tires."

"*Ya*, my stepfather brought it from New York when we moved here. I think it was his father's."

David nodded appreciatively. "Well, my friend Jared says the wagon is definitely worth saving. It will probably be next week before he gets it done, though. I hope that's okay?"

He was wearing aviator sunglasses, a blue plaid flannel shirt, and one of those goose down puffy vests *Englishers* wore. But he didn't look like an *Englisher*. There was something about his face that was very...wholesome. She wondered exactly how old he was.

"I know, I should have checked with you first," David continued. "But when I called Jared, he said he could do it, and since it was free, I figured, why not?"

"No, no. It's fine." She hugged the bundle of mail, hoping he didn't notice the trash sticking out of her pocket. Or the old clothing she was wearing. He didn't seem to, or maybe he just didn't care. That idea appealed to her. That maybe he was smiling at her because he liked who she was, not what she looked like. "Benjamin was tickled you found someone to look at the wagon because we don't have an Amish wheelwright around here anymore. There used to be one over in Seven Poplars but I guess that family moved to Kentucky last year."

"We had a wheelwright where I grew up in Wisconsin. He was good at his trade, but he was the crankiest man." David chuckled at the memory.

And Bay found herself smiling again. And for a moment, they were quiet, but it wasn't an uncomfortable silence.

David then tapped the door with his hand. "Hey, I want you to know how much I appreciate you offering a hand in friendship to my sister. Yesterday at supper she mentioned that it was nice to make a friend who didn't know her before Matthew died."

"Why's that?" Bay asked.

He took his time to answer and Bay appreciated that he thought before he spoke, something she was working on. She also liked that he could talk on a matter that involved feelings. She didn't often find that in men her own age.

"She feels like you want to be friends because of who she is. Not because you feel sorry for her."

Bay mulled that over. "I do feel empathy for her. I've never been married so I realize that I don't know what it's like to lose a husband." She met his gaze. "But I lost my father, so I know what it's like to lose someone you love, someone who is the center of your life." She shrugged. "But I just like her. And… I think I like her because, in some ways, she's different than anyone else I know. All of my friends are Amish." She wrinkled her nose. "Is that a terrible thing to say?"

He laughed. "It's not. I understand exactly what you mean. And even though you're Amish and we're Mennonite, because we all grew up Amish, I think we have a lot of things in common. Like having faith in the center of our lives."

Bay noticed that he was saying *we* now. "Because *we* grew up Amish…" Hearing him say that made her feel good—the idea that they both wanted to be friends with her.

He tapped the truck door with his hand again. "What are you doing today?"

His steady gaze made her slightly uncomfortable, but not in a bad way. It was a feeling she didn't recall experiencing before. "Me? Oh… I'm… I was mailing a check to one of our distributors. Getting the mail." She motioned to the bundle she held against her chest. "And my brother Joshua is replanting seedlings we grew from seed. Vinca, zinnias and geraniums, I think. When I get back, I'm going to mix up fertilizer."

"What do you use?"

Feeling less self-conscious talking about gardening rather than herself, she rattled the ingredients off the top of her head. "Gypsum, seed meal, dolomite lime and ag lime."

"You add bonemeal to that or kelp meal?" he asked.

"Both."

"So you use a dry fertilizer," he remarked thoughtfully. "I use liquid and dry. Depends on what I need it for. Of course, I don't grow annuals. Well, I haven't in the past. Though I think there's decent money in it around here, especially if you can sell them to the big-box stores." He glanced away, out the windshield, then back at her. "I'm kind of fascinated with hydroponic growing. I think it would be amazing to grow and sell annual flower and vegetable plants without soil."

"I don't know anything about hydroponics, but I'm intrigued by the idea of it, too," she told him. Without thinking, in her enthusiasm, she took a step closer to the window. "I've never seen hydroponic growing, but I've read all about it. And seen pictures. Joshua and I subscribe to a couple of commercial gardening magazines, and of course, I see the supplies in the sales catalogs. My *mam* says I'm the only woman she knows who reads gardening catalogs for fun. My sisters read every issue of *The Budget* front to back. That's an Amish newspaper."

"Annie says the same thing about me. And we get *The Budget*, too. Because it's a way for us to keep up with what's going on with friends all over the country. Annie reads it mostly, though. Does anyone grow hydroponically commercially around here?"

She shook her head. "I don't think so. I imagine you make money at it, though. People around here are really into organic growing. And anything progressive. And they're willing to pay a steeper price. My sister Lovey sells cage-free eggs, charges a dollar more a carton and she's got more customers than eggs."

He was quiet for a second, then he looked up at her again. "I talked to a guy on the phone the other day in Sussex County who's growing hydroponically. He invited me to come to see his greenhouse. What would you think about going with me? You know, to check out his operation, get an idea of the cost of setup and such."

Bay didn't take the time to think the invitation through or its consequences. "I would love that!" she told him, practically bouncing in her sneakers.

"You would?" He looked surprised. And pleased. "Okay, then." He was grinning, looking as excited as Bay felt. "Ronny—he's the grower—mentioned next Thursday. Would that work for you? Because if it doesn't, I could call him and reschedule for a better day."

"Nope. Next Thursday would be great."

"Okay, then. I guess I'll see you Thursday. Want me to pick you up?"

"How about if I come by your place?" The words came out of her mouth before she could think better of them. Of the whole idea of going somewhere with David. Alone. Something her mother might frown on and the town gossip would love. An unmarried Amish woman going somewhere unchaperoned with a single Mennonite man. That would be fodder for chatter for weeks in their little community. "I promised Anne I'd stop by next week, anyway," she added.

"Okay, well…" He seemed hesitant to go. "I guess I'll just turn around here and head home. I've got a list of things a mile long to do. Good talking to you."

"Good talking to you, too." Bay stepped back into

the grass and watched David turn around in his truck in the driveway. He put down the passenger side window as he slowly passed her. "See you next week!"

"See you next week!" Bay waved and watched him pull out onto the blacktop before turning to head back to the greenhouse.

She couldn't believe she'd agreed to go with him. Talk about impulsive. What was even harder to believe was that she had decided so quickly that she didn't want her mother to know about it. But her mother would never understand why she would want to see plants being grown hydroponically because she didn't understand Bay's passion for growing plants. And she might insist that Bay take one of her sisters or a brother as chaperone.

Of course, chaperones were only needed for dates. And this wasn't a date.

At least she didn't think it was...

As David pulled onto the blacktop, he glanced into the rearview mirror. Bay was still standing there in her driveway, watching him go. And smiling. Which made him smile.

With his eyes on the road ahead, he gripped the steering wheel. Did I just make a date? he wondered. *With Bay?*

Well, maybe it wasn't exactly a *date* date. But they were two single people going together somewhere, so it certainly could be a date. If that was what he wanted it to be.

But surely Bay didn't think it was a date. She was Amish. He wasn't. It wasn't done, he reminded himself.

A horse and wagon with an Amish man driving went by in the opposite direction. He waved at David, and David waved back. A neighbor probably.

David liked the idea that the man who had waved might be a neighbor. Even though David had moved from Wisconsin to Delaware four months ago, he had still felt like he was here visiting. He told himself he hadn't made any friends because he was busy, because he hadn't been here that long yet. But if he was truthful with himself, the fact was that he hadn't really gone out of his way to meet anyone. He didn't really talk much to the people he *did* meet. Because he really hadn't wanted to move, maybe he had been resisting the idea of it, even now that he was here.

After his brother-in-law died, he had seriously considered insisting Annie and Matty come to live with him in Wisconsin. And if she had agreed to it, that was probably where they would be now. But Anne had stubbornly refused. She had said she didn't want to uproot her son and leave her home, church and friends, especially not when she was expecting. He'd even enlisted the help of friends and relatives to try to convince Anne to move, but she'd still refused to give in. Everyone they knew had thought it would be foolish for him to pick up and move just because Anne didn't want to leave Delaware, but after many days of prayer, David felt led to come.

At the time when he made the choice to sell his place and move, he had told himself that if it wasn't God beckoning him to Kent County, Delaware, then it was his sense of responsibility to his sister and her family. Now he wondered, as he turned onto his road, if God wanted him to move to Delaware to meet Bay.

Chapter Five

The following week Bay climbed up into the antique courting buggy her stepbrother Levi had restored, as her *mam* watched her, frowning with obvious disapproval. Her mother and sisters didn't like the two-seater and felt it was unsafe, especially for a young woman. It was so lightweight in comparison to the bigger, enclosed family buggies that they thought it bounced around too much and it was easy to go too fast.

Bay liked it because she *could* go fast, especially with Levi and Eve's new gelding. Joe was a retired race-horse, but at only five years old, he could still fly down the road. Bay loved the feel of the wind in her face and the motion of the buggy as it sailed over the pavement and the trees and fields streaked by.

"I appreciate you running the potpie and biscuits over to Ginger," her mother said from the ground. She stood with her arms crossed over her chest. "I just wish you'd take one of the other buggies, or at least Sassa-fras, instead of this troublemaker." She lifted her chin at the gelding that was dancing in his traces, as excited as Bay was to be headed for the open road.

"I'm sure Ginger will appreciate not having to make supper tonight," Bay responded, wishing the horse would behave itself, at least until they got out of her *mam's* sight. "I know she has to be worn out, what with the new baby and the four other little ones. I don't know how she does it, and always with a smile on her face."

Bay's twin had married their widowed neighbor with four children, and now she and Eli had a *kinner* of their own. Just thinking about running a household with so many children and responsibilities made Bay think maybe she wasn't meant to be a mother and wife. But Ginger had taken all of the changes in her life in stride. She never seemed overwhelmed and she always had a smile on her face. She had stepped into motherhood as if it were a comfortable dress she had been wearing her whole life.

"How does Ginger manage it all? Love, that's how she does it," their mother answered simply. "Love for Eli, for the children, for God."

"I suppose it's hard to understand when I'm not in her place," Bay commented.

"Ya." Her mother stepped back. "Give Ginger my love. And my grandchildren, too. Tell your sister I'll see her Thursday for the quilting circle she's hosting." She tightened the knot of her headscarf at the nape of her neck. "Are you going with me? You haven't said. Tara and Nettie are."

Thursday, she was going with David. Bay took the

reins firmly in her gloved hands, avoiding eye contact. "*Ne*, I wasn't planning on it."

Her mother frowned. "I suppose it was foolish of me to ask. I know you avoid sewing like I do the dentist." She sighed. "But these days, a woman doesn't have to sew her own bedding, does she? It can be bought. And whoever you wed may not have a homemade quilt on his bed, but at least he'll have beautiful flowers in his window boxes."

Bay smiled, appreciating her mother's words, which also made her feel guilty. She knew it was wrong to keep her trip with David from her mother, but wasn't she too old to be asking permission from her parents for anything? Ginger certainly didn't ask them. Everyone assumed that because Ginger was married with children, she could make her own choices. It wasn't fair. But it was the way it was in their community.

"I'll give Ginger a hug from you. I promise! And kisses for all of the children, whether they want them or not. See you later." Bay gave Joe some rein and the horse leaped forward, causing the buggy to lurch and sway as they pulled into the lane that led to the road.

As Bay pulled away, her mother gave a loud *tut* of disapproval, but Bay didn't look back. She held the reins firmly, thankful for the old gloves that Levi had given her. The first time she had taken the courting buggy out, she'd returned with blisters on her hands from the leather reins and the gelding's enthusiasm. Her sister Tara had fussed over her like a mother hen, and then when Bay had refused the balm she offered, Tara had run to their mother to say she didn't think Bay ought to be driving that wild beast.

Bay sailed past the harness shop and her greenhouse, oyster shell from the driveway flying in every direction. Seeing there was no traffic on the country road, she turned onto the blacktop road toward Ginger's without stopping.

Bay loved Tara, but they were so different that she sometimes struggled to understand her. And she knew that Tara felt the same way about her. But the thing was, despite only being twenty-one, Tara knew who she was and exactly what she wanted in life. And Bay didn't. And that was causing the distance in their relationship. Of course, that could be said for all of Bay's relationships right now. No one in her family understood her. Except maybe Joshua, who loved her for who she was and kept telling her that God would reveal her place in His world and that she only had to be patient.

Patience was not one of Bay's virtues.

She laughed and gave Joe a little more rein as they reached the center of a curve, and the horse stretched his long neck and went even faster.

An hour later, Bay was back in the courting buggy. Her nephew, Simon, now ten years old, untied Joe from the hitching post in their yard. Ginger stood on the steps of her porch, baby Paul on her hip.

"You should come to the quilting on Thursday," Ginger called to her.

"I can't," Bay answered.

"You don't have to sew. I just want you to be here. I miss you, *Schweschder.*"

The moment the gelding realized the boy had released him, he started to back up, moving so quickly that Bay was afraid he would turn over the buggy. "Careful, Simon," Bay called as she tugged on the reins. "Easy, boy. Easy there, Joe." She made the gelding walk in a circle, moving them closer to the house.

"I know you don't like children, but they really are well-behaved," Ginger said, emotion in her voice. "And we can always send them outside to play now that it's getting warmer. Except for this one," she added, bouncing Paul, who was wearing a long white dress and baby bonnet.

"Who said I didn't like children?" Bay worked the reins, trying to make the gelding hold still. "I never said I didn't like children. I... I'm busy, Ginger. With the business. Joshua and I are a week behind our repotting and we want to open by Mother's Day." As exasperated with her sister as the horse, she took a deep breath. "I'm not coming because I have somewhere else to be."

"Oh, where are you going?" Ginger asked. "Somewhere fun, I hope. You work too much."

Finally, the gelding settled, and Bay gave her twin her full attention. She pressed her lips together, contemplating whether or not to say anything about David. Ginger would never tattle on her, unlike Tara or Nettie, but Bay didn't know if she wanted to share the news of her budding friendship with David and his sister or not. But she was so excited about seeing the hydroponic greenhouses with him that she wanted to tell *someone*.

"If I tell you where I'm going, you can't tell *Mam*. Or anyone else. *Oll recht?*"

Ginger narrowed her gaze as she came down the steps. "Is it something dangerous? You know *Mam's* rule. We all have a right to privacy, but not if it involves something dangerous. I know you and Jacob were talking about how you'd like to skydive someday..."

Bay laughed. "I'm not going skydiving. I'm going to look at greenhouses where someone is growing fruits and vegetables hydroponically. In water rather than soil."

"I know what hydroponic means." Ginger reached the bottom step but stayed there, safely out of the way of Joe's hooves. "Who are you going with?"

Bay glanced into the barnyard, where Ginger's boys were chasing each other, throwing bits of straw and laughing. She looked back at her sister. "The brother of a new friend." She hesitated. "They're Mennonite. But they grew up Amish," she added quickly. As if that made a difference.

"Recht." Ginger drew out the word. "And is this brother a single man?" She raised her brows.

"Ya."

Ginger nodded. "I agree, you shouldn't tell *Mam.*"

"That's what I decided. There's no need to worry her." Bay shrugged. "It's just a ride to Sussex County and back. I'll be back before *Mam* is home from your quilting."

Ginger kissed the top of her baby's head and said cautiously, "You need to be careful, *Schweschder.*"

"He's a good man, Ginger."

"I'm sure he is, but you know what *Mam* always told us. A woman can't fall in love with a man she doesn't know. That's why you stay away from single men who aren't acceptable husband material."

Their gazes met and Bay understood the warning. "Well, I don't think anyone needs to worry about me falling in love," she said. "It's just that David owns commercial greenhouses and he has the same interests I do. And he doesn't care that I'm a girl running a business. He doesn't see a problem with that."

"David, is it?" Ginger said thoughtfully. Then she inhaled and slowly let out her breath. "Promise me you'll be careful."

Bay rolled her eyes. "I'm an excellent judge of character. He's a good person. I'll be perfectly safe with him. And his sister will know where we're going and when we'll be back, and I trust her, too."

Just then, one of the boys began to howl and Ginger and Bay both looked his way.

"Oww, Mama! He's a bad boy." Phillip cried in Pennsylvania *Deitsch*, holding his eye. "I got straw in my eye. Andrew threw it at me." He leaned down and grabbed a handful of straw that was blowing across the yard and threw it at his brother.

Ginger looked at Bay and sighed. "Sorry, I best take care of this."

"It's okay." Bay lifted the reins. "See you soon?" she called as the courting buggy began to roll forward.

"See you soon," Ginger called after her as she walked across the yard. "And be careful!"

Bay smiled as she flew down the driveway toward the road. She was glad she had told Ginger about David. It felt good to share her happiness with someone else.

When Bay reached the road and pulled to a stop to look for cars, it crossed her mind that she could as easily take the long way home. And if she felt like it, she could stop in at David's and say hi to Anne and Matty. She had promised Anne she'd visit again. This was the perfect opportunity.

Bay urged the gelding onto the road in the direction of David's place. Who was she kidding? She wanted to see Anne and Matty, but she wanted to see David, too, and maybe he would just happen to be there. Then she wouldn't have to wait until Thursday to see him. The thought of getting to see him, maybe talking business, made her grin and give the gelding more rein.

Half an hour later, Bay was at David and Anne's back door. There was no sight of David's white truck in the barnyard and she tried not to feel disappointed as she knocked on the door.

When it opened, Matty was standing there looking up at her solemnly. "Hi, Matty," she said. "Is your mama here?"

He nodded and opened the door.

"Bay!" Anne greeted as Bay walked into the kitchen. "I'm so glad you came! I was afraid you would think I was being polite when I told you to stop anytime. You made my day!" She was wearing a plain dress that looked very similar to Bay's, but with a flowered apron tied around her rounded belly, and instead of a prayer *kapp*, she was wearing a bit of lace pinned to the back of her hair tied up in a bun.

"I was out delivering a meal to my sister Ginger. She

has a new baby and four small children, so my *mam* likes to give her a break once in a while from cooking."

"Oh, how nice," Anne sighed. "I'd love a break from cooking. But right now I need a break from cleaning. I was making myself some tea. Want some? We have fresh blueberry muffins, too, don't we, Matty?" She looked around. "Where did he go? He was here a minute ago."

"Down the hall, I think." Bay walked toward the kitchen counter. "How about if I make our tea and you sit down and rest for a minute."

"You sound like David."

Bay laughed and began to fill the kettle with water from the tap the way she had seen Anne do it. They didn't have an electric kettle in their home, of course, but Benjamin had bought one recently and set up a coffee and tea station in the shop. At first, it had been for customers, but now the entire family and employees were enjoying, too.

"Your brother's right. You need to get off your feet and rest." Bay wanted to ask her where David was, but she didn't want Anne to think she had only come to see him.

"Fine," Anne surrendered, dropping into one of the kitchen chairs. "Tea bags are in the canister on the counter." She pointed to a pretty crockery tub with a lid on it. "Mugs are in the top cabinet to the right of the sink."

Bay set the kettle back on its plate and flipped the switch to turn it on. She carried two mugs to the table and sat down across from Anne.

Anne leaned back in the chair and groaned with obvious pleasure as she rubbed her extended abdomen. "Oh, this feels so good. My feet are swollen." She propped them up on the seat of the chair beside her to reveal fuzzy pink slippers. "That's even better," she sighed with enjoyment.

At the sound of little footsteps, they both looked in the direction of the hall, from where Matty appeared. He was holding several books in his arms.

"Oh no," Anne groaned and looked at Bay. "You don't have to. Really."

"I don't have to do what?" Bay watched Matty walk around the table and come to her, not his mother.

The little boy looked up at her with his big brown eyes and offered the stack of books, which she could tell by his face were a great treasure to him.

"You want me to read you a book?" Bay asked, surprised he would come to her. It made her feel good, because no matter what her sister had said, she really *did* like children.

Matty nodded.

Bay glanced at Anne.

"You can if you want to, but really—" her new friend held up her hand "—you don't have to. I read to him several times a day and David reads to him for an hour every night."

"I want to." Bay looked down at Matty and put out her hands to accept the precious picture books. "Let's see what you have here," she said to the boy. She set the stack on the table and thumbed through them. "*Summertime in the Big Woods, Winter on the Farm, Going to Town*." She chuckled. "They're all Laura Ingalls Wilder books." Bay and her sisters had read the chapter books as little girls, quite progressive for their mother to allow it. What books Amish children could read was limited: nothing with undesirable *Englisher* ways, no animated animals that could talk, and nothing that went against the church's teachings.

"I don't know why, but he loves these books." Annie went on to explain how her son had become attached to and obsessed with the picture books after his father died. "You ought to be pleased that he's asking you to read to him. It means he likes you. He hasn't taken to strangers since Matthew died. It took him weeks to warm up to David."

"Okay, let me get your mother some tea and then I'll read to you," Bay told Matty. She got up and made tea for them both and, as per Anne's instructions, poured a cup of milk for the boy. Then she took plates out for the muffins and sat down again. "Do you want to sit on my lap while I read, or do you want to sit on the chair?" she asked Matty.

He pulled out the chair beside her and climbed up.

"*Oll recht*, I think that means you'll be sitting beside me." Bay glanced at Anne for confirmation and Annie smiled back, obviously pleased Bay was willing to read to her son. "Here we go," Bay told Matty, taking the book on the top of the stack.

Anne chuckled and peeled the paper off a blueberry muffin. "You're going to regret this," she warned, her tone teasing but kind and full of obvious love for her son.

Bay read a book to Matty. And then another. And another. She was ready to begin a fourth when she heard the back door open. David called from the mudroom, "Thank you for reading *Going to Town*. I don't think I have it in me to read it again today."

He appeared in the doorway in his stocking feet. "Bay, good to see you. Nice horse and buggy you've got out there." He hooked his thumb in the general direction. "Is that yours? I have to say it suits you better than the wagon and the old mare."

Bay felt herself blush. "It's my brother Levi's. He's a buggy maker. He found the buggy at an auction somewhere in Maryland and rebuilt it. It's an antique."

"Well, it's beautiful and I'm impressed that you can handle that gelding. That horse is spirited—I could see it in his eyes." He shifted his attention to Anne. "Are those blueberry muffins I smell?"

"They came out of the oven half an hour ago," Anne replied. "Would you like some tea?" She started to get up. "I can—"

"Anne," he interrupted, holding up a hand to stop her. "Please sit down. This must be the first time you've sat since you got up at dawn. She stands eating breakfast half the time," he told Bay before turning back to his sister. "What have I done to make you think I'm incapable of making my own coffee?"

Anne relaxed in the chair. "Tea," she corrected.

"What?" David looked at her, not following. "I was going to have coffee."

"No, you're not," she told him. "You had three cups this morning, which is one cup beyond your limit.

You're cut off. No more maple syrup for that one today."
She pointed at her son. "And no more coffee for you."

Watching this exchange, Bay had to press her lips
together to suppress a laugh. She loved how David and
Anne bickered the way she and her siblings did. Despite their minor disagreements, they obviously loved
each other dearly.

"Fine, I'll have tea, Miss Bossy," David told Annie,
then he looked at Bay. "I see the little man tricked you
into reading to him. Let me guess. Two books?"

Bay grinned back. "Three."

"When Bay arrived, he went right to his room and
brought her the books," Anne explained, gesturing to
her son. "I have no idea what's gotten into him. He's
been sitting there beside her ever since. What's gotten
into you, Matty?"

The boy said nothing.

"Wow." David turned on the teakettle. "You should
feel honored he trusts you, Bay. He's a good judge of
character, though." And then David winked at Bay. Just
like the day she had met him.

Was he flirting with her right in front of his sister?
A warmth of pleasure flushed her cheeks. Not know-
ing how to respond, she looked down at the little boy.
"Is that it, Matty? Are we done here?"

The boy shook his head, took another book from the
pile on the table and handed it to her.

"No more, Matty," Anne said. "The adults are going
to enjoy the blueberry muffins and tea. You can sit here
with us or go check to see if the kitties have water. You
know that's your job, right?"

Matty looked up at Bay.

She smiled and took the book from him. "How about if we save *County Fair* for next time? Would that be okay?" She flipped the hardback picture over and read the description. "I can't wait to find out why Almanzo is going to the fair."

Matty nodded, took the book from her and added it to his pile. Then he slid off the chair and carried the books out of the kitchen.

David brought his mug and a plate for himself to the table. He chose two fat muffins bursting with blueberries and covered in a crunchy cinnamon and brown sugar streusel, before taking his seat at the head of the rectangular table. "I'm serious, Bay. I can't believe he's taken to you like this. He likes to be read to, but he's very particular about the reader." He held her gaze. "I don't know what you did but thank you."

A little embarrassed, Bay smiled and reached for her cup of tea. "I didn't do anything."

"Well, he was obviously happy to see you." David peeled back the paper from one of his muffins and took a bite. "I hope we see you often."

Bay focused on the muffin that had been sitting on her plate untouched. And thankfully, David began telling them about a pear tree he had managed to graft back in Wisconsin that had survived the trip and was sprouting leaves. Apparently, he'd been on the property all along, but his truck had been parked back behind one of his greenhouses. That conversation led to a discussion about the best pear trees to grow in Delaware, and Anne giving her opinion on which pears made the best pear butter. The next thing Bay knew, she was staring at the clock on the kitchen wall.

"Is the clock right?" she asked, pointing. "Is it that late?"

By then Matty had wandered back into the kitchen. He was playing quietly on the floor with a couple of homemade wood toy trucks. He had filled the beds of them with bits of dry cat food.

David glanced over his shoulder at the clock and back at Bay. "Yup."

Bay jumped to her feet. "I have to go." She took her mug and plate as well as Anne's to the sink. "I didn't mean to stay this long." And truly she hadn't. Two hours? She'd only been there half an hour before David arrived, but the next hour and a half had seemed to evaporate.

Her mother was going to wonder where on earth she had been. Bay had only intended to be gone an hour or so and she'd been gone four.

"Oh my, it is getting late. I suppose I should think about supper. We're just having leftovers," Anne said, getting slowly to her feet. "But I have chores to do before I think about warming things up."

"Thank you so much for the tea and muffin," Bay said as she hurried toward the mudroom to put on her jacket.

David got up from the table, following her. "Glad you stopped by." He stepped into the laundry room and watched her put on her jacket. He lowered his voice. "I'm really looking forward to Thursday."

"Me, too," she said.

"You sure you don't want me to come by your place for you?"

"No need." She carefully took the scarf tied at the nape of her neck and retied beneath her chin without exposing her hair. She'd had no intention of coming here today when she dressed in the morning. She certainly hadn't planned to see David, but she was glad she was wearing one of her nicer everyday dresses and that she'd put on her sneakers that didn't have holes in the toes. "I'll be over after breakfast. That way, I can… see Matty. Maybe read one book."

He laughed and opened the door for her. "I'm glad you came," he repeated, still speaking quietly, his words only for her. "For Matty and Anne's sake, of course, but—" He hesitated. "But I'm glad I got to see you. Thursday seemed like a long way off when we said goodbye the other day."

Bay stepped out onto the porch, unsure what to say. She thought about telling him that she hadn't been able to wait to see him, either, but feeling self-conscious, she offered a quick smile. "See you Thursday." Then she hurried down the steps and across the yard toward the buggy, hoping her mother hadn't noticed how long she'd been gone.

If wishes were horses, Bay thought to herself as, forty-five minutes later, her mother hustled out of the house, meeting her halfway across the porch. "Where have you been, Bay Stutzman? I was worried to death. I was ready to send the boys out to look for your body in a ditch."

"I'm sorry, *Mudder*," she answered, using the more formal word for *mother*. "Time got away from me, is all. I'm fine." She kept the irritation out of her voice. Her mother was right, but it still irked her that her mother kept tabs on her as if she were a child.

"I sent Jesse over to Ginger and Eli's on his scooter two hours ago, looking for you. Ginger thought you were going straight home."

Bay tried to go around her mother, but her mother blocked her escape.

"Where were you?" her *mam* repeated. "Supper's ready to go on the table. If you weren't here by the time we sat down, I was thinking about calling the police." Her face was stern, her eyes practically sparking with anger.

"I'm really sorry," Bay repeated. "It was wrong of me. I should have called and left a message at the harness shop. Of course, I don't know what the chances were you would have gotten my message. Emily isn't getting any better at answering the phone. I don't know why Benjamin keeps letting her do it."

"We're not talking about Emily right now, we're talking about you, *dochter*."

Realizing she wasn't going to get past her mother without an explanation, Bay dropped her hands to her sides. "Remember Anne I told you about? She and her brother helped me with the wagon last week?" She went on without waiting for her mother to reply. "She asked me to stop by sometime. She's recently widowed with a little boy and a baby on the way. She's around my age and she doesn't have any friends who live nearby, and…and she could use a friend. And I like her," Bay added stubbornly.

Her mother crossed her arms over her chest. "That's wonderful that you would be friendly with her. What's her name again?"

"Anne."

Her mother nodded. "I think that's wonderful that you would go to see her, but you should have told me or at least your sister that you were going there."

"But I didn't decide to stop by until after I left Ginger's. It was a nice day for a ride."

"Your impulsiveness will get you into trouble," her mother warned. "I've told you that."

"*Ya*, I know. You're right, and I am sorry. I won't do it again. Next time I go see her, I'll tell you. In fact, I'll be going Thursday. Probably be gone the whole day." She stepped around her mother and darted for the door. "I'll help put supper on the table," she called.

"You know, this is why I'll sleep better at night once you find a husband," her *mam* called after her. "Then he can worry about your coming and goings, and I won't have to!"

Chapter Six

Bay leaned out the passenger-side window of David's truck, as she listened to music on the radio and enjoyed the feel of the wind on her face. The sound of smooth jazz, a kind of music she had never heard before, drifted through the speakers. She was so happy, the happiest she could remember in a very long time. She looked down at Matty, who was sound asleep in his car seat beside her, and she smiled and stroked his silky red hair. Her gaze shifted to David.

He had his window down, too, his arm resting on the door. He was wearing aviator sunglasses, a ball cap that read Clark Seeds, and a chambray shirt and jeans. The puffy vest she was growing accustomed to seeing on him was draped over Matty.

"I had a really good day today," she said.

David pushed a button on the steering wheel and the music got quieter. He looked at her, and she wished she could see his eyes. It was hard to believe she'd only known him a little more than a week. The trip that day to the town of Milton to see the hydroponic greenhouses had seemed to solidify their friendship. Four hours after they left David's place, she felt as if she had known him her whole life. And strangely enough, she felt the same about Matty. Today looking after the little boy, cutting up his chicken fingers at the diner where they ate lunch, and now cuddling him as he slept had felt natural.

"I had a really good day, too, Bay," David said. "I'm so glad you came with me. You had questions I hadn't even thought to ask."

"It was nice of Ronny to be so patient with me and all of my chatter," she said, referring to the owner of the greenhouses. "I didn't mean to be annoying." She studied his handsome face as she spoke. "I was just so fascinated. I would *love* to try growing that way."

"You weren't annoying." He glanced at her, smiling shyly. "I was kind of proud you were there with me, asking so many good questions. You're one smart lady, Bay. Smarter than me. Some of the things Ronny was saying, I'm still processing. I'm ordering those books he recommended. And I'm going to check out the websites."

"I'd love to have a look at the books, when you're done with them." She stared out the window at a field of horses. She was glad David had taken the back roads home. The highway was safe enough in a motor vehicle, but she still preferred the country roads. There was so much to see, and with the land beginning to turn green and blossom with spring, it was a nicer ride. "We don't have internet. Benjamin is trying to convince our bishop that he needs it for the family business, especially now that Joshua and I have the greenhouses and

Levi is building buggies. It's so much easier to order over the internet— that's what Levi says, at least. I don't know where he's getting the internet to do it, and I'm not asking."

She chuckled and David chuckled with her.

"So your bishop says no on the internet."

She exhaled. "So far, *ya*. He says it will be too hard to keep employees and family off websites. He says if he allows us to order horse liniment one day, the next day someone will be using the computer to stream movies." She laughed again. "I didn't even know what that meant until Joshua told me."

"I can understand both sides," David said thoughtfully. "There are serious vices that can be gotten online. Plus, it can just be a huge waste of time. And money." He settled both hands on the steering wheel. "We have internet in my office out in the barn, but not in the house. No TV. Anne said that she and Matthew had been discussing getting internet in the house for the business and maybe to stream something family-oriented on Saturday nights, but they never made a decision and then…"

His voice drifted to silence and Bay was quiet for several minutes, letting him deal with the emotion she heard in his voice as he spoke of his brother-in-law's death.

Matty shifted in his car seat between them, but didn't wake, and Bay tucked David's vest tighter around him. "I'm so glad you brought Matty today," she said. "It was a nice surprise. Did he ask to come?"

"You mean did he jump in the truck? Because you know, these days he doesn't ask for anything."

She nodded in understanding. She knew David and Anne were both worried about Matty not talking, but they were trying to trust in the pediatrician's assurances and God's will. "I wondered if he let you know he wanted to come with you or if Anne suggested it."

"Actually, I asked Anne if it was okay if he came with us." His tone sheepish, David took his eyes off the road for a moment to look at her. "I got to thinking, you being a single woman, me a single guy. I didn't know how your parents would feel about me whisking you away in my truck for the day. Or what your bishop would think."

"My parents trust my judgment," she answered carefully. "But I didn't tell them I was going with you today."

"You didn't? Why not?"

She thought on it for a moment before she answered. "I'm not sure. I think because I'm feeling a little hemmed in. By my age, most girls are married and don't have parents keeping an eye on them, telling them what to do and how to do it. Telling them it's time they marry."

"Ah, back to that. Your mother still giving you a hard time?"

"She means well. I know that," Bay told him. "And I know she's trying to understand my perspective. But we're so different. It's hard for both of us."

"Would she be upset if you told her you went with me today? I would never want to cause any problems between you and your family. I really like you, Bay, but if our friendship is a problem, I would understand—"

"It's not a problem," she interrupted. "Meeting you has been the best thing that's happened to me…ever." Surprised by her own words, she sneaked a peek at him to see his reaction.

He looked straight ahead, but he was smiling. "I feel the same way," he told her quietly. He glanced briefly at her and then back at the road. "And I have to admit, I'm a little conflicted because—" He stopped and started again. "Because, well… Well, I'm just going to say it, Bay. If you were Mennonite, I'd ask you on a date."

For a moment, Bay was silent. Stunned. But then she felt a warmth in the pit of her stomach, one that slowly radiated through her body. She had suspected he liked her—but she hadn't quite trusted her own instincts. What did she know about the attraction between a man and a woman? Sure, she had seen her sisters and brothers fall in love and marry but she knew how things looked from the outside were different from how they felt from the inside.

David gripped the steering wheel tightly. "I shouldn't have said that. Totally inappropriate. I'm so sorry."

"You'd ask me out on a date?" she asked, feeling bold with newfound confidence. She had been right! He *did* like her.

He came to a stop sign at a crossroad somewhere out in the country, west of Milford, and put the truck in Park, giving her his full attention. "I would," he said carefully.

"Well, I'd say yes. If you were Amish," she added quickly. "But I think my mother would have kittens if I came home and told her I wanted to go out with someone who wasn't Amish."

"And I'm not." He took a breath and slowly exhaled, holding her green-eyed gaze. "Is that the end of it?"

Feeling upended, Bay tried to think. Suddenly, she saw so many choices in her life, choices she hadn't contemplated before. "I don't know," she answered honestly. "Do we have to decide right now?"

He shook his head slowly. "We don't."

And then he smiled, and the warmth was there inside Bay again, radiating outward.

Just then, Matty opened his eyes, yawned and looked at her. She smiled down at him and he closed his eyes again.

"You know, that's why I brought Matty with us today," David went on. "Because I have feelings for you. I know in the church community we grew up in, if you were of marrying age and intended to spend an extended period of time with someone the opposite sex who was also single, we had to have a chaperone."

"I'm glad you brought him along, but it's not necessary. At my age, I don't think my *mam* cares about chaperones." She chuckled. "She just wants me out of the house."

A car approached the intersection behind them. "Aren't you going to go?" she asked David.

With obvious reluctance, he shifted the truck and went through the intersection. "Know how to drive, do you?" he teased.

"No. But I know the same rules apply to a truck as

a buggy. You can't sit at stop signs with people behind you."

He laughed as he speeded up. "If you wanted to learn, I could teach you."

"Really?" Bay asked with surprise. "You think I could learn?"

"Bay, I have a feeling you'd be a better driver than I am. Of course you could learn."

She sat back in the seat. Amish weren't supposed to drive, though a bishop occasionally gave a dispensation if a man needed to drive for work. She knew a few young men in Hickory Grove who had learned to drive, some with the bishop's approval, some without. But she didn't know of any women who could drive. The idea of it intrigued her. "Just on your property, right? Not on the road?" she asked.

"Wherever you'd feel the most comfortable."

"I wouldn't want to drive on the road. I'm not really supposed to do that." She flashed him a smile. "But at your place, if I was helping you move stuff in the truck or something, I think I'd like that."

Matty made a sound and Bay saw that he was awake and watching. "Hey, little man," she said. "Have a nice nap?"

The boy nodded and pushed off his uncle's vest.

Bay and David exchanged looks and went back to talking about Ronny's greenhouse setup, and before they knew it, they were back at David's place.

Anne met them in the yard. She had been out collecting eggs in the henhouse and when Bay lifted Matty out of his car seat, he ran into his mother's arms, nearly knocking the egg basket from her hand.

"Oh my," Anne cried, hugging her son. "Looks like you had a good day." She glanced up at Bay and David getting out of the truck. "Seems like you two had a good time, too," she said, looking from one of them to the other, grinning. "Want to stay for supper, Bay?"

"I'd love to, but I should get home."

David walked around the front of the truck. "How about tomorrow night?" he asked. "That would work, right, Anne? We don't have any plans?"

He held Bay's gaze and she wished she could stay. Because even though they'd been together most of the day, she didn't want to leave David. Not yet. It was a strange feeling for her. She'd never felt this way about a man before. But suddenly, so many things she had heard her sisters say made sense. She was attracted to David.

"Ya," Bay managed before she tore her gaze from him. "I can come tomorrow night."

"Great," Anne said, ushering Matty toward the house.

"Great," David repeated softly, still standing in front of Bay and watching her. "I can't wait."

"We'll eat about six," Anne called over her shoulder, too far away to hear her brother.

"See you at six," Bay repeated to David. As she stepped onto her push scooter, she calculated how long it would be until she could see him again. Only twenty-two hours! she thought happily.

A month later, Bay carried a chicken, rice and broccoli casserole to Anne's stove and slid it into the oven.

"How long does it cook?" She turned to her friend who was sitting at her kitchen table, sipping lemonade Bay had made with the fresh lemons she'd snitched from a big bag at home.

"Forty-five minutes."

"Forty-five minutes," Bay echoed, setting the timer on the stove. Unlike the egg timer they used at her house, this was on the stove and was digital. It was easy enough to use, though, once Anne showed her how.

"Thank you for popping that in." Anne set her glass on the table. "I feel like such a wimp, but I get so tired by this time of day."

"You're not a wimp," Bay insisted, going to the counter to chop the lettuce she'd rinsed off and wrapped in a clean towel to dry.

She knew how to dry it because her mother had taught her, but the chopping was Anne's trick. Bay had never had a chopped salad before she'd eaten it at Anne and David's. It was different from the tossed salads she was used to, but having everything cut into bite-size pieces made it seem wonderfully exotic.

"You're carrying an extra person around with you all day," Bay continued. "And putting the casserole into the oven is the easy part. You did the hard part. Left to me, I'd have made a mess of the recipe, and we'd be having grilled cheese for supper. I'm a terrible cook."

"You're not a terrible cook."

Bay cut her eyes at her.

She and Anne had become good friends. After that first supper Bay had eaten with David, Anne and Matty the day after the trip to Ronny's greenhouses, she had quickly become a regular fixture at the table. She ate with them two or three times a week, depending on her schedule and theirs. If Bay's *mam* thought anything of her spending so much time with Anne's family, or so many missed family dinners, she said nothing. Other than on several occasions, her mother suggested Bay invite them to have supper with her own family.

Bay didn't know why, but she wasn't ready to have David and his family over. Maybe because there was so much commotion with not one but two kitchen tables, three children and a houseful of adults. Not only did her adult siblings Nettie, Tara and Jacob still live at home, but Levi and Eve lived there, too, and there was always someone coming for supper, whether it was Ginger and Eli and their five children, or Lovey and Marshall and their little ones. Or Joshua and Phoebe and their toddler who lived on the property but frequently joined them because Phoebe missed all the tumult now that they were in their own house. Bay told herself it was the chaos she was trying to save David and Anne from, especially considering Anne's condition. Now nearly eight months pregnant, Anne was slowing down and always seemed so tired.

But the truth was that while all those things were true, Bay just wanted to have something of her own. Her friendship with David, Anne and Matty was the one aspect of her life that she didn't have to share with her parents, sisters, brothers, sisters-in-law, brothers-in-law, nieces and nephews. And while Bay loved being a part of a large family, there were days when she didn't want to be a piece of such a large puzzle. She wanted independence.

Seeing the look on Bay's face, Anne began to laugh. "Okay, so you're not the best cook in Kent County, but you're not the worst."

Again, Bay gave her the eye. And then they both laughed.

"You just need practice. And to pay attention to the recipe."

"You mean if it says two cups of cooked noodles, I should add two cups of *cooked* ones, not dry?" She'd made that mistake the week before while trying to help Anne make something called goulash. It hadn't turned into a total disaster, but only because Anne had intervened.

"Exactly." Anne continued to rub her swollen belly. "You're just like David. I write two cans of tomato paste on the grocery list and he brings me two cans of whole tomatoes."

At the mention of David, Bay threw a smile over her shoulder and went back to chopping a carrot for the salad. She and David hadn't spoken again of their attraction to each other since that day in the pickup truck, but she felt like it was an ongoing current continually running between them. She could feel it when she was near him and she could see in his eyes, when they were alone, that he felt it, too.

At first, she had nearly convinced herself it was a passing attraction, at least for her. She'd never liked anyone before and it was exciting. Wasn't it natural that she would feel a light-heartedness whenever they were together? But as the weeks passed, she began to realize that her feelings for David weren't a schoolgirl's infatuation. If she wasn't in love with him, she was falling in love with him. So while she enjoyed every minute she spent with him, whether it was alone in his greenhouse with him, or playing Candyland with him and Matty at the table, she was beginning to worry about where the relationship was going to go.

Of course it couldn't go anywhere. She was Amish. Her parents expected her to marry an Amish man. In fact, the week before, the local matchmaker had stopped by to visit and Bay's *mam* had asked—right in front of her—if Bay was interested in hiring her to find her a husband. Bay had been mortified and angry with her *mam* for embarrassing her, basically suggesting that the reason Bay wasn't married was that she couldn't manage to catch a man.

Bay had politely declined and found an excuse to escape the kitchen. Down at the garden shop, which she and Joshua had finally opened the Wednesday before Mother's Day, she'd taken her frustrations out on seedling trays that needed to be washed and dried. But her mother's suggestion had brought back to the forefront her feelings for David…and where she wanted them to go. Because when she acknowledged her feelings for him, she knew she wanted something more than friendship.

Did Bay want to marry David?

She'd told everyone who would listen that she wasn't ready to marry, so she'd been justifying her frequent visits with David by telling herself she was only seeking his friendship. It wasn't true. But what more could there be? There was no sense in dating because she and David couldn't marry. To marry, one of them would have to leave their church. And David had already left the Old Order Amish, so she would be the one who would have to leave.

Would she be willing to do that to marry David?

The idea had been keeping her up nights, the thought turning over and over in her head. Could she leave her church? What would it mean to her spiritually? And of nearly equal importance, what would it mean to her family? What would living the life of a Mennonite mean to her relationship with her mother and Benjamin? To her sisters and brothers? Sometimes, when a man or a woman who had been baptized left the order, they were shunned by their families. That meant that a person who left the church was no longer welcome at their family's table. Some families even went so far as to no longer speak with the fallen. Bay couldn't see her mother and stepfather doing that, but what if she was wrong?

"That a no?"

Bay spun around, David's voice startling her. He was standing in the doorway between the mudroom and the kitchen, the threshold beyond which muddy boots were not permitted. "I'm sorry." She laughed to cover her embarrassment. She hadn't heard him come in the back door. "Woolgathering again." She covered the salad bowl with its snap-on lid. "Probably why I'm such a terrible cook," she told Anne. Carrying the bowl toward the refrigerator, she said to David, "What's the question?"

"I was wondering, Bay, if you could come down to the greenhouse and help me with something. I'm trying to get some PVC water pipes put together and I need four hands to do it." He held up his hands. "But I've only got two."

Matty popped out from behind his uncle. He was wearing a hoodie sweatshirt and a pair of rubber boots. On the wrong feet, as usual.

"Oh no, little man," Anne warned from the chair. "Boots off. You know better than to track mud through the house."

"Those two hands weren't enough?" Bay asked, her tone teasing. She was thrilled David had come to get her help. He'd decided to set up a small hydroponic growing system on one end of one of his greenhouses, just to see how it went. Bay was fascinated by the whole process and had spent hours reading up on the subject, so much time that Joshua was teasing her about needing to hire another helper to make up for all of the tasks she wasn't getting to in their greenhouse these days.

"He's a good helper, but very short." David whispered the last two words loudly, his hand cupped to his mouth, and everyone laughed.

"I can come. If Anne doesn't need me to do anything else to get supper ready." Bay looked to her friend.

"Go!" Anne shooed. "The both of you. I'm tired of being fussed over."

Matty, who had gone back into the laundry room to get rid of his boots, walked into the kitchen.

"Not going with us, little man?" David asked his nephew.

Bay was so impressed with how good David was with Matty. No father could have been better to the boy, no father kinder and more patient. It was one of the reasons Bay loved…*liked* David so much.

Matty said nothing. Instead, he climbed into his chair and began to dump playdough from containers he'd left on the kitchen table earlier in the day.

David looked to Bay. "Guess that means it's just you and me." She pulled the full apron covered in white daisies over her head and hung it on a hook where Anne kept her aprons. She looked to Anne as she headed for the mudroom. "You need anything else?"

"No, thank you. Go, the both of you," she ordered, feigning impatience.

Bay checked the kitchen clock as she walked into the mudroom. David was waiting at the back door for her now. "I've only got an hour and then I have to head home."

"Not staying for supper?" David asked with obvious disappointment.

She stepped into her sneakers and leaned over to tie them. "Can't. Our bishop and his wife are coming for supper. *Mam* said if I wasn't there, she was going to cut off my ear."

David laughed. "I like her. I can't wait to meet her." He held open the door for Bay.

Outside, they crossed the barnyard. "We may as well take these other pipes down," he said, pointing to his truck loaded with plastic piping.

"Okay."

They were almost to the truck when David turned to her. "Hey, I have an idea. Want to learn to drive?"

Bay stopped. "What?"

"Do you want to learn to drive," he repeated. "You told me you wanted to. We could skip the work and do a little driving."

Before she could respond, he tossed her the keys. She threw out her hand, caught them in midair and smiled hesitantly. "You really think I can learn?"

He laughed and went to get in on the passenger's side. "Are you kidding? I don't think there's anything you *can't* learn to do."

Chapter Seven

David sat back in the passenger's side of his truck, his arm propped across the seat, not quite touching Bay's shoulder, though he wanted to. He watched her as she signaled and made a turn, driving between his first two greenhouses.

Bay was a natural. Like a duck on water.

"How was that?" she asked, glancing at him as she drove down the bumpy gravel lane along the side of his second greenhouse.

David was so proud of her that he couldn't stop smiling. Despite Bay's apprehension, he had known she'd be able to do it. They'd spent the last half hour driving around the farm and she hadn't made a single mistake.

"That was excellent. Except you don't have to signal on private property," he told her with amusement. "In a driveway."

She stuck her tongue at him, then focused on the road again and gave the truck a little more gas.

David laughed. "I told you you'd be able to do this.

And not everyone can. Poor Anne hasn't taken well to driving. I keep telling her how much easier her life would be after the baby is born if she could drive. She could leave Matty here with me, and she and the baby could go grocery shopping on their own. She could drive to the church for her ladies' meetings without having to worry about me taking her or catching a ride. I've tried and tried to teach her." He shook his head. "But every time she hits the gas instead of the brake—that's how we got the ding on the front bumper." He pointed to the right front bumper, where there was a small dent from when Anne had hit the milk house. "Or she turns left instead of right. I even took her to a school parking lot when no one was there, thinking it might be easier for her to learn out in the open so she didn't have to worry about hitting outbuildings. It was no use."

"Maybe she needs a little more practice," Bay suggested, trying not to laugh.

David smiled at her. She was such a good soul, always kind, always willing to pitch in to help no matter how hard or boring the work might be. But she could also be fun. The other day Bay had come to help Anne wash all the floors in the house and, over lunch, he had challenged her to a game of checkers. They'd played two games of checkers and then Bay had put Matty on her lap and tried to teach him how to play. When David had gotten up to answer the door, he'd returned to find Matty and Bay sitting across from each other, sliding checkers across the table at each other, knocking one checker into another. Matty had been howling with laughter. Bay was so good with him. She was so patient that, day by day, David could see her drawing the little boy out of the dark cloud he'd been hiding inside since his father's death.

At the end of the sixty-foot greenhouse, Bay braked and came to a gentle stop. "Maybe after the baby is born, her head will be clearer. When Ginger was expecting she said she couldn't add two and two together without getting it wrong, but after Paul was born, her head cleared."

David couldn't take his eyes off Bay's pretty face. She'd been out in the sun and a sprinkling of freckles had appeared across her nose and cheeks. "I don't know," he hemmed. "Anne might be hopeless."

"Nothing and no one is hopeless," Bay told him firmly. "That's what my *mam* always says." She looked up into the sky at the sun falling on the horizon. "I've already stayed too long. I better get home." She flashed him a smile. "This has been so much fun. I can't thank you enough. Want me to park near the door so you can carry all of the piping inside?" She indicated the greenhouse he planned to use for his hydroponic experiment. He wasn't entirely optimistic he could make it all work, but he wanted to try.

"Nah, I should get inside and help Anne set the table. I'll do it after supper. Now that it's getting warmer, I like to bring Matty outside for a little while after we eat. It wears him out for bedtime and gives Anne time to catch her breath." He pointed in the direction of the barnyard in the distance. "Just take us back to the house."

She nodded but made no move to put the truck in

gear again. She just sat there for a moment, looking at him while he looked at her.

David felt a flutter in his chest. One he could no longer deny. For weeks he'd been rationalizing its meaning, but he couldn't do that any longer.

The fact of the matter was, he was falling in love with Bay Stutzman.

And he didn't know what to do about it. His mind told him to keep his mouth shut as he had since the day they made the trip to Sussex County. But his heart... his heart told him he couldn't keep quiet. He wanted to talk to Bay about his feelings for her, if nothing else, then to settle the matter, because obviously this attraction was going nowhere.

Even though he suspected it was mutual.

He could see it in Bay's eyes. He could tell that she had feelings for him. There was a sparkle in her eyes, the faintest smile on her rosy lips. But that day they were driving back from Ronny's greenhouses, they had agreed not to talk about it.

What if she did want to talk about it now, though? That had been a month ago.

But what would be the point?

He'd been asking himself that question for days now.

She was Amish. He wasn't. They were practically Romeo and Juliet material.

But the look in her eyes as she watched him now... His heart fluttered again. Was it too much to hope that maybe they could figure out a way to make a life together? Was it too much to hope that it was what she wanted? He would never ask her to do anything she didn't want to do, certainly not leave her church and the life she had always known. He knew from experience how hard that could be. It still was, sometimes.

But the longer he knew Bay, the more he recognized the restlessness he had felt before leaving his Amish life to become Mennonite. She seemed to question many of the same aspects of Amish ways that he and Anne and their brothers Abe and Hiram had wrestled with, like the often subservient role of women and the belief that education was unnecessary beyond eighth grade.

Was it too much to think that Bay would consider becoming Mennonite to marry him? Just the thought of it nearly made him giddy.

If he and Bay were to marry, they could work together on the farm and run the wholesale nursery business. It was easy to imagine them working side by side each day, laughing and loving every moment of it. It would suit her independent personality. And give her the freedom he sensed she was looking for.

David knew that once she married an Amish man, her domain would go from her greenhouse business to the family home. Her days would be filled not with nurturing plants, but children and her husband. She would be responsible for her own home, the garden, the making of clothing and meals. And there would be little time for her passion for gardening, once the babies came.

Not that he didn't want children if God so blessed him. But he wanted his wife to be a companion, someone he could work beside each day and share in his daily tasks. He didn't want his marriage to be divided by traditional roles as his parents' had been.

David had no problem with the Amish way of life for others. In some ways, looking back, he knew his life had been simpler when he'd lived without electricity, and shared a bedroom with four brothers. But the path he had chosen as a young man of twenty had been the right one for him. He knew God had meant him to navigate the challenges of moving from the Amish world to the Mennonite one. And he knew now that Kent County, Delaware, was where he was meant to be, here with his sister and Matty...and maybe Bay, too.

There was no way for him to know these things if he didn't explore them, though. And that meant talking about it with Bay. As scary as the idea felt at that moment, he knew he needed to do it. If nothing else, then to know if all of his dreaming was for naught.

"Bay," he said, digging deep to find the courage to say what he wanted to say. "We need to talk. About... us. About what I think is going on here."

In silence, she held his gaze a moment and then looked away. Together they watched a sparrow hawk soar over the field. It flew in lazy circles and then drifted higher until it disappeared.

"*Ya*, I know we need to talk, David," she said quietly. When she looked at him, her eyes glistened with moisture. "But... I'm just not ready. Is that okay?"

He nodded, feeling light-headed. "Of course," he managed. His heart was suddenly pounding in his chest. He hadn't imagined it, this connection he'd been feeling with Bay these last weeks as they'd spent time getting to know each other in his sister's kitchen and in his greenhouses.

Bay settled her hands on the steering wheel, shifted into gear, and this time, she hit the gas pedal with more force. The truck shot forward, and David grabbed the door handle, thankful he was wearing his seat belt.

Grinning, Bay whipped his truck around the back of the last greenhouse and headed for the barnyard. She was only going maybe thirty miles an hour, but it felt like sixty as bits of gravel shot out from under the tires, and the whole truck rocked as it hit the gullies in the lane.

"Whoa!" David cried, laughing. "Easy."

"I've got this!"

She was laughing, too, as they sped between the greenhouses. He couldn't take his eyes off her. She was as beautiful as any woman he had ever known, with her bright red hair, covered mostly with a denim kerchief, little wisps framing her heart-shaped face. And her big green eyes were so expressive he sometimes felt he could read her mind, looking into them.

As they drove into the barnyard, David spotted his sister and Matty coming out of the first greenhouse. Anne was carrying a gathering basket heaped with fresh greens he'd grown and Matty was carrying a handful of parsley as if it were a bouquet.

Bay parked the truck and sat back with a satisfied sigh. "Leave the keys in the ignition?" she asked.

"Sure. I leave them in there all the time on the property." David got out of the truck. "Anne thinks I'm crazy. Says I'm too trusting. That one of these days, I'm going to come outside to find the truck gone."

Bay walked around the front of the vehicle. "I'm

going to head home," she called to Anne. Then to Matty, she raised her hand. "See you another day, little man."

Matty took off across the driveway toward Bay, clutching the parsley.

"You sure you can't stay for supper?" Anne asked, following Matty, but moving far slower than her son. "I'm making a salad with fresh greens David grew to go with the casserole."

Bay dropped her hands to her sides. "Sorry. I can't. I promised my *mam*." She looked down at Matty. "But I'll be back in the next few days." She waved at him. "So it's only bye for now."

Matty looked up at her and waved his free hand. "Bye-bye," he said so softly that for a moment, David thought maybe he'd imagined it.

But he hadn't. Matty had spoken for the first time in six months!

David's breath caught in his throat, and he glanced up at his sister. She looked as shocked as he felt, and he gave a little laugh of joy.

"He's talking," Anne murmured, tears sliding down her cheeks.

Bay grinned and crouched so that she was eye level with Matty. "Bye-bye yourself." She was smiling as hard as David and Anne were. "Can I give you a hug?"

Matty nodded and Bay put her arms around him and lifted him and spun him around the way David sometimes did. The boy squealed with laugher.

"I'm so happy to hear your voice, Matty," Bay told him. And for the second time that day, David saw her teary-eyed and it touched a place in his heart he hadn't even known existed.

Bay set Matty down, and Anne put her basket on the ground and rushed toward her son. "You talked! See, I knew you could do it. When you were ready," she added, repeating what the pediatrician had told them. She leaned down, one hand on her belly, the other caressing Matty's shoulder. "Can you say *Mama*?"

"Mama," Matty repeated so quietly that his voice barely reached David. But he had heard him.

Matty then pointed at David. "Uncle David." And then he turned to Bay and grinned up at her. "My Bay."

Anne looked up at Bay. "Thank you," she whispered, through her tears. "Thank you so much, Bay."

Bay wiped at her eyes. "No need to thank me. Matty was just taking his time, weren't you?" she said. Then she looked up to meet David's gaze.

"Thank you," he mouthed.

"You're welcome," she mouthed back.

David watched her get on her push scooter and head down the driveway, and he prayed that God would help him find a way to make Bay his wife.

It was almost a week before Bay was able to make it back to David and Anne's. It had been a crazy last few days. There had been one problem after another at the garden shop: the roof had sprung a leak, a stray dog that had gotten inside one of the greenhouses and knocked trays of flowers over, and the credit card system Jacob had convinced Benjamin to invest in had crashed. Then on Saturday, Bay had planned to visit them, but her mother had guilted her into staying home to help whitewash the house in anticipation of hosting church next month.

Hosting church was a big deal because it was usually only once a year. Folks spent months tidying up, painting and even doing landscaping, not for reasons of *hockmut*, a boastful pride, but because it was an honor to host services.

When Bay arrived at David's, she didn't know who was happier to see her: David, Matty or Anne. David waylaid her in the driveway, where they talked for at least half an hour before she made it into the house. The plan was to all go together to Byler's store to do the weekly grocery shopping and have an ice cream cone. However, when she and David went inside, they found Anne was resting on the couch in their living room after having a dizzy spell. Anne decided not to go into Dover but insisted they go without her. Bay and David weren't too happy with the idea of leaving her home alone, but Anne was adamant. And Matty was so excited about the ice cream that, in the end, David wasn't able to say no.

In Byler's store parking lot, Bay got out of the truck and reached in to help Matty from his car seat.

"Need help?" David asked, tucking his keys into his pants pocket as he walked around the front of the truck.

"*Ne*, we've got it." She tickled Matty under the chin. "Don't we?"

Matty giggled and pushed her hand away as she unsnapped the last strap. "Bay," he said and grinned at her.

The sound of his voice saying her name brought up

a well of emotions. It was so good to hear his voice, to know that he was going to be okay. Matty still wasn't saying a lot, but, according to David, he was talking more each day. He wasn't participating in conversations yet, but there were a lot of yeses and nos. He also had no problem talking when he wanted something, and he couldn't make his uncle or mother understand. Or they pretended not to understand.

When she turned around with Matty in her arms, David stood right behind them. He took his nephew from her and lowered the boy to the pavement. As he set the boy down between them, David removed his aviator sunglasses and looked into her eyes.

"I've missed you," he said, slipping the glasses into the pocket of his red shirt. He was wearing his Clark Seeds ball cap and jeans with work boots.

Bay felt her face grow warm. "I've missed you, too," she told him, enjoying the connection she felt between them when their gazes met.

And she *had* missed him; she'd been surprised how much. The whole week she'd felt frustrated because she couldn't get away. In retrospect, she realized the week apart had been good for her. It had given her time to examine her feelings for him and determine if she was simply infatuated with the man or if it was more than that. After all, he was the first adult male who had ever paid any attention to her. Sure, once in a while, a boy would try to talk to her at church or when he stopped by the greenhouse to buy flowers for his *mam*, but they rarely ever said more than a hello the second time they saw her. Bay always felt like she made men her own age uncomfortable—Amish men, at least.

But not David.

She stood there for a moment, looking into his eyes, enjoying the warmth of the sun on her face and the warmth of his gaze. She hadn't imagined her attraction to him nor his attraction to her. She had accepted that fact sometime over the last week. Then moved onto the next question.

Was she interested in seeing where the attraction led them?

Was she interested in pursuing marriage? She had been raised to believe that dating was only for a couple seriously considering marriage, and while she would not judge others, it was the only option for her. She wasn't interested in casual dating. If she did feel strongly for David, if she loved him, was she willing to leave her Amish faith to be his wife?

Bay had been asking herself that for days and she still wasn't sure of the answer. It was too much to wrap her head around it. But after sifting through her feelings for David, she was pretty sure she was in love with him. Which meant it was time they had the talk she'd been avoiding.

Suddenly, Matty darted out from between her and David, and David took off after his nephew.

"Matty, you know the rules," David admonished as he caught up to the boy and took the child's hand in his bigger one. "You have to hold an adult's hand in parking lots."

"Horse!" Matty said, pointing.

There was a small painted pony tied up at the hitching post near the side of the store. Bay recognized the pony at once. Chester belonged to Eunice Gruber's mother, who had recently moved in with Eunice and her family. Bay and her family had belonged to the same church district as the Grubers until recently, when the church divided because of so many new families moving into the area.

Bay glanced around, hoping Eunice hadn't come with her mother to Byler's. Bay liked Eunice, but she was a busybody and a gossip. If Eunice saw Bay there with David, it wouldn't be long before she was at Bay's *mam's* table tattling. And that would be a disaster.

Bay scanned the parking area for the older woman and saw nothing but cars and pickups in the larger lot, and then the pony and cart and one horse and black buggy tied up on the side of the building. There were a few *Englishers* in the parking lot, some pushing carts out of the store while others walked inside, but she didn't see any Amish.

"Come on, Matty." David tugged at his hand. "Let's get inside and get our groceries. I thought we'd have our ice cream in the truck on the way home." He looked over his shoulder at Bay. "If that's okay with you. I'm concerned about Anne. If she's not feeling better by the time we get home, I'm going to insist she call her doctor."

"That's fine," Bay agreed. She was worried about Anne, too. She hadn't looked good to her when she arrived. Anne's face had a gray cast.

Bay scanned the parking lot again for her nosy neighbor, wondering if she should have stayed at the house with Anne. Bay realized now that she hadn't thought about the possible consequences of going out in public with David.

Her mother would be hurt if someone else told her first that Bay was seeing a man. An *Englishe*r. Not that David was exactly an *Englisher*, but no matter what he was, Bay knew her mother would want to hear the information from her daughter and not a neighbor. And Bay knew it was time she told her *mam*. She was feeling guilty that she hadn't said anything already. She'd been waiting for the opportunity, or would be, once she figured out exactly what she was going to say.

"Horse," Matty repeated, stamping his foot. He was wearing new green Crocs on his bare feet. The weather had turned from spring to summer over the weekend, and it was in the high seventies that day. Bay hadn't even needed a sweater when she'd ridden over to David's on her push scooter.

"See horse," Matty told David emphatically.

David sighed, and Bay knew he would give in. Matty had asked with words. How could David deny him?

"Can I get a *please*, little man?" David asked.

Matty looked up, the cutest smile on his face. *"Pwease,"* he said clearly and loudly.

Bay laughed and shrugged. "He said *please*."

David exhaled and tugged on the brim of his ball cap. "Fine. But just a quick pet, and then we have to get our groceries and get home to your mama. Okay?"

Matty nodded.

So they went over to see the pony, and while Matty

petted him, Bay kept watching over her shoulder for Eunice. What she was going to do if she spotted the older woman, she wasn't sure, but she still kept an eye out for her.

"Looking for someone?" David asked.

She turned back quickly. "What? No…um… *Ya*, I know the lady who owns the pony and cart. She lives in Hickory Grove."

David crossed his arms over his chest as Matty continued to stroke the pony. "Ah." There was curiosity in his tone. He could tell that she wasn't going to be excited if she did spot Eunice.

Bay thought about changing the subject, but if she truly wanted to consider something beyond friendship with David, she knew she could never deceive him in any way. She pressed her lips together. "My family doesn't know," she said, feeling ashamed as she admitted it aloud.

His forehead creased. "Doesn't know what?"

Bay met David's gaze. "My mother, Benjamin, my brothers and sisters. They don't know about you. They think I come to your place to visit Anne."

He was quiet for a minute, then pushed his sunglasses up on his head and rubbed his eyes with his finger and thumb. "So you've been leaving me out of the conversations?"

She nodded.

"Can I ask why, though I've got a pretty good guess."

Bay watched Matty move from the pony to the cart. He was checking out the wooden wheels. She made herself look at David again. "Because I like you. A lot.

And I'm afraid," she admitted, struggling to keep emotion out of her voice.

He seemed to hold his breath for a moment. "You're afraid that if you tell your parents you're dating a Mennonite man, they'll forbid you. Because you know, Bay, that's sort of what we've been doing for weeks. Maybe not in a conventional way, but—" He tilted his head from side to side. "We're both pretending it's something else, but it's not."

He surprised her by taking her hand. It wasn't that they had never touched before. They touched when passing things to each other in the greenhouse as they worked on his hydroponic system. They touched when they passed Matty back and forth or when Bay gave David the mama cat in the house to take outside. But this touch was different. It was more personal. It made her heart pound in her chest and she wanted him to hold her hand forever.

She was in love and she couldn't deny it any longer.

"Is that why you're afraid? Because you think your mother and stepfather will tell you that you can't see me anymore?" David pressed.

"Not Benjamin. He'll stay out of it. And I don't think *Mam* will outright forbid me. She's always said that forbidding someone to do something is an invitation to do it." She paused and then went on. "But she's going to be very upset with me. Disappointed with me."

David didn't take his gaze from hers but he let go of her hand. "Bay, you have to tell her."

"I know," she murmured. Her hands felt sweaty and

she wiped them on her apron. "I realized today that I can't put it off any longer."

David looked away. "Matty, don't get inside the cart," he warned. "It isn't ours. One more minute, and then we go inside, okay?" He returned his attention to Bay. "Will you tell her today when you get home?"

She chewed on her lower lip. "I'll try."

He smiled. "I doubt it will be as bad as you think. From what you've told me about your mother, she loves you and only wants what's best for you. Worrying about this sort of thing is always worse than actually doing it."

"You're right." She lifted her hands and let them fall. "I just need to do it and get it over with."

"And what will you tell her?"

She looked up at him through her lashes. "That…that I really like you and—" She pressed her lips together. "That you like me and that's all I know right now. But that I want to keep seeing you."

"And I want to keep seeing you. You know that, right?" he asked.

She nodded.

David was quiet for a moment, then went on. "And I hope that you realize that my intentions are honorable. I know this is more complicated for you than for me, but—" He stopped and started again. "But we'll figure it out, Bay, once we talk about what we both want. I think we need to make time for that talk."

"*Ya,* we do." Bay sniffed and used the corner of her white apron to wipe her eyes. She was embarrassed that she was tearing up, but she couldn't help it. She'd never felt so emotional before. David made her feel this way.

Because she wanted to be with him. She wanted to be with him always.

"Well," David said slowly. "I'm glad you're ready, because I'm past ready. And Anne is always on me, telling me we need to do it sooner rather than later."

Bay cringed. "Anne knows?"

He laughed. "She says it's pretty obvious. And she adores you. She has this idea that you and I would make a couple." His tone had lightened. "So let's set some time aside."

She nodded, wishing she could feel his hand on hers again.

"But right now, here, is obviously not the place. And not with little ears nearby." He cocked his head in Matty's direction. "Let's go shopping and get home to check on Anne. Maybe you can come over tomorrow or the next day and we can sit down together alone."

"I can't come tomorrow. Joshua has a dentist appointment and I have to run the shop. Maybe Wednesday." She grimaced. "No, we're meeting with someone about buying flowers from us wholesale on Wednesday. Maybe Thursday?" she said hopefully.

"Let me know what day works for you. I can do it anytime. Maybe we can go for a ride in the truck, just you and me." She was looking into her eyes again. "Get a bite to eat. There's this food truck in Clayton that everyone has been saying is amazing."

She smiled shyly, not feeling quite herself, but more alive than she'd ever felt before. Suddenly, she could see a whole life in front of her with David. They could run his greenhouses together. And while she would no longer attend the Amish church, she could attend Mennonite services. Just as David and Anne did now. "I'd like that."

He held her gaze a moment longer, a moment she wanted to go on forever but then he looked to Matty.

"Ready to go inside, little man?" he called, putting out his hand to his nephew.

"Ice cream!" Matty cried happily and ran to take David's hand.

Together, the three of them set off down the sidewalk. As they walked through the automatic doors and into the store, Bay wondered which looming conversation she was more nervous about, the one with her mother or David. Because one or both might change her life forever.

Chapter Eight

A few days later, David stood in the middle of the kitchen, frowning at his sister. She stood in front of him, her arms crossed over her chest. She looked tired. Her skin wasn't the usual rosy color, and she had dark circles under her eyes. And she was angry with him for *fussing* over her.

"I'm not fussing," he defended.

He was, but only because he was worried about her. The baby was due in five weeks. Wasn't it time she started taking it easy? This little spat between them had begun when he'd innocently asked her what she thought about hiring someone to help her with the cleaning and gardening once the baby was born.

"You *are* fussing. It's like you think you're my *gross-mama*," Anne sputtered. "There's nothing wrong with me. I'm not sick. I'm having a baby, which is the most natural thing in the world. I know what I'm doing." She pointed a finger at him the way their mother used to. "I've done it before, you know."

David eyed Matty, who was sitting quietly in the doorway between the kitchen and hall, playing with a new green tractor and wagon he'd bought for him. The boy didn't seem to be paying any attention to them. Sadly, he was probably used to his mother and uncle's squabbles. They were happening with increasing frequency and always over the same subject.

"I'm just trying to be helpful," David told his sister, taking his voice down a notch.

"That's nice, but don't," Anne snapped back, obviously frustrated with him. She raised her hand in a stop motion. "Just don't."

He watched her turn away and go to the kitchen counter where she took out a mixing bowl and measuring cups from the cabinet above. "And stop being cranky with me," she tossed over her shoulder.

He opened his arms. "I'm not."

"You are. You haven't been yourself since you and Bay and Matty went to Byler's at the beginning of the week. Did you and Bay have a disagreement?" She walked to the refrigerator and pulled out a carton of eggs and a stick of butter. "Is that why she hasn't been here? Please don't tell me you've argued with her because if you chased her off—"

"We didn't argue," he interrupted.

Anne was really trying his patience now. Maybe because somewhere in the back of his mind, he was beginning to wonder if he *had* chased her off with his insistence it was time she told her mother about him. And time he and Bay discussed their relationship and where it was going.

"Bay's been busy," David said. "Yesterday we were supposed to go get lunch at that food truck I was telling you about, but she had to cancel. Something about her mother needing her. They're hosting church this summer and you remember what that's like."

Anne carried the eggs and butter to the counter. "Was it supposed to be a date?" Her tone had gone from one of irritation to concern.

David thought about it for a moment. "We were going to go for a ride, get something to eat, and talk. Like have *a talk*."

"About your future?" Anne asked.

He nodded.

"Good. I know it's probably harder for Bay than for you, but you need to discuss how you feel about each other so you can decide what's to be done. Have you told her you love her?" She went on without taking a breath. "Because that makes a difference to a woman. We need to hear the words, not just see the actions. But maybe that's true for men, too," she mused.

Did he tell Bay he loved her? Anne's question so surprised him that he barely heard what else she said. "I...haven't—" he sputtered. "I'm not—"

"You're not what?" she asked, peeling a ripe banana and dropping it into a bowl. "You're not in love with her? You most certainly are, and I suspect she's in love with you." Picking up a potato masher, Anne turned around, giving him a look he recognized as she shook the kitchen tool at him. Their mother had made the same face when challenging him. "There's no question. You both love each other, and she'd be a good wife to you, and I think you'd be a good husband to her. But there's that one *tiny* problem."

He exhaled loudly. "Right. Just a tiny problem. She's Amish, and I'm not." He frowned. "She hasn't told her parents anything about me. They don't know I exist, and that concerns me." He rocked his head from side to side. "Well, they know I helped her that day of the accident, but they think she's been coming here to see you."

Anne turned around, wiping her hand on her apron. "Oh dear."

"Yeah, and it worries me. Even though we haven't talked about it yet, obviously, the only thing that could be done if we are serious about each other would be for Bay to become Mennonite." He met her gaze, his heart feeling heavy. "I can't go back, Anne. Not even for Bay. If I did, I wouldn't be true to myself."

She offered a generous smile. "I know. But she knows that, too. Bay and I have talked about why I left the Amish way of life. Why you did. She said she's had some of the same feelings lately about her life. Like maybe she's been trying to make herself fit in when the fact of the matter is, it doesn't fit her."

"Really?" He'd had no idea that Anne and Bay had discussed the matter. "Why didn't you tell me?"

She added another banana to the bowl and began to mash it. "Because girl talk is not something meant to be shared with others."

"Not even me?" he asked. "I'm your brother."

"Not even you," she said as she added another soft banana to the bowl. "We didn't talk specifically about her leaving the church to marry you. We both kind of danced around the subject, but she knew that's what we were talking about."

He thought for a moment and then said, "Wow. And I was afraid she wasn't that interested in me. Or at least in marrying me." There it was. He'd said it out loud. He wanted to marry Bay.

She turned to him again. "What would make you think she wasn't interested in you?"

"I don't know. Maybe the fact that she's been sneaking behind her family's back, coming here. Don't you find that concerning? Her mother knows nothing about me, and her mother is the one pushing her to find a husband."

"Ah, that." Anne set the masher in the sink.

"Ah, that?" He raised an eyebrow. "I'm afraid that maybe I'm just, I don't know, a flirtation."

"A flirtation?" Anne laughed. "Maybe you don't know her as well as you think you do. Bay is not that kind of woman. Even though she may not feel like she fits into her world anymore, she still carries a lot of Amish beliefs. She'd never toy with your emotions, David."

"Then why hasn't she told her mother about me?"

"You forget how complicated it is. Leaving the life." She narrowed her gaze. "How long did you wrestle with the idea of leaving the church before you said a word even to me?"

David thought back to that time. He'd only been nineteen when he had realized he would never be the man he was meant to be if he remained Amish. Anne had been the first person he had taken into his confidence when he began considering leaving. "Months," he answered. "Maybe a year."

"Exactly. And once Bay tells her family she cares for you, she's made a declaration. They'll know that having left the Amish church, you have no intention of becoming Amish again. Even if that would be allowed, which is highly doubtful. Which means," she said slowly, "they'll know that she's considering leaving."

"You really think she is?" Hope fluttered in his chest. To leave the church for him would be a huge sacrifice for Bay. Would she do it? Every time he got his hopes up, he tried to temper them with logic, but it was becoming more difficult with each passing day.

Anne leaned against the kitchen cabinet, stroking her abdomen. "Why do you think she's been coming here all this time? Not in the hopes you'll run her off the road again."

"I did not run her off the road!"

Anne chuckled. "You know what I mean. She's coming here to see you. To be with you, David."

"But she really likes you. And Matty, too."

"I know she likes us. But she's fallen in love with you."

Even though David knew in his heart of hearts that he had fallen for Bay, he still found it hard to believe that a woman like her could be interested in a guy like him. She was so perfect and he wasn't. "So you don't think she hasn't told her parents about me because I'm just a passing fancy."

She laughed. "Bay hasn't told them because once

she does, you know what's going to happen. The bishop will be called in, and the preachers will be at the house. Everyone in the community will band together to convince her that our life as Mennonites is not the life for her. They'll try to persuade her that you're not the man for her."

"Her brother Levi is one of her preachers."

"That's even worse. Can you imagine sitting at the table three times a day with him?" She turned back to the counter and opened the egg carton. "Oh no."

"What?" David asked.

She held up two eggs. "I'm one short." She sighed. "I sold my last dozen this morning to Mae Driskel, and I didn't collect the eggs yet. I didn't have it in me," she admitted.

"What are you making?" David asked.

"Banana bread."

His eyes lit up. "With chocolate chips?"

"I could be persuaded to add chocolate chips. And some maraschino cherries," Anne said, "if you'd be willing to collect the eggs."

David looked to Matty, who had filled his toy tractor's wagon full of pink plastic piglets. "Hear that, Matty? Mama needs eggs so she can make us banana bread." He widened his eyes excitedly. "Should we go get eggs in the henhouse?"

"Get eggs for Mama!" Matty leaped to his feet.

David raised his brows at Annie, and they both laughed as Matty grabbed his hand and began pulling him in the direction of the back door.

Twenty minutes later, David and Matty walked

onto the back porch with a basketful of eggs. As David opened the back door, Matty spotted a line of ants on the edge of the step and crouched down in fascination to watch them.

"Bugs," Matty declared, pointing.

"Ants," David said. "Look at them all. Let me take these eggs into your mama, and then when I come back out, we'll see where those little guys are going. I think they're probably carrying some kind of food to their nest. Be right back. Stay on the porch, okay?"

Matty nodded, his eyes round with enthusiasm over his discovery.

David walked into the mudroom, letting the screen door close behind him. The hinges were squeaking, and he made a mental note to get out the WD-40 and lubricate them. "You're not going to believe how many eggs Matty and I found," he called to his sister. "Did you forget to collect—"

He halted just inside the kitchen and stared for a moment, trying to comprehend what he was seeing. Surely this was a bad dream. Surely—"Anne!" He raced toward her, the egg basket still in his hand. "Anne!"

His sister lay unconscious on her side, on the floor.

David dropped to his knees, the eggs rolling out of the basket as it tipped when he set it down on the floor. "No, no," he muttered, rolling his sister on to her back and touching her face. "Anne!" She was still breathing, but he didn't know what was wrong with her. She wouldn't wake up. "Anne! Please!" But she still didn't respond.

David yanked his cell phone from his back pocket and hit buttons.

A young woman spoke. "911, what's your emergency?"

Bay glanced at the clock on her mother's kitchen wall as she set a big basket of potatoes down next to a bin of onions on the floor. It was two o'clock and it would take her and Ginger at least another hour to finish cleaning out the pantry. This meant there was no way she would make it to David's today, either. And she'd already had to cancel the day before because instead of the 500 six-inch plastic pots suitable for geraniums that she'd ordered, she'd received 1000 three-inch pots. She'd had to arrange to have the delivery returned and the correct order sent again. When she spoke briefly with David on the phone from the harness shop, they agreed that their lunch date could be postponed. But he was as eager to talk as she was, and they had hoped she could come by this afternoon and go for a walk. There were trails in the woods on the back of his property he wanted to show her, anyway. But today wouldn't work, either.

"Why did *Mam* ask you to come over today to clean her pantry?" Bay questioned Ginger as she walked back in, trying not to sound too grumpy. "Doesn't she know you have enough to do in your own home?"

Ginger was busy washing off the floor-to-ceiling wooden shelves with a soapy rag. "She didn't ask me to clean out the pantry. I volunteered. You know how she can get worked up when it's her turn to host church. She pretends she isn't, but she is." She shrugged, dipped the rag into the water and wrung it out. "And I want to help. Remember how much time she spent helping me last winter when Eli and I were hosting? She scrubbed the grout in my bathroom, for goodness' sake."

Bay unfolded the step stool and climbed up to grab a tray of canned goods. "But you were a newlywed with four children and still carrying that one under your apron," she argued, pointing to baby Paul asleep in an infant seat in the middle of one of the kitchen tables.

"I like helping," Ginger said firmly. "And with Eli taking the boys to work with him today, it was a perfect opportunity for Lizzy and Paul and me to spend the day here. I like cleaning. I find a clean kitchen or closet or drawer very satisfying. And when *Mam* said she was going to get you to help with the pantry, I offered to help because I wanted to see you. I love my new life with Eli and the children, but I miss you, *Schweschder.*"

Bay exhaled impatiently as she carried the tray out to the table, setting it down carefully so as not to disturb her sleeping nephew. "I'm sorry. I don't mean to be cranky." She turned around to face Ginger. "It's just that I don't have time for all of this. Things have been crazy at the garden shop and—" A lump rose in her throat and she swallowed hard, suddenly fighting tears. What was wrong with her? She rarely cried, and when she did, it wasn't over something so trivial as a mistake in an order.

Ginger walked into the kitchen. "What's wrong?"

"Nothing," Bay argued, shaking her head. "I just…" Tears welled in her eyes, and she realized she needed to talk to someone. "I haven't told *Mam* about David," she

blurted. "And he says I need to. And we were supposed
to get together this week to talk about our relationship,
but I've been too busy, and—" She raised her hands
and let them fall. "And I… I think I'm in love with him,
but I'm afraid to tell *Mam* and Benjamin because—"
Her voice caught in her throat, and she couldn't finish.

"Oh, *Schweschder.*" Ginger took Bay's trembling
hand between her own and peered into her face. "You're
afraid because marrying David would mean leaving
your life here to begin a new one with him," she said.
"It would mean leaving our church."

Bay nodded, breathing deeply.

Ginger hugged her. "It's going to be all right."

"I know." Bay sniffed, clinging to her sister. She
paused for a moment to catch her breath and stepped
back. "I know I need to tell *Mam*. I keep trying to find
the chance, but she and I haven't seen eye to eye lately
and she's so worked up about hosting church and—"

"You have to tell her, Bay," Ginger said gently. "For
your own piece of mind. And David's."

"But she's going to be so angry."

The baby began to fuss, and Ginger reached out and
touched his infant seat. The seat began to bounce ever
so gently, soothing Paul, and he went back to sleep. Bay
was fascinated that her sister reacted so calmly to the
child's cries and wondered if that came naturally when
one had a baby or if it was learned. She didn't feel as if
she had any natural mothering instincts, but if she and
David had children of their own, would she learn to be
the kind of mother Ginger was?

"Bay," Ginger said. "*Mam's* not going to be angry

with you. She might even be able to help you figure out what you truly want to do."

Feeling flushed, Bay pressed her hand to her forehead. "I know. You're right." She met her sister's gaze. "But you know how she can be. She always thinks she knows what's best for me. She doesn't listen to me. She doesn't understand me. I don't think she really sees me for who I am."

"I don't know about any of that, but I can tell you, even though I'm new at this mothering, I would do anything to be sure our children feel comfortable in their own skin." Ginger's eyes suddenly grew moist. "Even let them go to the *Englisher* world if that was what was right for them. If that was where God called them."

Bay gave her a wry smile. "If I married David—and I'm not saying I'm going to—but if I did, I wouldn't exactly be joining the world of the English. David and Anne live much the way we do. God is still the center of their life. They just have electricity and a truck."

The back door opened, and Bay and Ginger looked at each other and, without speaking, moved into the pantry to return to what they were doing. Just in case it was their mother. She had gone down to the harness shop to speak to Benjamin about whether or not the chicken coop needed a fresh coat of paint.

Ginger picked up the wet rag and began to scrub a shelf.

Bay climbed the step stool again to be sure she'd not left anything on the top shelf that was out of sight. "If you hand me the rag, I'll wipe this shelf down," she told her sister.

"Bay." Their mother walked into the kitchen. Her cheeks were rosy, and she was slightly out of breath. "My goodness," she said, pressing her hand to her chest. "I don't know what made me think a woman my age ought to be walking that fast." She met Bay's gaze. "Phone call for you at the shop. Your friend Anne's brother." Her face softened. "He said it's urgent."

The words were barely out of her mother's mouth before Bay was off the step stool and running through the kitchen. She flew out the back door, across the porch and into the lane. It seemed like it took forever for her to make it all the way to the harness shop. The last steps between the shop door and the phone on the far side of the cash register counter seemed to take the longest.

She grabbed the cordless phone lying on the counter. "David?" she said, out of breath.

"Bay." His voice was barely recognizable. "I need you. Can you come?"

"Of course. To the house?" She gripped the phone. "What's happened?"

"Not the house," he said, speaking fast. "The hospital. Anne collapsed. She was unconscious when I found her. I called 911, and they took her by ambulance. I don't know what's wrong with her. She was awake by the time I got here, but they only let me see her for a second. I'm still waiting for the doctor to tell me what's going on."

Bay felt as if she couldn't breathe for a second. *Not her Anne.* "I'm coming. I'll be there just as fast as I can. Is Matty with you?"

"Um…no." He sounded disoriented. "A friend from church picked him up. I have no idea how long we'll be here, and I didn't want him to get scared. I'm not sure it was the right thing to do. Anne might be upset with me, but…"

"No, no. You did the right thing. I'm sure Anne will agree. I'm coming now. Is there anything you need me to bring you?"

"No. I'll either be in the waiting room of the emergency department or in the back with her."

"Don't worry, I'll find you," Bay said. "I'll be right there, David. All right?"

"All right," he repeated, his voice breathy. "Bay?"

"Yes?"

"Pray for her."

The tone of his voice scared her. This was serious. "I will, David."

The phone disconnected, and Bay stood there for a moment, frozen in fear for Anne and her baby. For Matty and for David. But then she pushed her emotions aside and moved into action. From the bulletin board behind the register, she grabbed the list of *English* drivers they used when a horse and buggy wasn't ideal. She called the first phone number on the list. If no one answered, she'd call the next one and the next one. She'd call a dozen if she had to until she found someone who could get her quickly to the hospital.

She got a recording at the first number, hung up, and dialed the second. As it rang, she heard the bell over the door jingle, and she saw her mother. Again, Bay got a recording and hung up.

"How is your friend?" her mother asked, genuine concern on her face.

"I don't know," Bay said, flustered. "Not good. She's due in five or six weeks and David—her brother," she added, "found her unconscious. She was taken to the hospital by ambulance. I'm trying to find a driver, so I can get there. To be with her. She must be so scared."

"Here. Give me the phone." Her mother put out her hand. "I'll make the calls. You run up to the house and get ready to go. I'll get you a driver."

"You will?" Bay felt as disoriented as David had sounded.

Her mother took the cordless phone from her. "I'll call Lucy. She's not as busy as some of the others. Some don't like her attitude."

Bay's mother walked around the counter as Emily, Benjamin's new hire, came out of the back. "I thought Jesse was covering me for my break."

Bay's mother gave her one of her looks. "I'm not here to run the cash register, dear. I'm making a call."

Emily looked to Bay.

"And she isn't here to cover you for your break, either." Bay's *mam* pointed to the door. "Go," she mouthed to Bay and then into the phone, she said, "Lucy, glad I caught you. It's Rosemary Miller in Hickory Grove. One of my daughters needs a ride to the hospital. No, she's fine. A friend, but it is an emergency. Can you come for her now?"

As her mother made the arrangements, Bay hurried out of the shop, eager to get to Anne.

And to be there for David.

Chapter Nine

Bay and David sat side by side in Anne's hospital room, talking quietly while she slept. In the background, there was the sound of two heart monitors beeping steadily: Anne's and the baby's. When Bay had arrived at the hospital, David was still sitting nervously in the emergency department waiting room. A few minutes later, a nurse called them back to see Anne and speak with the doctor. The nurse must have assumed Bay was either Anne's sister or David's wife, because, before seeing Anne, they were both ushered to a small office where Anne's midwife and an obstetrician from her office met with them.

Anne had been diagnosed with peripartum cardiomyopathy, a dangerous and rare type of heart failure. Anne's midwife, Julie, explained that it could develop during pregnancy or right after delivery and was a condition that weakened the heart muscle. The weakened heart would become enlarged, and blood wasn't pumped properly to the rest of her body. The diagnosis explained

Anne's increasing tiredness that went beyond the usual fatigue of the last trimester of pregnancy. It also explained other symptoms she'd kept from David and Bay, like feeling out of breath at times and severe swelling of her hands and feet. The condition was likely also the explanation for the dark circles that had appeared under her eyes recently.

After the condition was explained to David and Bay, they, Julie and the doctor joined Anne in her hospital room. Together, they went over the diagnosis and a treatment plan. Through the whole process David listened and nodded, but it was Bay and Anne who asked questions. Anne's first question was: Had she done anything to cause the heart condition? She had not. Bay asked if her condition would right itself once the baby was born. It would not, they were told, as her heart had already been damaged.

Anne was now being treated with several medications, and she and the baby were safe for the moment. However, the doctor explained, her tone grave, that if there wasn't improvement, the baby would need to be delivered by cesarean section within the next twenty-four hours. Otherwise, Anne would remain in the hospital on bed rest until she went into labor naturally.

Bay had been surprised by how calmly Anne had taken the diagnosis. There were no hysterics, no tears. Once the doctor and midwife left, Bay sat down on the edge of Anne's bed, took her hand, and asked her how she was doing, considering all that had been said. Anne had calmly declared that God's will would be done and that she was certain her and Matthew's second child would be born safely into the world. She insisted that they all needed to pray for her and the baby.

Once all of the commotion of Anne's admission to the hospital had quieted, Bay had offered to sit in the waiting room so Anne could rest. She had no intention of leaving David alone in the hospital, but she wanted to give them some privacy. Though David appeared to be taking the whole situation calmly, Bay knew he was a mess. She could see it in his eyes. And Bay suspected Anne could see it, too, because when David stepped out to get some ice, Anne had asked Bay to vow she would look after her brother and her son until she and the baby were home safely. Bay held her friend's hand and made that promise.

Bay and David had been together most of the day, and she didn't know whether it was the physical proximity or Anne's illness, but in the last hours, Bay felt their relationship had moved from one phase to another. They hadn't talked about what they were going to do about their feelings for each other. It didn't seem appropriate with Anne right there, even though she had slept most of the day. However, David and Bay were acutely aware of the undercurrent of emotion rippling between them.

"She looks better," David observed quietly. He looked to Bay. "Doesn't she? There's some color in her cheeks now. Maybe she just needed some rest. Maybe her heart's not as bad as the cardiologist thinks."

An hour ago, Anne's new cardiologist had stopped by to check on her. The woman was not as warm and personable as Julie, nor the obstetrician, but as Anne had pointed out when the doctor left, she wasn't looking for a best friend. She needed a doctor who could treat her medically.

"David," Bay said gently. "We've talked to three medical professionals today. They all gave the same diagnosis, and you saw the echocardiogram. It was easy to see what the cardiologist was talking about when she showed us what Anne's heart looked like and then the picture of what Anne's heart *should* look like."

Bay had never heard of an echocardiogram before that day, but she'd read all of the literature the cardiologist had provided. She then explained it all to David when he said he was too antsy to read through the pile of papers on Anne's nightstand.

"I can't believe this is happening." David took a deep breath and exhaled. "But it sounded like the medicine might help, right?" His eyes sought hers. "The cardiologist said the combination of medicines would keep her from going into heart failure."

The cardiologist had actually said that she was hopeful the drugs would prevent heart failure. Bay had read between the lines and understood that Anne's condition was grave, maybe graver than David understood, but she didn't know that it would help to explain that to him right now.

"I think we need to give the medicine time," Bay told David. He looked exhausted. "When did you last eat?" she asked.

"I had those peanut butter crackers a while ago," he reminded her. He had gotten a pack from a vending machine, and they'd shared them. Anne wasn't allowed to have anything to eat in case she had to have an emergency C-section.

Bay frowned. "I mean real food. Breakfast, I would guess."

He nodded. "Anne made us creamed beef and buttermilk biscuits. She knows Matty and I love fresh biscuits with our breakfast."

"I think you need to get something to eat," Bay told him. "Why don't you go down to the cafeteria? When my *mam* had foot surgery, Ginger and I ate there a couple of times. They have soups and salads and sandwiches and usually a hot dish like spaghetti. I was surprised how good it was."

David worked his hands. "I don't know. You think it's okay to leave her?"

"It'll be fine," Bay insisted. "She told us she didn't need us to sit here all day."

His gaze shifted to the monitors on both sides of the bed. "I don't know if I *can* leave her."

"Sure you can. I'll stay here with her. You need to keep up your strength, David. You're going to have your hands full when she and the baby come home."

He seemed to chew over the idea of that for a moment. "I guess you're right."

Bay kept her tone upbeat even though she was just as concerned about Anne and the baby as David was. "When you go to the cafeteria, you can call and check in on how Matty is doing. Take a little walk, maybe. It will be good for you to stretch your legs."

"I have to call Rich from church." David ran his fingers through his red hair. "He left me a phone message. He offered to take care of the animals, so I don't have to worry about getting home for feeding time. Anne said I should let him do it. That you have to let people help you."

"My *mam* always says that gifts have to work in both directions. That you can't do things for others but never be willing to accept others' help."

David smiled. "I'm going to like your mother. She seems like a wise woman."

"She says she's wise only because of all the mistakes she's made in her life," Bay said with a chuckle. "Now go on. Go get something to eat. I'll be right here when you get back."

David met her gaze again and then surprised her by taking her hand.

Bay glanced at Anne, but she was still asleep.

"Is this okay?" David asked, quietly. "I don't want to make you feel uncomfortable."

They both looked at their hands intertwined on the arm of her chair, and Bay realized how right it seemed, holding hands this way. His warm hand, bigger than hers and a little rougher, felt good. It felt comforting and, at the same time, sent shivers of warmth through her body.

"*Ya*, this is nice," she murmured.

He squeezed her hand. "I've wanted to do this for weeks. I've just been trying to get up the nerve to do it."

He hesitated and then went on. And even though they were in a hospital room with monitors beeping inside and outside the room and there were hushed voices and footfalls in the hallway, Bay felt like there was no one in the world but the two of them.

"I didn't know if holding hands would be okay. Anne said it would be, but I kept second-guessing myself." He fixed his gaze on the monitor that reflected the baby's heart rate. "I don't know if Anne told you, but… I've never had a relationship, never even had a girlfriend before."

"You've never met anyone you liked?" she asked, a little surprised by that. David was older than she was, and she was practically an old maid. It was hard to believe that at thirty years old, he hadn't found a woman who wanted to be his girlfriend.

He shrugged. "I won't say that no one was ever interested in me, but I never pursued it. I always had this feeling that God had already chosen a wife for me. That I had to be patient." He grimaced. "That sounds cheesy, doesn't it?"

Bay laughed and squeezed his hand. "It sounds honest. And maybe a little cheesy," she teased to lighten the moment.

"All right," he said, pressing his free hand to his leg. "You're right. I should grab something to eat and make a couple of phone calls. I'm sure Matty is having a great time at Susan's house. They have eleven children. But it's still got to be scary. He's never been there without his mother."

"Take your time. I'll sit right here and wait," Bay told him.

He nodded.

Bay gazed into his eyes, then down at their entwined

hands and into his eyes again. "You're going to have to let go of my hand for me to stay here," she pointed out.

They both laughed, and Bay imagined what it would be like to look into his eyes before she fell asleep every night and woke each morning. Suddenly, the idea of marriage was imminently more appealing and far less scary.

"All right, all right, I—"

"Bay Laurel Stutzman!"

The sound of Bay's name spoken from the doorway made them both turn around toward the door. Bay knew instantly who it was and she pulled her hand from David's as she leaped to her feet. *"Mam,"* she murmured.

Bay's mother wasn't looking at her. She was staring at David.

Bay hurried to her. "What are you doing here?"

Her mother held up a cloth satchel, slowly turning her gaze on her daughter. "I should ask you the same question," she replied, her voice low and terse. When Rosemary Miller got angry, she never raised her voice. She got quieter.

David rose from the chair beside Anne's bed and joined Bay. "You must be Rosemary," he said, offering a quick smile. "It's nice to meet you at last."

Bay's mother looked from Bay to David, then back to Bay. "I brought the two of you something to eat. Cafeterias are expensive," she said in Pennsylvania *Deitsch*. "I wanted to bring comfort to you and your friend, who I can see is more than a friend. What are you doing alone with this man, Daughter?"

"*Mam*, David speaks *Deitsch*. I told you, he and Anne grew up Amish."

Her mother's mouth twitched into a frown. "Ham sandwiches, macaroni salad, grapes and cookies," she said in English, thrusting the bag at David. "Come with me, *Dochter*. Into the hall." It was an order, not an invitation.

"I'm sorry about your sister," Bay's mother said to David, her voice and posture stiff. "We will keep her in our prayers, my husband and I."

"Danki," David said. "For the prayers and the meal." He held up the bag she had handed him. "I appreciate them both, Rosemary."

Bay's mother gave a curt nod and walked out of the room, beckoning her daughter with a tilt of her head.

Bay considered, for an instant, refusing to go. She could tell her mother they would talk when she got home. But she realized that would only delay the conversation, and if she gave her mother time to heat up, it would go even worse for Bay that evening. So she gave David a quick look of dread, and walked out into the hall.

The brightly lit hospital corridor was a beehive of activity with men and women in colorful scrubs hurrying up and down the hall. There were people in hospital gowns, walking and pushing IV poles and wheeling in wheelchairs. And visitors, too, looking for the rooms of their friends and loved ones.

"What is it, *Mudder*?" Bay asked, using the formal term of address.

"Aeckt net so dumm," her mother snapped, whipping around to face her. *Don't act so dumb.*

Bay groaned, rethinking her decision to speak with

her mother while she was so angry. "Could we do this later? Anne is very sick. She's in heart failure. She might have to have an emergency C-section."

"For that, I am sorry, but *ne*, this cannot wait." Her mother stood nearly nose to nose with Bay. Folks were beginning to slow down as they walked by, curious about the two Amish women who were obviously having a disagreement.

"Can we at least go somewhere more private?" Bay tempered her tone.

She was angry and upset, and a part of her was afraid of her mother, or at least of the potential actions she could take. If her mother forbade her to be here alone with David at Anne's bedside, what would she do? She'd promised Anne she would be there for David, and for her. She couldn't leave the hospital. She wouldn't, she realized, no matter what the consequences. Not until she felt Anne and David would both be all right without her. But despite all of that, Bay didn't want to be disrespectful to her mother. Many years ago, when Bay was thirteen or fourteen, she had learned, from her mother, an important rule of dealing with others. No matter how much you disagreed with someone, it was never, ever right to be ill-mannered.

When her mother didn't respond immediately, Bay walked past her. "There's a lounge down here, where it isn't so noisy."

Her mother was silent until they passed a bay of elevators and turned into a small waiting room. It was set up with a couch, several chairs and end tables, and a TV mounted to the wall. To Bay's relief, there was no one else there. The TV was on, though, and she picked up a remote control and hit the red button on it the way she had seen David do earlier in the day.

"You lied to me, *Dochter*." Her mother spoke half in English, half in Pennsylvania *Deitsch*, something she did only when she was very angry.

"I didn't lie to you." Bay settled her hands on her hips defensively. "When did I lie?"

Her mother crossed her arms over her chest. She was wearing a new dress of cornflower blue, a starched white apron, her best prayer *kapp* on her head, and new black canvas sneakers on her feet. "You purposely misled me. Misled all of us. You've been telling us all these weeks that you were seeing your friend Anne to help her out when you were sneaking around behind my back to see a man!"

"I *have* been spending time with Anne. *Mam*, she's been feeling poorly for weeks. I've cleaned, done laundry and looked after her son. I've even been cooking for the family."

"I'm glad that you've helped her, but that does not change the fact that you purposely did not tell me about this man. You are involved with him. I saw you holding hands!" her mother sputtered. "In front of anyone to see."

"We were alone in a hospital room, and Anne was asleep," Bay argued. "And I'm twenty-six years old! I have a right to choose who I hold hands with."

Her mother kept shaking her head. "Never in my life did I think I wouldn't be able to trust you, Bay. I thought I'd raised you better than to behave shamefully with a man."

"I've done nothing wrong with David!" Bay folded her arms over her chest, mimicking her mother's stance. "I care for him, and he cares for me."

Her mother's green eyes practically sparked with anger. "'Honor thy father and thy mother: that thy days may be long upon the land which the Lord thy God giveth thee,'" she quoted from Exodus. "Those are *Gott's* words."

"I'm old enough to make my own choices, *Mam*. That's why I didn't tell you about David. Because I knew you would be angry. I knew you wouldn't understand because you never understand me."

Her mother stood there for a long moment, looking at her, and Bay realized maybe for the first time ever that she was slightly taller. The observation was so unexpected that it caught her by surprise. Her whole life her mother had been bigger than she was, more imposing and always in control. And now, Bay realized, and she suspected her *mam* did, too, that her mother no longer had that control over her.

The thought was freeing.

But it was also intimidating. Bay's whole life, she'd had her mother, her father, then Benjamin and her siblings, and even her church to tell her what to do and what to think. And in a way, the control that she was fighting now had made her comfortable. It had made her feel safe. And now, standing here with her mother and defending her right to hold a man's hand, a man her family didn't know, she understood the dangers of making one's own decision. She was in uncharted territory here. Instead of having the wisdom of experience behind her, she was alone in her decision.

Would she leave her Amish life for David?

And once she made the choice she suspected she would, would it be the right one? Would her decision lead her to love and the freedom she yearned for or would it bring unhappiness and unfulfillment?

"You should have been honest with me," her mother said, bringing Bay back to the moment. "No matter what you thought my reaction might be, you should have been honest with me." She drew herself up, settling her black leather handbag on her elbow. "We'll talk about this at home." She started for the door. "I assume you'll be home this evening. That you're not spending the night here with *that* man."

Bay pulled a face in response to her mother's ridiculous implication. Holding hands with a man she cared for, especially a man who wanted to marry her, wasn't immoral. Her sisters had certainly done it with their husbands before they were married. But, of course, her brothers-in-law were all Amish. And that was all that mattered to her mother.

"*Ne*, I'm not spending the night here with a man," Bay countered, wondering what would make her mother say such a ridiculous thing. "I am going to stay here a while longer, though. The cardiologist said she would stop by at the end of the day. I want to hear what she has to say and see, when Anne wakes, if she needs me to bring her anything from home. Lucy said for me to call her no matter how late it was, and she'd bring me home."

Bay followed her *mam* into the busy hallway that

smelled of antiseptic, cleaning agents and anxiety. It had been her experience that while, occasionally, something good happened in the hospital, like the birth of a baby, most patients were sick or injured. Feeling her own stress over Anne's illness, she could only imagine what others were feeling here, and not just patients and their families but their caregivers, too. It had to be such a weight on the shoulders of doctors, nurses and other medical personnel, looking after those in their care.

Bay stopped as her mother approached the elevator. "Aren't you even going to say goodbye?" she blurted.

Her mother turned around, speaking stiffly in Pennsylvania *Deitsch*. "Goodbye. I will see you tonight."

Bay took a breath as she tried to calm herself. She hated fighting with her mother. She loved her so much. She didn't want to worry or disappoint her, but she had to be true to herself to serve her family and *Gott,* didn't she? And didn't *Gott* make her who she was? And He didn't make mistakes. Wasn't it said in Psalms: As for God, His way is perfect.

Pressing her lips together, Bay willed herself not to cry at the state of her relationship with her mother. "Thank you again for bringing us something to eat. It was kind of you, coming all the way into town. We were getting hungry." On impulse, she gave her a quick peck on the cheek, something she didn't often do. Then she watched the elevator close, wondering if her relationship with her mother could survive if she left the church.

Bay stared out the truck window as they wound their way down country roads toward Hickory Grove. The sun was setting, leaving a glow over freshly planted fields and pastures thick with new clover. It was a warm evening, so she and David both had their windows down. Bay could smell freshly turned soil and hear the first sounds of night insects and frogs chirping and croaking.

She had stayed well past supper, sharing the homemade food her mother had brought with David, while poor Anne had enjoyed a meal of chicken broth and Jell-O. David got Matty on the phone, and after he and Anne spoke to him, she'd been surprised when David handed her the phone.

"He's asking for you, Bay," David told her.

The conversation was short, with her doing most of the talking, but Bay had been touched that Matty needed to hear her voice as well as his mother's and uncle's. It was interesting how important the boy had become to her in such a short time. On days like today when she didn't see him, she missed his smile, his laughter and the opportunity to read one of his well-worn Little House books to him.

After the cardiologist stopped by Anne's room to say there was no change in her heart function but that the drugs needed time to work, Bay had asked to borrow David's phone to call the driver for a ride home. But Anne had ordered them both out of her room, telling David to take Bay home and then stop by their friend Susan's to hug Matty for her. It was decided that Matty would stay the night with Susan so David could be back at the hospital in the morning to hear the doctors' latest reports.

Bay rested her arm on the open window of the pickup.

"You didn't have to drive me home. I could have gotten the driver."

"I know I didn't have to bring you home." He reached across the bench seat and covered her hand with his. "I wanted to, Bay. After all you did for us today, it's the least I could do. I don't know what I would have done in the hospital today without you. You were so calm and asked such good questions."

She smiled at him. "You would have been fine." She glanced out the window again. "I feel bad, you taking me home when you still need to go back to your place to get Matty's nightclothes and his books."

David had decided that he should fetch a couple of Matty's books in case the boy got to feeling homesick. The plan was to take him the following day to see his mother at the hospital if she was up to it.

"After today, I needed this," David told her. "To be with you alone for a few minutes." He squeezed her hand.

Bay looked down at their hands entwined on the truck seat, and she was amazed by how well they fit together. By how good his touch felt. She was scared to death for Anne. The cardiologist hadn't been all that optimistic the medicines were going to work, but somehow being with David made it all less scary.

"Are you going back to the hospital tonight?" Bay asked as they turned onto her road.

"You heard my sister. She said I wasn't." He cut his eyes at her, still steering the truck with one hand while holding hers with the other.

"But you're going back by, anyway."

He shrugged. "The hospital is practically on my way home from Susan's."

She chuckled. She had known that no matter what Anne said, David was going to check on her once more before he went home. Had Bay been in his shoes, she'd have done the same.

"Listen," David said. "I'm sorry about what happened today. Your mother seeing us holding hands. I shouldn't have…it wasn't appropriate."

"But I wanted you to hold my hand," she answered stubbornly.

He removed his sunglasses and tucked them into a small slot on the dashboard. "I take it you didn't have the chance to tell her about us."

"Mam? Ne."

The shadows were lengthening quickly now. The sun had nearly set. She was afraid he was going to lecture her about why she should have said something before this, but he didn't. Instead, they rode the rest of the way to her house, holding hands in silence, both lost in thought.

When David pulled up in front of the farmhouse, she expected him to say good-night. They'd already made plans for her to meet him at the hospital in the morning, and she'd arranged a ride with Lucy. But he got out of his pickup and came around to walk her to the door.

"You should go," she told him, afraid he was going to want to come inside.

Then both her mother and Benjamin walked out onto the back porch, and she looked up at David, feeling as if she was walking into fire.

"There you are, *Dochter*. Home safe at last," her mother said. She wasn't smiling, but at least she wasn't scowling, either.

With a sigh, Bay spoke to her stepfather as she walked up the porch steps, "This is David Jansen, my friend Anne's brother." She looked to David. "You've already met my *mam*. And this is Benjamin."

"Good to meet you, Benjamin. I've heard a lot about you." David offered his hand and Benjamin shook it, smiling.

"All good, I hope," Benjamin joked.

"All good. Bay sings your praises."

Benjamin glanced at Bay. "I know she's not my daughter, but I love her the same as I love my own. When Rosemary and I wed, we agreed we would share our children. Though there are some days I'd like to pass a few of my sons to her entirely," he said, looking to his wife.

Rosemary crossed her arms over her chest, saying nothing, and Bay wondered if this was all a huge mistake—considering marrying David and all that entailed. She had never seen her mother like this. Certainly her *mam* could get angry in the heat of the moment, but she had never seemed like the person who stayed angry. Bay had been sure that her mother would never shun her, no matter what, but what if she was wrong? Could she find happiness in a life with David if she no longer had her mother? And would Benjamin follow in her footsteps? Her brothers and sisters? Would they turn their backs to her if she ran into them at Byler's?

"Bay has been such a help to my sister, Anne, and

me the last few weeks. And such good company for my nephew, Matty," David said, sliding his hand into the pocket of his jeans. "I don't know if Bay told you, but after my brother-in-law's death, Matty stopped talking." He looked at Bay with a hint of a smile, then back at Benjamin. "Bay got him back to talking when we couldn't. He adores her."

Benjamin smiled proudly. "Bay's got a way about her, doesn't she?"

David looked down, shuffling his feet. "I think you know now that I care for her, too." He looked up at Benjamin and then to her *mam*. "I want you to know that my intentions are honorable. But if you don't want me to see your daughter again, if you forbid her, I'll abide by your wishes."

Bay was so caught off-guard by David's words that she froze, her eyes widening. *He wouldn't see her anymore if her mother didn't approve?*

"*Forbid* her?" Bay's *mam* snorted. "If you think anyone could forbid that one from doing something, you don't know her as well as you ought to if you intend to continue seeing her." She turned to go back into the house. "You should come for supper when your sister is out of the hospital. Good night." A moment later, the screen door shut behind her.

Bay couldn't decide who she was more upset with at that moment, her mother or David.

"That's an excellent idea," Benjamin agreed, meeting David's gaze. "As soon as your sister is well, all of you should come for supper so we can get to know you better." He offered his hand. "Bark's worse than the bite with these Stutzman women." He flashed a smile as he shook David's hand, and then turned to the house. "A good night to you, David. And I'll see you inside, Bay. We're just about ready for evening prayers."

Bay waited until Benjamin went into the house, and then she marched down the porch steps. David followed her. "You won't see me again without their approval?" she demanded over her shoulder.

When he didn't answer, she strode toward his truck, determined to get an answer from him if it took all night.

Chapter Ten

David was surprised by Bay's anger. She was a spirited one, this woman of his. If she was his, and he hoped she was. Would be, he prayed.

"What about me?" she asked. When she reached the truck, she spun around to face him. "What about what *I* want, David? What would make you say such a thing to them? Don't you care what I think? What I want?"

He wasn't upset that she was angry with him. He knew Bay had to be worried about Anne and the baby. She and Anne had only been friends for a short time, but it seemed like a friendship that was solid and would be a long one. And nothing could please him more because, when he let his thoughts run wild, he imagined them all living in the big farmhouse together as a blended family—he and Bay, and Anne and her little ones.

"Why would you say that to them?" she repeated, crossing her arms the way she did when she was angry.

The funny thing was, he had seen her mother do the same thing at the hospital and again this evening on the porch. Bay thought she and her mother were opposites, but from his observations, they were very similar. Where did Bay think she got her stubbornness if not from Rosemary?

David took his time, choosing his response to Bay wisely. He didn't want her to be angry with him, but he had to be honest. It was who he was, and if she didn't like it, then maybe they weren't meant to be. "I said it because it was the right thing to do, considering the circumstances." He looked down at her, meeting her gaze. "If we were to marry, Bay, and have children, if we had a daughter, how would you feel about her seeing a man you disapproved of?"

"I would never forbid her!"

"And it doesn't appear your parents would ever do that, either."

Bay took a deep breath. "But if they did—I don't know if I can go against their wishes," she admitted softly. "Even if they don't forbid me."

"Wait. Are you saying you're considering marrying me?" His chest tightened. All day he'd been on such an emotional roller coaster. It was hard for him to keep up with all he was feeling, between his concerns for Anne and the baby and his desperate need to have Bay fall in love with him. He wanted her not just to love him, but to be brave enough to be willing to leave the life she had known for a life with him.

He waited for her response.

"I'm saying—" She hesitated. "I'm saying I'm considering it. But I won't lie to you, David. I'm torn." She pressed her hand to her forehead. "Not about you. You're a good man and we get along so well together. You understand me in a way that no one here understands me." She took a breath. "It's me I'm worried about. I didn't think I wanted to marry. And be a mother?" she scoffed. "I don't have a mothering bone in my body."

She was considering marrying him!

He smiled, deciding that while she hadn't declared her love for him, her considering marriage to him was good enough for now. Because right now, she offered hope. "I'd disagree with you on that. You're so good with Matty. But because I don't want to be the object of your wrath again tonight, I'll say good-night. It's been a long day." He walked around the front of his truck. "Will you come to the hospital tomorrow?"

"Of course." She followed him to the driver's side, seeming calmer now. "I just wish I had a phone," she fretted. "In case you need me. I know Anne's going to be fine, but—in case you need me," she repeated.

"I can call the harness shop." He opened the door. He didn't want to leave, but if he didn't get moving, he wouldn't make it to Susan's house before Matty went to bed.

"But that's only during business hours. What if you needed me in the middle of the night?"

"Bay, she's going to be fine. The doctors have everything under control." He got into his truck. "She says she's cautiously optimistic." He frowned. "Besides, you're not allowed to have a cell phone. Are you?"

She closed the driver's door and leaned in through the open window. "Our bishop wouldn't like it. Of course, half the men I know have one. I know Jacob and

Joshua both do. And Marshall and Eli." She frowned. "But, of course, they're men, and they need them for their jobs."

He lifted his brows. "Hit a nerve there, did I?" He chuckled, but she didn't. "I'm sorry, I shouldn't tease you like that, Bay."

She looked into his eyes and managed a smile. "Give Matty a big hug for me and tell him I'll see him tomorrow. Susan's going to bring him to the hospital to visit, right?"

"Yup."

"Okay, then. I'll see you both tomorrow." She waved goodbye as he pulled away.

As David drove down the long oyster-shell driveway, he couldn't help wondering what it would be like to kiss Bay. He had never kissed a girl before and now he was glad. Because, hopefully, Bay would be the first and last woman he'd ever kiss.

Bay stood in Anne's hospital room doorway and watched her friend as she read *The Deer in the Woods* to her son for the second time. Anne had steadily improved over the last week, and Bay and David felt better about her condition.

Anne had so improved that she was making tentative plans to return home, promising anyone who would listen that she would remain on bed rest. David wasn't thrilled with the idea, which Bay could understand. But she also understood Anne wanting to be home in her own bed to snuggle with her son each night and read him his favorite books.

Just in case his sister was able to go home, David had begun to make plans. He figured he could take care of his sister and Matty at night, but they were going to need help during the day with meals, cleaning, laundry and Matty, and Bay had volunteered. David and Anne's income was based on what he grew and sold, and he already had several big orders from a landscaping company, so he couldn't just take the month off until the baby was born. And once Anne had the baby, no one knew what kind of recovery time would be necessary. Bay had already talked to Joshua about only working weekends and early mornings at their shop and greenhouses. He had been very understanding, promising they would make it work, even if they needed to hire another employee, which they had been considering before Anne was hospitalized.

So far, the cardiologist had refused even to discuss the option of Anne going home. If anyone kept Anne from going home until it was time for the baby to be born, it would be the midwife, Julie, maybe because she knew Anne well enough that she doubted her patient would follow the rules of full bed rest. Bay wasn't so sure Anne *wouldn't* comply; after all, she would be risking her own life or that of the baby's if she didn't. Her friend was such a good mother she would never risk her child's life. And with David at her side, watching her every move like the mother cat still living in their mudroom, she could see them making it work at home.

David walked into the hospital room as Anne finished reading a book to Matty who was snuggled into the bed beside her.

"You're back. Get your mysterious errand done?" Bay asked, smiling up at him.

When Bay arrived at the hospital, he and Matty were already there. He'd then excused himself, saying he needed to run an errand and left Matty in Bay's care. Anne had asked him where he needed to go, but he'd told her it was none of her bee's wax, which had made them all laugh.

"I'm back." David looked down at Bay, his smile meant only for her and she suddenly felt warm all over.

David slipped past Bay as Matty looked up at his mother with his big brown eyes. "Again, Mama. Read again."

Anne laughed. "Not again." She groaned theatrically and dropped back onto her pillow, making her son giggle. She was still wearing two heart monitors and had an IV, so there were wires and tubes everywhere. "I can't read it again."

Matty accepted the book and held it to his chest. "But I *wike* it," he told her.

She hugged him. "And I like it, too, but Mama needs to rest." She looked up at her brother and Bay. "And Uncle David is back. I think he and Bay have a little surprise for you."

Matty's eyes lit up and he turned to look at them. "S'prise!"

"We do have a surprise for you," Bay said. "Now give Mama a hug and come along."

Matty threw his arms around his mother, and she hugged him tightly again, kissing the top of his head.

When her son pulled away, there were tears in Anne's eyes. "Thank you," she mouthed to Bay.

A lump rose in Bay's throat. If possible, she and David and Anne had all grown closer since Anne had been hospitalized. There was something about possibilities of new life and of death that made a person look past others' little quirks and their own worries and doubts to treasure the life God had given them. Bay was so thankful for Anne and David's friendship and for the possibility of a life with them both.

Bay had been at the hospital every day since Anne was admitted, even Sunday, to her mother's irritation, and she intended to continue coming. Bay didn't care how much it cost her to hire a van to bring her every morning or how far she was behind in her work at the shop. What mattered right now was Anne. And in being there for Anne, she was also there for David and Matty.

"We'll be back in two hours," David said as Bay lowered Matty from Anne's bed to the floor. "Get some rest."

"Take as much time as you like. Have some lunch while you're out. Matty needs to get plenty of fresh air. I want him behaving himself at Susan's and tired boys make well-behaved boys," Anne said. "I'll be right here when you get back, Matty." She raised her hands before lowering them to her rounded belly. "I've got nothing to do here. Nowhere to go."

"You've got something to do. *Rest*," David instructed.

Anne looked at Bay. "Please take my brother before I throw this book at him." She raised one of Matty's books he'd left on her bed.

Matty frowned. "No, no, Mama. No throw books," he told her sternly.

They all laughed, and then Bay, David and Matty left the hospital and walked down the street to an elementary school. Because school was out for the summer, Matty could play on the playground equipment. After taking turns pushing him on the swings, they took him to see a bright yellow slide. The first time he climbed the steps, he got scared, but Bay climbed up, set him in her lap, and together they flew down the little slide. Her *kapp* strings flying, she had found it exhilarating. They did it twice more, and then Matty took it solo. Then he was joined by two boys just slightly older than him, and their big sister, and Bay and David wandered over to a bench to sit and enjoy the June sun.

From the bench, they could still see Matty, and it allowed them to talk privately. Her favorite part of the day was when she and David stole a few moments to themselves. Sometimes they ate lunch together in the hospital cafeteria or waited in the little waiting room on Anne's floor while she had testing done. Sometimes they just sat together in her room, holding hands and whispering to each other while she slept. Had it not been for the fact that Anne was suffering from a severe condition, the days Bay spent with David would have been perfect.

"So," David said, drawling out the word. "Anne and I wanted to talk to you about something."

Bay could feel her brow furrowing. "What about?"

He put his hands together in his lap. Today he was wearing jeans and a teal-colored polo shirt. It was a brighter color than she was used to seeing on him, but she liked it. It made his green eyes seem even greener.

"Matty," David said. "Anne talked to Susan last night and then called me after I got home. Matty's been up at night crying for his mother." He shrugged. "Not unusual for a three-and-a-half-year-old. But Anne's worried about him staying so long. And she doesn't want to take advantage of Susan's kindness. She already has a house full of children of her own, and while she's a church friend, she and Anne aren't friends like, well, like you and she are. So we were wondering—and if this is too much, just say so," he added quickly. "But we were wondering if you would be willing to take him to spend the night with you for a few nights."

Bay didn't consider the question for a second. "Of course he can come home with me. I'd love that."

David smiled. "Anne knew you'd say that. Matty loves you and trusts you. And we were thinking that if he can't be with us at night, at least he could be with you."

"I'd love to take Matty home with me. He'd have such a good time playing with my twin brothers. They're all about the same age."

He leaned on his legs, his hands still together. "But I know you've got work to do. We're getting into a busy season with retail."

She waved his thought away as if it was insignificant. "I can still work. He can go to the shop with me or hang out with Josiah and James. There are plenty of people around to keep an eye on them. You know how it is with a big family. Everyone takes turns with the little ones."

"But what about your mother?" David asked thoughtfully. "How would she feel about another mouth to feed? Because I know Anne is talking about coming home, but I don't see that happening. And the baby isn't due for another month. They want to get her as close to term as they safely can."

"*Mam* would be fine with me bringing Matty home," she told him, covering his hands with one of hers.

They held hands all the time now. Even in public, which she knew her mother would disapprove of, but Bay didn't see anything wrong with it. Not if she loved him. Which she knew she did, even if she wasn't ready to admit it to him.

"I'm sorry if I made her out to be a bad person, because she's not," Bay continued. "She's good and kind and I wouldn't trade her for any *mudder* in the world. She wants me baptized and married to a nice Amish man because that's what Amish mothers want for their children. She'll be pleased to know that you and Anne would trust us with Matty."

"Okay, so it's settled." He took her hand in his. "Anne will be relieved. I think she'd prefer he stay with you. We tried to figure out some way to have him stay with me, but she's afraid I can't get my work done. And if anything were to happen here and Anne needed me—" his voice filled with emotion "—I wouldn't want Matty here."

"David, everything is going to be fine. The medications seem to be working," she told him. "We have to trust in *Gott*."

He took a deep breath. "You're right. She's going to be fine. We just have to get through the next few weeks. And keep her in the hospital if we can." He turned on the bench so that their knees were touching. "So that's settled. Now, do you want to know where I've been this morning?"

"I thought it was none of my bee's wax," she teased.

"It was none of *Anne's* business because my sister can't keep a secret, and I wanted it to be a surprise."

"A surprise for me?" Bay asked.

"Yup," he said, pulling his hand from hers to reach into his back pocket. "If anything about this makes you uncomfortable, I can take it back. Not a big deal."

Bay frowned. "I'm not sure I like this."

"Who doesn't like surprises?" he asked, drawing his head back.

"Me."

"Well, I think you're going to like this one." He whipped his hand around to reveal what was clearly a brand-new cell phone.

"A phone?" Bay asked in shock. "You got me a phone?" She was so excited and yet she immediately tempered it. "No, David. It's too much. It's not appropriate. That's too much money to spend."

He looked into her eyes. "You think? Even for the person I love?" He lowered his voice to almost a whisper. "Because I do love you, Bay. You know that, don't you? Now, I don't expect you to say it back. Not yet. I'm willing to give you all the time you need. But I hope," he went on solemnly, "I pray, that someday you could love me. Even half as much as I love you."

It was all Bay could do not to say, *I love you, too,* but she held her tongue because she had to be sure she was willing to leave her church, her family, her life, no matter what the consequences, before she said the words.

She bathed in his gaze for a moment and then said mischievously, "Can I see it and then decide if I'll keep it?"

He laughed and handed it to her. "I didn't go fancy because I knew you wouldn't like that, but I got one that would do everything you need it to do—calls, messaging and the internet."

She closed her fingers around the phone, staring at it in awe. "A phone of my own," she breathed.

"So here's my reasoning before you hand it back to me telling me stubbornly that it's too spendy a gift." He glanced up, checking on Matty, and then returned his attention to her. "No matter when Anne is released, before or after the baby is born, we're going to need your help. Me calling the harness shop, trying to get a message to you, you calling me back, it's not working very well."

"Especially when Emily forgets to pass on the message."

He chuckled. It had happened the day before, though, thankfully, it hadn't been anything too important. He had just wanted her to stop at the house and get some clean nightclothes for Anne after he had forgotten them.

"And even if we can make the harness shop phone work during business hours, as you said last week, what about at night? What happens if Anne gets home and needs to go back to the hospital and I've got a three-year-old and newborn baby in my arms? I would need you to either go to the hospital with Anne or stay with the children."

Bay stared at the phone in her palm. Their bishop didn't permit it. If the bishop found out she had it, she'd been in trouble with him and the whole church. Living in a community that knew everything about everyone was one way they were able to keep their lives as strict as they did. A woman with buttons on a dress or a cell phone in her apron pocket would not only be gossiped about but would get a talking-to by every woman in her church district. She'd get visits from the preacher and other church elders and be pressured into a confession. It wasn't a place any woman wanted to be.

"I can't believe you bought me a cell phone," Bay said softly. She looked up at him. "Thank you. But I want to pay you back."

"You'll do no such thing. I bought the phone because I need you to have one." Catching sight of Matty, he called out, "Sit down on the top of the slide! That's right, no standing." He looked back at Bay, who was swiping from screen to screen. "Does this mean you're keeping the phone?"

"I shouldn't," she said.

"But you will." He smiled at her. "You make me happy, Bay." He touched an icon on her phone that read Contacts. "I put my cell number in, the hospital number to Anne's room, and also our house number. I didn't know what other numbers you would want. Lucy's maybe, in case you need a ride somewhere?"

Bay couldn't stop touching the smooth, glass screen. It felt good in her hand, not evil, not even wrong. And her heart swelled as she looked at David, seeing her reflection in his sunglasses. It was on the tip of her tongue to just say it, to tell him that she loved him and that she wanted to marry him, no matter what. She was trying to get up the nerve when Matty cried out, not in joy but pain.

"Bay!" he cried in his little boy voice.

Bay and David were both on their feet instantly. Matty was crying as he clutched his arm, the big sister of the boys he had been playing with now standing over him. The children's mother ran toward them from the other direction.

"Matty, what's wrong?" David called to him as he hurried in his nephew's direction.

Matty was staring at the inside of his forearm. "Ow," he cried.

"I think he got stung by a bee," the little girl explained.

"Bay!" Matty sobbed as David reached him. "Want Bay."

Bay dropped her new phone into her apron pocket and scooped the little boy into her arms. "Oh, a bee sting. Can you show me?" she coaxed. "My poor Matty."

"Here," he sobbed, pointing to a red welt rising on his skin.

Bay bent her head to get a closer look, the little boy's tears wetting her full apron. "Oh dear, it is a bee sting."

"Owie. Hurts," Matty cried.

"Shhh," she hushed, pulling him close. "It's okay.

We'll get a little ice for it. It won't hurt for long." As she held him and he wrapped his arms around her, Bay looked over his shoulder to see David standing there watching them. Smiling.

In that moment, Bay knew she would marry him. She knew this was God's plan.

Chapter Eleven

Bay glanced at the clock on the wall in Anne's hospital room. She and Matty had ended up staying the whole day to spend time with his mother. David had gone home for a couple of hours after Bay and Anne had insisted he need not be there every waking hour.

"It's almost time to go, Matty," Bay said. "Do you need to go to the potty before we get in the car?" She had arranged for Lucy to pick them up at seven. When David had gone home, he'd grabbed some clean clothes and toys for Matty, and of course, his precious books.

Matty nodded his head. He was seated on his mother's bed beside her, busy coloring in a book one of Anne's nurses had kindly brought him.

"Is it time already?" Anne asked. "I hate to see you go." She gave Matty a quick hug.

"Sorry, but I don't want our driver waiting for us in the parking lot." Bay rose from her chair beside David. "And Mama needs her rest, right, Matty?"

Bay was concerned that having Matty there all day

had been too tiring for Anne, even though she had taken him for walks around the hospital several times. She worried that Anne was looking pale again, although Anne protested she felt fine.

"I can take Matty," David offered without looking up from his phone. "Just give me a second to finish this." He was using his cell phone to place an order for more hydroponic equipment. Even though he'd had little time to tend to it in the last two weeks, the few plants he'd planted were doing well, so well that he wanted to expand already.

"I don't mind." Bay picked up crayons Matty had dropped on the floor and placed them in the box.

"That would be nice if you'd take him, David," Anne said. "I need a minute alone with Bay."

Bay and David looked at each other and Bay could tell that they were wondering the same thing—what did Anne need to talk to her alone about?

"Um, okay. Not a problem." David looked down at his phone again. "And…order is placed!" He stood, sliding his phone into his back pocket. "Let's go, little man."

Bay picked up Matty from Anne's bed and lowered his feet to the floor.

"Here." Matty handed Bay the coloring book. He started to walk toward David, then turned back. "No *coworing*, Bay," he warned, waggling his finger at him. "My book."

"Hey, hey," Anne said, fighting a smile. "We share, right?" Shaking her head with a chuckle, she watched him walk out of the room with David. "He's going to have to get over being an only child, isn't he?"

"He'll be fine," Bay answered, tucking the last crayon into the box. "What did you want to talk to me about?" She slipped the crayons and coloring book into Matty's backpack and zipped it up.

"Come here." Anne patted the edge of her bed. "Sit with me."

Bay hung the backpack on her chair and sat down on the edge of the bed, surprised she didn't feel uncomfortable in such intimate circumstances. Anne was lying on her back in bed in a hospital nightgown, still hooked up to the monitors and an IV. With a house full of sisters and a twin, Bay was used to familiarity with them, but she'd never had a really close female friend before. She'd never slept in a bed or braided another girl's hair except her sister's. But sitting there beside Anne seemed…right.

"I wanted to thank you for agreeing to take Matty home with you." Anne took Bay's hand in hers. "It was very kind of Susan to keep him so long and I know he was safe with her, but he'd rather be with you. He loves you so much."

The idea that Matty loved her made Bay's chest tighten. "Like I told David, I'm happy to take him home with me. My little brothers will be thrilled to have a playmate their own age."

"I also want to thank you for loving my son," Anne went on. "Our *grossmama* always used to say that a child growing up couldn't have too many mothers."

Bay thought it was strange that Anne saw her in that role—a mother. But she was touched that she appreciated how much she cared for Matty. And Bay did love him. Somehow, the little boy had found his way under her skin. She didn't understand it, but she accepted it as well as her role as a temporary parent to Matty while his mother was in the hospital.

"You don't have to thank me. Matty is easy to love," Bay said.

"You might say the same thing about my brother," Anne teased, raising an eyebrow as she released Bay's hand. "How's that going? You two seem pretty cozy these days. I see you holding hands when you think I'm not paying attention."

Bay felt a warmth flush her cheeks. "You know, if David was here, he might say that was none of your bee's wax."

The two laughed together.

Anne was obviously not offended by Bay's teasing. "You know," she said, "David told me about the night he took you home and spoke with your mother and stepfather. It sounds like once this baby is born and I'm on my feet again, we might be joining your family for supper. If your church is like ours was, I'd think such a supper might lead to an official engagement."

Bay could feel herself blushing. "I don't know about that. I think Benjamin's idea was for the two families to get to know each other. And to appease my *mam*."

Anne was quiet for a moment. "Do you mean you're not interested in marrying my brother?" She held up her hand. "And I'm not saying this isn't a huge step, Bay. But would life be so different with David than an Amish man beyond electricity and a truck? You've seen how we live. Our lifestyle is simple, and church is still a very important part of our lives. God is still at the center of who we are."

"I know." Bay folded her hands in her lap, looking down. "I just want to be absolutely sure before I say yes."

"Sure that you love my brother or that you could go from being Amish to Mennonite?"

"Both." Bay looked at Anne. "I… I do have feelings for David, feelings I never expected. But I've only known him for two months. Is that enough time to know that you love someone, that you want to spend the rest of your life with him?"

"It can be. It was in my case. I met Matthew at a county fair. I was serving church dinners and he came in to eat. I ended up leaving my shift to walk the horse barns with him and ride a merry-go-round. Within hours, I knew that I loved him and that God had meant us to be husband and wife. And Matthew felt the same way. We had only known each other five months when we married."

Bay folded her hands together in thought.

"Can I ask you a question?" Anne said.

Bay nodded.

"You told me a few weeks ago that you haven't been baptized. Why not?"

The question took Bay by surprise. It wasn't something people outside their community asked. "We're not required to be baptized until marriage."

"It was the same in our church growing up. But you *could* be baptized without marriage plans. We knew several people from our congregation who were baptized and didn't marry until years later."

Bay thought a long moment before she answered, because she wanted to be honest with her friend and herself. She had told herself for years that she was putting off baptism because she didn't need to do it yet, but that wasn't the entire truth. "I wasn't sure… I'm not sure it's right the choice for me," she answered softly.

"Because maybe God had other plans for you?" Anne pressed.

"Maybe," Bay answered.

Anne sighed. "I'm not trying to put pressure on you," she said, meeting Bay's gaze. "But I don't want you to miss out if my brother is the love of your life. Do you love him?"

"I do," Bay whispered.

Anne smiled. "Then tell him. And then pray together asking God if marriage is what He wants for both of you."

At that moment, Matty burst into the room. "Candy!" he cried, a fun-size bag of fruit chews in each hand. "Goin' to share." He looked up at Bay. "*Wiff* new friends at Bay's house."

"I did not buy that candy," David defended as he walked into the room, his hands up as if in surrender. "Someone at the nurses' station gave them to him. And I got an extra so James and Josiah could both have their own." He held up a bag. "I hope that's okay," he directed to Bay. "I told him he had to ask their mother first."

Bay chuckled, getting up from Anne's bed, their private conversation over. "It'll be fine."

"Guess you better get going." David pointed to the clock on the wall.

Seeing that it was nearly seven, Bay looked back to Anne. "Get a good night's rest. We'll see you tomorrow."

Anne met her gaze. "Thank you for taking Matty. And for being my friend." She put out her arms.

Bay leaned down to hug her.

"Take care of my son," Anne whispered in her ear. "And my brother, too."

Bay pulled back to look into Anne's eyes that were filled with tears. "I will, but only while you're on the mend," she murmured. "You're going to be fine."

Anne hugged her one more time and then let go. "Come on. Kiss Mama, Matty. I'll see you tomorrow."

Bay lifted Matty onto the bed and Anne hugged him tightly, also whispering in his ear.

Matty struggled to get away, eager for his adventure with Bay. "Bye, Mama. *Wove* you."

"I'll walk you down," David said as Bay lifted Matty down and led him away. "Be right back, sis."

"I'll be right here. Where else can I go?" Anne asked.

By the time David had Matty strapped into his car seat in the hired minivan, it was after seven and the sun was slipping in the western sky. "See you tomorrow. Be good," he told his nephew, kissing the top of the head. "Can I talk to you for a second?" he asked Bay, closing the van door.

"Sure. I'll be ready in just a minute," Bay told the driver.

The severe-looking woman with close-cropped white hair put up her window and went back to reading her paperback book.

David took Bay's hand and led her a few steps away from the van to give them some privacy. "Anne tell you about her numbers?"

Bay frowned. "What numbers? No."

He drew his hand over his face. "I guess she didn't want to worry you. Her blood test results came back when you and Matty were down in the cafeteria having milk and cookies earlier." He looked into Bay's eyes, so thankful she was there to hear him voice his concerns. "She's not responding as well to the meds as she had been and there have been some irregular heart rhythms. The cardiologist has changed up her meds. If she doesn't improve, she may have to have the C-section sooner rather than later." The last words caught in his throat. He had stayed calm when he had heard the news because he didn't want to upset Anne, but she'd been surprisingly fine, insisting God would see Matthew's baby born safely. But inside, David was so worried about his sister that his fear was coming in waves.

"Oh, David," Bay breathed.

And then she surprised him by putting her arms around him, hugging him tightly. David slipped his arms around her waist. Feeling her in his arms brought a calmness no spoken words would have given him. The only bad thing about her hug was that he never wanted to let go.

"Bay," he breathed. "I wish I could kiss you." It came out of his mouth before he could stop it.

Her hands still on his shoulders, she drew back, looking into his eyes. "You know I'm not supposed to kiss any man but my husband." Her tone was mischievous.

"So agree to marry me. Then I'll *almost* be your husband and maybe I could have a little kiss."

Her green eyes danced in the fading light. "I didn't say you couldn't kiss me. And I wasn't looking for a marriage proposal. At least not tonight," she added.

With one arm still around her, David brushed the backs of his fingers across her cheek. And then, looking into her beautiful eyes, he kissed her gently on the lips. "How was that?" he whispered.

Bay's eyes fluttered and she touched her mouth. "I liked it."

He smiled down at her, wishing he could kiss her a hundred times more. "I'm serious about marrying you, Bay. Say the word and I'll call our pastor tomorrow. I'll call him tonight if you say yes."

"I thought we were going to wait to make that decision, David."

"Does that mean you're still thinking about it?" He let go of her and took her hand. "Can I at least hope you're considering making me the happiest man alive?"

She smiled, her cheeks flushed. She was wearing a blue dress today and no apron, the strings of her prayer *kapp* tied at the nape of her neck. To him, there was no woman more beautiful than Bay.

"*Ya*, I'm considering it. I've been thinking a lot about what it would mean to leave my church, and I think… I think this is the direction God is leading me," she told him, speaking slowly. "We're raised to believe that our way is the only way, but I don't think I agree. I think that's why I was never ready to be baptized. Does that make sense?"

"To a man who wrestled with those questions ten years ago? It makes complete sense." He thought for a moment. "Maybe I should talk to my pastor about meeting with us. Talking with us about the possibility of the two of us marrying. He might have some good insight. He was raised Amish, too, though he left the order with his parents when he was a teenager. What would you think about that?"

"I think I would like that," she answered. "But we need to hold off until things settle down with Anne. Okay?"

He sighed. All she was asking was for him to be patient. He knew that wasn't too much to ask, but it was so hard because he loved her and he wanted to wake every morning to her lying beside him, looking at him the way she looked at him now.

"I need to go," Bay said. "But I'll see you tomorrow. I have a shipment of geraniums going out in the morning. After that, I'll come to the hospital. Hopefully, Anne's doctors will have some good news about the new medications."

"All right." He held up one finger. "But my marriage proposal stands. You say the word and I'll meet you at the altar."

"A church wedding," she mused. "I'd never considered that before. I always thought I'd marry in my mother's parlor."

"I'll marry you anywhere you want, Bay."

She smiled up at him and then hand in hand, they walked to the van and he opened the door for her. "See you tomorrow, Matty," he called, waving to his nephew.

"'Morrow." Matty blew him a kiss.

As Bay got into the van and buckled in, David had to resist the urge to kiss her goodbye. A stolen peck in the parking lot was one thing, but the beliefs he had grown up with about intimacy remained. He wouldn't kiss her in front of the driver or anyone else. Instead, he had to be satisfied with a quick squeeze of her hand.

"See you tomorrow," she told him.

"See you tomorrow," he echoed, feeling at that moment like the most blessed man on earth.

The following morning, while Bay waited for the delivery truck to take the trays of geraniums to a nearby gardening shop, she decided to make up some more planter pots. They sold out as fast as she could make them, and Joshua had told her that morning as she cut up Matty's eggs and sausage that they profited the highest percentage from her planters than any other item they were selling. That had surprised Bay, as they seemed so simple to make. She filled a big terracotta pot with potting soil, then planted flowers and greenery that complimented each other in color, height and texture. Sometimes she made one with a color theme, like with white geraniums, a spider plant and plenty of white vinca. Other times, she created planters in a burst of color like red, white and blue, which was always popular, especially around July Fourth. The fun thing was that no two planters ever looked alike.

While Bay combined New Guinea impatiens, blue salvia and pink petunias, Matty and her three-year-old brothers created their own flowerpots. Her sister Nettie had offered to watch all three boys so Bay could work, but Matty was more comfortable when she was nearby, so she'd taken them all to work with her. Bay's plan was for Matty to take the flowers he planted himself to his mother later in the day.

Josiah and James were making a large pot to go on their mother's front porch. While there had been a couple of blooms snapped off and some tears when Josiah had accidentally hit his brother's hand with the spoon he was using as a trowel, the project seemed to be going well.

The best part about their morning was that Matty was having a wonderful time. She'd never seen him so animated and he was talking nonstop with her little brothers. She loved seeing the three of them taking turns watering their flowers with an old plastic watering can they had found. As they played in the dirt, they chattered in little boy talk. While often Amish children didn't learn to speak English until they went to school because Pennsylvania *Deitsch* was spoken in the home, their parents believed it was important that their children be bilingual from birth.

Finished with the planter she was working on, Bay took a step back to have a good look at it, wanting to be sure it was properly filled in to allow for growth but also look good now. Satisfied with it, she began pulling through stacks of new planters, trying to decide if she wanted to do a shallow dish or another large one, when her mother burst out of the back door of the greenhouse.

"Here you are," her *mam* said, out of breath. "I've

been calling you and calling you. No one knew where you were."

Bay stared at her mother, who seemed flustered, and her mother never got flustered. "Sorry, the boys were talking and… I didn't hear you with the greenhouse doors closed, I guess." She walked toward her mother, a terrible sentence of dread coming over her. "What's wrong?"

Bay's mother met her gaze. "David is here," she said, clasping her hands over her strawberry-stained apron. She'd been picking berries that morning, promising strawberry shortcake with homemade whipped cream for dessert that night.

"Oh." Bay had planned to meet David at the hospital later and wondered what was up. "Could you tell him to come on back? The boys aren't quite done with their—"

"Bay, you need to go to him," she said soberly. "He's out in the parking lot." She glanced at the boys, who had abandoned their project and were busy stacking plastic pots into towers.

Bay frowned. "What—"

"He needs you. Go now."

The look on her mother's face made her rush through the open door of the greenhouse, past the rows of flowers and vegetables and out the front door. She spotted David's white truck and saw him leaning on the back bumper, his head down. Lifting her skirt, she ran the last steps.

"David?" She stopped short in front of him.

When he lifted his head to meet her gaze, she knew. *She just knew.*

"She's gone," he murmured, tears running down his

cheeks. "The baby's fine. A little girl. Born a little while ago." He smiled through his tears. "But Anne's gone, Bay. She went into cardiac arrest and they couldn't save her."

Bay felt as if her heart was shattering into a thousand pieces. *"Ne,"* she whispered, her own eyes filling with tears. And then she put her arms around him, and they held each other and cried together.

Chapter Twelve

As David went through the process of preparing to bury his sister, Bay remained at his side. She made phone calls, arranged to have Anne's burial clothing delivered to the funeral home, and rocked Matty to sleep in her arms as he clutched his favorite picture books. The hospital had agreed to keep the baby until after her mother's funeral. Afterward, David would have to bring home the healthy, seven-pound, red-haired infant, whom he had named Annie.

Three days after Anne died, she was buried in the local Mennonite churchyard. At the graveside service, the pastor had spoken words he hoped would comfort the congregation. "In my house are many mansions. I go to prepare a place for you." As he spoke, folks who had gathered tried to hold back their tears and come to terms with a mother taken to heaven before her thirtieth birthday.

Dressed in her black church dress and bonnet, Bay had stood beside David and listened to God's word, relayed by the somber pastor. Matty stood between them, holding both of their hands.

During the service, Bay's mind had wandered, and the pastor's voice had faded in her head, replaced by morning birdsong. Her gaze had shifted to the wild-flowers growing along the line of woods beyond the cemetery, and she had lifted her face toward the sun to feel its reassuring warmth. She had wondered how the world could be so full of life when such a beautiful life had ended. She had sought comfort in the holy words and her belief in a life beyond the world she lived in and in Matty's small hand in hers.

In the days following the funeral, David's house was full of people wanting to help. Little Annie came home from the hospital and there was a limitless number of people from the Mennonite church and their family, many who had traveled from Wisconsin, wanting to hold her, make supper and help any way they could. But within two weeks, everyone returned to their lives. David and Anne's family went home, their church friends went back to their work and families, and the visits became less frequent, the casseroles fewer.

Two and a half weeks after Anne's death, Bay sat at the kitchen table with Annie in her arms as she tried to comfort the fussy baby. David had taken his young-est sister, Maggie, to the Philadelphia airport to return home to Wisconsin, where she lived with their older sister Ruth. Maggie, who had stayed after their fam-ily had gone, had been a considerable help to David in the days following Anne's death. She had cared for the children, keeping Annie with her day and night, and reheated meals and played and read to Matty. But now she was gone, and David would be alone in the house at night with his nephew and niece. Bay didn't envy him. Annie wouldn't be sleeping through the night for a while, which meant he would be doing night feedings.

That morning before breakfast, Bay had spoken with her mother about coming to David's every day to care for the house and children while he worked. Ironically, as his personal life had fallen to pieces, his business had taken off. He was selling his late brother-in-law's inventory of flowering bushes and fruit trees as fast as he could get them out the door. Several of his commercial clients had also expressed interest in his hydroponic experiment and offered to sign contracts even before David had produced his first fruits, vegetables or flowers.

Bay's mam had frowned as Bay explained her schedule for the coming week—how she would go to David's every morning and stay all day until after suppertime, when he would take over the children's care. Her mam had said nothing until Bay, impatient with her mother's attitude, finally asked, "Do you not think I should be there for him? Anne was such a good friend. How could I not care for her children?"

"I think it's good of you to offer to help, but he's going to need a plan, Bay," she had responded. "And it can't include you, a single woman, long-term. What will people think with you there all hours of the day and night?"

"Did you not hear anything I said?" Bay had asked in frustration. "I won't be there *all hours of the night*.

Seven in the morning until six in the evening. Maybe seven if David is having a busy day." She had then lowered her hands to her hips, standing much the same way her mother was, and asked, "And how is this different than when Ginger was at Eli's *all hours of the day and nigh*t watching *his* children?"

Her mother's mouth had twitched. "Eli was a member of our congregation," she said finally.

"Ah, so Eli was Amish, and David isn't. Is that it? We should only lend a hand to Amish friends?"

"I don't know why you even ask my opinion," her mother had then said. "You're going to do what you want, *Dochter*, no matter what I say." She had then picked up the basket of dirty laundry at her feet and walked away. "At least take someone with you, James and Josiah, or one of your sisters so no one can say you're unchaperoned in a single man's house. One day I can come with you and we can do some deep cleaning. You said the little sister who had been staying with him wasn't much with a scrub brush."

Bay had just stood there watching her mother go, not knowing how to respond. Not knowing how she should feel.

Right now she was feeling overwhelmed. Annie was still fussing although she'd had a bottle and her diaper was fresh. Bay needed to start supper and she had clothes in the washer and dryer that she needed to take care of before David got home from the airport. She also needed to collect the eggs from the henhouse and pick the green beans in the garden she meant to cook for supper.

Yet here she sat, cuddling Annie, breathing her precious baby scent and whispering in her ear that she was all right. That she would be all right because while humans didn't always understand God's way, He was good, and her life would be full of love and goodness.

Matty sat at Bay's feet playing with wooden farm animals as he leaned against her. He hadn't stopped talking after his mother's death, but he was clingy and cried easily. If Bay left him to fetch a diaper for Annie, he began to wail. He didn't want to be alone. And bedtime had become a nightmare for David. Matty cried incessantly for his mother and Bay, and it didn't matter how long David read to him; he didn't want to go to sleep. And just about the time Matty fell asleep from exhaustion, David said Annie would wake up, wanting attention.

Bay felt so bad for David. She didn't know what to do for him other than be there. Since Anne's death, they hadn't talked about anything personal, hadn't held hands. The romance seemed to be on hold. Which she knew was to be expected, because David was grieving and overwhelmed. He was taking life one day at a time, trying to do for his niece and nephew as Anne would have wanted. He loved Matty and Annie as if they were his own, and that was what kept him going. Which made Bay love him all the more. Though his sister's passing was still a fresh wound, he found a way to smile, to play with his nephew, and snuggle Annie close and whisper to her how much her mother and father had loved her.

Bay was grieving, as well. And as hard as it had been understanding her feelings for David, understanding this emotional pull toward these two children was harder. No matter how difficult her days here were, she wanted to be there with them. When she was home working at the garden shop, all she could think about was hurrying to finish so she could be with Annie and Matty. And David.

Though she and David hadn't spoken of marriage since the night before Anne died, she knew it had to be on his mind. It was on hers. But every time it popped up, she pushed it aside, afraid to contemplate the decision before her that had only become more critical with Anne's death. Because if David were going to keep Annie and Matty, as she assumed Anne would want, that would mean Bay would be marrying into an already-made family. With *two* children. And while her sister had found it easy to slip into Eli and his four children's lives, she wasn't Ginger. But she loved David and the children. That would be enough to make it work, wouldn't it?

The screen door slapped shut and Bay heard David's footsteps. She listened to him remove his shoes, and a moment later, he walked into the kitchen. The first thing she noticed was how tired he looked. The second was how handsome. Just seeing him made her heart skip a beat. How could she be so blessed to have this handsome, smart, wonderful man love her?

There was no denying she loved him. And over the last two and a half weeks she had thought long and hard about leaving the Amish church, and she had concluded she could do it. She knew her mother would be opposed, but she also knew her mother loved her and would accept her decision. At least eventually she would. So all she had left to do was to talk to David. Bay needed to tell him she would marry him and all of this worry and confusion she'd experienced over the last months would be over. The decision would be made.

"Sorry I'm late," David said, brushing his red hair off his forehead. He needed a haircut. He'd been so busy the last month with Anne's hospitalization and then everything that had followed that he hadn't gotten a chance to go to the barbershop. She was amazed he could even get out of bed in the morning. Yet he did, and usually with a smile, albeit a sad one.

"The plane Maggie was taking out of Philly was late landing, and I didn't want to leave her in the airport until we knew her flight wasn't canceled." His sister Maggie was still Amish and had been raised by their oldest sister since their parents passed. She had come in a hired van with the family for the funeral, but she was flying home because she'd stayed behind.

David put out his arms, and Matty popped up off the floor and hurled himself at his uncle. David lifted him high in the air, and the little boy giggled.

Bay looked down at Annie in her arms. The infant was sound asleep, at last. Her eyes were closed, and she pursed her rosebud lips rhythmically. Getting up carefully so as not to wake her, Bay slid her into a battery-operated baby swing someone from the church had gifted. "It's just as well you're late." Bay hit the switch and gave the swing a small push. It began to swing steadily, making a soothing clicking sound. "Supper's not even close to being ready. Clothes are wrinkling in the dryer and…" Her voice waned. She was tired. And sad. She missed Anne and she missed the idea of the life she had begun to envision with David as newlyweds without the responsibility of children of their own. At least for a while.

He waved his hand dismissively. "I'm not that hungry, anyway. And this one—" he set Matty on the floor "—he wants peanut butter and jam for dinner most nights. I give it to him. And there are leftovers from yesterday's supper." He stood there for a moment, hands at his sides, looking as lost as Bay felt. "Do you have to go yet? I had an unsettling conversation with my sister Ruth. I called her on the way home to let her know that Maggie was safely on the plane, and apparently, she and my brother Hiram have come up with a plan. Without any input from me," he added.

Bay didn't bother to look at the clock on the wall. David needed her. "I can stay a while longer. Want something to drink? I made lemonade. We could sit on the porch swing. Let Matty run around outside."

"What about this one?" He walked over to the baby swing, leaned down and planted a kiss on the top of Annie's hair that was so red that it looked like one of Matty's red crayons.

Bay watched David with Annie and felt a crushing wave of emotion. How was it possible that she could love this baby so much? And why did her feelings for David seem stronger since Anne died?

"Annie will be fine," Bay answered. "The window's open. You know how loud she cries. The neighbors half a mile away will hear her if she wakes."

He groaned. "Of course. You're right." He looked down at Matty, who was playing with his toys again. "Hey, little man. How about we go outside and play before supper?"

The boy nodded.

Five minutes later, Bay had put a leftover chicken and dumpling casserole in the oven to reheat and poured two glasses and one sippy cup of lemonade. Out on the porch, she found David seated on the wood-slat swing. Matty was out in the grass, playing with the mother cat and kittens that now spent part of each day outside.

Bay set Matty's lemonade on the steps for him and then passed a glass to David.

He patted the seat beside him. "Thank you for being here through all of this, Bay. I don't know what I would have done without you."

"Nonsense," she said, sitting down beside him. "You had plenty of people here to help you—your sisters and brothers, all of your friends at church."

"Not the same thing," he told her, taking a swallow of lemonade before he set the glass on the table beside the swing. "They don't know me like you do. Like Anne did," he said quietly.

She wanted to argue that they were his family, but she understood what he meant. She loved her family, but right now, it felt as if David was the only person who really knew her. He was the only person who knew her hopes and fears and understood them.

She relaxed and lifted her bare feet as he put the swing in motion. "Tell me what your sister Ruth had to say." She had liked Ruth, who was ten years older than

David, but the woman was rather rigid and had none of David and Anne's light-heartedness.

"She doesn't think I can take care of the children." David looked at her. His blue eyes were still the eyes she knew, but with a sadness that had taken hold after they lost Anne. "My brother Hiram wants to take Matty."

She frowned. "Take him where?"

"Adopt him."

"Adopt him?" she asked, her eyes widening in disbelief. "But Hiram and his wife live in Ohio. How would Matty see you?"

"Oh, it gets better. Ruth is willing to take Annie off my hands."

Bay stared. "And she lives in Wisconsin! She'd separate Matty and Annie?"

He shrugged. "Ruth said that Hiram told her he could take Matty but not Annie. He said his wife wasn't willing to have another baby in the house. She just potty-trained their sixth child."

It was beginning to cool off with evening coming, but it was still warm and humid—a typical June day in central Delaware. She watched a honeybee flit from one white blossom of a buttonbush at the corner of the porch to the next. "What did you say?"

He exhaled. "Nothing. I was stunned. When Ruth said she had a plan to help me, I assumed she would offer to have Maggie come back and stay with me. You saw Maggie. She loved it here."

"She loved riding in your truck and flipping the light switch instead of lighting an oil lamp," Bay countered.

"Good point. But you know what I mean. And I'm

not sure the Amish life is what she wants, and I thought that might be a way for Maggie to find out."

"But being Amish is what Ruth wants for her," Bay observed.

"It is." He shrugged. "I can't fault her. You know how it is with a big sister. They think they know what's best for everyone in the family. Even a thirty-year-old like me."

Bay sipped her lemonade. "You haven't met my older sister Lovey yet. She's pretty bossy."

He was quiet for a long moment and then said, "You probably already know this, Bay, but I can't let the children go. They're all I have left of Anne. And I don't think Anne would want them to leave here. I certainly know she wouldn't want her and Matthew's children separated." His voice cracked with emotion and Bay reached over and threaded her fingers through his.

She didn't say anything, though. Instead, she sat quietly and watched Matty lying in the grass, three black-and-white kittens climbing on him. The child's laughter rang in the quiet yard and she couldn't help but smile. Life really did go on, didn't it? Even after the tragedy of losing someone as dear as Anne.

"So," David said with a heavy exhalation, "it's time to have that talk, Bay." He turned to her. "I can't send Annie and Matty away. But I also know that Ruth is right—I can't care for them completely on my own. Not the way they deserve to be cared for. So, will you marry me? Now? As soon as it can be arranged?"

His question was so abrupt that it startled Bay.

"Will you take me to be your husband, take Matty

and Annie to be our children?" he continued. "Because they will become ours. I know that. Annie never knew her parents and Matty... I'm not sure he'll even remember them when he gets older."

Bay fought tears, the sense of the children's loss washing over her.

"I know it won't be easy, but we can do it," David continued. "The two of us together. We can take care of these two and run this business. I could do it with you at my side and I think I could be a good father with you helping me. I don't know a thing about babies."

The way he said it made her bristle. He wanted to marry her so he would have someone to care for the children while he worked in the greenhouses. Was he just like everyone else? Did he think that the only thing she was good for was doing laundry and changing diapers? "I don't know anything about babies, either," she said.

"Sure you do. When I rock Annie, she cries. When you do it, she goes right to sleep. Look at her in there right now." He pointed toward the kitchen. "Sound asleep. I can promise you she won't be doing that tonight when it's bedtime."

Bay felt a sense of panic building in her. She imagined Annie awake and crying in the middle of the night. She imagined herself awake in the wee hours of the morning, walking the baby, up at dawn making breakfast, working in the house all day long caring for the children. And never getting to work again at what she loved.

Was this what she wanted?

Before she met David, she had been sure of what she wanted, and more important, what she didn't want. She wanted to work in her greenhouses and run the business. She hadn't even been sure she wanted marriage and children. Fifteen minutes ago, she had wanted to tell David she would marry him. But was that because she really wanted to marry him, or because she felt sorry for him and the children?

She was so confused. Was she in love with David, or had she loved Anne so much that she would marry his brother to care for Anne's children?

"What do you think?" David asked. "Shall we get married?"

Bay felt a buzzing in her ears, and she pressed the heel of her hand to her forehead. She hadn't been sleeping well. She'd been going to bed late and getting up early. Burning the candle at both ends, that was what her mother called it.

David watched her. Waiting.

"I… I don't know, David," she said, not daring to look at him for fear she would burst into tears. "Can I have time to think about it?"

David stiffened. Bay still wanted to think about it? After all the time they had spent together in the last month, she still didn't know how she felt about him?

He felt sick to his stomach. It was time he saw the reality of his situation.

She didn't love him. She would never love him. It had all been false hope.

He had fallen for Bay so fast. So easily. But it hadn't

been mutual. When he and Bay talked about marriage before Anne died, he had assumed it was her hesitation to leave the Amish church that was holding her back. Which he sympathized with because he had struggled with his understanding of his own faith, too. But apparently that hadn't been it.

She hesitated now because she didn't love him.

And that was what the *English* called a deal-breaker. No matter how much he loved and needed Bay, he would not marry a woman who didn't love him back. His parents had never been in love. Theirs had been an arranged marriage and though they came to respect each other and love each other in the way a family does, there had never been a romantic love. And the day David had left his black, wide-brimmed church hat on his neatly made childhood bed, he had promised himself he would only marry for love.

He rose suddenly from the swing, sending Bay flying backward. "You know what, Bay? You're right. That's a bad idea." His tone was so cool that he barely recognized it as his own. "It was a bad idea from the beginning."

She pushed out of the swing. "What?" She stared at him. "No, I didn't say that. It's only that—" She squeezed her eyes closed, then opened them again. "I'm so tired, David, and sad and I… I don't want to make a mistake that will ruin all of our lives."

He strode across the porch, away from her. "Matty, come on inside." He waved to the boy. "Let's get some supper on the table. Come on," he repeated when Matty didn't get up out of the grass immediately.

"David," Bay said behind him, her voice thick with emotion. "Please don't do this."

"Go home, Bay. Go back to your single, carefree life. There's no need for you to come here again. I'll manage with the children."

She darted around him, blocking his path to the door. "David, please, I only—" She exhaled, dropping one hand to her hip in anger. "How are you going to manage the children if I don't come back?"

"I'll get some of the women from the church. Susan said she had a niece looking for work as a nanny." He stepped around her. "Or Maggie can come back. Problem solved." When he reached the back door and turned to wait for Matty, who was now coming up the porch steps, Bay was still standing where he had left her. "Go home, Bay," he repeated. "I've got this."

Annie began to wail, the sound of her distress coming through the open windows.

"Inside, little man." David opened the door and pushed Matty in ahead of him.

In the kitchen, he lifted Annie onto his shoulder. She burped and he felt a warm wetness run down the back of his shirt. Tears filling his eyes, he hugged the infant, patting her back and whispering in her ear. "Shhh. It's all right, sweetie," he hushed. "Uncle David is here. I've got you, and I'm not going to let you go."

As he cuddled Anne's newborn, he turned to the windows and watched Bay get on her push scooter and head down the driveway. As she disappeared, he was choked with emotion, realizing that not only had he lost his sister but now he had lost the love of his life, as well.

Chapter Thirteen

That night Bay went to bed early without bothering to eat supper. Her *mam* must have sensed it wasn't a good time to question her, because when Bay announced she was going straight to bed, her mother gave her a quick hug but said nothing.

Bay slept so late the next morning that breakfast was over by the time she got downstairs. The kitchen was empty, except for her mother and James and Josiah. The sight of her little brothers immediately made her think of Matty and Annie, and she feared she would begin her day the same way she had ended the last—in tears.

Earlier, as she brushed her teeth and prepared for the day, she told herself that she had been foolish to think that things with David would ever work out. It had been a mistake to think that a man like him could ever love an unconventional woman like her. It was better it ended now. This way he could find the kind of woman he needed, one who would care for Anne's children, have a baby every year, and keep the house neat and clean, with meals on the table on time.

The talk she gave herself was a good one, so good that she nearly convinced herself that she was right, but by the time she made it downstairs, she could feel that she was on the verge of another good cry. After twelve full hours of sleep, she realized now that she'd made a terrible mistake. She *did* love David, and she wanted to marry him. She wanted to be a mother to Matty and Annie. But now she'd made such a mess of things. David had been her one chance at love and she had let it go. Let him go.

"Breakfast, *Dochter*?" Her mother was putting away the last of the clean breakfast dishes as Bay entered the kitchen.

Bay shook her head. "Just coffee. Where are Nettie and Tara?"

"Gone to Fifer's Orchard to see if there are any flats of strawberries. Tara wants to make strawberry syrup to add to her cache of jams." Her mother took a white mug from the dish rack and poured a cup of coffee.

"I can get it myself," Bay said.

"I know you can, but I want to do it for you. It doesn't matter how old a mother's child is, she still likes to do things for her. You'll feel the same way someday."

Bay dropped into a kitchen chair. "That seems unlikely now."

"Why do you say that?"

Bay didn't answer.

"Has something happened between you and David?" her mother pressed.

"We've broken up," Bay said softly. Tears filled her eyes as she reached for the mug in front of her.

"What happened?" Her *mam* took the chair beside her.

"I don't know. I guess we both realized I would make a terrible wife and mother. With David now having the responsibility of Annie and Matty, he needs someone who can do that. Someone who can cook and clean and be satisfied with that." Bay cupped her hands around the hot mug but didn't drink.

Her *mam* knitted her brows. "David said that?"

"Not in those words, but I know that's what he was thinking."

"Ah." Her mother leaned back in her chair, crossing her arms. "I've learned the hard way not to assume I know what people are thinking, not even those closest to me."

Bay stared straight ahead, saying nothing.

"Sounds to me like you're the one who's worried you'll be a poor mother." Her *mam* was silent for a moment and then went on. "You want to know what I think?" She chuckled. "Probably not, but I'm going to tell you, anyway. I think you would be a wonderful mother to Annie and Matty. I saw how you were when Matty stayed here with us and again at the funeral. He loves you and you love him. And that precious baby? I see the love in your eyes when you talk about her."

"But is that enough?" Bay's voice cracked, because she was thinking of David, as well. "I'm afraid it isn't."

"Of course it's enough. With love, you can do anything, including be a mother. Now, you might not be the mother I was to you, or the mother Ginger is to her flock, but *Gott* didn't create us to all be the same. I think, Bay, that you could be a different kind of mother than what you saw growing up. And I think you could be a good wife, just a different kind than I've been. You could be a wife who works beside her husband in their business. If anyone could do it, have a family and work, it's you."

Bay lifted her gaze, surprised by what she was hearing come from her mother's mouth.

"You know," her mother continued, "becoming Mennonite might be the way for you to find the independence you're looking for."

"Do you think so?"

"I do."

Bay couldn't believe what she was hearing and she stared at her mother. "But…but you were so angry when you found out I was seeing David."

"I was angry because you weren't honest with us. Because you were sneaking behind our backs."

"Because I knew you wouldn't understand. I knew you would never approve of the match with a man who wasn't Amish."

"And you were wrong." Now her *mam's* voice was laced with emotion, too. "You want a bigger world than the one you were born to. You always have. So I want that for you because all a mother wants is for her children to be safe and happy and to know *Gott*. You already know Him, and He will be with you, even on a pew in the Mennonite church."

Bay met her gaze. "You think I should marry David?"

"*Ya*, I do."

Bay sat there for a moment, stunned by her mother's words. She wondered why they hadn't had this conversation weeks ago. "None of it matters now," she said, hanging her head. "Last night, David told me to go home and never come back."

Her *mam* got up from the table, shaking her head. "Well, it sounds like he can be as impulsive as you." She rested her hands on her hips. "Don't be stubborn, *Dochter*. If you love David and those children, fight for them. Sometimes you have to fight for love."

An hour later, Bay was busy transplanting dahlias, thinking over what her mother had said. Praying. She felt so miserable about the mess she had made with David that she didn't know what to do. Did she just go to him and tell him she was sorry and that she did want to marry him? Did she tell him she wanted them to have a marriage that was an equal partnership where they shared everything—work, the children, household chores?

Would he even listen to her now? What if he didn't love her? What if he'd only asked her to marry him yesterday to solve the problem with the children?

But she was usually so good at reading people. It had *seemed* like he loved her.

Bay was so frustrated and confused. She sat down on a tarp she'd laid out to keep from spilling potting soil all over the ground in the greenhouse. It was warm and humid inside and it occurred to her that she should open some windows or at least the back door. Instead, feeling so tired that she could have climbed back in bed, she stretched out on the tarp. No one would see her. Joshua was busy in the shop, tending to customers.

It felt good to lie down, so good that she told herself it would be okay to close her eyes for just a minute. She deserved it after the last month of running nonstop with not enough sleep. Just a minute, she told herself. Five at the most.

Bay had barely closed her eyes when she sensed someone was there. Someone had caught her napping in the middle of the day. Horrified, her eyes flew open and she found herself staring at Matty.

Matty? It had to be a dream. How would Matty get there alone?

"Bay, you *sweepy?*" Matty asked in his sweet little boy voice, squatting in front of her.

Startled, she sat up. It wasn't a dream.

"Matty, what are you—" Her gaze shifted upward.

Matty wasn't there alone. Of course he wasn't. David stood beside a table of potted dahlias, Annie asleep in his arms.

"David," she breathed.

"I see you found her," Bay's *mam* announced, strolling into the greenhouse.

"I did. Thank you," David said, seeming unsure of himself.

Bay got to her feet, looking from David to her mother and back to David again. "Tell me she didn't call you."

"I'm right here. I can hear you," her mother said as she put out her arms. "Give me that little one. Matty and I are going to find the boys, and I think Annie better help us."

"*Mam*, please tell me you didn't call him." Mortified, Bay covered her face with her hand.

"It's a good thing Rosemary did," David said, handing off the newborn. "Otherwise, I don't know how long it would have taken me to get the courage to come and say I was sorry."

"Matty, would you like to come with Rosemary?" Bay's mother asked cheerfully. "I think the boys are playing with our new kittens. Would you like to play with kittens with James and Josiah?"

Matty nodded excitedly, then looked back to Bay. "You wanna come *pway wif* kitties?"

Bay cut her eyes at David, then looked back at Matty. "How about if you go find James and Josiah and the kittens, and Uncle David and I will be along in a few minutes?"

Matty seemed to consider the suggestion before nodding.

"Come on, Matty." Bay's mother shifted the newborn to her shoulder and put out her hand to Matty.

David and Bay watched them go before being forced to look at each other when they were alone.

"Oh, Bay," David sighed, his arms slack at his sides. "I am so sorry. I don't know what happened yesterday. I was tired and worried and…and so sad." He adjusted his ball cap. "I was only thinking of myself and not you, not thinking about how stressed and sad you had to be, too. We both miss Anne so much. It was wrong of me to put that kind of pressure on you about marrying me."

Bay clasped her hands together, looking down at her bare feet. "No, I'm sorry. I think I took it the wrong way. I thought you were asking me to marry you so you could have a babysitter."

"What?" he asked in horrified surprise. "Bay, look at me."

She slowly lifted her head until they were eye to eye.

"I was *not* asking you to marry me so I would have someone to watch the children. I can hire someone to do that. I asked because I couldn't stand the thought of you coming to the house every day and then leaving every night. I asked because since Anne died, I've felt so lost. I was afraid if I didn't ask you, you'd think that I no longer wanted to marry you because of everything that's happened."

As she exhaled, she felt a weight falling from her shoulders. "I'm sorry, too. I was tired, and then I got upset about Ruth and Hiram wanting to take the children. And then I… I got scared, David." Tears clouded her eyes.

"Come here." He opened his arms. "What are you afraid of?"

She went to him and rested her head on his shoulder. "That…that I won't be a good mother to Matty and Annie. That…" The warmth of his embrace gave her the courage to go on. "I was afraid, *am* afraid I can't be the mother the little ones need or the wife you want. I don't want to have twelve children. I don't want to spend every day in the house cooking and cleaning."

One arm still around her, he brushed a tear from her cheek with the pad of his thumb. "What would make you think I would want any of that from you? I want you to be happy, and I want you to be you. I want a wife who wants to be at my side, a wife who likes playing in the dirt like I do."

She gave a little laugh, sniffling. "I do like to play in the dirt."

"I can see now that I should have been clear, early on, when I realized we had feelings for each other, what I was looking for in a wife. What I dreamed our life would be. I want a wife who wants to work in the greenhouses with me, who can get as excited as me about cloning a fruit tree. I want a wife who can talk with our customers and take the truck into town to get groceries. I don't care if the house isn't perfect. I don't care about meals—I like macaroni and cheese from a box. It's what I've been eating since I left home ten years ago. And as for children—" he gazed into her eyes "—I know this wasn't what you had in mind, a newborn and toddler on the day you married, but more children? We'll make that decision together. And we don't have to do that anytime soon. If you ask me if I want children of our own, it would be a lie to say I don't. But Bay, I want you. More than I want more children."

"You want me," she breathed.

"I do. And just as you are. Feisty and independent."

She laughed and laid her head on his chest. He felt so warm, his arms around her so comforting. "But you told me to go home and never come back."

"I did. And that was a mistake. I was so upset about my sister and brother wanting to take Matty and Annie away from me that I thought they must not care about me. Not love me. And then when you said you weren't ready to give me an answer, I somehow made the ridiculous leap to think you didn't love me. Or the children."

"I do love Matty and Annie. I love them so much." She raised her head to look into his eyes again. "And I love you, David. And I want to marry you. And I don't care how messy it gets. I want to be with you for the rest of my life."

"Bay," he whispered, pulling her tight.

"Ask me again," she told him, resting her head on his chest.

"What?"

"Ask me again, David. If I'll marry you."

"Will you marry me, Bay?" he whispered in her ear.

She hugged him tightly, suddenly seeing the life she would share with him would be the life she had dreamed of. The life she had never thought possible. "*Ya*, I'll marry you, David. And no long betrothal."

"Because of the children," he said, holding her against him.

"*Ne*. Because I can't wait to be your wife." Then she kissed him, and knew in her heart of hearts that God would always be with them.

Epilogue

Two years later

"Can you pour some water in this one?" Bay asked, showing Annie a planter she'd made with colorful dahlias and green herbs, something that was selling well at the shop she still owned with Joshua.

Annie toddled toward her, carrying a little pink plastic watering can. "Pretty," she said with a giggle, spilling water onto her dirty toes.

Bay laughed and carried a tray of basil to the potting bench David had built the winter before. "Keep pouring," she encouraged as Annie sprinkled water over the plants. "Mama will get you more water if you need it."

When she and David had first married, she'd felt guilty referring to herself as Annie and Matty's mother, but as time passed, it had become second nature. At first, Matty had called her Mama Bay, but eventually, he dropped her name and their pediatrician had promised it was perfectly natural for him to call her mama.

As time passed, while hopefully Matty wouldn't forget his mother entirely, his memories would fade and some might even be replaced by Bay's face, the doctor had explained. Bay and David were careful to talk about Anne regularly to both children so they would always hold her in their hearts, but the truth was that Annie had never known her birth mother. To Annie, Bay *was* her mother. And Bay felt honored and humbled by that each and every day. And blessed. So blessed.

"More *wawa*," Annie announced, holding up her watering can. *"Pwease?"*

Bay gave one of her red-haired daughter's stubby braids a playful tug. "More water? I can do that." She accepted the watering can and began to refill it with the hose. "Wonder what Papa and Matty are making for supper. Are you hungry?"

Annie was busy poking her finger into the wet soil in the flowerpot that was nearly half as tall as she was. "Hun-gry," she mimicked.

It was David's turn to make supper. After they married, they'd quickly realized that while it sounded like a wonderful idea to work in the greenhouses all day side by side, it wasn't always practical. No matter how much they and the children enjoyed the work, laundry still had to be washed, shopping had to be done, and meals needed to be cooked.

Now they worked together most of each weekday but set time aside for housework. It had been David's idea to share in the household and barn chores. He had no problem throwing a load of clothes into the wash before they sat down to have breakfast, which was often just cereal, or an egg-and-sausage casserole made the night before. And he was becoming quite the cook, with his sous-chef, Matty, at his side. So now, three days a week Bay and Annie made supper and three days a week David and Matty made it. Then once a week, they cooked together. Of course, sometimes one of them ended up with both children in the greenhouse or the kitchen, but that worked out fine because that meant the children received the attention they needed.

As Bay turned off the hose and handed Annie her watering can, Matty burst through the greenhouse door. "Supper's ready!"

A few steps behind him, David appeared in the doorway. "Supper's ready," he called with the same enthusiasm as Matty.

Bay looked down at her daughter. "Sounds like supper's ready."

"Supper, supper, supper," Annie sang, abandoning the flowerpot to water her bare foot.

David walked over to where Bay stood and casually put an arm around her. He kissed her cheek. "How's it going?"

"Great." She plucked off her gardening gloves. "I've got five more flower and herb pots ready to go to the shop in the morning. How'd things go in the kitchen?"

"Just fine."

David kissed her again and she laughed, still learning his way with physical attention. "I thought as much since we didn't see any smoke?" she teased.

Marriage was nothing like what she had feared it would be. She was still amazed by how easily she and

David had transitioned to married life and how right it had felt from the very first day. It had been surprisingly easy to move from the life of an Amish woman to a Mennonite one. While not everyone in the Amish community of Hickory Grove had approved of her decision, her family had embraced it with open, loving arms. And they had embraced David and the children with the same acceptance that quickly turned to love.

David gazed into her eyes. "I missed you."

She eyed him. "Missed me? You only went up to the house an hour ago."

He shrugged. "I still missed you."

"We made cheeseburgers on the grill," Matty told Bay. "And we put French fries in the oven."

Bay looked at David with surprise. "You guys cut up potatoes and made fries?"

"Of course not." He laughed. "But we did manage to open a bag of frozen fries. And there's fresh broccoli ready to be steamed in the microwave when we get up to the house."

"I guess we'd best go, then." Bay turned to her daughter. "Ready to have some supper, Annie?"

The little girl with eyes the color of David's looked up, beaming. *"Weady!"*

"Race you to the house!" Matty told David.

Before David could respond, Matty took off.

"Race? You want to race?" David called to his son as he ran after him.

"Come on, Annie!" Bay said, swinging her into the air and onto her hip.

Annie squealed with laughter. *"Wace!"*

Bay caught up to her men as they went through the greenhouse door and passed them outside in the grass.

"No fair," Matty cried. "You're bigger than me."

Then David lifted Matty onto his shoulders and Bay slowed to a walk. When David caught up, he reached out and took Bay's free hand in his. They made eye contact and he smiled.

"I love you," David said softly. "Thank you for being my wife. For making me the happiest man alive."

Bay gazed at him, her heart swelling with joy. "I love you, too. More every day," she told him, her eyes growing moist.

"Hey, I thought we were racing," Matty protested from David's shoulders.

Bay took off. "We are!" she called over her shoulder and both children burst into peals of laughter.

"Wait, no fair!" David called, running after them.

And side by side, Bay and David ran toward the house, sunshine on their faces, surrounded by all that was good and right in the world.

* * * * *